Tree Soldier

A Novel of Love, Forgiveness and the Great Depression

J.L. Oakley

ISBN:13: 978-1453896471
Library of Congress Control Number: 2010919418.

DEDICATION

To my sons Matt, John-Rolf and Brent
and husband Rolf who loved me.

ACKNOWLEDGMENTS

Many thanks to those who made this work possible: Margaret Hillard, Andrew Shattuck McBride and Anne Mini, for editing, Jeff Fielder for the cover, and Hank Reasoner for his insight into forestry practice in the 1930s. To all the CCC boys I interviewed, thanks for sharing your stories about life in FDR's Tree Army.

I went to the woods because I wished to

live deliberately, to front only the essentials of life, and

to see if I could not learn what it had to teach...

Walden, Henry David Thoreau

....while we help grow

More woods for ages yet to come

...when the bugle and the drum

Again calls forth we'll answer, "Here"..

-*Happy Days*, CCC magazine 1933

PROLOGUE

From inside the farmhouse, John Hardesty heard the car door slam and the engine roar to life. He got off the floor and rubbed his sore cheek. Paul had hit him hard, but it hurt more to think about the rift between them. They were so close. It was all Marie's fault. Well, it was his fault too. He started it.

He staggered to the front door and turned on the porch light before going out. The snow was falling in a steady sheet of soft flakes, the wind on the rise. On the passenger side of the '29 Chevy coupe, Marie Bertin got in, her cloche hat already collecting a thick layer. Between the snow and the dim light of mid-winter dusk, he could barely make out the ruff on her fur coat enfolding her neck like a lion's mane. No time to be leaving.

He jumped down off the porch, slipping in his street shoes as he came alongside the driver's side. He pounded on the door. His brother rolled the window down.

"Paul. Wait. You're in no shape to be driving."

"Too bad, pal. Why don't you shut up? S'matter of fact, good riddance to you."

"Marie?" John stared into the car.

The woman gave him a weak smile. "I am going, cheri. *C'est la vie.*"

Paul hit the accelerator. For a moment, the car's wheels spun around before they got footing, sending out clods of packed snow. It fishtailed down to the main road and gathered speed. There was nothing to guide it. The rail fences were piled up with snow.

Hardesty watched the red tail lights swish and weave, then suddenly bump up into the air.

To his horror, the car skidded across the snowy lane before it hit the corner. Its back end went out first like the Chevy was trying to slide into home plate backwards, going slowly, slowly, then suddenly the front end swinging hard to the right. There was no sound, just the snow coming down. The car spun until it hit the snow-clogged ditch and bounced. Then the screams began.

John ran as fast as he could. The frigid night air knifed his lungs. In the ghostly light, the car lay half way on its side like it was just resting, but the windshield was broken, naked headlights beaming into a void. The only thing real to John was his brother's yelling and the strong odor of gasoline.

"I'm here, Paul," John shouted as he pulled the awful weight of the door up. Paul struggled inside, screaming, smelling of alcohol. John caught a flailing arm.

"Marie!" Paul's voice was chaotic agony.

Underneath him was Marie. An odd, flickering glow highlighted her bloodied head which had broken through the car door window and was shoved into the snow bank. Her shoulders hunkered in, like she was trying to get into the fetal position. He wondered if she was already dead.

There was a sudden bang and in an instant a bright flash licked up from the passenger side and underneath the dashboard. Flames grabbed hold of his brother's coat sleeve, exploding like a winter's night bonfire. John pulled. His brother pulled back, shouting,

"I hate you! I hate your bloody guts! You killed her, you bastard. You killed Marie."

"Stop! You're not making sense. Let me get you out. Then I

can get her."

Flames engulfed the whole inside of the car now. Like a maelstrom of roiling fury, it caught Paul's coat sleeve and collar coming off the cloth like a line of seraphim wings, searing the skin on Paul's face, scorching his hair. John tried to pull him out, but his brother fought him, scratching his face, and screaming obscenities at him. Finally, other hands appeared to pull his brother out onto the snow.

A neighbor from the farm next door rolled Paul around, giving John the freedom to go back into the car. When he touched the handle of the car door, he burned his hands. He tried again. Using his coat sleeves to shield his palms, he tugged and pulled, but the door stuck. A tower of black smoke poured out the driver's window, dwarfing the mounded hills of snow on either side of the country road and flashing them with huge, golden lights. Through the flames Marie's head seemed to have shifted, exposing a jagged piece of glass slicing her throat.

There was another explosion, this time blowing out the back window. Someone wrenched him back from the heat.

"Too late," a voice said. His voice. John looked down at Paul. His brother lay moaning, staring up into the snowflakes. By the intense firelight, John could see that the skin on Paul's face and neck was peeling. Then he noticed his own palms. Quarter-sized blisters were bubbling up.

"Let's get you to the side, son. Looks like some nasty burns."

John obeyed. He felt like he was not part of the scene, but above it. The fire flicked and flashed. The snow swirled. The smell of cooking flesh made him gag. "I didn't think…"

"What'd you say?"

He gave no answer. He dropped into the cold, wet snow.

CHAPTER 1

Washington State 1935

The big canvas-backed, bug-eyed Ford truck shook like a malaria victim in the last throes of dying as John Hardesty and the gaggle of boys behind him pushed it towards the angled steps of the general store ahead. "Almost there," his companion on the other side of the cab called out. "Frazier straight ahead."

Hardesty craned his neck from his stance at the open door of driver's side, hand on the steering wheel. The sign over the steps spelled out Alford's General Store and Mercantile in fading white capital letters. It sat on what Hardesty supposed was a corner of the village crossroad, dwarfed by the giant fir trees behind it. He aimed the trunk past the steps, putting his back into his effort.

"Friggin' truck! Are we there yet?" "

"We better be. I gonna friggin' kill it."

"Cut it out, boys and push. That means you, Costello." He felt the truck wobble as twenty hands marshaled forces to move the heavy vehicle to its last stop when suddenly it lurched so hard he had to fling into the cab and pull the brake. The truck hit the log curb, dislodging a couple of kids onto the dirt road before the front tires caught.

"Everyone okay?"

The group standing behind him didn't look so sure. Dressed in newly-issued khaki shirts and olive drab pants of the Civilian Conservation Corps, they looked like they had been picked up by a steam shovel off the streets of New York City and dumped in the middle of the North Cascades dirt road. Their haircuts were new, their tall, laced boots were new. Some of the boys looked in awe at the hundred-foot tall Douglas fir trees lining the little village like a gigantic fort's palisade. Others dusted themselves off and stared at the dozen weathered buildings glowing in the sunlight.

"Now what?" someone muttered.

Hardesty shut the cab door. "We'll have to wait until it cools." They'd only met a few hours before at a small town train station and he didn't have all the names straight.

He went to the front and opened the hood. A cloud of steam escaped. A dark haired man from the passenger side of the truck joined him. "How's it look, Park?"

Hardesty answered easily to his chosen name. "Well, maybe it'll cool down again, Jack. I don't know. Can I call the camp? This is ridiculous. We were expected an hour ago."

Turner gave the front tire a good kick. "Aw," he chuckled. "I know the commander. He's all right. I'll see if we can't get another truck to come down and pick you fellows up."

"Thanks. 'Preciate it. I'll let the boys buy sodas. They can eat their sack lunches while they wait."

"Great. I'll call, you watch the crowd."

Hardesty gathered the boys at the front. "Take a break, guys. We'll find out about another truck. Hey -- Spinelli, where are you going?"

"Hell, I thought I was a See-See boy. Live out in the woods. Or hike there."

"You're not in the Tree Army yet. You have to get your shots."

That stopped the wiry, dark-haired kid in his tracks.

The recruits went into Alford's to see what was available.

Hardesty monkeyed under the hood for a while, but it would do no good. The truck would have to be towed. He put the hood down and tried to clean his hands, but the grease wouldn't come off the burn scars under the calluses, so he went in search of a public outhouse or pump.

Behind the store, a thick grove of cedar trees, with roots that clutched the earth with long thick toes broke open enough to suggest a stream or river there.

"Gravel will work," he thought and went in search of it.

Kate Alford sat on a large smooth boulder and watched her horse drink water from the river. Here the cedar trees gave way to scrubby alder and vine maple that lined the gray stones of the riverbed.

So peaceful. A kingfisher dived from the trees on the other shore, making way for a raven gliding out from the woods behind her. Not a crow, but a true raven, it was much larger than its more common cousin and steeped in lore.

"You trickster." She thought. It back-sculled its coal black wings in the air as it landed in a tall red alder. As it settled, it made a clacking noise like large knitting needles banging together. The horse raised its head.

"See any Dolly Varden, Elsa?" The mare pointed her ears forward like she was studying the small calm eddies on the opposite side of the river. Where it ran low and clear over its stony bed, an occasional steelhead rippled the water as it made its silent way in to spawn. When her horse finished drinking, Kate led it by its reins up to the grassy bank behind her and let it graze. A calm animal, it wouldn't stray. She sat back down on the boulder and resumed reading her book.

The raven called again. Something's near, she thought, then realized she wasn't alone.

A German Shepherd appeared on the opposite bank and climbed down to the low gravelly shore to drink. Bob Walton's dog. Half grown and surprisingly dumb for the breed.

Kate put her hair up and tightened her bootlaces. She started to pick up her things when suddenly the mare nervously shot her head up and stiffened towards the river. Turning, Kate saw to her amazement two young bear cubs tumble down to the water and over to the gravel bar. Though not uncommon, bears usually came to the river a little higher up and later in the spring. For a moment she watched with fascination as the small cubs played at the water's edge.

Suddenly to her horror, she remembered the dog. The German shepherd was still there, its hackles raised now as it lowered its head and faced the cubs.

"Oh, my God! Buster! Come! Buster!"

The dog turned and wagged its tail, then swung back with bared teeth as the cubs discovered it and charged. Playfully, they surrounded the dog, one of them clambering on the dog's back as if it thought the dog was another cub. The dog snarled and snapped, sending the cub away with a squeal. The other cub continued to play.

"Buster!" Kate shouted. Without thinking she dashed into the water. "Buster!"

Behind her, Elsa snorted and bolted away, leaving her alone in the water, trying to get the dog to come. Buster dropped his head, his brows crinkled in worry and confusion. Kate went further into the stream, wondering if she could physically pull the dog away. "Buster, come." She waved the dog to come to her, but it was too late.

The sow bear burst through the willow saplings, its coat gleaming like oily satin in the sunlight. It was one of the things Kate would remember for a long time. The gleaming black coat and the bear's powerful muscles rippling under it. She wanted to touch it. To ask for the bear's blessing and send it on its way, no one hurt for the worst. But of course, it couldn't be that way. The mother bear was awesome in her strength and fury.

The dog didn't have a chance. Trying to shake off the second cub, it didn't see the danger until there was no escape. For a brief moment it stood bravely against the bear, then shrieked when a paw slapped it to oblivion in the river. Whining pitifully, it tried to paddle away, but its back was broken. The bear slammed her bulk through flowing water and crushed the dog's neck with her jaws.

For a moment, Kate stood transfixed. She knew that she was in danger, but her legs didn't want to move. Finally, she got a grip on her nerves and backed away to the shore, mindful she could slip on the slippery stones under her boots. Never taking her eyes off the bear, she began to ease her way back to the bushes. The bear pawed at the carcass of the dog around on the rocks, then looked up. Suddenly, Kate was seized by strong arms and without ceremony hauled back through the salmonberry bushes.

"Get your hands off of me." She twisted her shoulders away, but whoever it was the kept pulling her back.

"I'm sorry," the man whispered. "Don't mean to be fresh. Keep moving. I've got your mare further back."

"I was doing just fine. Bears come here all the time."

"Mama Bear didn't look so thrilled to see you." They retreated to the safety of the woods, but he continued to march her through the trees to the trail back up to her parent's store. To her surprise Elsa was there, tied to a tree. Kate looked at her shoulders. There were greasy handprints on them. What the hell had he been doing?

"You from the camp?" He was definitely a CC boy with the uniform, but he was older than most of the enrollees she saw around Frazier. His work-hardened shoulders and arms filled his khaki shirt, yet he didn't look like someone who was accustomed to a hard life, but like many, thrown into it by the Depression.

"Not quite. Our truck broke down. Want some water?" He offered her a canteen.

"That's very kind, but I'm okay." Well, not quite. She kept seeing the bear and the mangled body of the dog. The dog's agonized whimper rang in her head over and over again. She patted Elsa for reassurance.

He took a swig and stored the canteen away in his rucksack. "That's an interesting horse. Is it a Palouse horse?"

"Appaloosa."

"It's nice. Like the blanket on its rump." He pointed to the large white patch in which a field of black blotches had been splattered. "It has good markings."

She wondered how he knew that. "Thank you, Mr..."

"Hardesty. Park Hardesty. And you?"

"I'm Kate Alford. And that's Elsa."

"Glad to meet you both." He gently stroked the animal's nose. "You're not related to the folks that run the general store in Frazier?"

"Yes, I am. Have you been there?"

"Truck's right out in front." He put the rucksack on his back. "I was going to go down to the river and get this grease off my hands, but don't think I'll do it quite yet. If you don't mind, I'll head back to my mates. Bunch of teenagers, all of them, fresh out of the city."

"Thank you Mr. Hardesty. As I said, I usually can take care of myself."

Hardesty smiled. "I gather you can."

A couple of hours later, Hardesty was standing along the edge of the camp parade ground with the rest of his young squad mates. They all looked like they wanted to bolt. He followed their line of sight. Behind the camp craggy, white mountains painted amber by the afternoon sun leered over trees most likely bigger than anything they'd ever seen. They had startled him too when he first came out.

"Holy cow. Do you see them trees?" Costello dropped his duffle next to Hardesty with a thud.

"I see them," Spinelli said on the other of him. "Wonder which place is ours?"

Hardesty wondered too. The long wooden buildings lined up in neat rows looked no different from the last camp he had been in. Even the smoke brought the smell of roasted ham out of a building that suggested the cook house. It made his stomach growl.

A military type officer showed up with a clipboard and ordered the group to gather around. "Welcome to Camp Kulshan, F-23, one of the oldest Civilian Conservation Corps camps in the state of Washington. We make campgrounds, roads, bridges and fight fires. Three departments run it here: the Army, Department of Agriculture and Department of Labor. During your time here you'll not only be sending money home to your folks, but will have the opportunity to finish high school and learn a trade. There'll be more about that later. For now…"

Spinelli turned to Hardesty. "That true about the girl and the bear?" he whispered.

"Where'd you hear that?" Hardesty was surprised news traveled so fast.

"At the store. I didn't know there were bears there. Only bear I seen was at the Bronx Zoo."

"I think you're safe," Hardesty said.

"…shots. You'll line up at the infirmary and get your paperwork put away. Dinner is being held for you in mess."

Spinelli slapped his arm. "I'm doomed."

Hardesty followed the group into the barracks and once given the parameters of his new world, tossed his duffel on the nearest lower bunk. Identical to the last one he had been in, the barracks had double-decker bunks lining the fir plank walls on both sides, twenty-five to a side. The fir floors were worn and creaky. In the middle, trunks had been dragged in and left in a jumbled stack. He spied the worn army-drab one that was his.

My whole life's in it. That's all I have left.

"Hey," Spinelli said. He held in his hand the mimeographed camp paper, *The Mountain Call: An Avalanche of Events*. "Mind if I go up?"

"Nope. The place is all yours." Hardesty smiled. He liked Mario Spinelli the minute they met at the train station in Seattle. He acted tough, but he had seen the kid's eyes when they left the train two hours later and headed east into the rugged Cascade Mountains. He was scared. The whole lot of them, their false bravado trying to cover the fact that they were about to meet their match: the forests of the Pacific Northwest. For some reason, at the camp orientation, the kids started following him around.

Hardesty just wasn't sure he wanted to be nursemaid. All he

wanted to do was mind his own business and keep his head low.

Spinelli spread out his bedding and slapped his pillow before climbing down. "Do you remember where we take a leak?"

"Bath house. Out the front door to the left. How's your arm?"

"Not a twinge," he answered, even though he moved his shoulder like it had been struck with a bat.

Lights were out at 9:45. Taps called not long after. Soon the camp descended into snores and stirrings. Except for a family of raccoons ambling forth in the direction of the mess hall's garbage cans, no one was out. While the camp slept, the woods leaned over the buildings and grounds, jagged black guardians poking into the starry night sky. For once there was no hint of rain.

A faint light appeared at one of the barracks doors as a figure stepped out onto the small porch and slipped down the stairs. When he was sure of the direction he wanted to go, the flashlight went out. A few yards and he was in the forest.

It was chilly under the boughs of cedar and hemlock, a musky scent of lichen and moss caught in the damp air. At an old stump, some ten feet across, Hardesty found a spot on the other side, where he threw down his jacket on a log. When he became accustomed to the space around him, he turned the flashlight back on.

He didn't like breaking curfew, but he had a hard time sleeping. Too much crowding in after a long day. Thirty hours ago he had been in Oregon. Now he was as far away as he could get without leaving a region he had grown to love. He hoped that he could start fresh again.

He took a brass medallion about the size of a silver dollar out of his pocket. He rubbed the hard, stamped surface between his fingers and read the words like Braille:

••LOYALTY•CHARACTER•SERVICE••

Honor Award

C.C.C.

The words rose in an arch over two wooden barracks set in the woods. Smoke from a chimney curled up to touch the middle

"R" in the word "CHARACTER" overhead.

Hardesty knew the words by heart just like he knew the way the scars lay on the palms of his hands.

He had been proud when he was given it, but truth be told, some days he didn't feel like he deserved it.

And why he ran away again.

CHAPTER 2

Camp life began ruthlessly at 6:00 a.m. with the playing of reveille blasted over the camp PA system about ten decibels too loud. Groaning, the new enrollees rolled out of bed in various states of dress and went through the motions of preparing for breakfast. The education assistant had explained the routine to them the night before, but the group around Hardesty's bunk just followed him like baby ducks after their mother.

Hardesty got out of bed, tired from staying up so late. He had ended his time in the woods by writing in his journal, slipping back in before light. Since camp life wasn't different from the last place he was in, he fell into the familiarity of the program without thinking. When he put on the blue denim work suit issued to them the night before, Spinelli and his buddies followed his example, then scrambled out the door when he headed towards the bathhouse.

The day outside was chilly and gray with the promise of rain. Morning dew dampened the grass and mist hung low on the sharp, forested mountains overlooking the camp.

"Man, it's cold," Spinelli said as he walked along the dirt path.

The tips of his canvas slippers were dark from the dew. "Is this all it does around here?"

"No," Hardesty said. "Sometimes it rains hard."

Trudging over to the bathhouse, the group from Barracks II met up with a small batch from the neighboring barracks and filed in to clean up. Since most of the camp was on weekend leave, there were only about fifty men including Hardesty's batch of new enrollees. When assembly sounded twenty minutes later, the groups gathered on the main ground in the center of camp and fell into a routine of physical training that lasted nearly twenty minutes. At the end of the exercise or as one of the boys put it, "physical torture," Commander Taylor came out and said a few words to the new arrivals. When he was finished, they trooped off to the mess hall.

Inside, Hardesty guided them to their assigned seating, a long table at which six to twelve men could be seated. As they sat down, some enrollees, obviously old hands at the place, started to call out to them from their table.

"Ellllmer. You'll be sor--ree."

"What's an Elmer?" Spinelli asked Hardesty as he reached to pour coffee into his cup.

"Means someone who makes foolish mistakes."

"I ain't making no -- any mistakes," Spinelli grumbled. "They better not meet me in the dark."

A crew on KP duty brought the food to them to the tune of clinking silverware, ceramic plates, and scraping benches on the concrete floor.

"Holy cow, look at this," Costello's face looked like he couldn't believe the fare: ham and eggs, stewed prunes, cereal, coffee and milk.

While Hardesty nursed his coffee, the kids fell onto the food, their travel fatigue over. They acted like they hadn't had a meal like this since the Depression hit. It was nothing to laugh about. He had been so hungry once that he made a soup out of grass. He quietly helped himself to the plate of ham sent around, then watched them for a bit. After twenty-four hours, he was beginning to sort them out.

Sitting next to him was Mario Spinelli, a dark-haired olive skinned youth of eighteen. From Newark, Jersey, he was one of several in the group from that state. He was a tough kid but never had been fifty miles west of his home. On Park's left was Jeff Staubach, a second generation German from eastern Pennsylvania. He was a big blonde fellow who looked like an underfed farm boy. His Pennsylvanian accent was as familiar to Hardesty as his own. Sometimes, Pennsylvania Dutch terms like "I'm going to red up the room" would slip in to the blank stares of the others, but then again not everyone could understand the New Jersey boys.

There were six in all, including Mario: Sal Lorenzo, Tim O'Connell, Jacob Golden, Haskell Werner and Steve Costello. The rest were from upstate New York with one lone boy from Chicago. Their average age was nineteen, making Hardesty feel like a mother hen. Between the two tables, there were sixteen easterners, enough to form two squads. Hardesty had been told they would most likely stay intact and at the camp. That he'd been added to them didn't bother him, but he knew when the rest of the camp returned in the afternoon, the hazing would begin. Already he had caught glances from the other tables. The fun could begin even sometime before or after Sunday services.

"Wacha got in your lap, Spinelli?" Costello asked around a load of pancakes in his mouth.

"The Mountain Call." Spinelli put the two-page mimeographed camp paper on the table. "Listen to this item. How to Stay Sober. One, don't drink in the first place. Two, don't look for no beer parlors."

"Where we gonna find that?" Lorenzo wondered.

"Not in that town -- Frazier," Spinelli answered. "Three, know your own ca- pass-ity."

A couple of the boys laughed at that.

"Four, get yourself a girl. If you can." The table erupted into laughter.

"I think we get the drift, Spinelli," Hardesty said. "You better finish eating. Your morning's just begun. The rest of you calm down. The other squads are watching."

Spinelli started to say something, but shut up and started shoveling eggs and ham into his mouth. The other boys followed suit.

After breakfast, they were marshaled out to police the grounds and tidy their huts, but because it was Sunday Hardesty explained they didn't have to line up in platoons for roll call and inspection. Instead, they stayed in their barracks and listened to the barracks leader, a seasoned enrollee, give them a lecture on camp policies and programs. Afterwards there was a tour of the grounds. Lorenzo and Costello inspected the heavy pool table, Werner, the library, but Spinelli said he liked the baseball field best of all. "The New York Giants are my favorite team." Nobody, however, looked forward to KP duty, including Hardesty who had done his share of peeling potatoes in the last two years.

At nine-thirty they broke off to change into their Army olive drab uniforms for Sunday service after which the rest of the morning was theirs. Lunch was at noon. Bladstad, the camp forester and projects manager, would meet with them at one to discuss their work assignment the next morning. Drawing on his experience, Hardesty thought it might be clearing trail or bucking logs. They might work with a regular crew for awhile until the squads were broken in and their shots taken hold. He looked forward to the work and the solace it gave him.

The rest of the day settled down to predictable routine. Camp Kulshan was back to full complement of one hundred and ninety-two by dinner at 5:30 and by ten at least three incidents of hazing had come and gone. Coming back from service, Staubach found his new work boots nailed to the floor. During an impromptu baseball game in the overcast afternoon, Sal Lorenzo had a banana slug stuffed into his mitt. And after dinner, four of the boys had their clothes stolen from the bath house and naked and without towels, they had to dash for the barracks about the time the commander's wife was returning from town.

"Lights out" was signaled and at ten, turned off. Tired from their first real day, the new squads fell easily asleep. Only

Hardesty lay awake, waiting for sleep to come.

He was still awake at eleven when the camp commander made a final bed check, but feigned sleep until he was gone. When the crunch of his boots on the gravel path between the barracks faded, Park lay awake looking up at the ghostly pattern of springs above him. He was tired, but wary of falling asleep and dreaming. More than anything else, he wanted peace of mind. Maybe, he thought, it was time to stop running, to put down roots and call it home. He had a glimpse of it yesterday when he met the Alfords at their store. They were firmly planted with that strongest of all tap roots: family affection and love.

Hardesty rolled onto his side and curled up, remembering what he'd done to his.

CHAPTER 3

"Honestly, Kate...Someday..."

"Mom, it was no big thing. I think getting lost with Cory was much worse and you know it."

"But there were no angry, unpredictable animals...even if you were nine."

"There was Dad. I've never seen him so mad or so scared for that matter before or since."

Caroline Alford laughed. What was she going to do with this bright, lovely, totally unconventional daughter of hers? She had been gone for the weekend and had just learned of the bear and her cubs at the river. She kept her voice light and coming into the house, put the mail down on the dining room table.

"Betty Olsen called. I think she wants you to come to her class again. You were a hit."

"I think Elsa was. I let the kids ride her. I'll give Betts a call."

Her son Cory came in from the kitchen. "So you heard about the bear that got Bob Walton's dog. That's what happens when you go to town."

Caroline picked out a bill and opened it. "You're grown up now, but we're not in the city."

"It was nothing, really, Mom. Elsa panicked, but I had help."

"Oh?" Caroline said.

"One of the See-See boys was out. He stopped her when she ran away. Then came and… checked… on me."

Caroline stopped and stared. "You didn't say anything earlier."

"Oh, Mom, what was the point? It's no big thing." Agitated, Kate headed off towards the kitchen past her brother. Caroline lifted her eyes heavenward in exasperation. Cory leaned around her and looked through the mail.

"Better lay off, Mom. She's still prickling over breaking off with David. She knows you don't approve."

Caroline sighed. "It's not that I don't approve. I just want her to be happy."

"Then let her be happy." He found the letter he wanted and patted his mother on the shoulder. "She's got to make her own choices. Betty Olsen's got her pegged. She should be teaching or doing something with her forestry interests. I've heard she's great with the kids at school. Besides, I'm not so sure David Callister was the best man for her."

"Oh?"

He shrugged. "He's smart and all that, but I don't think he really cares about who my sister is. I think he just wants her."

"Shh. Don't talk so crude."

"Well, it's my opinion. Just like a woman shouldn't go around changing a man, I think it works both ways. Kate is Kate and I love her for it. Callister just doesn't understand. All he sees is this beautiful dish." He opened the letter, quieting as he read.

"How's Mary?" Caroline asked.

"Her grandma's still the same. They won't know until Monday if she can go home. Maybe never. There's still infection in her hip."

"What a shame… I'm so sorry. Look, I have soup on the stove."

"I know. I stole some." He grinned like a boy caught stealing cookie dough. "I've got some things upstairs to put away. I'll come down in a few minutes." He closed the letter lovingly.

Caroline touched his cheek. “Of course, dear. Don’t be long.”

Kate was standing at the window looking outside to the river when Caroline came in. It was still sunny out but a breeze was stirring up. She didn’t turn, but after a while she said,

“I’m sorry I snapped at you, Mom.” Kate gave Caroline a faint smile. “I know you mean well, but I just don’t like feeling that somehow everything I do is wrong for me. That I can’t make decisions for myself. I’m not going to be some dried up old maid, but I’m not going to be sitting around listening to other wives talk about their miscarriages and tilted uteruses either. You certainly don’t, even though this place was the other side of the moon for you when you married Daddy.”

Caroline started to argue about Kate’s choice of words, and then thought better of it.

“I want a marriage like you and Daddy have. One that gives and takes. Every man I’ve met in the past ten years has been a taker. They are nice and all, but dully predictable. I want to be loved for me and for what I like and have to say. And I want to like and love back. Is that so unrealistic?”

Caroline sighed. “All I want for you is someone who is smart and can do something with his life. God knows how hard it is for the men right now. I guess I thought David was the one.”

“David’s a friend. And he’s always welcomed here. Invite him any time. But I don’t love him. I never have.”

“All right, dear.”

The sun picked up strength and suddenly burst through the tall windows. It struck her daughter’s hair in such a way that it appeared a deep molten red, like a chestnut. What a beautiful young lady you are, Caroline thought. She respected her daughter’s decision, but still hoped for a life that was away from all this. Maybe a nice home in Tacoma or Seattle. She stopped, and laughed silently. Cory was right. Trust Kate to make her own decisions and trust that they would be right because they had brought her up right.

“Friends?”

“Best friends.” Kate came into her mother’s arms and they embraced.

"Now," Caroline said. "How about some lunch?"

The day after the boys got back from their first weekend leave, Joisey Squad was trucked up to Big Fir high up in the mountains and initiated into that other aspect of CCC life, the side camp.

After three weeks, they had settled into the near-Army discipline of Camp Kulshan, accepting its order as a part of being an enrollee. At Big Fir, they soon discovered that life was much more relaxed, largely because it was under the auspices of the Forest Service. The side camp or "spike" camp as it was called -- because the camp was "just a spike to hang a man on"-- was much smaller in size. It accommodated about 50 men at the most. Although the layout was the same, its purpose was to put men close to where the work projects were. And there was work. Most of the young men were involved in the building of a new fire road that cut through a thick forest of fir. Eventually it would come out on an open range far above, cross and then descend down again into the forest on the other side of the mountains. It was hard physical labor that involved felling trees, clearing, widening and eventually grading. In some cases, bridges had to be built.

The boys arrived at the spike camp around 9:00 am and were shown where to put their gear in their tents - eighteen foot pyramid types with shiplap floors. Then they were loaded back on the truck and taken about five miles away to where a bridge was being constructed. Hardesty sat up front with Bladstad and listened to the forester explain the project. One thing Hardesty knew: the CCC in this neck of the woods and elsewhere built solid, lasting constructions.

"The kids are taught well here," Bladstad said as they bumped along. "We try to instill pride in their work, but I think that comes naturally. In the past two years, they've built two campground shelters and a ranger's station."

"I've seen the ranger's station. Nice building. Stonework's great."

When the truck pulled up to their destination - a cut through a steep forest grade - Hardesty knew what needed to be done.

Hardesty had not seen them in the main camp since last week, but knew their reputation. They were a tough lot, capable of giving back what any streetwise kid from back east could give out. The boys stopped working and watched Joisey Squad get down. A couple of them sat on the long squared-off logs laid on the pebble creek bed and dangled their legs. The rest stayed down in the creek and leaned on their shovels. Bladstad called out one of them to come up.

"Hank Spenser, this is Park Hardesty," Bladstad said. "He's straw boss for this outfit. You'll find him experienced. He was down in Rouge River before this."

"Glad to meet you," replied the lean muscular brunette. He was wearing a tank shirt sagging with dirt and sweat. His face was tanned and hardened, but the lines about his eyes belied a natural friendliness and good humor. He couldn't have been more than twenty-two. Spenser offered his hand to Hardesty then introduced his crew.

"This is Jim LaPlante, Carl Gilhausen, Roy Thompson…" He went around the group of young men no older than Hardesty's squad, the names slipping by too fast to remember. When Mario and the rest of the boys were alongside him, Hardesty did the same. Hank Spenser showed them where they were in the project and then made assignments. Bringing additional tools from the truck, the newer enrollees soon were working.

For a time, they worked separately. The bridge's footing had already been constructed, and what was needed next was the planking.

"See those boards?" Hardesty pointed out the thick wide boards of Douglas fir stacked by the side of the existing road. "We have to drill them by hand, set them in place and nail them with spikes to those squared-off logs supporting the bridge. After that, they'll need to be sealed with creosote."

It was a long morning. Some of the squads worked under the bridge, the rest on top. Except for a water break, Hardesty's squad worked straight until noon when a truck brought out a hot lunch of soup and sandwiches. Another crew working above them with a big cat joined them at that time. Sitting around the bridge, the groups ate and for the first time tried to learn about each other. It wasn't long before talk got around to the subject of family and home. It was obvious who was local and who was not. When it got a little too personal, Hardesty kept the talk friendly by answering Spenser's questions about Rouge River and the camps he had been in down there.

"You've got it made at Camp Kulshan," Hardesty said. "At our main camp we had to sleep on mattresses stuffed with hay. First thing you did when you showed up, they gave you a tick. We had to go to a hay pile to stuff our own bedding."

"We got straw here at Big Fir."

"I noticed."

"Didn't they have some trouble down there?" a boy asked.

"Not any more than any other place." Hardesty took a bite on his meatloaf sandwich. "On the whole they have good relations with the locals. The boys are the same all over. They're basically good kids."

"What about the girls? Did they like their girls dating foreigners? "

Hardesty looked at this new face from the other crew. He was a tough looking enrollee from the Skagit area. He was big with a thick neck and a thatch of red hair. They hadn't been introduced, but Hardesty guessed the type. "I suppose."

"Hell," another kid from the same bunch said. "I heard that a girl got murdered."

"That true, Hardesty?" Spenser's brown eyes deepened with shock.

"Not murdered, but died from exposure, yes," Hardesty said, shifting uncomfortably on his log.

"What happened?"

"I know what happened," the other enrollee sneered. "A girl got kidnapped. Someone played funny with her. Betcha it was some foreigner."

"It happened that it wasn't," Hardesty said quietly. "It was a great tragedy and… some time ago."

"Did they find the bastard?"

An instinctive wariness began to rise in Hardesty's gut. He

wiped his mouth. “No.”

“Sure you ain’t suspect?”

“McGill! That’s enough.” Spenser put his hand on his squad mate’s shoulder.

“It’s all right, Spenser,” Hardesty said. “He’s just checking the competition and finding his own backyard wanting. Just wants to stir things up.” He looked at the boys from the other patrol. “Look, they never found the fellow. Just bad luck. The family was pretty torn up.”

And so was I, Hardesty thought. “Things did settle down,” he went on. “It's a good camp. Like here. You have your dances. The girls are even trucked up here and the boys get along. Same down there. There have been a number of squads from back east and they've done fine. Been a few marriages even …"

"Not here. Not with our girls," someone said. "How can you trust anyone who can't tell the difference between a cow and a horse and thinks an elk is a moose? Or a pasture on a stump farm a lawn?"

"Now why don't you let the ladies decide?" Spinelli asked. He puffed his chest out, grinning from ear to ear. His dark good looks seemed to make the others nervous.

"Ladies? You're the ladies,” the Tar Heel sneered. “You can't even do half the work one of us can do in hour in a day."

"Says who?" Staubach jumped up. "I challenge anyone to prove it." He looked at the others from his squad, especially Hardesty for support. Mario and Sal Lorenzo joined him.

"Well?"

Hardesty could see it coming and sighed. The next few days were going to be hell. A spike camp was often like the Foreign Legion. It ran on kangaroo court rules. The Forest Service let the enrollees police themselves. Joisey Squad had to start proving itself now. He looked over at Spenser. The two of them would have to maintain some sort of order.

"How about a bucking match?" Hardesty pointed up the roughed out road to a large fir down by its edge. It was over two feet thick. "Two teams, each team rotating its manpower. Like a relay race. The crosscut saws are in mint condition. First team to cut four rounds wins. This time."

"We'll do it," one of Spenser's men said.

"So will we." another said from the other group.

"Done," Spenser said. "Get up and shake on it, but hurry. We still have 'til four to finish up before we go back to camp. Lunch is about over."

"Then see how many rounds can be done by one," Hardesty said. "That's fifteen minutes."

The teams were made up while Mario figured out the order they'd go in. "You're included, Park. You're straw boss." Hardesty couldn't say no. When they were ready, the teams went up to the fir. It was decided that they would cut rounds that were eighteen inches in length so that they could be split and used as firewood. A watch was produced and a whistle. The first two pairs set up at each end of the tall fir and on signal began to saw.

It was a wild race of strength and skill. The thick bark of the fir was tough and Joisey Squad made a couple of false starts before the teeth of the saw found its path and began to slice with real determination. Stripped to the waist, the teams put their backs literally into their work pulling and drawing the long saws through the down tree. About a foot into it, the cut was beginning to close above the saw, causing it to pinch. Team members then hammered wedges into the gap as the sawing continued. There was a technique to doing it, something the easterners had learned by trial and error.

"You don't force a saw," Hardesty once told his squad. "There's a give and take with your partner and when the proper rhythm gets going, the saw sounds like a piece of heavy canvas being ripped over and over. A pull one way will make the cut, drawing back kicks the wood out into long thin pieces. Old loggers call them noodles."

Joisey Squad began to make good noodles.

After four minutes of hard sawing, the first round fell and was rolled away. The locals won that one, the next two boys immediately stepping in and setting up their saw. Lorenzo and Golden finished not long after and were replaced by Spinelli and Steve Costello. Getting their rhythm early on, they buzzed through the fir to the cheers of the others. They missed the local squad by a short margin.

The third team ran into trouble almost right off. Hitting a knot inside the tree, Hoss Werner and O'Connell were powerless to go any faster than a slug's pace until they were free. The local squad was already on their last round when Joisey Squad cut through theirs.

Hardesty and Staubach went last, picked because they were taller and in most respects, stronger, but mostly they were used to teaming up together. Both being Pennsylvanians, they had gravitated towards each other naturally and it showed now as they put their backs into their work. Their bodies sweating, their rock hard muscles rippled under glistening tanned skin while they both put all their effort into the rhythm and flow of the eight foot saw. Though behind, their concentration began to pay off each time the saw raked deeper into the wood. The noodles were flying and so was Joisey Squad as they shouted rough encouragement.

Hardesty didn't hear them. He closed out all other sounds and eventually his eyes, as he felt only the saw as it glided back and forth between his partner. There was only motion and then Staubach was yelling at him.

"We gotta give more. More!"

Hardesty gave more. In the order of things, the race was ridiculous, but it suddenly made him absurdly happy. He wanted to beat those local boys and put them in their place. He was tired of the jokes and remarks. He was good as any of them. He belonged here as much they did and maybe more because he loved this rugged mountain and forest country. Grunting, he gathered all his strength and increased their tempo to exhausting limits. The tree trunk began to tremble. Lifting his head, he glanced at the other team and became aware for the first time of the cheering and the noise. The other boys, one of whom was Spenser, were sawing furiously and for a sinking moment, Hardesty thought they had cut all the way through.

"Don't slack, Park!" Spinelli shouted. "Watch your position." He gave the wedge above the saw couple of more hard raps, freeing the space where the hot blade tore up the wood. He stepped out of the way and joined his hooting mates. "Not much more, Jeff! Go! GO!"

Hardesty put his head down again and fought against the strain in his shoulders and upper arms. Sweat poured from his hairline down the sides of his jaws. He was nearing a point of either utter exhaustion or a new level of exertion when he heard the boys around the other team begin to chant. It seemed the end was very near and his squad was going to lose. Shouting to Staubach, without pinching the saw, he bore down on the wood in a final effort and cut through to the ground. The round rolled away just as the other squad finished. Joisey Squad had won.

Yelling and slamming hearty pats on Staubach's and Hardesty's shoulders, the group of Joisey boys jumped and crowed their triumph. Hardesty begged for mercy and a canteen after awhile.

"Sure, Park." Lorenzo and Hoss obliged him by pouring a bucket of water from the stream over him as he sat on the log. When Costello attempted to do the same, Hardesty grabbed the pail and threw the remainder back at him.

"Yowl." Costello arched his back then grabbed another bucket. A full-scale water fight broke out, the Joisey boys laughing and throwing insults at each other. Some of the others from the other squad joined in immediately, but when it threatened to come to blows, Spenser blew his whistle and called the escalating war off.

"Enough. I think Hardesty will agree. The race was won fair and square, although round for round, I think we had you beat."

Spinelli jumped up and protested, his posture resembling a wet bantam rooster. Hardesty reined him in by his belt.

"I'd say that was almost true," Hardesty said. "But no one asks that of the horse that placed. We came from behind and won." He came away from the log and offered his hand to Spenser. "There'll be another time," he said. "Hopefully, fighting on the same side when fire season comes. No hard feelings."

"Naw, no hard feelings."

Soon they were all back to work on the bridge and road. But

there were hard feelings, most of which were unearned and unjustified. Come afternoon, the local squad got their revenge.

The trucks brought the squads back to Big Fir camp around four, letting them out on the parade ground in the middle of the camp. It took a moment for Hardesty and his crew to get their bearings, but they soon located their tents and gathering up gear, headed over to the bathhouse.

The spike camp was more rustic than Camp Kulshan, situated on a narrow prairie track close to a fork of the river and surrounded by a thick mixed forest of fir and deciduous trees. All around and above were high jagged peaks. It was more remote than Kulshan and from experience, Hardesty knew that it ran on its own rules. It would do its own policing and like the other spike camps he had been in, would have its own kangaroo court. That necessarily wasn't bad, just a fact of life Joisey Squad would have to be aware of.

The bathhouse was smaller than main camp's and the boys had to jostle with the other squads for a spot in the showers. "Someone watch the clothes, in case they're run off," Hardesty said as he stripped and joined the mass of stinking bodies along the concrete wall. To a man, each sported white thighs and buttocks where the sun hadn't turned them brown. Spinelli and Staubach squeezed in somewhere near him and carried on a conversation of sorts above the showers' hiss and drumming. Spinelli had managed to lay some bets during the race and was bragging about how he had collected enough bits to take the bus into the city if he wanted or better, pick up something special for the next dame he was going to meet at the dance. He stepped under the shower to rinse off his head and bumped into an enrollee from the squad he had beaten. The Skagit Tarheel.

"Watch it," the red-haired enrollee said.

"No offense," Spinelli replied and went back to talking to Staubach.

"You didn't say sorry," the other countered. "Say it nice."

"Sorry. *Ecusi.*"

"Say it in American."

"Oh, dry up, McGill," a new voice said. Stepping into the

space next to his mate, Spenser lathered up his lean frame as he turned under the shower stream. "I said lay off," he said again when McGill didn't. "Wait 'til later," he reminded his friend.

"Wait for what?" Hardesty asked as he stepped out for his towel.

"None of your beeswax," McGill spat as he looked across the naked backs of Staubach and Mario.

"It's nothing, Park." Spenser gave Hardesty a conciliatory smile as he gave himself a final rub with the soap and wash rag. "Just squad business. You going to the canteen?"

"Thinking about it."

"Good."

Hardesty dressed quickly and went outside. He took a deep breath of the mountain air to rid of his nostrils of the newly sprinkled chlorine inside. In front of him the boys were spread out like ants going home from a picnic across the company "street" where the tents were laid out in double rows facing each other. He stopped by the bathhouse window and dried his ears. He was about to move on when he heard voices inside. It was Spenser and McGill.

"You done?" McGill's voice.

"Yeah," Spenser said.

"I'll alert the welcoming committee."

"All right. Just don't get rough with these boys. They did a hell of a job out there."

After dressing, Joisey Squad returned to their tents where they organized their gear before going out on their free time. Someone had mentioned that there might be a ball game at the field down near the river and Staubach and Golden were interested in that, but first they all wanted to go to the canteen such as it was and get a soda. They were all dry and thirsty. After the contest, Joisey Squad had put in a full afternoon, having felt it important to present a good showing as regards to work. The contest was only symbolic. Everyone was sore and walked a bit stiff. They had really put on the heat in that last leg. As a group, they made their way over to the wooden building set up on brick posts. Inside, they found some of the boys from McGill's squad playing pool. Hardesty put his nickel on the counter and got the bottle of soda he wanted. He nodded to Spenser who was working behind the counter.

"You on duty?"

"Yeah. There'll be a list for you too."

"KP?"

"That's how it works."

Hardesty grinned wryly and borrowed an opener for his soda. "You keep this?" he asked as he put the metal cap down.

"Sure. We make boot scrapers with them. Toss it in the bucket over there."

Hardesty took aim at a metal bucket in the corner by the counter wall and pitched it in square. Taking a swig of his soda, he turned around and watched the rest of his crew settle in.

"I hear you're from Pennsylvania," Spenser said."You from a coal mining town?"

"No, a small place. Mostly farms."

"Near Philadelphia?"

"No, the other side. South of Pittsburgh."

"How you end up out here?"

"I wanted to come. I've always wanted to see the West. Went to eastern Oregon first, then to the Idaho border for a while. Last place was Rouge River."

"You seem to know your way around a tree. Did you ever do it before?"

"Sure, but not home. Oregon." Hardesty took another swig, wanting to change the subject.

"Didn't mean to pry."

"It's OK. A man's bound to be curious about someone who out-bucked him."

Spenser laughed. "Say, about McGill. Don't pay him no mind. He's a Tar Heel."

"What's that?"

"Someone who came out from North Carolina to work out our woods a few years back. They're rough and tumble some of them. Scottish and proud of it." Spenser lifted up the counter top and came out. "You going to watch the game down by the river?"

"Planning to."

"Then watch out. You boys are going to get baptized. It's tradition. There's no avoiding it. I'd just get it over with. Go down to the game. They'll hunt you otherwise."

Hardesty stared at him for a moment. "All right. Thanks for the tip. I'm not sure who all can swim."

"Don't worry, they'll tie a rope around you if you don't."

"How civilized." Hardesty came away from the counter taking his bottle with him. The pool game was over. Spinelli and Staubach along with the others gave him the high sign and they headed over to the door.

"See you all at the game." McGill's voice was as sweet as lemonade.

Sure, thought Hardesty. Only we're it.

CHAPTER 4

The game was in the third ending when McGill and some others struck. It was all supposed to be a joke, a tradition, but from the start, it turned ugly. Surrounding the group of eight, a crowd of local enrollees began to ask questions of the boys and when Costello or Spinelli spoke they got teased for their accents.

"Hey, they did all right," a blonde local named Larsen said. "They did their share."

McGill knocked the enrollee's cap off. "Sure they did. You're gonna get dunked."

"So?" Staubach said. The big blonde Pennsylvanian straightened his back. He was a farm boy, but not the hayseed they thought he was. He put up his dukes. "We've got bigger rivers where I come from."

"Yeah, but we've got man eating fish. Ever wonder why a salmon looks so threadbare by the time it spawns? It's the little fishes in the water that nibble at them, bit by bit. They can take off your toes if you're not watching. If the cold don't get you, they will."

"Where do I sign up?" Staubach asked.

"Why, over there," one of McGill's buddies said. He pointed to the willow-lined bank at the end of the field, some fifty feet away.

"Come on fellows, let's show them what we can take," Staubach said.

"Now wait a damn minute," McGill growled. "You got to be done proper."

"Then carry me there." Staubach swaggered his shoulders.

McGill looked annoyed but instantly several enrollees seized and carried Staubach like a plank of wood to the river. There they swung and tossed him out into the river. When he yelled as he hit the water, some of the locals began to cheer and chant, "Dunk them, dunk them." The boys pushed on Joisey Squad, edging them toward the water. Joisey Squad pushed back.

Careful, Hardesty thought. He didn't like the feel of the whole situation. A strange electricity prickled around the water's edge.

"You're next," McGill said to Jacob Golden.

"Where's Jeff?" Golden craned his neck and looked down river.

"He's okay," someone said. "He's making his way down to the next stop."

"How fast is it here?" Hardesty asked.

"You worried?" McGill sneered, his face puckered up like a Boston terrier's.

"No, I'm just inquiring whether I should dog-paddle or display my Tarzan-like swimming skills."

"It's not too fast," an enrollee said. "And it's deep."

"Stop talking," McGill said. "You, Toland. Get some of the boys to bring up Golden and O'Connell."

"Don't sweat it," Golden said and let himself and O'Connell be thrown in. Hoss Werner was next. He stood at the edge and held his nose before jumping off. Some of the locals laughed. A ways downstream Staubach waved as he climbed out and then turned around as Golden and O'Connell came paddling by. They had narrowly missed a big snag in the water, coming around it backwards.

Up on the bank, it was Costello's turn. McGill's squad charged him, but he fooled them all and twisting out of their hands, took a flying leap and went blind into the water. Fortunately, he avoided going out into the river's faster middle.

"How's the water?" Spinelli yelled to Costello. He got an answer quicker than intended when he was pushed in. He grabbed onto an enrollee from Spenser's squad and they went in together. The local man came up sputtering to the roars of the others. Both young men made it down to the stony shore several hundred yards down, safely making it around the snag. Costello and Werner were there to pull them in.

"That leaves you two," McGill said. He looked really steamed. Turned around and looked sharply at Hardesty and Sal Lorenzo. "Who goes first?"

Hardesty shrugged. At this point, they had no choice, but go in. The honor of squad at stake. He looked over at Lorenzo and was surprised to see him pale and drawn. A tough, wiry Puerto Rican from Newark, what bravado he normally carried was long gone. He worked his mouth constantly, his dark eyes on the water. Sensing Hardesty's gaze, he looked up at his straw boss and instantly Hardesty knew what was wrong. Lorenzo couldn't swim.

"I'll go," Hardesty said. "I'll wait for you, Sal," he said directly to him, ignoring McGill's curious look.

"I'd rather not go at all," the eighteen-year-old replied.

"You gotta. It's tradition," a local enrollee next to him said. "Unless you're chicken."

"I ain't chicken." Lorenzo spat.

McGill suddenly understood. "Aw, he can't swim. That's what he's afraid of." His eyes grew wide. "Hey, Larsen. Get that clothesline rope."

"What for?" Lorenzo asked.

"To snag a fish."

"Do I have to?" Lorenzo asked Hardesty.

"No," Hardesty said. "You don't have to."

"It's okay," Larsen said. "I'll tie you good. You'll only get wet." Squeezing through the group around the remaining enrollees from Joisey Squad, the blonde put the rope around Lorenzo's waist and tied it in front. "We'll hold onto you. I won't let go. I promise."

Lorenzo seemed resigned to his fate. Hardesty could see it on his face and appreciated the fact that he had probably faced worse things in the streets back home.

"You going in, Park?" Lorenzo asked.

"Sure. I'll go in." He took the rope in his hands. It didn't seem strong. Its cotton fibers looked old and rotten. "You got another?"

"This'll do," McGill said. "Quit babying him. You going in?"

"Sure... I'll do it," Lorenzo said. "When Park's ready."

"Ready?" McGill nodded to two of his friends and before Hardesty could react, Lorenzo was picked up and tossed far out into the river. He went down, then came up sputtering, grabbing desperately for the taunt rope.

"That was a dirty trick." Hardesty got right in McGill's face and slammed him on his shoulders. "What the hell did you do it for? What was the point?"

McGill shrugged him off. "Watch your paws."

Hardesty watched the boy flounder in the water and hoped Larsen and the two others that held him would bring him in quickly. He hesitated, wondering if it would do any good at all to go in, when he could help haul him in here on shore.

"Bring him in, Larsen," he finally asked. "He's done his time."

"Yeah, sure."

"No wait," McGill said. "He's not done."

"He's done." Hardesty reached for the rope but before he could lay hold of it, in one sickening moment, it broke, causing Larsen and the others to fall to the ground. Lorenzo went spinning out into the middle of the river, thrashing his arms wildly where the rope had once been secured.

"Park!" The boy screamed, then quit when he got a mouthful of water.

"You bastard, McGill." Hardesty tore along the edge of the bank, looking for a place to go in, watching in horror as Lorenzo swung back into shore directly in line with the snag. For a moment, he seemed to be held in place there, before swinging out into the current again and crashing back into the weathered gray roots of the old tree.

"The rope!" Careless of his safety, Hardesty dove into the water and let the current take him down to the snag. At the last minute he stroked over to where Lorenzo was caught on some roots. The boy's head was bleeding and half-submerged under the water. Hardesty came alongside and kicking out, clung onto one of the roots while desperately lifting Lorenzo's chin out of the water.

"Sal!" he shouted above the water's noise. He slapped him on his cheek and the boy's eyes opened. "Hold on. I'll cut you free. Can you do it?"

The boy nodded, choking and spitting out water. "I think so..." He had one of his arms wrapped around a gnarly root, but when he brought up his free arm, he cried out in pain. One glance told Hardesty that it was broken. "Just hold on."

Hardesty got his knife from its soggy scabbard and sawed on the rope. The water was a numbing cold and he found it hard to concentrate as it pulled relentlessly on his clothes and body. His feet were in danger of slipping off the root he stood on. He did not notice that Spenser had joined him until he was beside him. Together they got the boy untangled from the snag.

"Dumb tradition!" Spenser yelled over the water's torrent. "You did good, Sal. No one's going to give you a hard time."

The boy smiled weakly. He looked like he was going to pass out and Hardesty feared shock. When he was completely free, Hardesty asked if anyone had gone to get a doctor.

“Yes,” Spenser said.

"Then let's get him away from this." Knowing that it would probably hurt him, Hardesty chose the best lifesaving hold he could think of for this water and kicked out into the river with Lorenzo. Spenser stayed close and together they were swept downstream to the low bank. By now most of Joisey Squad was standing there ready to help as well as a crowd of boys from the other squads. The dunking had turned ugly and many were ashamed. As soon as the three were within grabbing distance, there were hands to help pull them in safely to shore. Groaning, Lorenzo was gently lifted out of the water and brought up on the bank. A blanket was produced and the boy wrapped up. A group of enrollees volunteered to take him to the infirmary, but Hardesty checked him again for shock. The boy looked cold and pale, but Spenser okayed the move and Lorenzo was quickly taken away.

"What happened?" Spinelli asked.

"That happened," Hardesty replied pointing to McGill as water dripped off his head and nose. His sopping wet clothes clung to him like he had just emerged fully clothed from a bathtub. His skin was like goose flesh. As they walked back up towards the field, McGill was standing with his little group. Larsen off to the side looked horrified, but McGill didn't look particularly perturbed. There was a sly smile on his face when Hardesty came up to him.

"He couldn't take it," McGill sneered.

"He took it all right. Here's his answer." Hardesty slugged the Tar Heel in the mouth in a single movement that sent McGill to the ground. Hardesty stepped over him and walked on, gathering people as he went. His own squad stayed close to him, clearing the way as he went back into the camp. Something roared behind him, yelling at him to stop. Hardesty turned in time to see McGill charging up to him.

"No one lays a hand on me!" he shouted. "No one!"

"All right, I won't."

McGill didn't see Hardesty's foot until too late. Tripping, he lost his balance and went rolling down the bank to the pebbly narrow beach below.

"I'll get you, you dirty foreigner," McGill shouted as he climbed back up, but Hardesty was already across the field. He held his hands up in the air.

"No hands," he yelled back, his squad laughing beside him.

Bladstad was in Callister's office when the truck pulled up in front of the infirmary.

"Isn't that truck from the spike camp?" Callister said getting up from his desk.

"Appears to be," the forester said. "That looked like Park

Hardesty in the back."

Bladstad watched the Pennsylvanian get down from the canvas covered truck bed and go to the infirmary door. Doc Sorenson came out and with two enrollees from first aid went into the back of the truck and brought out Lorenzo on a stretcher. He was wrapped with wool blankets and sporting a temporary sling. Bladstad watched them take the boy inside with Hardesty helping.

"Think I'll go over," he said.

Hardesty was standing at the door to the examining room when Bladstad came in.

"What happened?" he asked.

Hardesty told him.

Bladstad shook his head. "That McGill. He ought to be disciplined. He's a good worker, one of the best fire fighters, but he's unprincipled. He must not like you very much."

Hardesty shrugged. "Our squads had a bucking contest. We won."

"Figures..." He looked at Hardesty curiously. "What are your plans? Going back?"

"No, I can stay down for the night. I'll probably go back at noon. Sal will have to stay here while we're at the spike camp. He might be able to join us next week."

"Let's see. You're working on the new fire road."

"Yeah."

"He'll be back. It'll take three weeks. What did Spenser have to say about all this?"

"He was mad. Pretty apologetic. I don't think the other squads will give us much more trouble now. Mine proved it can pull its own weight."

The front door screeched and Callister came in. He nodded at Hardesty.

"Hard day in the woods?"

"Sort of. We're getting retreaded." Hardesty turned to Bladstad. "I think I'll go see if anything is left in the mess to eat. We left before I could get dinner."

"Look," Bladstad said. "When you're done, come on over to

my place. You're welcome to relax with me and my wife."

Hardesty smiled. "Thanks. I appreciate that, though I won't make a great conversationalist. I think I'll hit the hay before lights are out. It's been a full day."

"Come anyway."

Hardesty nodded at both of them and before slipping out the door, called into the room.

"See you later, Sal."

Callister watched Hardesty go. "Interesting fellow."

"I like him," Bladstad said. "I rode up with him today. Pretty level-headed guy, not the usual stuff we get out here."

"How's that?"

"He's educated. I swear he is."

"You mean college?"

"Yes."

"What's a man like that doing in the Three C's?"

"Dunno, though it's not against the law. The Depression hurt everyone and I've met many enrollees who had to quit school to help their families. Only this one has me intrigued. He's no freshman in college."

Callister looked thoughtful.

"Of course neither are you, Mr. Education Officer. All that studying in Illinois."

"Chicago," Callister murmured. "Northwestern."

"I keep forgetting you're back from there. You've been with us so long you've got lichen growing on you."

Callister laughed. "I suppose so."

Doc Sorenson came over to the door. "Are you the mourning party?"

"No," Bladstad said. "Just wondered how the boy was doing."

"It's a clean break. I'm going to set it now, then get him to bed. He's worn out and sore. You can stay if you like."

Remembering Doc's way with setting bones, Bladstad politely declined. "The missus expects me home." He patted Callister's shoulder. "See ya, David."

Hardesty found peanut butter and blackberry jam in the kitchen and had to settle for that. Afterwards, he headed back to his barracks to change. As he crossed the parade ground, Jim Taylor, the camp commander, came out of the camp office and called him over.

"Have a moment?"

"It's yours, sir." Not sure what to expect, Hardesty followed the burly ex-policeman inside. Since the incident at the river, he had been half-expecting a meeting with Taylor. Although he was viewed with affection by enrollees and staff, the commander was also a strong, though even-handed disciplinarian. As Hardesty was led into the man's office he couldn't help but think the gray-haired commander reminded him of a WWI general about to call him on the carpet. He wore his CCC corps uniform like a military officer.

"Heard you had an incident up at Big Fir. I was in the city. Mind telling me about it?"

Standing with his hands behind his back, Hardesty told him, leaving no details out. When he was finished, Taylor asked him a few questions, in particular about McGill. Hardesty answered them straightforward, then waited for Taylor's response.

"He'll be disciplined, of course. As for you, I'm not so sure your response was appropriate, though understandable. When you get back to the spike camp, I want you to report to Williams there and ask for some disciplinary duty. Understood?"

"Yes, sir."

Taylor moved some papers on his desk with his big rough hands, then cleared his throat.

"You've been in a while, haven't you?"

"Yes, sir. Since '33."

"Then you know the rules and the way things are." He looked sharply at Hardesty for a moment, then softened. "McGill's a hard case. He's had hard times with his family. Dirt poor - made even poorer by these times. But being here has helped both him and his family. Done him some good. That's the point of all this. I want you to remember that."

"I do already, sir."

"If you're wondering why I'm saying this, it's because that it's the good things I've heard about you. You've whipped your squad into good shape these last weeks. Bladstad said that you've been an excellent straw boss and that you've shown knowledge about things that we're trying to accomplish here. People like McGill are out there. It takes a leader to handle them and keep them going the direction they should take. Handle this and you can consider yourself in for the long haul. What do you think about this part of the country?"

"I like it very much, sir. It's beautiful."

"Then you should know that there might be opportunities beyond the corps. Especially here in the woods."

"Thank you, sir. I'll think about it. May I be excused, sir?"

"You may. Goodnight to you, Mr. Hardesty."

CHAPTER 5

Hardesty went over to Bladstad's at eight, wearing his dress uniform. Amy Bladstad greeted him at the screen door and let him into their small log bungalow nestled in a cedar grove at the end of Camp Kulshan. She was a petite woman with a full, sweet face and short blonde hair held back with a barrette. Bladstad got up from his armchair, newspaper in hand to welcome him.

"Care for coffee?"

"Thanks. That would be nice." He inclined his head politely at Mrs. Bladstad and went over to where he was invited to sit. There were some pictures on the wall and he looked at them before sitting down.

"That Darcy Meadows?"

"That's right. That picture was taken in 1908. Hiking club my folks used to belong to. They explored all over the mountain and its flanks."

"I hear there's copper and gold up there."

"That's true. More to the Canadian border. My brother had a claim up there before he got killed in an avalanche. Took him and all his buildings out."

"Geez, I'm sorry." Hardesty didn't know what else to say, but he felt of wave of guilt. Bladstad had lost his brother. Hardesty didn't really know what state his brother Paul was in. He looked at the next picture.

"Those are the ice caves up there and that's the largest glacier." Bladstad pointed out some features.

"Pretty impressive." Down in the corner of the picture Hardesty saw a smudge of blue next under a steep incline of fir and hemlock. "What's this? A lake?"

"There are scores up there. The Forest Service likes to keep them stocked."

"How do you get them up there?"

"You take them up on your back in tanks and put the fry in. I'll be doing that in mid-June. Most of the lakes will be nearly unthawed from winter."

"I always forget that. June, July seems so late. What kind of fish?"

"Trout, mostly. We've been trying a type from Montana. They have to be re-stocked every year."

Amy Bladstad came in with his coffee.

"Would you like cream or sugar, Mr. Hardesty?"

"No, thank you. I like it black."

She visited with them for a few minutes, then got up. "Excuse me. I've got a little one to put to bed."

"I didn't know you had family." Hardesty said after she was gone.

"Just getting started. Been married about fifteen months. Amy's an old high school sweetheart. We just got reacquainted a couple of years ago. Like we never been apart."

"That's nice... You been in forestry long?"

"Since '28. My family's been involved with logging and forestry since the 1880s. My grandfather came over from Sweden to work in the Northwest woods. My father logged too and later managed sawmills, but I... I was drawn to the trees. I wanted to see how to stop all the over-harvesting. Some areas around here were devastated before the Great War. It was so bad that there were programs to entice people from the cities to move on the lands and try to farm them. It was hopeless, of course. Too many stumps and poor soil. Me, I liked the scientific end of forestry. I wanted to see things work. Get a real replanting program going and tackle the problems of soil erosion."

"You from Frazier originally?"

"No. Down the valley way. By Twin Forks."

There was a comfortable silence. Hardesty savored his coffee and leaned back in his chair. It was nice being in a home. He had almost forgotten what home was like. He liked Bladstad and was curious about his ideas on forestry.

"Where are you from, Park?"

"A small place in western Pennsylvania. You probably never heard of it."

"Try me."

Hardesty started to say something, then changed his mind and gave the name of another town. "Fair Chance."

“No, I haven't," Bladstad laughed. "Interesting name, though."

"Yes. Downright inspiring."

"I know you told me you'd been out here since the summer of '33. You must have signed on right away."

"As soon as feasible. I thought it would do some good."

"For your family?"

Hardesty stiffened very slightly. "Yes," he mumbled. He looked at his coffee for safety and was relieved when there was a knock on the front door. Bladstad went over to the screen door and pushed it out.

"Why Cory and...Kate."

From outside, Hardesty could hear voices, then the screen door whined. Cory and Kate Alford came into the small living room. Hardesty got up and offered his hand to Cory when he came over.

"Evening, Miss Alford."

"Mr. Hardesty."

"We aren't interrupting anything, are we?" Cory asked.

"Nope," Bladstad replied. "Hardesty's down in the camp for the night. One of the boys in his squad broke his arm at the spike camp. They brought him in to set it."

"How badly was he hurt?"

"He's all right," Hardesty said. "It wasn't a bad break."

"That's good news."

They all stood in the little space designated as living room and talked. Hardesty stole a glance at Kate and admired her once again. She was wearing riding pants but had on a soft coral sweater with a Peter Pan collar and tiny silver earrings. She had even added a little lipstick. Her fair oval face looked golden from being outdoors and he followed the flow of her curly auburn hair pulled off her forehead with a barrette. She caught his gaze.

"How are things working out for you?" she said.

"Fine. How about you?"

"Oh, busy as usual. I'm helping to pack materials up to one of the mining camps and I've been asked to collect some alpine flower samples later this summer for an artist."

"Elsa treating you well?"

"Yes. She's working hard these days."

Hardesty leaned over. "Any bears in her nightmares?"

Kate laughed. "Not recently. I won't tell either."

"Neither will I."

"Why Kate and Cory," exclaimed Amy Bladstad as she came into the room. "I thought I heard someone at the door."

"Where's that sweet Andy?" Kate asked.

"Why don't you see for yourself?"

Linking arms, the two women left, leaving the three men standing in the middle of the room.

"How you been?" Cory stuck his hands into his pants' pockets and studied Hardesty with a mild smile. "Kate says she met you a couple of weeks ago under stressful conditions."

Hardesty grinned. "It was a bit unusual."

"I hope now that you're settled in, you'll take the time to come to the store. I'd like to show you around."

"Thanks. I'd like that. Things have calmed down a bit, although there's the spike camp to adjust to, but the weekends should be more stable."

Cory looked over at Bladstad, then back. "Word that I heard was that you had a run-in up there," he said in a low voice.

Hardesty was astonished that he even knew about it.

"Oh, things like that get around pretty quickly. I knew an enrollee had gotten hurt, but the news was about how you laid McGill out flat. You did a good thing putting him in his place, but it's not going to make life easy for you from now on."

"How does he get away with it?"

"I'm not sure if he'll be able to do much more," Bladstad said. "He's a great fire fighter. One of the best. Absolutely fearless, but he's beginning to wear a little thin with the camp commander. As long as he doesn't rape or murder, he can stay in, but I think Big Jim's glad he's in the spike camp most of the time."

The men stopped talking when the women came back into the room. More coffee was offered. When pinochle was suggested, they started a game that went on for an hour more. Eventually, Hardesty noticed his watch.

"I better go," he said. "It's been a long day and it's close to lights out."

Everyone stood up at once, disappointed that things had come to an end so fast.

"Thanks for everything," Hardesty said to Amy Bladstad.

"Oh, you're most welcome. You play a good hand, Mr. Hardesty. Please come again."

"Thanks, ma'am. Mr. Bladstad," he said as he retrieved his jacket. He started for the door when Kate called to him.

"Mr. Hardesty, would you mind so much if I went with you? My car's over by the camp office."

"You coming, Cory?" Hardesty asked.

"Later. Bladstad wants to show me a new fly he's invented. Just take a couple of pans with you to scare off the bears. Kate won't mind." Cory positively beamed from his chair at the dining table.

Kate gasped. Hardesty could have sworn she had blushed. Amused, he held the door for her, then led the way out to the trail back to the parade grounds.

Hardesty didn't go back to Big Fir until afternoon the next day. By then Lorenzo was feeling better and resting more comfortably. Getting his arm set had been tough. Hardesty came by to see him before lunch and promised to let him know how things were going up on the fire road project. They would see him in about two weeks. In the meantime, he could practice his tap dancing routine. Sal threw a book at him. The boy wouldn't admit it, but Hardesty knew he secretly aspired to do it.

After lunch, Hardesty had an hour to kill before the truck came to take him up, so he chose to spend it down by a creek that flowed into the river a quarter mile away. Sitting on a rock above the creek bed, he took out a book he had picked up in the camp library. Most of the stuff there was newspapers like the *Seattle Times*, *Seattle Post-Intelligencer* and *Christian Science Monitor*, government publications, popular novels, and textbooks although there was a worn copy of *Ivanhoe*. Hardesty had found a book on forestry and he thought he'd give it a try. For Spinelli, he picked up *Captain Blood*, some swashbuckling adventure, and a mechanics magazine for Staubach. He hadn't been sitting very long when a chipmunk came out and tried to steal some cake he had brought from the mess hall in a bandanna. The little rascal darted around the rocks and bushes, sometimes stopping to sit and look at him, its tail jerking like the tip of a tiny whip. When Hardesty started reading, it dashed in close to the rock he was sitting on and snatched a piece laying on the cloth before tearing away.

"Hey. Pretty daring, aren't you?" Hardesty said out loud. He watched the piece disappear into its fat jowls. He pinched off some more cake and laid it near him and went back to reading. Immediately, the chipmunk came back and shot away with its prize. Hardesty threw a little pebble at it and narrowly missed. He tried again and hit it on its tiny rump. The little creature jerked its tail and then ran.

"Gotcha!"

"Got who?"

Hardesty turned around. "Miss Alford..." He jumped to his feet.

"Mr. Hardesty. You weren't talking to yourself, were you?

"Hush, don't tell. In the woods too long. No, I've just been robbed by a *Tamias striatus*."

Kate laughed and Hardesty decided that he liked the sound. "Mr. Hardesty. You've been hiding. Are you are a biologist?"

"No..."

"Well, you're not far off. About the *Tamias*. Being an easterner, you would naturally name the eastern variety of chipmunk, but unfortunately..."

"Ah, then the... *Tamias.... minimus*, although if I were a chipmunk, I wouldn't particularly want to be called a "least" chipmunk. I'd take offense."

"Don't worry." Her laugh was infectious. "We don't really have chipmunks on this side of the Cascades. They're actually ground squirrels. *Spermophilus lateralis*."

Hardesty grinned. He liked the verbal sparring. "It still wants my cake. And its name is much too big for its size."

"He doesn't seem to mind," Kate said. The disputed mammal had come back.

"He looks like a chipmunk to me." Hardesty reached for the handkerchief. The tiny animal scurried around the rocks, then hunkered down to watch them.

"I think we're being observed," Hardesty said.

"You're avoiding my question. You said that scientific name like you're used to it."

"A hobby of mine," Hardesty countered gently. "I enjoy natural science."

"Then you are in the most perfect place...."

They stopped talking and stared at the trees along the stony bank on the other side.

"Not collecting specimens these days?"

Kate picked up a twig. "No. That's later. I came up to see Jim Taylor on some business for Cory. My brother was a LEM -- you know -- "local experienced man." He still occasionally works for the camp."

"That something you'd like to do, Miss Alford? The Forest Service? I would think that would be something that would interest you."

"Why, Mr. Hardesty. You hardly know me, but I thank you

for considering that. It does interest me. Folks don't know it, but Cory sends things my way."

"How did you get interested?"

"In part from growing up here. My dad says it's all the fault of a great-aunt of my mother's. She was a proper Bostonian who was a naturalist some seventy years ago. She was a published writer, but wrote under a man's name. Are you familiar with New England, Mr. Hardesty?"

"I've been to Boston."

"Lucky. This woman, Sara Colton, hiked and climbed all over New Hampshire looking for inspiration in the White Mountains. I'd love to see them."

"So you've never been there?"

"No. I haven't been east of Yakima."

Hardesty's bunched his brows. "Where's that?"

"It's southeast of here. On the other side of the mountains."

"Oh." He glanced back at the brush next to the rocks. The chipmunk had suddenly disappeared. When a red-tail hawk glided out of the trees behind him, Hardesty understood why.

"How long have the Alfords been up here?" Hardesty asked after awhile.

"Since around the turn of the century. My grandparents were immigrants."

"English?"

"No, actually Scandinavian."

"I thought Alford was English."

"It's not our real name. It used to be Alfjord. It got changed at Ellis Island."

"Heard that before." He cocked his head. "You said your mother's family was from New England."

"Oh, yes. So very proper. They came out to Oregon a long time ago and became proper pioneers of Portland. It caused quite a lot of comment when my mother married my father.

Hardesty reached down for his rucksack. "It was nice seeing you again Miss Alford."

"You're leaving now?"

"Yes. I should see my friend before I go."

“Is your friend all right?”

“He’s going to be fine."

"I'm glad. Cory always said the spike camps can be tough sometimes. "

"I think things will take care of themselves. There are usually ways to settle disputes."

He shook his bandanna out. "Peace offering for *Spermophilus*." He smiled when she laughed.

CHAPTER 6

The next two weeks at Big Fir passed without incident. True to his word, Jim Taylor had spoken to McGill and had him disciplined. For two weeks he would not be allowed to go on weekend leave. He would spend it on KP and other maintenance duties. McGill appeared to take the news calmly, especially when Hardesty got assigned to the laundry for a day. But as Hardesty was to find out, he was only biding his time, waiting to confront the Pennsylvanian legitimately.

After the hazing at the river, Joisey Squad had settled into the routine of the spike camp without too much difficulty. Still foreigners to most in the camp, they grudgingly earned their place there and both as a squad and individuals made friends. Spinelli with his enthusiasm and street smarts made him an easy favorite with several of the local boys and both Staubach and Golden gained acceptance for their musical ability. Like at many of the CCC camps, enrollees provided a lot of their own entertainment. Golden played a solid jazz clarinet. Staubach played guitar. Together they became involved in a camp band.

The work on the fire road continued for two weeks. During

this time, the squad went out regularly with Spenser's and McGill's squads. After finishing the bridge, they continued to cut out the road by felling and clearing trees. When the rains came, they still went until the trucks couldn't get in through the mud. A day off was declared and work continued in the camp around the buildings. When the weekend came, most of the squads were allowed to go down to Kulshan, but crews were needed to repair some damage on outbuildings at the camp and it was decided that Spenser, McGill's and Hardesty's squads would stay behind. They would work half-day shifts, having the afternoons off to themselves. A senior leader, himself an enrollee, was left to watch the camp while Williams, the head of the spike camp, went down to Frazier to meet with other forestry personnel.

Hardesty woke Saturday twenty minutes late and in a gloomy frame of mind. He hadn't slept well the night before, waking from time to time after dreaming things he could not remember. Only the sensation of guilt. It had been over two years since he had left home and jumped a train where he rode on "cushions going west" like countless other young men. In that time he sometimes thought he had put everything behind him. He had not only gained strength and new skills, he had found a new confidence in himself and often, a peace of mind. He had made friends and met people who had faith in him. He had been especially happy here the last few weeks, genuinely liking the younger enrollees in his squad and his workload. He enjoyed helping them and being their mentor, acknowledging they were changing him too. He liked the responsibilities of being a straw boss and the work in general.

He had joined the CCC in 1933 to find himself and to make amends for what he had done. There were long periods of time when he felt that he was accomplishing that, but sometimes in the still quiet of early morning, visions of the car on its side in the snowstorm and his brother's half-face would come and then he feared that he would never be forgiven. No matter what he did, he would always be guilty.

"Hey, Park!" Spinelli yelled. "Get up! It's late. You'll miss breakfast."

Hardesty rolled out of bed, putting his bare feet on the fir floorboards. The tent was cool, but someone had started up a fire in the Sibley stove set in a sandbox in the center of the tent. The wood popped and crackled near the foot of his bed.

"Man, you look beat. Bad night?" Spinelli sat on the plank board bed next to him. The mattresses were ticks stuffed with hay.

"No, not really," Hardesty lied as he dressed. "Where's Staubach?"

"He's washing up. The rest of the guys are already out and ready to go. According to Spenser there'll be no formal drill. We're just to get over to breakfast as soon as possible."

"Everyone else is over there?"

"Almost. Some of McGill's squad is here." Spinelli looked at his friend. "I'll wait."

Hardesty grinned and changed into his work outfit. When he was ready, he joined the boy at the stove and combed his hair. "What's the weather like?"

"Cool and misty. Should burn off according to Spenser."

"He been talking to you?"

"Yeah…He's all right. That McGill, though. He's a bad apple. I don't like him at all. You ready?"

"Sure."

Spinelli went ahead with two other mates from the tent. Hardesty followed, then remembered his shaving kit and went back to retrieve it. He was back near the tall opening when a shadow suddenly filled it. It was McGill. His face looked flushed and his square body seemed to cover every corner of the opening as he leaned in with hands on the flaps.

"I was waiting for this, Hardesty. Just wanted to remind you that I haven't forgotten. I'm going to get you."

"How? Why take the risk?"

"Oh, it'll be all right. The camp has its rules. I'll dust you, Hardesty."

"Here or later?"

"Oh, not here. But in time. Just remember that I'm watching."

"All right, I'm warned," Hardesty said. "Look, I'm hungry. We can talk later." Ignoring McGill's threatening stance, he slipped under the edge of a flap and stepped down off the low tent platform. Behind him he could feel McGill fuming, but the man did nothing. Later, though, true to his word, McGill followed, watched and waited.

After breakfast, the squads loaded up wheelbarrows with lumber and cedar shingles and took them over to a storage area that was being re-roofed. Some of the boys set up a station where they could make additional shingles while the old roof was removed with crowbars. Hardesty got his squad started by showing them how to use a beetle and froe.

"You hold it like this," Hardesty said as he placed the 'L'-shaped froe on top of a cedar bolt quartered and cut to twenty-four inches tall. "Then you take the beetle and bash the top of the metal blade."

"That beetle looks like some caveman's club" one the boys said. The rest of the squad laughed.

Hardesty went on to show how the froe was placed on the bolt a half inch in from the edge and beaten with the wood beetle until it sunk into the cedar and caused it to split into a plank or shake. When it popped off, the bolt was flipped and the procedure repeated. This way, the shingles were cut uniformly, the ends always being tapered. He helped them set up additional splitting stations. When the boys looked like they knew what they were doing, Hardesty looked to the roof. By coincidence, both McGill and Hardesty ended up on top.

For several minutes they worked side by side with neither one of them saying anything, but as work progressed, they had to interact for safety's sake. The old rotten shingles flew down, exposing perlins that were halfway decent. Working from the peak down, the two young men eventually cleared the roof down to hastily set up scaffolding. Sitting at its edge, they waited for the shingles to be passed up and a line run on the outside of the roof. The sky was still overcast and the day cool, but the men sat and drank cold water from canteens. McGill was silent, ignoring Hardesty all together, but spying a leather band on the

Pennsylvanian's wrist, he asked about it.

"What is that?"

"Rawhide. White tail deer."

"What did you do? Buy it at the store?"

"No, I shot it. Skinned and tanned it myself."

"That a fact."

Hardesty looked straight at McGill. "That's a fact. You're from the Skagit. You ought to know. Ever go elk hunting?"

"Have you?"

"Yes."

A load of shingles was tossed on the scaffolding plank, momentarily distracting them.

"Where was that?" McGill sneered. "The city zoo?"

"Oregon."

McGill reached over for a can of nails. "You're in my way, Hardesty." He shoved into him and retrieved a can. "I'll start laying them this end. Double layered, first row. Then we'll snap a line."

"All right. Just don't forget to use roofing nails. Those are twenty penny."

"Aw, give the other can, dammit." McGill yanked the can away, smoldering over his mistake.

Hardesty handed them over politely, saying nothing.

For the next hour, they worked as a reluctant team, laying up the beginnings of the shingled roof. The air continued to be cool and damp, but it carried the wonderful smell of freshly cut cedar as the shakes were split below. After a while, Hardesty called up Spinelli and had him take over. After showing him how to lay them so the rain wouldn't work its way down through the cracks, Hardesty got down and got a drink of water from a water jug. The camp assistant came over and asked how it was going.

"We can put another two up on the top on either side. No sense working it short. Mine or McGill's squad can send someone up."

"Looks like everything is under control. You and McGill getting along?"

"As sweet as honey with dead bees in it."

The roof was halfway finished by noon. When the lunch bell rang, the openings were covered up with canvas and the tools put away. Inside the mess hall, the three squads bunched down near the serving counter, keeping to themselves in the big hall. Joisey Squad hunkered down at its table, occasionally exchanging words with friends in Spenser's crew. McGill's group was quiet.

Golden leaned over the table, his wire eyeglasses slipping on his nose. "That McGill giving anyone a hard time?"

Spinelli shrugged. "Not much different than the last two days. He was almost nice up on top." He looked over at Hardesty who was wiping his gravy up with a slice of bread. "How about you, Park?"

Hardesty was as noncommittal as Spinelli. "He's biding his time. I wouldn't put it past him to pull something off while Williams was away." He asked for the pitcher of milk and poured himself a glass. It was all so sophomoric. Like some Saturday afternoon serial western. Big showdown in Big Fir, only McGill would do it legal. Get him in some sort of flap where they would end up punching it out. Hardesty looked at his hands. He hadn't used gloves in awhile and he wondered how good the big Tarheel was.

After lunch they were supposed to be on their own to do what they wanted. The sky had cleared up and the dazzling peaks that surrounded the camp caught the sun on their snowy fields. In some spots not even the summer sun would melt their hidden crevasses. Walking outside with the rest of his squad, Hardesty heard that some of the boys wanted to play touch football. They ambled their way down to the field and when they had the numbers they needed, began to play. Hardesty stayed uninvolved until Spinelli and Staubach yelled at him to come in, then for more than thirty minutes they played a hard round that kept them all running and laughing. Hank Spenser was there and all of his squad. McGill was notoriously absent until he showed up an hour later with two others from his squad. By then, they had all switched to baseball.

"Got a spot?" he hollered.

Hardesty wished someone would say no, but no one objected

and McGill came into the game opposite his team. Joining the outfield, McGill eventually traded with one of his mates on second base.

"Hey, skinny," he yelled to Spinelli who was just stepping up. "Don't forget which end of the bat is up. We don't use any 2 by 4's. This here is real baseball. Not some city back lot. See. We even have bases."

Spinelli winked at Hardesty waiting his turn in the lineup. "Aw, take a ride, McGill," he shouted. "You don't even know what a baseball stadium looks like. All you've got is fir trees and raccoons. We've got the real stuff. The New York Giants. Even the Brooklyn Dodgers." He took a couple of practice swings then turned to Larsen who was catching. Since the incident at the river, the enrollee from McGill's squad had been friendly. "Whatcha guys got around here anyway?"

"We've got some minor leagues. The Seattle Indians."

"That a fact?" He took a final practice swing, then held back when the ball came through for ball one. "So who's big?"

"Mike Hunt." Larsen said. "I saw him once. He's a right fielder. A couple of weeks ago they beat Portland 12-11."

The ball came by again for ball two. Spinelli checked again. "What's his average?"

Larsen told him, then threw the ball back to the pitcher. He squatted down again and said, "Maybe I could take you some time when they come to Everett. It's not that far away."

"'Preciate that." Spinelli swung at the next ball and hitting it square, sent it out into the outfield for a double.

Costello was up next, but he was out on a fly ball. Spinelli made it back to second on a dive and got his fingers tromped by McGill. In an instant, the boy was up on his feet. Slamming into the older, heavier enrollee, he tried to push him over, but McGill laughed it off.

Hardesty watched ruefully from the makeshift batter's circle. Spinelli was on his own, but he was getting tired of his squad being badgered.

"What's the matter with you? You want to be out?" McGill yelled.

Spinelli continued to fight him. "You bastard," he said. His words got increasingly hotter. Some of the boys from both sides came over and tried to get the game back on track. McGill just kept turning around, trying to swing the boy off. Finally, some of the enrollees pulled him off.

"I'll get you for that!" Spinelli shouted.

"For what? Did you hear that, Spense?"

"Just stay cool. Both of you." Spenser tried to keep Spinelli away from the other, but the boy struggled back. McGill pulled away highly amused. He looked across the infield to Hardesty who was standing next to the plate.

Hardesty caught his smirk and shaking his head, tapped the bat in the dirt.

"Let's play ball," McGill said. He backed away, giving the boy room.

Hardesty watched Spinelli wrestle away from Spenser and rubbing his aching hand, go back to his position by the base.

"Batter up," someone yelled and play resumed.

Hardesty stepped into the batter's box, hastily scratched out in the muddy dirt and got into his batter's stance. He let the first pitch go by for a ball, then fouled the next one back for a strike. On the next pitch, he hit a line drive that got him around towards second, but he had to head back to first. Spinelli, in the meantime, came running home for the run just ahead of the ball and slid across the plate. The rest of his team cheered. The run had tied them with the other team.

"Just luck, Hardesty," McGill hollered. "You won't get past me." He swung around to the others from his squad. "You watch him, now. Don't let him get past."

Staubach was up next, but tapped to first and got thrown out at first. Hardesty charged second, trying to outrun the double play. At the last minute he slid for the muddy plate. McGill came deliberately after him and even though Hardesty was safe, the Tarheel fell on him for a tag, digging his knee hard into his lower back before pulling back. Gasping in pain, Hardesty rolled away and stood up as fast as he could, but seeing stars, he nearly blacked out.

"Feeling a little low?" McGill asked as he dusted himself off.

"Don't count on it," Hardesty said, spitting on the ground. "Do that one more time and you won't be able to cry Mama."

"Try me."

Hardesty flashed his eyes at him. "You really want it, don't you?"

"Yeah... Show me you're not some eastern tinhorn. You don't belong out here. None of you do."

Hardesty rubbed his back. The pain came in hot waves and he wondered if a kidney had been hit. He looked across the infield. The other boys were watching, waiting to see what would happen. He knew that if he backed off now, McGill would be on him the rest of his tour here. He needed to be put in his place and for good.

"Okay. Three rounds or whoever tires first. No matter who wins, truce is called. This is a spike camp. There's too much work to do."

"You lose, you do my KP."

"I win, end of conversation. Until then, let's finish the game."

The game ended in a tie when Golden got a hit, but was out at second on the next play for the third out. When it was announced that Hardesty and McGill were going to settle their differences like gentlemen, the game ended abruptly and the boys marched back with them to the canteen where the sports equipment was kept.

Spinelli opened the trunk and two pairs of boxing gloves were brought out. "I'm your manager," he told Hardesty." I know all the tricks."

Hardesty stripped down to his sleeveless undershirt, the narrow shoulder straps accenting the work-hardened, tanned muscles in his arms. He took the gloves from Spinelli and put them on, oblivious to the patter around him. His lower back still hurt, but he hadn't passed blood when he dropped by the bathhouse, so he assumed everything was all right. He watched with half-amusement as Spinelli tied on the gloves. The boy was chattering non-stop, carrying on a conversation with a half-dozen others. Everyone had an opinion where the fight should take place. One of the boys suggested that they go outside by the flagpole. There was plenty of space there.

"For who?" Hardesty asked.

"Your audience."

The boys went outside. The match had by now created so much excitement that the boys working in the kitchen came out to watch. The camp assistant came out of the office and standing on the porch, asked what was going on. "Anyone approve this?"

"Oh, it's all legal," an enrollee said. "No one's called anyone a rat yet, but they need to settle their differences."

The camp assistant looked at Hardesty and McGill. "Whatever you do, it's got to be fair."

"Of course." McGill smiled at Hardesty. He was bigger, heavier, and very sure of himself.

McGill took off his work shirt so that he was in his undershirt like Hardesty. He looked powerful. Curly red-gold hair on his chest peeked over the top of the undershirt's u-shaped neck and his shoulders were freckled, but he was tough and hard, as a forester should be. He put up his fists and then toed the line along with Hardesty near the flagpole.

Staubach had a watch. Spenser had a whistle. Together, as the circle around the fighters formed, they tried to bring some order to the dispute. The rules were hastily explained but when the whistle blew, the circle around them surged as Hardesty and McGill both danced away and came together moments later to test each other with their first blows. Neither wasted any time, each of them quickly laying blows that were successfully blocked. After several series, they separated. Moving away, Hardesty danced lightly around, his hands up in front of his face. He had learned one thing. McGill was bigger and heavier, but he had the longer reach.

"Not bad, Hardesty, but don't count your chickens. You know, buck, buck."

"Why don't you shut up, before you lose some teeth. Your mouth is gaping."

McGill reacted on that and threw a punch, but Hardesty saw a hole and got in the first real hit, a solid right to the Tarheel's cheek. Wasting no time, McGill came back with a left and a right which were blocked, but hard enough to knock Hardesty back. Hardesty recovered quickly, but McGill was back again and this time he scored with a left then a right into the Pennsylvanian's side. Hardesty danced away, then came back with his own hit into the other's stomach.

"Get him, Park!" Mario crowed. "Don't pay him no mind."

The fighters danced around, then became serious again with an exchange of blows that left both men smarting. Behind them the boys cheered their favorites on. Hardesty came in again with a good solid hit to McGill's jaw and came back again with a left to the other side that sent McGill back. One thing about McGill: he didn't take "no" for an answer. He charged with a ferocity that forced Hardesty to protect himself. Again and again he was struck, until he pushed back against the bigger enrollee. They locked against each other, attempting to get in blows as they did so. Spenser had to come in and separate them.

"Anyone getting tired?"

"Aw, dry up," McGill said and threw a punch at Hardesty that caught him on the side of his eye. His head turning, Hardesty stumbled back to the shock of Mario and the others, but he regained quickly and came back to dance lightly around again.

"Stubborn," McGill said.

"Willing," came back Hardesty.

Then he grinned. Maybe he didn't like getting beat up, but like the bucking match, there was something in him that always made him come back and meet the challenge. For the hell of it. He had always been that way with his brother Paul. And they had fought and scratched from the time he could walk and talk. If it wasn't fists, there was always the mouth.

For the next couple of minutes, they danced around exchanging punches and moving the circle further out into the parade ground.

"Tiring, Hardesty?" McGill taunted. He was getting annoyed that he hadn't settled the dispute in one flat knockout.

"Hell, no." To prove it, he increased his tempo, coming at

McGill with a heavier barrage that almost knocked the Tarheel down. A couple of boys from his squad pushed him back in.

"You caught me off-guard, foreigner. You're not a Max Bauer, but you're not bad."

McGill winked at his supporters, then laid in a good hit to Hardesty's mid-section. He beamed when Hardesty grunted loudly, but Hardesty took the smirk off McGill's face when he came back again and again. He was making better contact with his reach. Angered by his continual harassment, McGill put his weight to use and succeeded in hitting Hardesty so hard in his shoulder that he fell back. A follow-up to his right cheek sent him down.

"Oo-ohh," the crowd said.

The circle of boys collapsed as they surged in to see the damage, but Hardesty had rolled out and was up. Sweat poured down into his eyes and mouth. He felt heavy with it, but he quickly wiped it dry with his arm and came back in. The circle held for a moment then inched back at Spenser's hollering.

"Get back! Way back! Hey, Van Houten! I said back!" Spenser hit the enrollee with his cap, and then the crowd to make them widen the ring.

The boys moved, yelling at their favorites as they went, but Spenser had to spin away when Hardesty and McGill nearly mowed him down. They were hitting pretty hard now, the sweat and blood coming regularly. A cut on Hardesty's cheekbone had opened, blood welling from the split and the skin on the eye socket was bruised, but McGill looked no better. His nose was bleeding on one side and his lip was cut.

"Give in?' McGill shouted.

"No way."

The crowd cheered with joy.

Sometime during the exchanges, Hardesty's mood shifted and occasionally he found himself laughing after an especially hairy encounter. There was something exhilarating about it, because it no longer made any sense. He was so tired, but McGill was tired too. Despite the cool air of the late afternoon, their shirts and pants were soaked, their hair plastered to their skulls.

"The three rounds are over," someone said, but no one was going to give up. There would be no knockout. They'd just go until they dropped dead.

There was one time when it looked like it would be all over. Hardesty had landed a series of punches that made McGill slip on the muddy ground. He fell down and lashed out with his feet. The heavy boot hit Hardesty on his shinbone causing Hardesty to swear and nearly loose his footing, but he staggered back and waited for the Tarheel to wobble up. After that, they were so tired they leaned against each other and flailed away, neither of them making any headway.

"Give up?" McGill said, his breath coming in jagged little puffs.

"Do you?" Hardesty felt equally winded.

McGill pounded Hardesty in his side, but he was pushed away before causing further damage. Finally, neither one of them could move. They rocked around, hugging each other as boxers do, like two leaning bookends with nothing in-between to hold them up.

Spenser who seemed to have forgotten all about his whistle and the rounds in all this, suddenly remembered it.

"Had enough?"

"No!" Hardesty and McGill shouted, but it was over. They were exhausted. Hardesty was beginning to realize the scope of their cuts and bruises.

"Well, I call it done," Spenser said. "No honor lost on either side. I say you stop and shake hands."

Some in the crowd protested, but when Spenser blew his whistle, friends from both squads came out and began to separate the fighters. McGill tried to get in one more lick, but at the last minute it looked more like a pat on the back. In the end, they touched each other's glove and then staggered off with their supporters literally holding them up.

"Jesus," said Spinelli. "You've really got a shiner, Park. Oughta get that cut looked at too." He yelled at Staubach to get the first aid room opened. "We're coming over, but first we're gonna hit the showers."

"Could someone get me a soda?" Hardesty asked as he limped over. His lower back throbbed and he felt light-headed.

"Sure, sure." Spinelli yelled at someone to go get one then grabbed onto Hardesty when he sagged. "It's okay Park. Just keep marching."

"Just point me." Hardesty thought Spinelli gave out orders like he was experienced doing this. Then he remembered the boy saying he had hung around the boxing ring at the Newark `Y' where he had so proudly learned to swim and knew a thing or two.

"You did good, Park," Spinelli said as he shooed people back, "and you're all right in my book. Even if you're literate and a Pennsylvanian."

Hardesty spent the remaining time until supper with a hot water bottle filled with crushed ice on his left eye. Stripped out of his damp clothes, he had stayed under the shower stream where he half fell asleep. There were bruises on his chest and shoulders and the area around the eye where he had been hit was shiny and fast turning black. He didn't bother to soap, only let the hot water eased the soreness and the hurt. When he was done, one of the boys gave him a towel and waited with his robe like he was some sort of royalty. Hardesty felt like shit but as he plodded out the door and over to the infirmary, he was relieved to see that McGill didn't look much better. Still, there was some feeling of resolution. At mess, the animosity between the two squads lessened. Since neither side had lost face, boys at either table could in all conscience talk to each other and actually admit a friendship or two.

After dinner, Saturday night ended on a pleasant note with several rounds of pool and cribbage in the little canteen, but Hardesty only heard about it later. Having defended the honor of the East Coast in general and Joisey Squad in particular, he promptly went to bed and fell sound asleep.

CHAPTER 7

The lights were on at the Alford home when Callister parked the camp truck along the picket fence. In the fading twilight, they made long, weird blocks of gold on the lawn and against the dark cedar and fir that huddled close to the two-story gabled house. He came through the gate and up to the porch where a small group of men was gathered. From inside the house, a piano pounded out "Roll Out The Barrel," almost loud enough to drown out the tree frogs creaking like rusty hinges in the cedars.

"Say, David. We wondered when you'd get here. What hung you up?" one of the porch sitters said.

"Had to go to the spike camp and check on the afterhours programs. They were late getting in and late to mess." Callister took the flask of whiskey offered him and took a swig before handing it back. "There was fight among the enrollees."

"Who won?"

"Some foreigner from back East."

"Well, drinks here, food's inside-- smoked salmon, potato salad. The usual suspects."

The screen door whined and Cory Alford came out.

"Hey, David. Glad you got here. Want to go fishing in the morning?"

"Wish I could, but work's spilled over onto Sunday again. Another time."

Talk about fishing on one of the best steelhead rivers in the state bloomed around him. Callister listened for appearance's sake. He had gone fishing, but these men were local. They lived and breathed the mountains, forests, and river. He didn't. A year and a half ago, he'd been an outside man.

Eighteen months, he thought. I've been here eighteen months as head education officer. Who'd had thought they'd buy my ideas after Dwyer blew it? Won me a place right here on this porch.

"- it was about this big and took my line clear out to the end before I could get a handle on it. It fought and leaped all the way in. I got it up to me close enough to nab it - but dammit –the hook slipped out. It must've been stuck in its tail." The speaker demonstrated to roars of laughter.

Callister laughed along with the others. He'd heard the stories before. Hiding his boredom, he looked into the big window behind him where the old oak table had been covered with a lace cloth. Around it people leaned over and sampled plates of food. Some of the men had brought their wives and he recognized Dolores Taylor, the commander's wife. The Osborne twins were here as well, gracing the gathering with their version of female society learned largely from Hollywood musicals. Their short blonde hair permed as tight as the day it was done and pale chiffon dresses looked wildly out of place. One of them curtsied above a platter of smoked salmon and waved her fingertips at him. David waved back, thinking her perm as attractive as a cocker spaniel's back, then stood still when another figure came into the dining room carrying something red wiggling on a bed of lettuce.

He didn't have to look beyond the auburn hair to know that it was Kate Alford. She could unsettle him even before she walked into a room, and she unsettled him frequently. Right now, there was an uncomfortable twinge somewhere between his stomach and groin. People thought of them as a couple, but truth was, despite what the community thought, there was no romance. She'd made that clear from the beginning, even though he'd kissed her good night a time or two. That would change, he thought. He'd bring her more his way.

He watched her arrange the plate on the table, then go back into the kitchen. She was wearing a forest green pullover sweater and plaid skirt that complimented her hair and complexion.

Thank goodness, he thought. No pants.

That disturbed him. She was too damned independent and tended to dress like her brother too much to suit him. Even more irritating, she liked forestry work. She could make a trail, pack a horse, and put down a tree as good as the forestry boys, but Callister couldn't understand why she preferred living the rough life. She was one of the most beautiful girls he had ever met. Smart and levelheaded too. She was wasting her time here.

When she came back into the room with her mother, Callister felt the overwhelming urge to go in and get her. To drag her out and declare his love for her. Couldn't she see? He hadn't been so taken with anyone in years.

"Say, David. I forgot." Cory said from his perch on the porch glider.

"Oh?"

"Yeah. Some conflict, I guess. Something to do with the school."

"All right...Guess I'm hungry too. You coming?" he asked the others. To a man, they put their hands on their stomachs and said they were full.

Kate saw David come into the house and felt a twinge of irritation. She'd have to explain to him again why he shouldn't expect to see her all the time. One, she didn't love him though he was educated and charming. Two, he was making assumptions of their friendship that were not true and she had to correct them. He had been a pleasant friend at first, but recently, she felt a subtle, stifling presence that sought control over her.

Many people in the community and at the camp admired him, but she wasn't sure how much he was interested in them. In an unguarded moment, she had seen the disdain in his eyes more than once when he dealt with some of the less educated in her community. Their unsophisticated ways seemed to offend him. Or had she misunderstood?

These were people that she'd known all her life and her parents had taught her to care about neighbors. In a crunch, neighbors counted more than all the diplomas on the wall. That didn't mean that they didn't care about getting an education. Everyone had worked hard to get a school and keep it going. From a tiny pioneer log cabin from before the Great War, the schools had grown. Some students had even graduated and either went to the Normal School in the city or the University of Washington.

No, there was more to David Callister than people saw. Maybe that was why she was uncomfortable. She slipped back into the kitchen. It didn't take long for him to find her.

"Hi, Kate."

Grabbing a large can of peaches from the pantry, Kate turned around to greet him, feigning surprise.

"Oh, David. There you are. I tried calling you to say that I can't come to the dance this Friday. I'm spending the night with Betty Olsen's fifth grade class. I'm helping to teach a unit on biology - frogs and other wildlife stuff."

"You camping?"

"Of course. We got some old Army tents from Jim Taylor and we'll use them whether it rains or not."

"It'll probably rain..."

Kate laughed, trying to be friendly and not offend a guest in her parent's home. "It usually does, but we're not called 'webbed footed' out here for nothing." She spied a can opener on the worktable. "Say, could you open this for me?" She handed him the can of peaches while she found a bowl.

"Sure. Uh, how many kids?"

"Twelve, I think. Twenty if all the sixth graders come. It'll be fun. I hope you understand."

"Sure." He jabbed the opener into the top and turned the key around.

"Thanks. You're a pal." Putting a glass bowl on the worktable, she stepped back, but he took her hand and pulled her to him. He gave her a soft kiss on the mouth.

"Any time -- pal."

"David." She stiffened in his arms. "Please."

"You know I'm crazy about you."

"I appreciate that, but..."

David pushed back a strand of hair off her face. His fingertips felt clammy. His eyes shone with an unnatural glint.

"David. Stop. We've been through this before. Please."

"Please what?"

She pushed away from his chest, but he continued to hold her.

"David."

"Oh, there you are, Kate. What's this, Biology 101? You two! Look, David, I'm going to have to borrow her for awhile."

One of Kate's best friends, Betty Olsen, stepped into the kitchen. She was a petite blonde with dimples that put Shirley Temple to shame.

Kate pushed down Callister's hands. He let go, but Kate felt his hands shake. "Evening, Mrs. Olsen," David said. What's this about frogs?"

"Oh, that. It's the annual overnight. That's where I take a contingent of wild near-adolescents out in the woods and teach them about wildlife --as if they don't know. Kate's doing life cycles. Bob Reilly's going to show them how to plant trees. Can you believe it? Surrounded by several million of them and some don't know the difference between a pinecone and a catkin. We'll put in seedlings." She folded her arms and grinned as Kate broke away.

Kate gave her a silent thank you.

"It won't take long." Betty said. "I promised."

"It's all right. We were just finishing up." David turned to Kate. "See you later?"

"David. All right. But just for a moment. That's it." And the last time, she thought.

Once David was out of the kitchen, Betty turned to her. "What was that all about? I thought you two broke up."

Kate sighed. "We did. Just that he hasn't got the message." She poured the peaches into the bowl. "I used to think he was nice. A breath of fresh air. Then he got too possessive. Wanted to control what I did." She put a serving spoon into the bowl with a splash. "I don't want to see him again."

"Why meet him later?"

"To tell him that I mean it. I don't want to see him again. If we could be friends, we could be friends, but..." She gave her friend a weak smile. "I'm going to have to stay low for a while. Avoid the male population all together."

"What if he presses you?"

"I'll tell Cory. He'll make him understand."

"What about the guy with the bear?"

Kate laughed and shook the spoon at her. "Oooh. I'm going to get you."

CHAPTER 8

Joisey Squad was back in the main camp the following weekend and having come through the fire, found the other squads according them a newer degree of respect.

"Hell," said Staubach, "anyone can run a river and split shakes. What it takes is style. We've got style."

"That a fact? Next time you go swimming just remember to tuck your shirt in and take off your corks. You looked like a hayseed," Spinelli said from the safety of his bunk.

"I ain't no hayseed. At least I can swim. Where did you learn your strokes? The Newark Water Department?"

"At the Y'," Spinelli said.

"Hey," Golden said, "you ladies fighting? We've had enough fighting." He came between their bunks, wearing his corduroy bathrobe and boots, scuffing his feet like he was wearing slippers because the heavy corks were unlaced. He flung his towel up on his upper bunk. "You ought to devote your time reading like I do. It's more cultured. Besides, it'll impress the girls. I just got word. There's going to be a dance up here next week."

Spinelli rolled over on his bed and propped his head on his hand. "That a fact?"

"They're coming here?" Hoss Werner asked.

"Yeah. Some of the boys are already planning what they're going to play. There may be two bands this time."

"How do you like them apples?" O'Connell said.

"Apples?" Spinelli reached under his pillow for a newspaper. "You mean roses. Look at this picture I saw in the city paper. Take a look at that dame. Ain't that something?"

In unison Joisey Squad crowded around the top bunk and stared. On the page filled with news items from around the country, there was a picture of a beautiful girl dressed in a swimming suit made of roses.

"Santa Rosa, California, it says. Do you suppose they all look like that down there?" Costello wondered.

"There won't be any rose swimming suits like that up here, but I've seen a girl or two down in Frazier," Staubach said. "Not bad looking, considering the scarcity of the population."

"As long as they got legs."

"They've got legs -- although you might not know it with all the clothing they sometimes wear. You can't walk two feet behind your house before getting scratched or stung. Girl told me so herself."

Other enrollees came in from the showers, getting ready to unwind for the rest of the day. Being Friday, they would have the weekend to themselves. Nothing but a movie was planned for the evening and twilight would be late tonight.

Hardesty came into the hut with Spenser. He greeted the boys with a nod and put away his shaving kit. His hair still wet, he gave himself a final rub before putting on a clean uniform shirt. Spinelli pointed to his eye. Hardesty still had the shiner.

"Won't wash off," Hardesty said.

"Then you'll have to use makeup. You hear about the dance, Park?"

"Sort of. I heard it's next week." He ran his comb through his hair a couple of times. "I suppose you have your wardrobe all figured out."

"Do you?"

"What I hear is regulation only."

"You going?" Golden asked.

Hardesty shrugged. "I don't know."

"You gotta go," Spinelli said.

"We'll see." Hardesty put away his kit and smoothed out the blanket tucked tight on the bed. Someone had been sitting on it. "Anyone get the mail?" he asked.

"I did," said Werner. "Sorry. Forgot there was something for you." The big twenty-year old picked an envelope off his bed and handed it over. "I don't think it came through the post, though." He passed it past O'Connell's face. O'Connell sniffed at it.

"And it's not from some girl."

Hardesty grinned. Some days he felt like a den mother. Taking the envelope, he glanced at the handwriting briefly then walked away from them, his heart pounding.

So he had been found.

Standing by the cold wood stove, he carefully opened the letter up. It was a short note, friendly but to the point. It must have come up yesterday from the city through the camp post, he thought. He glanced at his watch. He had about an hour to drop everything and go to meet him.

"Good news?" Spinelli asked.

"Just a line from someone I knew in one of the camps. Any news about duties?"

"I think you're clear, Park," Staubach answered. "Nothing for you until tomorrow night."

"Thanks. There's no first aid tonight. Anyone needing help can ask me later." He folded up the note and put it into his pants pocket. "I think I'll take a walk before mess. If anyone asks, I'm going into Frazier." He picked up his camp-issued jacket and hung it over his arm. "It shouldn't take long. In the meantime, you could organize a committee for the dance. Golden can take down ideas for a theme. I'm sure Spinelli has several hundred, although I suppose it's a tossup between *Naughty Marietta* and that Jean Harlow movie, *Reckless*."

"Heck, I was favoring *G-Men*. You see that, Jeff?"

Hardesty left them talking about their last time-off in town. As usual, he hadn't gone in, despite the invitations.

Outside on the barracks' steps, Hardesty looked across the

barracks, and felt an increasing oppression. Garrison. The man was so damned persistent. All Hardesty wanted to do was to be left alone, but the older man wouldn't hear of it.

It's for your own good.

Someone shouted to him as he stepped down. It was Larsen from McGill's squad.

"Where you headed Park?" the towhead called as he walked over.

"For a walk."

"Spinelli around?"

"In the hut."

Hardesty waved him off and started out to the road. Once beyond the log gate he headed down the graded gravel road towards Frazier. It was a pleasant afternoon. As he descended down through the forest growing close to the banks along the road, his boots scrunched on the bits of rock. Except for an occasional call of a crow or Steller's Jay, it was remarkably silent. Hardesty liked that -- the solitude. Shouldering his jacket, he walked along looking for animal sign in these forests he had come to love.

About a mile down the road, he stopped and looked his watch. It was nearly four-thirty. Garrison would be around somewhere. He started up again when he heard the sound of a car approaching, its motor chugging on the hill. Down a ways came an old Model A Ford, its bug lights rattling as the car trembled over the rough road. As it came up, he looked inside at the driver and saw that it was some local man. It wasn't Garrison. No one from the camp, either. As it passed, he gave the driver a wave and went on.

The road curved around and crossed a single lane bridge made of logs that had been built just a few years before. Halfway across, Hardesty stopped and leaning over the rail, looked down at the creek below. It was rushing high after a night's rain, sounding and smelling sweet and fresh. He became so engrossed that he didn't hear the second car until it was almost up to the bridge. When he turned, he straightened up at the sight of a light truck with a small flat bed. It was marked CCC on the outside panel. It pulled up alongside him and stopped to idle. The driver rolled the window down.

"Afternoon, Park. I see you got my message in time," the driver said. "I didn't know if you'd come or not. You're looking fit."

Hardesty nodded back, not sure why he was nervous. "How're you, Floyd? Looks like you're doing well. Well fed, that is. Lily must be cooking up a storm."

The driver chuckled and signaled him to get in. Once Park was in, Floyd backed up.

"I saw a road a ways back. Maybe we can take a ride. Figured you might not want to be seen with me."

"It's not that, Floyd. I'll meet with you any day. But I appreciate the consideration. No one knows I know you."

Garrison turned around and a few hundred yards down the road, drove onto a fire road put in about a year ago. It took off on a steep grade that drove onto a forested ridge that went back into a canyon area several miles back. It was noisy inside the cab, so neither man spoke. Maybe there was nothing to say. Not yet. Hardesty hadn't seen him in about five months, but he was amazed that Garrison cared that much to run him down.

Floyd Garrison was forty-nine, and a man who had devoted a long time to the Forest Service. His work in the Northwest was well known and he was greatly admired. He had also seen action in France during the Great War, had even received a commendation. As a result he worked easily with the military heads at Camp Lewis, Washington which served as one of the Army centers that helped distribute young men arriving for assignments to CCC camps throughout Region 6. A conservationist with a military bent might have seemed odd, but the business of organizing young men from a diversity of backgrounds required such experiences. He knew his trees and mountains. He also knew his men. He moved with ease from camp to camp, but in the early years, he had been stationed in camps in Oregon. That is where he had met Hardesty.

About a mile back into the wilderness, Garrison stopped the truck and got out. Below them on the left of the truck, the ridge dropped several hundred feet to a tight valley floor that resembled a canyon more than a valley. On top, it was forested, but below it had been heavily logged and it looked quite bare. The road that eventually met it from above was fairly new and still under construction.

Hardesty joined him at the edge of the ridge. Neither man spoke at first; eventually Garrison asked, "You work on this?"

"No. Some other crew. I think they'll do some planting too. It was logged some time back, and erosion has hurt it. There was a wash out two years ago."

They became silent again. Garrison fished in his jacket pocket for his pipe and began to stuff it. Hardesty focused on movement in the scrubby brush across the canyon, waiting for Garrison to speak. When he did, the older man wasted no time getting to the point.

"I don't know how you thought you'd get away from me, Park. Sneaking off like that."

"I didn't sneak off. I got a transfer."

"You never said anything to me or Lily. She's worried about you ever since."

"I'm sorry. I truly am. She's a lovely person. I respect her enormously."

"I'll tell her that. I'm relieved that it was not just the home baking."

Hardesty grinned and kicked a rock in front of him. "How did you find me?"

"Records. Almost a fluke actually. I've been transferred myself -- back to Washington State. It sets better with Lily and her family." Garrison tamped his pipe and began to light it. "I didn't think you'd leave the Corps entirely and I was right. I saw your name on a list two weeks ago at Camp Lewis. When I knew I had to come up here, I took a chance."

Hardesty nodded. He said nothing. What could he say? This man knew more about him than his own father. What he really thought or felt.

Or what hurt him.

He had been like a father, giving Hardesty some answers and

direction he needed when he didn't think he had anywhere to go any more.

Garrison looked Hardesty's face over and noticed the bruise near his eye for the first time.

"Say, that's quite a shiner you got there. What happened?"

"A camp dispute, neatly solved by bashing in my opponent."

"He still standing?"

"It was a draw."

"Friends?"

"Hardly. But I'll sleep better at night."

Garrison laughed. "You're a survivor. You always manage to come out on top."

Hardesty became quiet. It wasn't always that way. Once he had been shaken to the core, his actions and very soul put into disrepute and censored. He had been close to drowning, with no hope for him on the third time he went down.

"Why did you come?" Hardesty asked.

"Now, Park, you know why. You don't have to ask that question. I care about you, son. We're not only eternally grateful for what you did for us, I just couldn't stand to see a soul slip away because like heart rot in an alder, you'd eaten yourself inside out with grief. You need to get beyond that."

"I'm not grieving. Not anymore."

"That why you left? Because I was making you face up to it at last and stop the running?"

Hardesty sighed. Stuffing his hands in his pockets, he moved away. Garrison could be so personal. So clear to the point. He changed the subject.

"I'm in with a good bunch. All easterners, every last one of them. 'Joisey Squad' we're called. A bunch of kids, though. Not a one over nineteen and five minutes."

"How they doing?"

"Except for some tracc of homesickness, they're doing fine."

"That how you got your shiner?"

Hardesty turned around and grinned. "You sure are nosy."

"You sure are obstinate." Garrison looked out over the canyon. Far off a small creek meandered down through its center. Hardesty followed his eye. Something moved near it and he saw a doe and her young fawn move up from the brush. "What do you think of this place?"

"Beautiful. Great camp. Good people too. I like the head forester a lot."

"Let's see. That would be Bladstad. You know, you could be one too. You've got the skills and that's good. Time was only the toughest could be out here, but that's changing. You have that new ingredient - a college education."

Hardesty shrugged. "I didn't get so far..."

"You can always go back."

"That what you came to tell me?" He was irritated, yet moved by Garrison's ceaseless concern. Like he was worth it.

"No, Park. I only came to say that I'm around when you need me. I'll be working with CCC camps on this side of the Cascades mostly. I've been to Darrington south of here several times already and the camps at Skagit and Cornet Bay. If ever you need a friend or someone to talk to, write me or call. I'll come. It's as simple as that."

Hardesty said nothing. He just let the silence fall again.

"When's mess?" Garrison asked.

"Same time everywhere else."

"I'll drive you down to the road or -- unless you want to go into the village."

"Actually, I just might do that. Are you going to be up here for awhile?"

"As a matter of fact, I am. I've been invited to dinner at the commander's. I'm going to stay on through Sunday morning. Is this an invite to meet again?"

"I wouldn't want to disappoint Lily. I'll write her a note and bring it down tomorrow to the store."

"Good. That's good."

Garrison started back to his side of the truck, stopping to lean on its roof. "I'm glad I came and I hope you are too. You're a fine young man, John Parker Hardesty. Don't you lose sight of that. Without sounding maudlin, you've had some difficult experiences that would test anyone's character, but you've come through them." Garrison opened the car door. "Tell me something, though. Do you still send your paycheck back east to the drop in Pittsburgh?"

"Yes. Why?"

"Just wondered if you had finally let your folks know where you are."

"Nothing's changed, Floyd."

"Oh, I think you're wrong. You've changed. You're not the same young man I met two years ago." He patted the top of the truck and got in.

Hardesty followed suit knowing that as far as Garrison was concerned, the subject was over. He had made his point and that was that.

The Alford General Store on a late afternoon was as busy as it got. With school out, a collection of teenagers and an equal number of bicycles occupied the front steps. Hardesty had to make his way through the crowd of legs to the swinging doors without stepping on someone. One of the girls looked at him and his uniform. She started to smile, but was nudged by one of her friends. When she stared at the shiner next to his eye, Hardesty smiled wryly at her and went in.

He knew what she was thinking. CCC boys were interesting, but some in the community thought that a number had police records, especially the boys from back east. Rough young men they were, with rough ways and language. The Army life was supposed to keep them in line and although manners and cleanliness were a part of their daily education in the camp, who knew what sort of boys they were?

The store was dim and cool inside, the smells of food and floor wax mixing with Hardesty's memories of a country general store he had walked to as a child growing up in Western Pennsylvania. There were a number of posters advertising products, including Hanes underwear for 50 cents apiece. Fryers went for 65 cents, roosters 13 cents. Over in a section devoted to that pantheon of childhood--the candy shelf with jars for selecting treats--there was a poster advertising Radio KJR's Signal

Tarzan Club. (Back east he had listened to KDKA as a teenager.) Underneath, there were some boxed toys. Hardesty looked to the back where the outdoor equipment was displayed. Behind the counter there, he caught a glimpse of the elder Alford and he tried to recall his first name. He was talking with a customer.

Hardesty made his way slowly back, taking his time to look at some of the fishing equipment on the shelves. The store did a big business in steelhead and salmon fishing when in season, but there was tackle for the Dolly Varden and rainbow trout that were also around. From the looks of it, there were equal supplies for both fly-fishing and live bait so no one would get into any sort of philosophical debate with the owner. He was looking at some of the dry flies in a box when a voice surprised him.

"That you, Hardesty?"

He turned to face Jack Turner. "Hey, Jack."

"How's the camp?"

"Fine. Good bunch. Can't complain about the work. And you?"

"Aw, more bad luck," His companion on the ride up from the train station said. "The lumber strike is still going on. Everything is closed down except for you fellows. No mills running, no loggers cutting. It's affecting the building of the new highway over the pass at Snoqualmie."

"So you're not working at all?"

"I'm doing some work for my folks and for a man with a stump ranch. The one Cory told me about. Say, have you seen him lately?"

"I saw him about a week ago."

Turner lowered his voice. "He's a good man. Nice family too. You ever meet his sister, Katriana?"

"Katriana?"

Turner beamed. "Kate to you. She'll kill me for divulging a family secret. All the kids have these strange names, Cory included. Funny spellings. Scandahovians." When Hardesty looked puzzled, Turner said, "Sorry, local joke."

"I've met her." Hardesty was about to comment, but Turner was talking again.

"Kate's a real sweetheart, although I've known a guy or two to be left in the dust. She can pack a horse as good as any man and knows the trails up there like the bull of the woods. That tends to trip a fellow."

"You ever date her?"

"Oh, a long time ago in high school. We went to a dance or two, but mostly we're friends. She's a good friend to have too. Thing about her...she's an absolute lady under that hat."

Hardesty studied one of the flies from the box, wondering how they had gotten on this subject. Turner leaned over the box to see what Hardesty was looking at.

"Say; that's a wooly bear tie. I heard about your bear," he chuckled. "I'd say you two were off to a good start."

"We've barely met." Hardesty didn't know whether to laugh and feign indignation. To tell the truth, he wished he did know Kate Alford better. She was beautiful.

"Don't let that keep you apart. Maybe I shouldn't tell you, but my sister Betty Olsen is one of her best friends. Kate wouldn't have said anything about the bear to Betts unless she was trying to talk about something else. She was asking about you."

Hardesty put the box of flies down and felt his face flush. "I had no idea," he said.

Hardesty stayed down at the store until the last possible moment before he would have to walk back to the camp, visiting with Turner and the senior Alford at the back counter. Mr. Alford was very friendly, asking about the camp and the projects that were going on. He appeared to have no prejudices against him for being an enrollee, which Hardesty remembered in some communities had been a mark against him no matter how much the program was admired. Because he wasn't a local.

While they were talking, Cory Alford came back from guiding some city people on the river. When he saw Turner and Hardesty, he invited them upstairs to the apartment there and offered them bottles of Olympia beer.

"It's okay, isn't it?" he asked Hardesty when they were upstairs. "You didn't take some oath up there, did ya'? Got to watch out for morals here." He settled down on an arm of a sofa in the living room. "I saw a survey once about the very first bunch at Camp Lewis. About two thirds of the CCC boys had graduated from high school, the rest only grammar school. More than half hadn't worked in six months to two years. What the survey didn't publicly acknowledge was that boys will be boys. Smoking, drinking and generally chasing after women. That true?"

Hardesty shrugged. "On leave, the boys go where they want. Most behave in the manner expected of full-blooded males, but with discretion. Trouble comes with those who are lost being out here in the woods or just plain homesick. Maybe want an excuse to go home."

"That true of your squad?"

"The kids are fine. They're a little rough around the edges sometimes, but they're good kids. None in my group's been in serious trouble with the law, although a year or two ago, being in the three C's might have been an option to spending time in jail."

"You talk like a mother hen."

Hardesty took a sip of his beer. "I am a mother hen."

"That how you got that shiner?" Alford asked.

Turner laughed. "You've been on the river too long, Cory. Park had a hell of a fight at the spike camp. Some disagreement."

"You're kidding."

Hardesty looked at his beer bottle, but he hadn't missed the look of concern on Alford's face. Probably didn't like brawling. "It was nothing. Things have calmed down considerably."

"Who was it?"

"Jonas McGill."

"Oh, McGill. Figures. I'd say you came out fine."

Hardesty tossed the rest of his beer down and got up. "I've got to walk back for mess. It'll take about thirty minutes."

"Want a ride?" Cory asked. "I'm going that way."

"Sure. Thanks." Hardesty collected his knapsack loaded with some things he had bought in the store and followed the two friends downstairs. After saying goodbye to Turner, they climbed into Cory's truck and took off for the camp. They were quiet for a bit, but by the time they reached the camp, they had discussed every bit of news from the radio and newspapers. The new Social Security Act had been voted in and other reforms were happening. As they had the night they had played pinochle together with the Bladstad's, Hardesty felt a mutual friendship. When Hardesty got out at the gate, they shook on it.

"Please, Kate. Will you do it?"

Kate put down her towel and began brushing her wet hair as she sat on the edge of the claw-foot tub. "Does mother know?"

"She'll let me go if I'm escorted."

"Is anyone else going from Frazier?"

"The whole senior class. Meg and Peg Reilly are going too and their parents are strict. Lots and lots of people are going. It's the first dance in a long while. The CCC boys have been busy this summer."

"I haven't been to one of those things since -"

"- You broke off with David. Are you worried about that?"

"David and I are friends. It doesn't bother me."

"That why you're brushing your hair too hard?"

Kate shook the brush at her younger sister. "Oooo, you're impossible. I'm not going to discuss this with you."

"You won't mind if he's there?"

Kate put a hand on Karin's shoulder. "No, I'll be too busy watching you."

"Oh, then you'll do it! Oh, Kate!" Karin jumped up. "I'll have to make a dress or re-do that blue one I have. You have a dress, don't you?"

"I've been known to wear one." Kate worked at one of the ends of her curly hair. She smiled, her eyes twinkling. "When is this affair?"

"This Saturday. At the camp. It's going to be won-der-ful."

"Not if I can help it. You're going to have to stay with me."

Karin didn't pay attention. "Meg met one of the boys at the store the other day. He was buying some gum. His name is Carl and he's from somewhere near Chicago. His dad owned a jeweler's shop, but it went bust."

"What about some of our boys?"

"Oh, Kate. They're...oh, you wouldn't understand."

Kate raised her eyebrows, but didn't say anything. She wasn't sure, but she thought she had been sixteen once too. However, she had favored a different sort of beau. Usually someone with more brains than brawn, although Jack Turner was smart and he was a logger now.

Kate stood up. "I've got to get dressed. Father is having company over -- Mr. Taylor from Camp Kulshan and a district officer. I promised Mom that I'd help. You can too. You can check the silverware."

"Must I?"

"Does it rain in the Northwest?"

CHAPTER 9

THE DANCE became the discussion of the week at dinner tables in Frazier and at mess in the camps. Civic minded folk thought it would be nice to participate because they wished to thank the boys for the work done on the roads and new campgrounds. Every time a new road opened up, it seemed that there was increase in the number of cars that braved their way out to the mountains. A hiking club in the city fifty miles away was particularly active, having been busy making repairs to the cabin they retained higher up. Families drove out now, taking advantage of the ability to drive further into the forests for a picnic or camping at one of the campgrounds. Where there had been tangles of brush and forest, there were now tables and pavilions. The city folk came and they brought commerce to the store, hotel and gasoline station. Frazier recognized the impact and wanted to act accordingly.

On the whole, relations were good with the camp, although rumor had it that there was an increase in boys who were not from the county. So far, they had behaved themselves. The high school baseball team from down the way was looking forward to playing a game with them later on in the summer and most folks were looking forward to the dance.

Interest was equally high at Camp Kulshan. By Thursday, it was a logistics frenzy in the best democratic tradition. There were committees for decorating, committees for food (some donations were being offered by a local church) and committees for committees. Joisey Squad, like all the others, was in the thick of it, providing an important part of the band. For that, Golden said there was going to be a surprise. Each evening, after work and camp duties, projects were suspended so things could get done on THE DANCE. By Friday, things were in good shape. All they had to do was to hang things up in the large hall that served as mess hall. It was big enough to accommodate the numbers that were anticipated.

Dinner was over early on Saturday so the last minute touches could be put in place in the room. Crates were draped with pillow covers and given a jar filled with ferns for a centerpiece. "Naughty Marietta" had prevailed and there was a decided lavish look to the posters put up around the big space. When the crews had everything in place, the boys went back to their barracks. Some of them hurried. They had to warm up the band.

At 7:30, the lights were on in the hall, part of the band already playing a few strains. Over at the barracks, Spinelli finished tying his tie while he talked to Staubach who was polishing his shoes. They all wore dress uniforms and as a group looked groomed and as handsome as they could get.

"Wonder if that girl I saw at the store will be there?" Staubach said out loud.

"What did she look like?" Spinelli asked.

"She was real pretty. A red head with the nicest…" He made the shape with his hands. "You wouldn't know it, but she's the same girl we saw up at Darcy Meadows when we were cutting trail by there."

"The one with the horse."

"Same one."

"That's the storekeeper's daughter," commented Lorenzo who said he was planning on going to the dance despite the broken arm because the girls would feel sorry for him. "I heard she used to go with Callister."

"Callister," Spinelli spat. "That guy really causes me grief. I told him I wanted to take an advanced class, but he said my writing was poor. Hell, I can spell."

"But did you finish high school?" countered Golden.

"Naw, I'm short," Spinelli said quietly. "Not much, though. I could do it." He finished up his dressing and combed his hair. Ignoring the last exchange, he asked where Hardesty was. "If he doesn't go, I'll kill him."

"Aw, leave him alone," Staubach said. "He doesn't have to prove anything. Besides, he told me he would go. He won't let the squad down." He tightened his belt. "I gotta go. I'm in the band. See you guys later..."

Joisey Squad went over ten minutes later.

On the long end of the wall away from the band, a gaggle of girls sat at the tables or chairs set up for them. Dressed in the style of the day, they wore light patterned dresses made of cotton or even chiffon with high heels. A couple had purses that they could carry under their arms, others hats. A picture of femininity that had been sorely missing around here. A couple of them stood up when the CCC boys began to drift into the hall and took their arms when greeted. Obviously, there had been some fraternizing elsewhere. When the band started playing, they went out to the dance floor.

Joisey Squad came up the cement steps and paused at the opened door. The younger boys just stood there and stared. It was a warm June evening with sunset many hours away.

"What time you said it gets to twilight around here?" Werner asked.

"Spenser says 10:30," Spinelli answered. "Trees'll probably stop that."

"Plus that new Daylight Savings Time. That means legal closing time is 2:00 AM."

"A whole night of possibilities."

"If you'd stop gawking, you could let the ladies through," a voice said behind them. It was Spenser with his squad. In front of them was a group of matrons and some girls from the surrounding community. The boys let them pass into the golden glow of the hall, then squeezed back in after them.

"Some place," murmured Lorenzo when he saw the decorations. Spying a lone table, he went and sat down. He had changed into a black sling that added more depth to his predicament. Some of the squad sat down next to him. Spinelli was already to go. He sat at the table, tapping out the beat with the flat of his hand. The band sounded good and the dancers on the floor moved in time to the driving rhythm. He surveyed the opposite side of the room and spied two girls who were dressed exactly alike. Twins, he thought. They were dressed real nice, like they were from some movie or something. He watched an enrollee go over and ask one of them to dance. The girl with the permed hair played shy, then rose to the occasion.

"Where's Hardesty?" he asked Staubach.

"I think he's at the door talking to someone."

"He ought to come in here. If he does, tell him I'm dancing." The eighteen year old got up and wove through the dancers over to where the remaining twin sat.

"Wanna dance?" Spinelli had to repeat it because she couldn't understand him, but when he led her out to the dance floor, she had no trouble following. Spinelli could dance.

"Well, there goes the evening," griped Werner. "Figures he'd be the first on the floor."

"Why don't you go ask one of the ladies over there?"

Werner looked. The matrons. Their charges were out on the floor. "No thanks."

"Then buy me a drink. What do they have in that punch bowl any way?"

“I'll look. Don't think it's alcohol.”

By eight, the dance was literally in full swing. While some on both sides held back, there was a good deal of mingling. Hardesty came in and sat with them, but he didn't dance until there was ladies choice and one of the twins came over to pick him. When he stood up, he stood well over her.

"My," she said and nothing more. He did cut a good figure. His sandy hair was streaked with blonde and he filled out his uniform. The only thing out of place was the bruise on his eye and cut cheekbone. "My name's Agatha Osborne," she said as she led him out. It was a moderately lively dance on the next number, but she got him to stay for the one after that which was slow. The rest of Joisey Squad sitting at the table watched with fascination. Hardesty had already demonstrated his abilities in the woods and they knew he liked to read, but this was a side they hadn't seen. An ease with the social scene.

"Now where do you suppose he learned that?" Lorenzo asked. So far his strategy for attracting beautiful women wasn't working.

"He's a Pennsylvanian. We're all like that," Staubach answered.

To prove it, he got up and went looking for his own partner on the next dance. Spinelli had finished escorting his back to her chair, but Hardesty was still talking to the other twin. Staubach decided to cut.

"Mind?" he asked as the music started up. Hardesty didn't. He looked relieved. He patted his mate on his shoulder and headed back to the squad. That is when he first saw Kate Alford and her sister come into the hall.

Karin was dressed in a simple blue print dress that made her fair hair and skin glow. He had never seen her before, but instinctively knew that she was related by the way Kate stayed close to her and by the way they leaned into each other and whispered. She was a pretty girl, just on the verge of young womanhood and unlike some girls that grew up in rural areas, she lacked the ripeness that comes early on, then fades before twenty. He knew it because he had seen it in his own female cousins. There was a sweetness about her with staying power that made her both attractive and vulnerable.

But it was Kate Alford who made him physically weak and stirred feelings that he hadn't felt in a long time. She was, like her sister, attired in a simple dress with padded shoulders. Its rich forest green seemed to drape from her body like silk, its boat neck accenting her lovely smooth throat and shoulders. She was tanned, but it was a creamy honey-gold against her rich palette of auburn hair. Carefully held back with tortoise shell barrettes, it framed her face, and made her appear more alive than any other creature in the room. It seemed that the music stopped along with the talking and every male who had eyeballs, took a second take. She froze in his own eyes, but when he looked again, she had stepped alongside the wall and over to some chairs where a number of girls and matrons were sitting. He lost sight of her after that and nearly got mowed down when the dancing kicked into a livelier tune. From up on the stage, Golden began to play his clarinet and the room rocked in time.

"Hey, Park! Are you deaf?"

Hardesty turned. Werner was making signs at him. "I got you something to drink."

"Thanks." Hardesty sat down on the wooden folding chair with a thud. Lorenzo leaned over. "You see her?"

Hardesty said nothing, but his face betrayed his interest.

"See what I mean? I'm going to ask right now."

"With that arm? You got to be kidding," Werner said.

Lorenzo got up. "Watch." He went around the edge of the dancing mass. They could see his head eventually on the other side. A few moments later, he moved into the crowd of dancers. With him was Kate.

"Damn!" Spinelli said just sitting down. The squad stared. Lorenzo had taken his broken arm out of the sling and had it around her waist. It was a slow dance, so they just moved about in one spot. Hardesty laughed. Lorenzo was only eighteen, but he seemed to have mastered the fine art of dancing etiquette. The couple seemed to be getting along fine and Hardesty imagined that she would be gracious to someone more of a pup than a man. She listened to him and occasionally laughed. They danced through the first number and a second, but before it went any further, another enrollee cut in. To Spinelli, it was becoming old.

"I'm going over."

"And do what?" Staubach asked as he rejoined them.

"Dance. See ya'"

Staubach picked a flowerette off the bouquet of foxglove

stuffed it into a jar on the table. He stuck his forefinger into the back of it and made it jump around like a little Thumbelina."How long do you think he'll last?" the puppet asked Werner."Aw, dry up. Look someone's cut in already."

Staubach turned around. "Hey, it's Callister."

So it was. He deftly took her in his arms and danced away from the side into the center of floor.

Hardesty couldn't explain it, but he didn't like Callister being with her. She appeared quieter and subdued, not herself. When Callister spoke to her, she lowered her head and nodded. He was a good dancer, and he made good use of the floor, all the time holding her in a gentlemanly fashion. When the number ended, she acted like she wanted to sit down, but he continued to keep his arm around her slim waist. She turned and the squad saw Mario come up beside her, but he didn't cut in. He had acquired her sister and looked perfectly content.

"You going to do something, Park?" Staubach asked.

"Am I supposed to?"

Staubach shrugged. "What do I know? Guess it's none of my business."

The music started up. The band, recognizing the successful mingling of the sexes, settled down to gentler tunes that would ensure longer contact. Mario said something to Kate's sister and they moved away from Kate and began their own encounter. Callister coaxed Kate into going with him again, and she gave in.

"How long do you think he's going to hold onto her?" Werner wondered.

Hardesty said nothing. He took his punch and downed it like a shot of whisky, then sat back as best he could on the folding chair.

"Two bits, he'll do it again," commented Staubach.

"Done," Hardesty said. He looked for change in his pockets and put it on the table. "We'll see." He waited for the dance to be nearly over, then got up suddenly and went through the wall of couples on the dance floor. When the music stopped, he went over to Kate and Callister and tapped her shoulder.

"May I cut in, Miss Alford?"

Callister started to say something, but Kate said yes and thanked Callister for the dance. All he could do was bow and let her go. She accepted Hardesty's arm, but as soon as he took her away, he asked if she would like to sit.

"Why, yes I would... Would you mind?"

"My cut," he answered.

They walked down to the tables where the punch was being served and he got her a cup. Behind him he could feel Callister's eyes boring into him, but he didn't care.

"Cheers," he said, then drank the overly sweet drink again. The kitchen crew must have put a ton of sugar in the mix. They moved away from the table to the corner, then sat down. She visibly relaxed, raising her shoulders in a big sigh, then as if remembering her duty, sought out Karin on the floor.

"That enrollee. You know him?"

"Sure, that's Mario Spinelli."

"Sp- spinelli?"

"Yeah. He's a nice kid. He's from New Jersey, although everyone in my squad is from New Jersey except me and Staubach. Makes for interesting communication. Sometimes you'd never know there was only a state border between us."

Kate laughed. "How old is he?"

"Eighteen, although I think he snuck in underage. If not, he's one of the youngest, if eighteen is positively old age." He smiled, glad to have this time with her. "Is that your sister?"

"Yes. That's Karin. It was her idea to come."

"You mean you wouldn't have come?"

Kate grinned. "I don't know what to say now."

"Say that when you're ready, you'll dance with me. You can choose any time tonight. I won't hold you to now."

Kate took a drink and smiled over the cup. He smiled back.

"Oh," she said, "you've hurt your eye."

Hardesty touched the bruise. He had forgotten about it. "Camp life. It can be exciting."

Kate didn't say anything. Instead, she watched her sister and Spinelli resume dancing. Hardesty saw an enrollee try to cut in, but the two teenagers continued to dance. Karin was chattering, but Mario was quiet. He seemed totally struck by her and Hardesty wasn't sure if that was good or bad. Mario would probably be put in the "rough" category by her parents, although he thought the boy could be a gentleman.

"Mr. Hardesty? A penny for your thoughts."

"Just thinking about that dance and how I wish you would say yes now."

Kate put the cup down. "I may be fair game again for cutting."

"Let them. If they can correctly identify a *Rattus norvegicus*, I say let them."

"Mr. Hardesty, that's a Norway Rat!"

He beamed, then offered his arm, but she asked to sit out one more and he complied. The music started up again and they talked over the saxophones that had taken over the melody, but soon the drum solo drowned them out. When it was finished, they put down their cups and went out onto the floor.

It was moment he would ever forget. Something as simple as taking a hand and placing it on a waist or shoulder. To look at someone opposite you and then as the music begins a mellow strain, to step out across the floor as one. Someone lowered the lights it seemed, and after a while, he no longer was aware of anyone else. As the music became more drowsy and saxophone-laden, he drew her deeper into his arms until her head rested on his shoulder. She didn't seem aware of this simple crossing of the line, but he was. This slip of a woman at a river with her horse and bear, this person who loved the woods as deeply as he did, touched him and for the first time, in a long time, he cared. For a moment, he was sublimely happy until Callister stepped in. Hardesty hadn't been aware that the music had stopped, but apparently it had.

"My turn," Callister announced. He seemed glad to be back in control.

"Miss Alford?" Hardesty asked.

"Kate will be fine, Mr. Hardesty," Callister said. "As you were..."

He started to take her away, but Hardesty said "*Rattus*

norvegius."

"Now what does that mean?" Callister wondered.

"I don't know," Hardesty said. "Ask Miss Alford."

"It's all right, Mr. Hardesty. Thank you. I'm going to check on my sister if you don't mind, David." She backed away and left both of them standing there. Callister looked non-plussed, but Hardesty thought, "Touché."

He didn't see her until later and then she was out in front of the mess hall with Karin, getting ready to go home. It was very late, but the dance was still going on strong, the music blaring out of the open windows. Hardesty, however, was tired and was seriously considering retiring for the night. He had been waylaid several times by the Osborne twins who seemed to think he was swell stuff, but he supposed that if they couldn't get a real military uniform, maybe a tree soldier was okay.

He came out into the cool of the night and into the parade ground. A black outline of tall trees against the starry sky surrounded him. Twinkling and glowing, the stars seemed to grow and expand before him. Suddenly, a brilliant light shot across the sky. A shooting star.

"Did you see that?" a young girl's voice said. Hardesty turned and saw Kate over by a car. In the dim light, he was still able to pick her out as she opened the door to her sister.

"Yes, it was lovely." She started to go to the driver's side, then stopped. "Who's there?"

"Park Hardesty. Are you leaving?" he asked as he came up.

"Time to get a certain lady home. It was fun, though. I'm sorry not to have seen you again."

"Perhaps another time." He came up close so he could see her face and figure like a ghost in the starlit light.

"Oh, I think I've had my dance quota for awhile."

He chuckled. "Me too. I forgot it takes certain muscles, which hacking through brush and falling trees does not concentrate on."

"Will you be in the main camp for awhile?"

"I think so, though Bladstad was thinking of assigning me to some special trips up to the lakes. Did you ever hear of Bear

Lake?"

"Yes. It's an alpine lake up near Darcy Meadows. I've packed there before."

"Of course. Dumb question."

"It's not dumb. If you like, I can show you some maps sometime. My dad has old ones that were used before the Forest Service even existed. They're very interesting."

Hardesty said he would and they parted on a "Good night."

He saw Kate a couple of times after that -- once at the store and once when he was down by the river where the bear had terrorized the horse.

"I've brought Elsa to help her get over her jitters about the place," Kate said.

"I've come to try my hand at fishing."

While he cast out, they talked, but he was torn between paying attention to his line or to her. She won out when the line got caught in a willow across the water. While he waded across the cold low water to untangle it, she gave him encouraging words about his technique.

"Don't think willow at two o'clock is in the manual, Miss Alford."

"No, but look how easily you got everything back. The mark of an experienced fisherman. Even my dad has lost a few."

He joined her on one of the numerous drift logs and they talked about whatever came into their heads.

"Tell me again about the young man Karin met at the dance. My sister is head-over-heels in love with him. I'm not sure if my parents will approve."

"Because he's an enrollee?"

"Because they're both young and he comes from so far away."

Hardesty put his rod away. "It's not the end of the earth. It's just another piece of it."

"Is that how you view it?"

"What would your naturalist great aunt say? The one with a man's name?"

"She'd say it was home. I do worry, though. Karin's been very sheltered. This boy comes from a rougher world. Even at his age, he may have had experiences with women that are not acceptable out here."

"Does that bother you?"

"My sister is special. I wouldn't want anything to happen to her."

"No one would, especially Mario. Despite hardship, from what he says, his family is a good one with solid values. I'll talk to him if you like. Remind him of some rules - although Mario is a sensitive person. We get enough lectures as it is."

"Are you lectured, Mr. Hardesty?"

He grinned. "I'm just one of the boys," he said, wishing he wasn't.

CHAPTER 10

The days after the dance were busy for the squads. Rotating the boys so they could learn different skills, the new squads were given the task of planting trees. Some of the over-logged or burned off areas desperately needed trees to reclaim the land before erosion and run-off from the rains caused the mass of logs jamming the creeks to give way and destroy some of the homesteads below. There was no legislation that promoted the re-seeding -- loggers traditionally cut everything and occasionally left a seed tree for every forty acres -- but the Forest Service tried to encourage the logging companies to do more.

From a nursery two hundred and fifty miles away in Wind River near the Columbia, seedlings were trucked up in canvas backed trucks and stored at a warehouse at the camp. There they were kept in their gunny sack bales on two by six boards to keep the air circulation going, then stacked as high as ten feet so the growing seedlings wouldn't generate heat and eventually create mold. Planting usually took place in early spring and sometimes as early as February, but this year due to a cool spring, they could still plant these last two days of April.

On the Monday after the dance, Joisey Squad spent the afternoon preparing the trucks for transporting seedlings. Each bale had twenty-five to fifty of them laying root to root in peat moss with the limbs sticking out. The boys hand-carried and loaded the sixty pound bales onto the trucks destined for the field. To prevent air circulation around them, a canvas tarp was put over them. On the following day, the squads were driven out to a steep mountainous region after breakfast and began the first of several grueling days.

Planting, Spinelli soon learned, was no picnic. The main tool, the mattock, was heavy and unwieldy. Essentially a grubbing tool, it was an adze, ax, and pick all in one. To haul it around, was to invite the most original of swearing and after working seven and a half hours and planting nearly a thousand trees a day, there were blisters and backaches as well. At noon on the first day when the bull cook made up lunch, some of the boys flung themselves on the hill spread eagle with their boots sticking toe up and just laid there, too tired to move. But they had to move, so they traded off with the boys packing the seedlings at the truck. Spinelli found a boulder to sit on, afraid if he lay down he would not get up.

Each enrollee carried a canvas bag - like a water bag except it was not flat. With its sides, it could hold about one hundred trees. At the top of the bag were loops and they could be looped onto a belt. At the truck, the bags were filled and picked up by the enrollees for planting. As they moved along down the mountainous hills in lines, they each dug a hole and put the seedling in, then tamped it down and moved on.

"Bend, dig, put in, stand up and move on." That's all this is, Spinelli thought.

By three in the afternoon, it was hard to move on. He and the otherwise fit crew were a mass of aching limbs and muscles. Going back to the camp, no one in any of the four squads said anything. Some of them sprawled on the truck floor, too tired to sit up. The second day was worse but the third was better and at lunch, Spinelli moved over to Hardesty who was off reading a book while he ate.

"Good book?" he asked for starters. It was a high, bright day now that the morning mist had burned off and the logged-off mountain was alive with birds and bugs flitting and crawling in the remaining vegetation. Far down they could see the river twisting like a silver white ribbon through the steep sides of the valley. It continued to amaze him.

Hardesty turned his book over. "Passing. The camp library's not a literary treasure house."

"You're always reading."

Hardesty raised his eyebrow and put the book face down on his denim pants." I enjoy it. It's also a good way to keep my mind off the work…"

Spinelli picked a blade of grass growing next to a gray, weathered stump, and chewed on it. "I like reading, but books was always expensive in my town. I couldn't get a library card."

"You interested?"

"Yeah." He looked away, a little bit embarrassed.

"That's good."

"Yeah, but I'd like to do better." Spinelli cleared his throat. "You see that girl I was with at the dance?"

"Uh-huh."

"Well, I saw her again on Sunday. She's real nice. I'd like to see her again, but I'm afraid that she'll think I'm stupid or something."

"You're not stupid."

"But she could think that. I didn't finish high school."

Spinelli was glad when Hardesty made no comment and just let him talk.

"I'm real close, though. Real close. I had good grades too. And you know something? I'd like to go college. Does that sound dumb?"

"No." Hardesty smiled. "I don't think so."

Spinelli felt his face flush. "I've always had this idea that I could do it. Be the first in my family. I had to drop out of high school my senior year so I could help in my dad's business, but things got so tough I had to sign up for this. At first, I thought it would be bad, but now I see that I can finish school here."

Hardesty nodded his head as a way of encouragement.

"....only trouble is, Callister is giving me grief. He says I have to improve my writing before I can take more classes. I only need one or two. That's all." He cleared his throat. "You're a good straw boss, Park. All the guys like you because you're fair and you explain things without making us feel stupid. Some of the guys in the other squads say they get grief all the time because they're new -- and 'foreigners.' But you... you're fair and you work as much as the next guy. I've been thinking a lot lately. I'd like to finish school, but Callister is all high and mighty just because he's got college schooling. He just gives me grief." Spinelli looked sheepish as he pointed to the book. "That's what I wanted to talk about--I was wondering if you could help me out."

Hardesty used a leaf to mark his place and put the book away in his knapsack. His eyes twinkled. "For the girl?"

Spinelli grinned. "And myself."

"The best reasons in the world."

The planting went on for a week and a half more, despite the fluctuations in the weather, and the two of them made it a practice to spend their lunch time going over papers Spinelli had picked up from the education office. Hardesty found that the kid could spell well, but had some trouble with writing paragraphs and organizing his thoughts, so he gave him some writing assignments after demonstrating some principle of writing he should know.

"What should I write about?"

"What you know."

Mario wrote about the mean streets of his home, of his brothers and sisters and his Uncle Jerome, of the time he stole candy from the corner store and got caught by his mother.

"My old lady's a stickler," he wrote. "Acted like I stole candles from the vestry. She marched me back, pulling me by my ear all the way down the street. Every nona putting out the wash two stories up called down to my mother to wish her courage. To me they behaved like it was Judgment Day. Scared me to death. Fortunately, instead of one hundred Hail Mary's, I got to stack cans in Georgio Margoloti's storeroom for a whole week. I was eight years old."

Hardesty would read each assignment and show him how to proofread. When they were in their final form, he bound them into a notebook for keeping. Then he asked Mario to write about something that happened at the camp and had him compare it to something back east. At the end of the first week, Hardesty gave back his papers and told him he was improving, but if he wanted to practice, maybe he should write something for the camp paper.

"There's the national paper too, *Happy Days*. You could look into that." He showed him copies of the *Seattle Times* and had him look over some of the better articles and stories and had him figure out why they might be good. Then he found books in the library and pointed out pieces in those.

Lunchtime began to look like study session because some of the other boys in the squad were taking interest. Joisey Squad suddenly had a serious mission in life -- to pass high school. Of the eight, only three had finished, including Hardesty. Sitting in a group on the bare steep hills above a valley whose sides dove deep down to the river like the petals of a green-throated lily, they did their workbooks while eating. When they picked up their bags of seedlings for the afternoon, they all seemed refreshed and energized.

"What's the matter with them?" Hardesty heard McGill grumble up behind him. In the clear air, voices drifted down like disembodied spirits. "They've gone soft. That Hardesty."

"Oh, it's not Hardesty. It's Spinelli," corrected Spenser. "Wouldn't hurt you either. What are you going to do when you get out of the Corps?"

"Log."

"What if the mills stay down longer? Then what?"

Hardesty slung the seed bag on his shoulder and started down to his new position. For one last time he heard McGill's voice. "Lousy foreigners."

Hardesty wondered if that were directed at the whole squad or just him in particular.

The squads returned from planting for the last time on the eighth of May. The season was over for now and something different was about to start. While the projects list was always expanding, Joisey Squad and two other new groups had been at Kulshan for two months and could now sign up for whatever training that interested them. The boys discussed it among themselves and began to make decisions on their own. There was a mechanics class, something that interested Jeff Staubach. Golden wanted to learn about wireless radios. Steve Costello and Hoss Werner were interested in the woodworking classes. O'Connell favored cooking. In addition to taking some high school completion classes, Joisey Squad began to spread out and diversify.

One evening, a week after they got back, Hardesty was asked to go over to Bladstad's office. The main door creaking behind him as it closed on its spring, he walked down the narrow hall. The building was quiet. His boots sounded hollow on the wood floor. In the third door down he found the forester making some tea on a little hot plate. Papers were strewn all over his desk and a metal side table.

"Come in, come in," Bladstad said. "Don't pay any attention to the mess. The maid's coming over in the morning."

Hardesty removed his cap and stood at ease.

"Oh, brother. Just sit, Park. Please" the forester said, quickly clearing away a chair.

"You wanted to see me, officially?"

"Yes." Bladstad went over and closed his office door, then came back to rescue the boiling tea pot from spilling water all over the hot plate.

"I heard something the other day and I must say that I'm impressed."

Hardesty looked at him curiously, wondering what it might be.

"We had an important visitor up here a while back, a man by the name of Floyd Garrison. I don't expect you to know him, but he is a moving force in the Forest Service. He is a district supervisor for the CCC program in this state, a liaison."

“I think I’ve heard of him,” Hardesty muttered, but Bladstad had already gone on.

"He does, however, know you."

Hardesty stiffened.

"Oh, don't look so stricken. No bad reports. In fact, very complimentary. He remembers you from Rouge River. Said you'd done a good job as a junior down there." Bladstad poured his tea and offered some to Hardesty, but Hardesty was not a tea drinker and declined. Bladstad cleared his throat. "Some of us have felt the same here, including Taylor and myself."

"I appreciate your confidence in me."

"It’s more than that. I want you to consider staying on after your tour is up." Bladstad sipped his tea. "How old are you?"

"Almost twenty-five."

"Then you know the cut-off is close."

Hardesty nodded. It was something that worried him, because he wasn't sure what he'd do next. When he turned twenty-five, he could no longer be in the CCC’s.

"I picked up something last week. How you're helping some of your boys in your squad."

"It's nothing. Nothing big."

"Perhaps, but in my book, it measures a man."

Hardesty looked straight at him, feeling uncomfortable about the direction this was going. His privacy. He kneaded his cap between his fingers. "You don't know me, sir. Not really."

"I like what I see. Look. Everyone is signing up for classes for the next few weeks. I was wondering if you want to work with me on forestry procedures. Most of it's science; the rest, policies. In particular, I want to train you for a project that involves stocking the lakes with fish. The one I told you about. Interested?"

Hardesty was, but he had the nagging suspicion that Garrison had something to do with this. He was silent for a moment -- too long for Bladstad after awhile.

"You could always let me know later."

"No, it's all right. I'd like to do it."

"Great! We can begin right away."

"Sure... Tell me something, though. This Garrison. You know him well?"

"Not real well, but professionally since the twenties. He's been with CCC camps down in Oregon for the past two years. He's just been transferred." Bladstad sat down and drank his tea. "Remarkable man. A visionary and a gentleman. An optimist. You'd never know that he has experienced tragedy in his life."

Hardesty became quiet, his heart pounding as he waited for Bladstad to continue, but he did not say anything more to his relief.

"I've got some books here if you want to look at them. Tomorrow after evening mess, we can go over and look at the fishery south of Frazier. If there's anyone else in your squad who might be interested, let me know."

Hardesty stood up. "By the way, have you seen Cory Alford?"

"I was at the Alford's yesterday as a matter of fact. You haven't seen him in awhile?"

"Been out with tree planting so much, that I didn't even leave camp this last weekend. I was beat."

"I don't remember, but did he go to the dance?"

"I didn't see him."

Bladstad shrugged. "Probably with his girl, Mary. Too bad about her grandmother. She passed away."

"Oh, I didn't know. I'm sorry. Well, if you see him before I do, give him my condolences. We go to the spike camp next week, don't we? I suspect we'll be there most of the month."

"At least until the thirtieth. After that time, we can look into the lake-stocking project. Some might be opening up by then."

"I look forward to it. I like being out in the mountains."

Hardesty left a few moments later. Standing out on the porch, he put on his cap. It was still light out. From far off, he could hear cheering, signs that an announced baseball game was underway. Everywhere else, the camp looked deserted, making him feel alone.

Bladstad's offer about joining the Forest Service was very tempting, but he would have to make a decision soon about everything else in his life. Garrison was right, he couldn't keep running, when he was mainly running from himself. What was done was done. He could not go back and change it, but at least, he should try to go forward without the past always dragging him down. He had a new life now. And new opportunities -

He closed his eyes in shock as the image struck him: the face that heat had erased and replaced with shrunken flesh, the hand mangled with only half its fingers.

Bastard. Leave me alone.

Anger exploding in him, Hardesty stepped down off the porch and marched over to his barracks. Relieved to find it deserted, he went to his bunk and threw his duffel bag on his bed. He quickly found the notebook and opened it up. Between its weathered leaves, he had stuffed news clippings. Holding it by its spine, he shook them all out onto the blankets, the honor award medallion plunging down onto the blanket beside them, and began to go through them.

He wondered why he continued to keep them. It was better if they were burned, but as he shifted through them he could see clearly the end and the beginning. Some were from his days down in Oregon when he had come to the CCC's green and out of shape. He had been so lost and angry because he truly had been running then -- until he met Garrison and his family.

Had some tragedy.

Garrison had his share all right, but in an odd way, it had saved him. There were more clippings about that too.

Then there were the others, the ones that pained him the most. Paul's accident had happened so suddenly, but the printer who made up the headline made it sound like an eternity

FAMILY WAITS IN VIGIL. POLICE SEARCH FOR YOUNGEST SON.

The news stories went on for days, then weeks.

Loyalty, Honor, Service.

Some award.

Hardesty looked at the face in the newspaper photograph before it was burned. We look the same, he thought. That is why they hurt him so and why he did not throw away the clippings.

For the next six weeks, Joisey Squad and some of the other squads were gone from Camp Kulshan, working on projects out of the spike camp at Big Tree and south in Skagit County. On two occasions they were unable to leave on the weekends so when they finally did during the first weekend in June, the boys all took off, including Hardesty. For once, he caught the stage line out of Frazier into the city with them where they found cheap rooms for the night and took in a movie or two at fifteen cents apiece. There were other temptations, but with loitering laws, the more adventuresome played it safe and hung out at a pool hall.

Staubach found a Chinese shop selling herbs and other unusual things in bottles and bought some ginseng tea. While he was inside with Staubach, Costello bought a paper lantern to hang up in the barracks. When they met up with the rest of the squad, they found a diner and had lunch together. Hardesty bought a newspaper. Huddling over it, they tried to get a sense of what was going on in the outside world. Locally, there was a lumber strike, but across the land there seemed to be more interest in kidnappings, gangsters, the lives of movie actors and the economy. Abroad, Hitler and all his pack flexed muscle in a number of places in Germany and Europe.

The weekend went fast and it wasn't long before they were back on the bus heading out to the mountains. When they arrived in Frazier, they had enough time to hoof it back before dinner. Joisey Squad at that moment was as solid as it would get and they had high hopes for the summer.

The rest of June was busy as they began a new campground project up near Kulshan Falls as well as preparing for the fire season. More often than not the squad was out all week at one of the spike camps, making it in late Friday afternoon. There was barely any time for socializing, but some of the boys managed to go into Frazier and meet with girls they had met at the dance. Some even managed to go a dance at the local Grange down the way, but Hardesty in accepting Bladstad's offer was stuck and could not go.

Once he went into Frazier and he saw Kate Alford at the store. They talked for a bit, but that was all. As usual, it was a funny, friendly visit.

"Heard you put in seedlings," Kate said from behind the counter. "How did it go?"

"Ask my back. We put in thousands. We've moved onto the next project, a new campground. Been spending a lot of time out at the spike camp."

They continued the verbal sparring of scientific words. She was very warm towards him, but when she declined an offer to go out with him the following weekend he sensed that she liked their friendship the way it was. He wondered if it had to do with Callister who might still have a claim on her and decided that it was none of his business. He'd take the friendship for now because he enjoyed seeing her.

"Looks like I'm going to be hauling fish up into the mountain lakes for the Forest Service," he told her.

Kate laughed. "Don't get lost and watch out for the trees."

She didn't know how true those words would be.

Near the end of June, Hardesty along with Spinelli and Steve Costello were given the assignment of hauling fish fry up into the mountain lakes. During the summer when Forest Service crews were up there, some of the men liked to fish, so when the lakes became free of ice, fish were transported up there in water metal carriers and released. Several varieties of trout were tried, but cutthroat and the black spot from Montana were favorites. The lakes had to be restocked every year, however.

One evening, they drove down to the hatchery where Bladstad showed them how to pack the fish. Using ordinary five-gallon water cans fitted with a wider mouth than normal, the fingerlings would be poured into it and the top sealed. The metal can was then strapped onto the packer's back. In order to ensure the health of the fish, packers were instructed to leave early in the morning before the sun was up to prevent the can from heating up. During the trek in, however, the water would need to be tempered. Stopping by a stream, some of the water could be bailed out with new water added from the stream. If the water was deep enough, a makeshift screen could be put over the top and the entire can immersed into the water. Once the water was tempered, the packer could move onto his destination, where the fingerlings would be released.

On the first run, Bladstad went with them, hiking back to a lake not far from the spike camp. They hiked and spent the day there. After releasing the fish, they explored the mountains around it before returning to their truck several miles away.

The second run, Spinelli and Hardesty went together. They spent the night at Sooner Lake and returned the following day. On the third run during the first week of July, Hardesty and Costello started out together, but near the trailhead, Costello hurt his ankle, so Hardesty went on without him. This was the longest run of the group, so he was prepared to spend the night again, carrying everything he would need for a change of weather. June had been relatively warm, but the last two days of the month brought cooler weather and some morning drizzle. When Hardesty left for this trip, however, it had been sunny. He traveled several miles before he came upon a steep, forested area with convoluted switchbacks. Here the trees were mostly alder and some maple, none of which looked very stable to him. Some of the trees leaned way out, while others had already fallen against their neighbors, putting them in danger of falling themselves. It was a haunted place, and Hardesty heard the call of a raven occasionally and sound of water cascading down a ravine below. In a way it was like a mysterious gateway to the meadow above, for once on top, the view was breathtaking. Beyond that, it was several more miles to Bear Lake. It was early afternoon when he got there. After releasing the fish, he set up his tent and made camp.

Hardesty was up early, making a fire for coffee before he took the camp down. As he cleaned up, he watched the sky for the coming day and found it unsettled. Gray and overcast, the weather looked as though it was going to stay that way. The trees around the bowl quivered as wind raked their tops. He wondered if it would rain. After a cold, light breakfast, he strapped his bedroll and tarp onto the top of the fish carrier then set it against a small cedar near the fire. Standing up and stretching, he looked across the little lake and decided he would walk around it one more time.

The water in the lake was clear and deep, but under the gray cover of clouds it appeared cold. Out in the middle, the surface shivered then broke as one of the old denizens jumped and dived under again. Hardesty wondered if it was the old trout Cory had talked about. The ring it left was large.

At eight, he was back at the campsite. Shooing away a gang of robber jays, he filled his coffeepot with lake water and put the fire out. Five minutes later, he was gone.

The hike down to Darcy Meadows took two hours. At the creek, he stopped to take a drink and rest, then taking up the empty metal container again, descended down into the forest. The day continued to be dark, increasing in its coolness as the next hour passed. As he approached the switchback, a strong wind came up bringing a threat of rain. For a moment he hesitated at its edge, watching the leaves and branches of the alder and big maple shimmer in the mix of fir and hemlock. The forest was full of eerie sounds as the limbs of some tree rubbed against another. The creek gurgled down below but there were no sounds of birds in the undergrowth. The crows and ravens were oddly distant. Adjusting his burden, Hardesty headed down the damp trail.

He made it down through the first two bends with no problems, despite the hardening wind. He did not like the way some of the alders, many over sixty feet tall, swayed above him. They creaked hard as their tops moved about in a circle. Wary of their notorious instability, he made it to the last turn with no small sense of relief. Glad to be out of their line of fire, he stopped briefly to tie his boot laces then rose sharply at the strange cracking sound above him. But it was too late.

With awesome speed, an old alder, rotted at its heart and weak in its roots, broke away from the earth. It plunged head down from the hill above him. Crossing two bends of the switch back, its heavy branches charged its full sixty-five foot length at him. Attempting to avoid the top of the tree rushing at him, he jumped down the steep incline below the trail, but he had no chance. The upper branches caught up with him and turning him around slammed him on his back into the earth. For a brief, pain-numbing moment he was pushed head down the hill. Then he hit solid rock and was knocked unconscious.

Hardesty woke with a jolt, coming to hard edged reality. On his back, he lay head down on a slope. Encased in the branches of the tree, he was partially draped over the fish carrier. The impact of the slide down the hill had been so hard that the strap on his left shoulder broke. The container under his neck and upper back was like an iron pillow. Its hard edges dug into him, but when he attempted to move, he felt the most excruciating pain in his shoulder.

Pushing leaves and small twigs away from his face, he tried to locate the placement of his legs under the tree whose branches had pinned him down tight. His right leg above him was free and able to move, but the other was bent up towards his hip and caught under one of the heavier limbs. Fearing it broken, he decided to try moving it anyway. When he attempted to straighten it, however, he discovered that it was dead. Gingerly, he willed it to unbend, but a heavy limb was in the way. He shifted his weight to ease his predicament and was suddenly hit with waves of tingling pain through his leg as blood circulation improved. Gasping, he lay still. At least it wasn't broken.

Christ, he thought. Now what? How long had he lain here?

He tried to lift his head to scan the sky, but all he could do was lay head down and look at the forest on the opposite hill. Any attempts to raise his head any higher resulted in more pain. He was stuck. For a moment he closed his eyes and rested, but the pain in his shoulder was relentless. Any movement produced a nauseating sensation of bone moving against bone and he soon realized that his collarbone must be broken. Alarmed, he fought down a rising panic and told himself to remain calm. Help would come. If not shortly, then hours when he was reported AWOL.

The trail was well known and his destination was on record. Others might guess he was in trouble. In the meantime, he would have to help himself.

The tree that held him was an old red alder. Its upper limbs were like the Crooked Man's pitchfork and two of its tines had him fairly stuck around the middle. Even worse, some of its branches had broken off in the slide down the hill and he realized how lucky he was not to have become impaled on one of them. One of them was close to his face. Instinctively, he knew he was in serious trouble, but he wondered if he could clear space around him and slide out. At best, he could at least lay sideways and not head down like he had been. It would clear his head and stop the pounding in his temple. He pulled some dangling lichen away from his face and began snapping small branches around him. He would dig his way out from under with his knife if he had to.

"You see Hardesty?" Spinelli asked as he came into the bathhouse.

Lorenzo was shaving at the sinks. "What?"

Spinelli turned off the running water. Sal lowered his razor.

"I said, Hardesty. He here?"

"Naw. He took off yesterday for Bear Lake. Should be back any time or by dinner."

Spinelli looked off, tapping his hands.

"Something up?"

"No... Just wanted to talk to him, that's all." He made a face.

"Trouble?"

"Ain't no big deal. I thought he'd be back before I was."

Lorenzo started shaving again then stopped. "How was town?"

"All right. Took in a movie last night. Went to Mass this morning. Staubach and I found a cheap place to stay."

He walked across the concrete floor to the door and leaned against it. Across the grounds, the mountains seemed to fill the sky, something that continued to amaze him. There was a slight stir in the air as a chilly wind came through. He looked higher up.

The sky was black.

"You're sure restless," Lorenzo commented as he wiped extra shaving cream off his face. "What time is it?"

"Four…"

"A hour and a half to mess. Look, I'll finish up and we can go and play pool."

"Okay. .." Mario straightened up suddenly. "Holy smokes. Hardesty better hustle. It looks like its going to rain up there."

Equally worried about the rain was Caroline Alford. She watched the dark clouds move in from her kitchen window and hoped that Kate was under cover. She wished Kate had stayed at the cabin, but knew she wanted to keep her promise to Betty and go into town with her tomorrow. Kate would have started in. Caroline trusted her daughter's common sense to see her safely home. The screen door to the front of the house creaked, then banged. Wiping her hands on her apron, Caroline went quickly to the hall.

"Kate?"

"Just us, Mom," Cory called back. "Karin's here."

"Have you seen Kate yet?"

"No."

Cory came into the hallway and seeing his mother's worried look, told her that Kate would probably call from the new ranger's station as soon as she got in. "She was prepared when she left, Mom. She always is."

Caroline sighed. "You kids."

Cory came by her, aiming for the Kelvinator, giving her a peck on the cheek as he passed. "When's dinner?" he asked. She gave him a pat on his rump for an answer.

Karin all this time had stayed back, finally coming into the kitchen when Cory got into the pantry looking for something to munch on.

"There you are, sweetheart," said Caroline when she spied her. "And how was your day?"

"All right."

"Not really," Cory replied. "Her new love went to town

yesterday."

"Cory! You promised!"

"Oops." He ducked when she threw a kitchen towel at him.

"Someone I know?" Caroline asked. She scowled at Cory long enough to make him pick up the towel. It didn't matter if he was a grown man. When he was in this house ...

"No, but he's very nice."

"And how did you meet him?"

"At the dance."

"That's nice." She sounded non-committal for now. She brushed back her youngest daughter's silky hair and gave her a reassuring smile. "Why don't you help me get dinner finished and tell me about him. Hmm?"

Karin seemed reluctant at first to say anything then relented. She passed by her brother and implored him with wide eyes to leave. Taking a slice of bread and butter with him, he winked at her and left.

"Now," said Caroline conspiratorially as she handed Karin a peeler and a carrot. "Tell, me about your young gentleman."

Hardesty woke to a cold splatter on his face. Looking up, he saw a black cloud hanging low over the cedar trees. A thick mist like dry ice vapor drifted silently through the pointed dark green tops. As it settled, it muffled all sounds except for the wind that had begun to shake the wet leaves on the alder that pinned him down. A shower of droplets fell on him, adding to his misery.

Seven hours hadn't changed much. He had managed to clear the nearest branches away from his head and chest and using his knife cut out the soil around his hips. It was exhausting work, however. To move his arms was to invite fiery pain in his shoulder and chest and frequently a deep stabbing sensation that took his breath and concentration away. More than twice he had attempted to pull himself out but his left leg was placed in such a way under the alder's limbs that he could not straighten it. As the hours passed the strain it put on his thigh muscles had become intolerable. His head hurt too and exploring with his right hand, he had found a goose egg lump at the back. When he removed his fingers, there was blood on them. It was a bad situation, growing worse by the coming storm, but he wouldn't give up.

He managed to get the strap off his right shoulder on the last try. The effort caused him to black out. Wakening now, the pack lay underneath his right shoulder. He hoped to push it away, giving him more room to turn his body. Then he remembered the tarp and the bedroll. He needed them to stay dry. The ferns he had pulled over him were only a thin barrier against any downpour and with the way the clouds were threatening that was a distinct possibility. Here in the deep mountains, the tarp could mean the difference between life and death.

Taking a deep breath, he braced himself for the inevitable jab of pain, then reached behind his head to the straps below him. After several minutes, he managed to undo the buckle on the right with his fingers. The left side was much more difficult. With his feet always higher than his head as he lay trapped on the slope, he worked behind his head to release the remaining buckle. As he worked, a breeze continued to stir the trees, causing large drops of water to splatter on the leaves and limbs dangling over his head and torso. Muddy and cold, they slid off and hit him in the face. That made him work harder. Finally, after much struggling, the rolled tarp was free and he brought it over his head to his belly. Hurting, he laid back cold and exhausted on the damp earth. He closed his eyes to rest, feeling light-headed and nauseated but when the dripping water increased, he aroused himself to action again. He reached back for the bedroll just inches from his head, but he couldn't touch it no matter how hard he tried. He finally decided that it was better that he got covered. He'd get the pack pushed away, then see if he could turn his body and lay laterally, instead of head down. After that he would cover himself with the tarp. Steeling himself, he raised his shoulders forward and in one motion pulled the metal container out from under him, but he was not prepared for the racking pain that shot through his left shoulder. Gasping, he fell back too quickly, putting his full weight onto his injured shoulder. Slamming into the wet layer of fern, leaves and sticks, he let out of a loud cry of agony and passed out.

When he came to, Hardesty was chilled and disoriented until he was rudely reminded where he was when a soft rain began to fall onto his face. Rain! He needed to get covered.

Warily, he shifted his position and found that he could move his body away from its downward slant. After some struggling, he was able to lie in a more comfortable position in his branchy cage. Satisfied for the moment, he opened the tarp one-handed and covered himself with it as best as possible. He didn't want to repeat having to bend forward to cover his upper legs, so he did the best he could. The tarp brought immediate relief from the drizzle, but he swore at himself for being so cowardly. In his pain, he could not reach the bedroll.

He closed his eyes and began to pull the tarp over his head when he heard a strange sound above on the trail--like a large heavy animal. The weight of hooves was very distinctive. Were there elk there? He listened carefully then was stunned when someone called out,

"Hello? Is someone there?"

In disbelief, Hardesty found his voice and croaked out, “Here! I'm down here!"

There were sounds of movement on the trail above him, but he couldn't see around the trees and other brush. Afraid he wouldn't be seen, he called out again and was relieved to get an answer.

"I'm coming. Hold on!"

Gasping with relief, he laid back on the ground, oblivious to the pain washing through him. He was found. One of the CCC boys no doubt. Anxiously, he wondered what time it was. Hell, maybe it wasn't as late as he thought it was. He listened to the sounds of someone coming through the brush and he called again unaware how hoarse he sounded. The person scrambled down alongside the alder and coming around to where he was pinned, found him.

To his surprise, it was Kate Alford.

"Oh, my gosh. Mr. Hardesty!"

"Miss Alford - Sorry I can't rise to greet you."

She smiled weakly at him as she scrambled over the limbs to

appraise the damage. More water shook down on him as she came through.

"Sorry. Oh, dear... How long have you been like this?"

"Since this morning. Sometime after ten. My leg's caught. What time is it now?"

"About six thirty in the evening."

He looked at her from his position on the ground. She was wearing dungarees, a cattleman's hat, and a rubberized cloth poncho. Underneath the hat, her curly hair was pulled back in a single braid. She looked so slight and feminine. He wondered how in the hell she'd get him out alive. She was his only hope and the thought was unnerving.

"Is Cory with you?"

"Oh, no. I'm quite alone...except for Elsa.... but never fear." She inspected the tree's angle and position. "You're pretty well pinned here."

Hardesty swallowed. His mouth was dry. "Tell me about it. How did you find me? How did you know?"

"I didn't. I was coming from my parent's cabin from a trail across the ravine. I heard someone holler. It was too unusual to ignore. No one's out. There's a storm coming. When I saw the downed tree..."

She knelt beside him. "May I look? Are you hurt?"

Carefully, Kate removed the tarp from Hardesty. His leg was stuck all right, bent at the knee and folded back towards him. Part of a tree limb held it in place. The pants leg as far as she could see was ripped. Both legs looked scraped and stained with reddish brown marks made from the alder bark. A boot was missing.

"Think it's broken?" she asked.

"I don't think so. My hip is strained though. All that pressure holding it in place."

"You've got some scrapes. Bruises, I'm sure too."

"My shoulder - something's broken."

Kate chewed her lip, then reaching over, unbuttoned his wool shirt and long underwear top underneath, and expertly felt around with her fingertips. When she touched his left shoulder, a jolt went through him. He barely stifled a groan.

"You don't have to be all heroic with me, Mr. Hardesty. I can feel that the collarbone is broken. It must really hurt."

"It's not been my favorite day."

She laughed softly. "Then I'll make it so. I'm going to get you out." She stood up and the tree shivered again. The rain had halted, but more drops from the alder's branches fell on him.

"But first you better stay covered." She replaced the tarp and started around the tree to go back.

"Where are you going?" Hardesty didn't want to sound like he was panicking, but the thought of her leaving …

"To Elsa. Your day's improving already. I'm packing a buck saw." She smiled reassuringly at him. "I've got a canteen. I'll bring some water too."

He nodded his thanks and pulled the tarp around him. Closing his eyes, he rested until she came back, if lying on the cold, wet ground was rest. She gave him some water, then told him she was going to cut away some of the limbs.

"Even if only a few of them are removed they should still release some of the weight of the main fork that's pinning you around your waist."

She helped him to rearrange himself, placing the bedroll under his neck and head, then began limbing with the saw.

For what seemed hours, she worked. Hardesty hadn't known what to expect, but after a few minutes it was obvious that she knew what she was doing as the small branches began to disappear. His confidence in her grew. Lying as he did, he found it oddly comforting with her working around him. She was very graceful and her slight body moved wonderfully to the rhythm of the saw. What power she might lack in her arms she made up for in determination and skill, but he no longer thought of her a tomboy who occasionally showed up at dances. Kate Alford was a beauty.

From time to time she said something to him or smiled at him and as she heated up, her face began to glow. The rain started lightly again, forcing her to work harder, but she never wasted any motion. Soon some of the medium-sized limbs were cut and tossed away and with each limbing, the weight of the main fork began to lessen.

"Can you move your leg?" she asked.

"Not sure." He tried to straighten it, but in moving his body, a jolt of pain went through him that made him swear and bite his lips.

"Excuse my French." he muttered.

"You're excused. How does the limb feel now?"

"Which one? Mine or the tree's?"

"The tree's," she laughed.

"It's lighter. It feels lighter..."

"Good. I'm going to take out the larger branch on the left now, but I don't want it to fall on your face. I thought I'd tie a rope to Elsa and keep some tension on it. Are you cold?"

"I'm all right. Just want to get out."

"You will." She smiled sweetly at him.

Hardesty thought her smile dazzling and incongruous. How could a woman in a wet poncho and hat with wet hair look so good? Tough but every inch a lady? She patted his good shoulder lightly and left. Five minutes later she was back with a rope which she tied to a branch. Like a surgeon about to perform an operation, she explained the procedure to him.

"I'm going to saw through the limb. Elsa will keep the rope taunt and hold the limb away from you. Are you ready?"

Wearily, Hardesty nodded that he was.

She set the saw where she wanted and began working above him.

"Better close your eyes. There will be sawdust."

He closed his eyes and listened to the light patter of the rain on the tarp and her poncho. The sound of the saw cutting became steady and it made him drowsy.

"Give Elsa," he heard her say unexpectedly. He felt the tree move slightly as she continued to saw. Opening his eyes, he could see that she was half through. She grunted once but kept on going through. The tension in the tree changed and suddenly she shouted,

"Go Elsa! GO!"

She stepped to the side of him and handled the saw and blade with both hands. The limb suddenly gave as it was cut off the main fork, but the horse had moved on command and pulled it away from him. She put the saw down behind him and pushed on the limb.

"Go Elsa!"

The mare responded and the heavy limb was free of the tree. The main fork lifted. It shifted and Hardesty groaned with relief. For the first time in nearly nine hours, his leg was free of the weight. His relief was short lived, however, as the muscles in his leg cramped. Trying to straighten it was agony. He bit down on his lips.

"Don't give in yet, Mr. Hardesty. I'm going to pull you out, but you've got to help with your feet."

She put her arms under his and on the count of three he kicked back while she pulled.

"Aruh," he grunted. She dragged him down and away from the tree. When he was resting completely free of the alder, she untied the rope and told the horse to stay.

"Phew," she said as she sat down. "That was tough. Now to get you up there."

For a moment Hardesty lay precariously on his back, saying nothing. A pulsing throb banged through his body and in places he hadn't noticed before. He was battered and scraped from his fall far worse than he had realized. Finally, he opened his eyes. "Where's the elevator?"

"I'm afraid I'm it. Do you think you can stand? I'll help you climb all the way."

"I'll try."

When he was up on top and resting, she went back to get the rope, his boot and bedroll. On top again, she busied herself around the horse, then came to him and asked to look at his shoulder again.

"I want to get the bone in place and the arm secured. Doc can set it proper."

"Stinker."

"Mr. Hardesty."

"I'll be good."

Holding onto a stick he had found, he clenched it tightly while she opened his shirt. Gritting his teeth, he sat rigidly while she popped the collarbone in place then folded his left arm on his chest. When she was satisfied with the way it lay, she bound it firmly with one of her extra jersey shirts. Hardesty became overly quiet as she finished up and when she looked at him, he felt as though he had been quartered. His face was sweaty. When he let go of the stick, it fell to the ground in two pieces.

"How about a ride Mr. Hardesty?"

"I'm not sure I can get up..."

"Elsa can get down."

"What is she, a trick horse?"

"Some days. I hope this is one."

Kate helped him to his feet and brought the horse over. The Appaloosa mare was carrying a packsaddle with crossbucks for holding saddlebags. There were makeshift stirrups made of rope. It was not a riding saddle and it looked uncomfortable, but there was room for him to sit.

"Down, Elsa," the young woman said and the horse sat, then lay down. Kate helped Hardesty to the horse. He limped awkwardly over to the Appaloosa on the left side as she instructed, but getting on was very difficult. By the time the horse was standing with him mounted, he was sick. He held onto the wood packsaddle with his free hand and leaned over in pain.

Kate covered him with the tarp. "Do you have dry clothes?"

"In – my - bedroll," he said haltingly.

"Good. We'll save them for a worse scenario."

"This isn't worse?" The rain was falling lightly and it was getting chilly.

"It could be, but really -- you're doing fine. It's six miles to the ranger station as the crow flies, though you know, it's up and down in between. That means more miles. Do you think you can hold on?"

He nodded his head yes. He'd make it.

Kate smiled sweetly at him and took the mare's reins. She wouldn't let him see how worried she was.

The storm hit just as Spinelli made a combination shot into the corner pocket. He had made a perfect bank, forcing Staubach to put two more Chesterfield cigarettes on the edge of the pool table.

"Damn, I'm good!" he chortled and set up for the next shot. Staubach groaned, rubbing the tip of his stick into the chalk extra hard. Behind him, Lorenzo and the others in the Joisey Squad laughed.

"That's four," Golden taunted, then looked up when a blast of rain hit against the windows and roof like gravel being thrown against the glass. It roared a crescendo.

"Jesus. Listen to that! What time is it?" he asked Lorenzo.

"Eight."

"Time flies when you're having fun," Spinelli said over the rain's roar. His next shot was a cut shot in the corner with a full follow. The winning stroke was just moments away.

"Get ready for pay off," the slight Italian said as he leaned over the table.

Staubach rolled his eyes. The others gave him no help. Spinelli set it up and started to stroke when there was a loud crashing sound as thunder sounded directly overhead. It was loud enough to make him miss and dig the stick into the felt. Golden started to laugh, but a blinding light followed by a second crash made everyone in the room freeze.

"Someone make sure the windows are shut," an enrollee shouted from the canteen. "That last one was a killer."

The little group stood uneasily around the table and looked outside warily. It had grown dark suddenly as the rain drove down in sheets. Some of the boys from their barracks came over from the canteen and stared alongside them.

"That for real?" someone asked.

The outside door creaked faintly over the noise of the rain, letting two rain-soaked figures into the entryway. They were covered head to foot in rain gear. One of them had a sou'wester on. The taller of the two stamped his feet then came into the rec room. He removed his coat and looked around. It was Bladstad.

"Anyone see Hardesty?" he asked.

"Naw. Not at mess," Lorenzo said in a loud voice. "He ain't AWOL, is he?"

"No," replied the forester, "but I expected him back some time ago."

"Think he's caught in this stuff?" Staubach frowned as he tried to resume the game. "If he's still up there, it'll be unavoidable."

"Damn," Spinelli said when another round of thunder crashed over them. "That was close."

The lights flickered between dark and bright, then steadied. Outside across the parade ground, they heard something like shouting followed by a terrible thrashing sound. A few minutes later, Callister came into the building, his slicker shining and dripping water.

"Bladstad. There's a big fir down on the ball field." He started to say something more when the thunder crashed again, a little further away. The lights flickered wildly finally going into total darkness.

"Someone get the lanterns behind the canteen counter," Callister ordered. "You, Spinelli, check and make sure all the windows are secured, then stay away from them." He handed him a flashlight, then turned to Bladstad.

"Got a call from Caroline Alford," Mario heard him say above the storm. "She wondered if anyone had heard from the ranger's station. Kate went up to the family cabin yesterday. She's overdue."

"I haven't," Bladstad said, "but there's no reason why we can't make a call on the phone unless the lightning's interfering. Ed has the short-wave radio it set up. You can call if you like and if they haven't heard, the lookout tower might know something."

Staubach and Golden brought in some lamps and set them down on the pool table for lighting.

"Don't touch anything," Staubach said. "The game's not over yet." He got the first lantern going and hung it up on a nail in the rafters. Golden put his up too, illuminating the table.

"Ball's still in place. It's your turn."

"Not until everything's settled," Callister said. He seemed to enjoy getting things organized and eventually took off for the little office behind the canteen counter.

Steve Lorenzo made a face. "Putting on airs again. Forgets where he comes from," he said then clammed up when he saw Bladstad.

Bladstad put a log in the stove. Out at the entryway, more people arrived bringing news about storm damage. Callister came back in.

"Hardesty not in, Dick?"

"That's what I heard. I hope he's found cover. Conditions in the mountains are murder. If he doesn't appear in the next hour, I think I'll organize a search party first light."

"Excuse me, sir" Spinelli said. "Are you talking about Park?"

"Yes," Bladstad replied.

"I'm going. You just tell me when."

The thunder crashed again and Bladstad had to shout, "First thing in the morning."

CHAPTER 11

Kate knew they were in trouble before the storm even hit. Bringing Hardesty down was much more difficult than she realized. He didn't say, but she knew he was in considerable pain by the way he carried himself on the horse. She couldn't keep the pace she wanted for fear it would cause him to black out and as the time lengthened, she wished she had taken the time to make a litter and drag it behind the mare. Hardesty would have been more comfortable. Yet she knew no matter what she tried, the weather would go against them and soon she would have to make another decision that could have grave consequences for him. When the approaching storm began to threaten more violently, she had no choice. She had to get him into shelter.

The forest through which they descended was thick, but relatively stable. No winter-weakened trees here. In some places there were openings in the cedar and fir mix where big leaf and vine maple grew on their edges. It was here she spotted a cleared and level place where she could pitch her tent. It was close to the trail, but provided the extra shelter she desired without the danger of windfall limbs landing on them. Clicking to the horse, she led her up on the little knoll. Holding on with some difficulty, Hardesty looked out of his rain-slicked cocoon.

"What's going on?"

"A storm's coming, Mr. Hardesty. You've got to get under cover. You're chilled already. Do you think you can climb down? I'm not sure if Elsa's up for a repeat performance."

When he nodded that he'd try, she helped him down, an effort that seemed to exhaust and hurt him more. He leaned against the wet horse, clutching the crossbucks one handed while she undid a pup tent. Dully, he watched her set it up in the increasingly harder rain. It was a little two-man tent with a floor. When it was ready, she got his bedroll and under the cover of the tent, took it out of its oilcloth covering. She spread it out, then got her own. When everything was set, she helped him to sit inside the tent, taking away the tarp at the last minute.

"You've got to get dry," she said after bringing back her rucksack and setting it inside. "Take off your pants and boots and crawl inside the bed roll. Do you think you can manage?"

Hardesty looked at her with weary eyes, like the cold and the rain finally got to him. He said, faintly, "No. I can't."

She said nothing for a moment. "All right, I'll help you scoot back, then get you undressed." At least I think I can.

He didn't object, gingerly pushing aside the covers as he moved back. Each movement seemed to send bolts of agony to his shoulder and chest for he grimaced each time, but said nothing. When he was set, he undid his buttons and fly while she took off his boots.

"Ready?" she asked when she was done. All Hardesty could do was nod. Leaning on his free hand, he painfully shifted his weight off his hips and let her pull the canvas pants off, then put the covers over himself. She folded the pants and put them with his boots. As an afterthought, she removed his socks and put new ones on.

"There," she said.

"Thanks," he murmured. "I'm going to lie down." He lay down with a soft groan, pulling the blanket around him. Cradling his bound arm, he closed his eyes and was quiet.

"All right," said Kate. "I'm going to rig up a fly for the tent and check on Elsa. I'll be back." She looked in his direction for a reply, but Hardesty was asleep.

The storm broke ten minutes later with a flash of lightning, followed by a loud crash that made the mare pull at her stake. Kate checked her one last time, then scrambled for the tent when the rain began to fall with a vengeance. Crawling inside she closed the flap and removed her hat and poncho in the low, cramped space. Putting them aside, she retrieved her flashlight and a change of pants from her rucksack. A few minutes later she was under her own covers.

Beside her, Hardesty slept on his back, his feet resting next to her right shoulder. He was very still, but above the hollow sound of the rain slamming on their canvas roof, she thought she could hear him moan. For awhile, she listened to the rain and wind, wondering if a search was being organized -- not for her -- there would be no alarm until tomorrow -- but for him. He was probably overdue and would be AWOL now. Only he wasn't the type. She had heard Jim Taylor say how responsible he was. With the way the storm pounded the mountains, there would be concerns for his safety.

Sometime around midnight, Kate woke at the sound of the mare as she came close to the tent ropes. Lifting up the flap, she poked the flashlight out and shined it on the horse. Elsa brought her wet head up and whinnied. Speaking to her reassuringly, Kate pointed the shaft of light around the clearing. The rain had diminished to a light drizzle, but where the light hit, the leaves of the trees and ferns gleamed brightly.

"Good girl," she clucked to the horse. She withdrew into the tent, carefully avoiding Hardesty's feet behind her. Wondering about him, she shined the light indirectly on his face. He was still asleep, with his head to the side. The scratched face didn't look changed, but his hair lay damp on his forehead. Curious, she got out of her covers and crawled over to him. Holding the flashlight away from his face, she touched his forehead and was shocked to feel a damp chilliness. Keeping the light directed away from him, she touched his unshaven cheek and found the same.

Darn! Now what?

She decided to loosen the blankets around him to make him

more comfortable and in doing so, he stirred and opened his eyes. For a moment, he furrowed his brows at the space above him, then looked at her face half-lit by the flashlight's glare. Smiling wanly, he raised his free hand to her. It trembled in the light.

"How are you feeling?" she asked.

"Rotten. I ache everywhere," he answered hoarsely.

"Sorry to disturb you, but you looked uncomfortable. Are you cold?"

He nodded. "A little. Feel a bit shivery. I could use some water."

She found her canteen and helped him to drink by lifting his head, but the pain in his shoulder cut him short. He swore, then apologized, sputtering as he laid his head down.

"Are you okay?" she asked.

"Yes," he gasped. His eyes half closed, he murmured, "I am thirsty."

She cupped her hand and poured water into it. "Here," she said and guided it into his mouth. Afterwards when he had his fill, she wiped his chin dry with a bandanna and sat back.

Hardesty lay limp on his makeshift bed and turned towards her. His face looked pale and ghostly in the dim light beyond the flashlight's range, but he smiled at her.

"You're a nice person, Miss Alford. I appreciate this."

"I'm glad I came along." She fiddled with the blankets for a bit then said, "Why don't you call me Kate? It would be so much easier. Not such a mouthful."

"All right, if you return the same." He was silent for a moment, but his head shook. “Is it still raining and blowing?”

"It's calmed down considerably. When morning comes, I'll build a fire, rework the tarp so I can get some things dried."

"Do you think someone will come?"

"Absolutely. I don't think it's a good idea to try to move you again. As long as you can stay warm, you'll be fine. Help will come soon enough. It's not that far to the trailhead. If I have to, though, I'll go and get help. We'll decide in the morning."

He nodded his head. “Good idea,” he said, then with his free hand pulled the blankets around him. "Water made me cold," he murmured and then closing his eyes, drifted to sleep.

Kate woke abruptly a few couple of hours later and found that Hardesty had kicked her shoulder with his feet. Fumbling for the flashlight, she shined it on him and found him stirring restlessly under his covers. He was still asleep, but hardly peaceful. His whole body was trembling like a horse’s skin flicking off a swarm of flies. His face was pale and his head moved with agitation. Slipping out of her bedroll, she crawled over. Hardesty held one of the top blankets tightly in his hand, but it shook like he had palsy. Alarmed, she touched his good shoulder and found that he felt damp and cold. His sandy hair was plastered on his forehead and his breathing was shallow.

“Mr. -- Park," she corrected. "Park?"

When he didn't respond, she went back to her rucksack and took out a flannel shirt. Coming back, she wiped his face and neck, wondering how she'd change his shirt without disturbing his shoulder if she had to do that. When she touched his forehead, it felt cold.

"Park?" She sat back, uncomfortable about his worsening condition. She looked at her watch: two-thirty with two and one half-hours to go until daylight. She had nothing else to give him except her own bedding. She pulled the wool camp blankets across his body and rearranged the ones beneath. Sitting back near the tent wall, she turned off the light and listened to the light tap of the rain outside as it resumed again. She wanted to sleep, but knew that she couldn't until this crisis was over. And it was a crisis.

Increasingly as the time passed, Hardesty's breathing became more and more audible above the patter as he breathed through his teeth. Suddenly, he began to mutter. At first, she couldn't understand him, but when the words became clearer, she realized that he wasn't speaking English. She wasn't sure, but it sounded like French. Whatever it was, she was sure that he was addressing a woman. For awhile he spoke to her in a low voice, then seemed to argue with her or was it with himself?

"Marie!" he called suddenly. "Marie!" His actions became

agitated, his legs moving under the blankets. His words were slurred.

"*Arrete,* Marie. *Je t'en pris. Mon frère* - Paul!" Hardesty flung his arm out, hitting Kate's knee. She took it without thinking and holding his hand, sought to comfort him in the dark. He felt both cold and clammy to her and when his struggles continued, she spoke to him a soothing voice.

"Park, please listen. Park. You're all right. You mustn't be afraid."

"*Quoi?*"

She heard him turn in the dark space and wondered if his eyes were opened. He acted as though he were awake, but when he continued muttering in French, she felt increasing alarm and confusion because he wasn't fully conscious.

"Mr. Hardesty, you must be still. You'll hurt yourself."

She felt for his forehead with her other hand and continued to talk above his stream of foreign words. Suddenly, he stiffened and cried out in anguish.

"*Mon frère. Quest-ce j'avais fait? Tu est mort. Tu est mort*!" He came forward at that, then collapsed back holding his shoulder. When Kate hastily got the flashlight on she found him out cold.

The next hour was awful. He shivered for some time, then fell into a disturbed sleep going from chills to listlessness and back. Finally, he became quiet and lying limp, no longer called out nor shivered. Alarmed, Kate did her best to revive him as she sat cross-legged, her head bent under the slant of the tent's roof. She removed his damp shirt and knit underwear top by cutting it off him. After drying him, she lay one of her own shirts over him, sculpting it around his sides, then put the blankets back on. It was a hellish attempt, for any movement seemed to hurt him more, but sometime after three, there was a change. Noticing it, Kate turned on the flashlight.

Hardesty lay weakly in his blankets, his eyes half opened. When the light glanced off the side of his head, he opened them wider and stared into the yellow orb of the flashlight like he did not see nor recognize her. Eventually he did turn and look at her.

For a moment he stared at her, then unexpectedly reached

out and with some effort touched her hair. In the gloom created at the edge of the flashlight's beam, it was hard to tell what exactly he saw, but the auburn color of her hair seemed to fascinate him. He rubbed it stiffly between his fingers but never connected with her. She was someone else. For awhile, he seemed calm then subtlety he stopped playing with her hair and eventually in a clear voice said,

"My God, Holly Garrison. You always were a pretty thing. I thought you were dead." He breathed raggedly through his mouth, his eyebrows crinkled as he tried to figure out something. He touched her cheek.

"You are dead, aren't you? You - you were killed. I -" He stroked her skin, tanned by the sun. "Funny, you're not cold." Hardesty shivered and his eyes went unfocused. "You're not cold at all..." He paused, then murmured, "I'm cold, Holly. I'm so damned cold."

Like a frightened boy, he shrank back, taking his hand away. He began to shiver violently. "You're supposed to be dead!"

He became agitated, but Kate spoke to him in a strong, calm voice,

"Park, it's Kate Alford. You got hurt and you're having chills. Look at me, Park. I'm not Holly, whoever she is. I'm Kate. From Frazier."

He squinted his eyes at her, trying to make her out.

Kate took his free hand and held it.

"Miss... Al..ford?" he asked.

"Yes...Kate Alford. You're going to be all right. There's help in the morning. We'll get you to camp, to the infirmary."

"Camp," he murmured. "The ... C … CC … camp."

"That's right. I want you to stay awake and talk to me. Remember where you are? We're still in the mountains. I had to set up the tent because of the storm."

"I'm cold."

"I know you are." And she would have to do something about it quickly or he would die. She'd seen enough in rescue operations to know how the rain and chill of the Northwest lowered the body temperature. Lethargy and babbling were symptoms of a dangerous condition. There was no name for it, but she knew a cure taught by an uncle who had mined in Alaska and in the North Cascades. She'd have to do it. It was the only thing that would save him. Swallowing, she made the decision to do it. It was her reputation or his life.

"Park. Mr. Hardesty. I'll help to get you warm. But you must trust me, as I trust you."

He looked at her unfocused, but obeyed her when she pulled back the covers and crept in next to him. She removed her shirt and pants so that all she had on was her bra and knit undershorts. She took a deep breath and closing her eyes, she slipped out of her brassiere. Very carefully, she coaxed him onto his good side, an effort that hurt him. It made him gasp and clutch at her rigidly, but finally she could pull him to her chest and body and cradle him. His skin felt cold to her. His limbs were becoming stiff. But she could feel his heart beat and it was still strong. Giving her warmth to him, she soothed him as she held him. She talked to him in an attempt to keep him awake in the real world, not some horror he was remembering and to her great relief, it began to work. A quarter-hour after she started, he felt warm to her touch again.

For a brief time, he shivered, then the stiffness went out of him. His eyes remained half opened and he responded more lucidly to her as the time passed. About an hour after she had climbed in, he began to drift and fall asleep. For a bit longer, she kept him focused. She needed to be sure that if he should fall asleep, he would wake. When the lethargy was no longer present, she let him rest, cradled in her arms against her breasts. Soon he was sound asleep. She held him a while longer even though her left arm was in danger of going dead. Finally she slipped it out, continuing to lie beside him to prevent his body temperature from dropping.

It was semi-dark in the tent. Outside the rain had stopped again and the wind had died down. For the first time in hours, she was attuned to it as well as the mare who cropped on a small plat of grass under the vine maples. Above all, she was attuned to him and the idea that a man lay next to her. She was conscious of his breathing, the smooth, hard muscles of his arms, his long bare legs. She put her hands on her mouth and shook her head. It was so unreal, but she had done it. Saved his life too and she knew it, but what would people think? What would he think? It suddenly mattered very much what he thought.

She had liked Park Hardesty for some time. Especially since the dance, but she had decided after breaking it off with David that she wouldn't see anyone else for awhile. Even if she liked Hardesty's quiet self-assurance and surprising interest in the things she liked. Even if he was good-looking enough to turn a girl's head when he came into a room. Like he had with the Osborne twins.

She had listened to what Cory had said about him and knew he was a solid man, someone who could take care of himself. Yet she had made her decision to concentrate on studying and working on projects in the woods. Funny how something could change all that, she thought. What had happened in the last couple of hours had shaken her. His anguish had touched her and the thought of losing him before she even got to know him was disturbing. It would have broken her heart, but what did all that babbling mean? Who were Marie and Holly? And Paul?

Elsa nickered and stamped. Kate chanced shining her flashlight on her watch's dial. It was four-thirty. It would be getting lighter now. Restless, she wondered if she should get up and start a fire and get some of his clothes dried. Sleeping was beyond question now, even though she was very tired. Help, she hoped, would get organized at first light. Maybe there was concern for her as well. Sighing, she mentally made a list of what she should do, but Hardesty distracted her when he stirred and shifted his weight. Groaning when he rolled back on his back, Kate thought he had awakened, but he resumed sleeping. Touching his arm softly, she was relieved to feel warmth. She slipped her hand to his wrist and felt his pulse. It was steady. He groaned again, then was silent. Kate decided she'd better get dressed.

Hardesty woke around five-thirty asking for water and the time. Fully clothed, Kate satisfied both requests, then sat back on the tent floor.

"You looked tired," he commented. "I hope I haven't been a bother."

"No, you haven't," she said, relieved that perhaps he hadn't remembered everything. "You did have a rough time early this morning, but you're O.K. now. You were out of your head for a while."

"Did I talk?"

"Yes."

"Nothing embarrassing, I hope."

"I won't tell. I promise." She smiled softly, but kept her expression otherwise blank. Hardesty glanced at her briefly, trying hard to read her, but she gave him no clue. Finally, he asked if she had made a decision.

"I've made a fire and I'm drying your clothes. It hasn't rained in more than an hour. I can make something hot for you now."

"How soon until the cavalry comes?"

"No later than noon. I'm sure of that. We'll get you down to Doc's as soon as we can."

Hardesty didn't say anything. He became withdrawn. Kate asked him what was wrong.

He started to shrug, but he winced. "Just wondering if I'll get busted or get medical leave."

"I don't know..." she answered, "but I really don't see them drumming you out, Park Hardesty."

He smiled at her. Their eyes locked for a moment and helpless, she smiled back.

Cory Alford found them first around nine-thirty leading the way on horseback. A party of CCC boys and Doc trailed down below him. When he saw Kate sitting by a fire under a tarp, he raised a Colt .38 and fired it into the air three times.

"Sis!" he said. "Am I glad I found you. Mom and Dad have been worried sick. That was some storm. A Douglas fir fell across the ball field at camp. We lost power in Frazier. Trees are down everywhere."

"Were you looking just for me?"

"No. I figured you'd lay low -- though I thought you'd be at the cabin. We're looking for Park Hardesty."

"We?"

"A bunch of boys from the camp."

Oh, thank God. Then you can help for sure. I've got him in the tent. He's been hurt. A tree fell and nearly killed him."

"Last night?" Cory was incredulous.

"No, yesterday morning. I didn't find him until almost five in the evening. He was pinned."

Cory looked at his sister in amazement. "You've got him out. Kate..."

"That isn't all -- and Cory, please, please don't say anything. We stopped here when the storm broke last night. He was cold and exhausted and in pain. I bound his arm and I got him out of his wet gear, but he turned bad this morning. You remember that trick Uncle Lars told us about mountain chill?"

Cory nodded.

"I did it. Oh, don't look at me like that. I wasn't buck naked, but folks will talk. Please don't say a thing, okay?"

"Will Hardesty?"

"I don't think he remembers. He was out of his head."

"He says anything and I'll break his nose."

Kate cringed. "Oh, Cory, don't do anything. I couldn't bear it. Just don't say anything, all right?"

Cory gave her hug and a peck on her forehead. "Sure, Sis. Is he decent?"

"He's in his underwear."

Cory shook his head. "My Kate. My beautiful Kate." He hugged her again. "I'll take care of the censorship committee. We'll get him out as soon as we can."

Hardesty was awake when Cory crawled in.

"Say old man. This any way to spend Monday morning?"

Hardesty grinned. "Anything to avoid splitting shakes."

Cory laughed. "You may live to regret that when Doc is done with you."

Hardesty turned a bit pale. "You serious? I'm not out am I?"

"Heck no. I'd say medical leave, then soft duty, like bull cook or KP--light stuff."

When Hardesty noticeably relaxed, Cory asked if he would like to go home on leave.

"I don't have a home. I left long ago."

"Well, maybe we'll take you in."

Hardesty shot his head up then clutched his shoulder in pain.

"Hey, don't get so charged up. It's only an offer."

Hardesty put his hand on his bound shoulder and grimaced. Through his teeth he said, "It's a very kind one, but I'd hate to impose."

"It's no problem. Really. There's my place over the store."

Cory pulled in some clothing from outside. "I'll help you dress. Doc'll be here shortly. You might as well get used to feeling like minced meat. His father was a baker so his hands can poke like he was kneading dough."

"Don't worry. I've been a human punching bag since yesterday. Nothing's going to make a difference."

A few hours later, Hardesty almost ate his words.

CHAPTER 12

Standing at his window, Callister watched the slim figure of Kate Alford go into the infirmary and in irritation, stacked a set of papers a second time at his desk. For the past week, both the camp and community of Frazier had been talking about the storm and the dramatic rescue of Park Hardesty. It had taken more than a day to restore power to the community when the transformer received damage from a fallen tree and there was excitement at the camp when the backstop in the ball field was crushed by a massive fir tree. The twelve-inch dent it put into the ground had been sobering. But Hardesty's rescue had been another matter. He was already six hours late when the storm broke and an effort had been made to locate his whereabouts by radio. Neither the ranger or spike camp had seen him. All foot traffic had been down by around three in the afternoon. Concern increased by ten p.m. when flooding had reported around the bridge going towards the trailhead to Darcy Meadows and Bear Lake. Hardesty was thought to be a careful and cautious man, someone who prepared well before going into the wilderness, but he was also an easterner, and not a local man who would know the area intimately. Bad weather was an enemy to all up there, but everyone thought the Pennsylvanian would fare worse.

Mixed with a concern for Kate Alford, at daybreak, a rescue party was formed and took off when the rain was abating.

It had taken most of the morning to bring him down by stretcher. Advanced word had arrived that Hardesty had been found alive, but injured. With him was Kate Alford.

Callister frowned. At first, he didn't believe it, but from the initial report given by a CCC boy, he learned of Kate's role in the whole affair and that had sent tongues wagging. When Hardesty finally arrived - pale and half asleep - after lunch there wasn't anyone in either the camp or the village who didn't know. With work projects suspended to focus on the myriad of downed trees around Camp Kulshan, the majority of the camp was on hand when the search party returned.

They took Hardesty to Doc to look over his collarbone and stitch wounds on his head and leg, then put him to bed in the infirmary. With some of the road to the city inaccessible due to the storm, hospitalizing him there was not possible. Besides, Doc thought he was worn out enough as it was. Rest and quiet was what he needed, not a jarring, fifty mile trip to town. So Hardesty stayed, and to Callister's suspicions, so did Kate.

"See that report?" Bladstad asked coming into the office.

Callister started, then recovered. "Yeah, I saw it. We can make some adjustments in the classes for the fall."

"How about the spike camp?"

"We can add on more classes for high school completion."

"I'd like to do something for the rest of the summer. Like add on a forestry class."

"We need a teacher."

"I think we got him." Bladstad paused. "Park Hardesty."

"He isn't qualified."

"Oh, I think he is. I keep telling you, he's college educated. He knows his natural sciences very well. I know he's been helping some of the boys with reading. I've seen him with some of them. He's a natural teacher. Patient."

"I didn't think he was the type." Callister was getting tired of the subject already, then thought of Kate. "How is he this morning?"

"Much improved. The danger of infection is passing. He's more alert, though he's stiff and sore. Moves like he was beat up."

By a tree, thought Callister sarcastically. "How long until he reports to work?"

"He's been given leave. About three weeks' worth, then I think he'll be bull cook until he's more mended."

"He cook as well as he teaches?"

"Callister, I detect a jealous streak."

"I just think he's too good to be true." Callister jammed his hands into his uniform pants pockets and looked across the grounds to the infirmary. And he better stay away from Kate.

Hearing the door click behind him, Hardesty looked up from where he sat on the bed's edge in his bathrobe, and braced for another one of Doc's unflinching examinations. After a week he was still tired and stiff, but he was also leery of passing another day here. All the poking and prodding had worn him out further. Doc was O.K., but Cory was right. The man had slapped the hell out of bread dough in his younger days, and never quite got over it. Setting his collarbone had been a more painful exercise than Hardesty had anticipated.

"Doc?"

"No, Kate Alford."

Hardesty swung around a little too fast, causing him to grunt at the pull on his shoulder. The collarbone had been set with a strap. It went up over his shoulder and across his back where it looped under the armpit and back up again, forming an eight shape. A cinch on his back held everything in place, pulling the shoulders back. With both arms placed in slings, he had as much mobility as an armless slug sitting up in a chair. Feeling somewhat vulnerable, he started to carefully rise, feeling stiff and uncomfortable.

"I didn't mean to barge in. I can come back later." She began to back out.

"Wait. Please. I'd like to speak to you."

"All right." She came further into the infirmary's sick bay and stood by a screen that separated the next bed. She was dressed simply in riding pants and blouse, her hair held back with a barrette. Hardesty thought she looked beautiful.

"You're looking better," she commented.

He settled back down on the bed, "Still tender, but I have no complaints. I know what the outcome would have been if you hadn't come by and for that I'm eternally grateful."

"It's nothing," she laughed. "Let's just say we're even. You rescued me from a bear."

"Even? It doesn't come close. You saved me from a tree. Trees are inanimate."

"But gnarlier than my bear."

He chuckled. "Done. Still, there is my image to maintain."

"Being attacked by a tree or me rescuing you?"

Hardesty looked straight at her. "Maybe, but it doesn't matter. I can live with it."

The conversation stopped dead after that, both of them self-conscious. He was wearing his flannel pajamas bottoms, but under the bathrobe, he was bare-chested. Most of the sling was visible to her.

"I heard you're going on medical leave."

"Yes, three weeks' worth."

"Cory also said he had asked my father about you staying with him above the store."

"That an imposition?"

"No. Technically, that's Cory's home. Dad likes it for the night security."

"In Frazier?"

Kate laughed. "Dad has a long memory. A drunken logger broke into it in '25 and stole a case of vanilla. We found the empty bottles down by the river the next day. The logger was in the brush passed out."

"And Prohibition, no less. Well, I'll just have to hold down the fort and put the cases of vanilla under my bed there."

"Sweet dreams for sure."

Kate cleared her throat. "Well, I better go. I'm awfully glad you are looking well."

Hardesty smiled. In a wood framed mirror across the room, his face appeared pale and his eyes weary. There were scratches just beginning to scab on his cheeks. Not so well. He struggled further to the edge of the bed, but she came over and stayed him lightly on his arm.

"You don't have to get up for me."

"I know. Just wanted to thank you again. I really mean it. If I can ever do something for you or that horse, let me know."

Kate laughed brightly, then blushed.

"Anything wrong?" he asked.

"Oh, no. I just remembered something about Elsa I'm supposed to do about. I really should be going." She moved away from him, smiling bravely. "Bye."

"Bye."

After she left, Hardesty went over to the window and waited until he saw her go out across the grounds.

Damn, he thought.

"You decent?"

Kate hadn't been gone more than ten minutes when Hardesty had company again. He had attempted to lie down and take a nap when there was a knock on the door. It was Garrison. He came into the room after quietly closing the door behind him.

"What are you doing here?" Hardesty asked as he struggled up into a sitting position.

"Heard you had an accident. It was in the news."

"The news?"

"Yeah, the local city paper. I saw it when I came up the other day. Didn't you know?"

Hardesty sighed. No, he hadn't.

"Well, don't look too gol darn happy about it. You should be glad. You're really part of the bunch now."

"I'd rather not have the publicity."

"You're too sensitive. Which surprises me. I always thought you were a thick skinned sort of guy."

"Tell that to my backside. I left part of my leg and shoulder on a hill."

Garrison looked sympathetic. "So I heard." The forester shook his head. "Lucky you were found. With that weather socked in....That was close, John." He took out a little bag of tobacco and began to tamp it down in his pipe.

Hardesty gave a halfway shrug. "I'm alive." He got gingerly off the bed, self-conscious of his inability to tighten up his bathrobe. He limped from a large bruise on his inner left thigh.

"Am I disrupting anything?"

"Just my beauty sleep." Hardesty grinned wryly. "It's okay. I'm going to be out of here tomorrow and I can get a good sleep then. Too many interruptions here." He limped over to the window, lurching like a mummy the way his shoulders were bound. Outside on the parade ground some enrollees were sawing up the last of the downed limbs that had sailed into it during the storm. After a moment he cleared his throat. "You talk to anyone here? Won't they be curious?"

"The office thinks I just dropped by to see the enrollee who got caught by a tree. Quite a story. I've been making the rounds of the camps in the state. No big deal."

"Maybe to you."

"Park. You're starting to sound testy."

Hardesty turned around. "I am."

Garrison smiled. "Don't worry. I'll get out of here before I do something stupid. What are your plans?"

"I'm going to be in Frazier for a few weeks' stay. I've got medical leave."

"No chance on going home?"

"Floyd, I don't have a home and you know it."

"No, I don't know it and neither do you. Things may have changed."

"They'll never change. They're better off without me." His voice broke and he looked away. Garrison sighed, then said he was going. "Take care of yourself, son. Hope you get a good rest." He went over to the door. "By the way, Bladstad said you're interested in the Forest Service when your tour is up. I'm glad. He said you've done a hell of a job with the fishery project and that you're getting good marks in the forestry class he's doing with you. We can talk about it some time."

"All right...." Hardesty turned. "Sorry to be so grumpy. I hurt just about everywhere. Thanks for coming, Floyd. Did Lily ever get my note?"

"Sure thing. She says hello."

Hardesty nodded. He limped over cautiously and offered his elbow in jest since he couldn't shake hands. Garrison put his hand on Hardesty's good shoulder and gently drew him into a hug.

"Don't be a stranger," he said.

"Betts?" Kate called through the screen door. "You there?"

"In the back, Kate! Come on in!"

Avoiding the washing machine that had been pulled out on the back porch, Kate made her way around the pile of clothes lying in a basket there.

"What's going on?"

"Wash day," said Betty as she came out into the kitchen. "Honestly, you'd think I would have him trained now. Look at these. I found them under the bed." She threw some dirty socks into the basket, then stepping onto the porch put a clean, wet shirt through the wringer mounted on top of the washer.

"Want some coffee?" she asked after she hung it up over a wash tub.

"Sure."

"You look nice. Where are you going?"

"To the city with Cory." Kate followed her back into the house.

"We were just there."

"I know. His girl is finally coming back. All that time. Her grandmother passed away a week ago. She stayed to help settle things for the family."

"Poor Mary. I'm so sorry."

Betty Olson picked the enamel coffeepot off the stove and poured them cups of coffee. Pushing her hair back off her forehead, she sat down heavily on her railback chair. She pushed away some books and sighed.

"What's up?"

"The annual struggle. Do I stay in teaching which I absolutely love or do I have to stop forever because I want to have a baby with a man I absolutely adore, namely my husband?"

Kate chewed her lip. She had her own opinion, which was essentially that it was crazy that a perfectly fine teacher like Bette had to make that kind of decision. It was ludicrous, just like it was ludicrous that she could be allowed to man a fire tower, but couldn't do other things with the Forest Service.

Betty folded some tea towels lying in front of her. "Silly isn't it?"

"Ah-hmm." Kate sipped her coffee. Her lackluster response made her friend look at her.

"Something up?"

Kate blew out a big sigh. "I don't know yet. I mean, I'm not sure."

Betty gave her a quizzical look. "David?"

"Oh, goodness no. Although... He's called a couple of times since the dance and doesn't take no for an answer."

"Men. So it isn't about men."

"Well, yes. Yes it is."

"Katriana Alfjord. I've never in my life known you to stutter or blush. My God, girl, you're blushing."

Kate began to laugh and grabbing a tea towel put it over her face. When she shot her eyes at Betty over the top of her cover, she began to howl again with laughter to the point of tears.

Betty's face burst into smiles and dimples. "You're in love! That's what's different about all this. You're honestly in love."

Kate nodded from behind the towel. "Uh-uh," she murmured, then laughed again.

"Are you going to tell me? Or do I have to laugh it out of you?"

"No," Kate answered calming down. "You don't. Just let me get my breath..." She continued to hold the towel in front of her for safety's sake. Her green eyes were wild with sparks.

"So?" Bette coaxed.

"You wouldn't believe it." she said through the towel.

"Who?"

"Park Hardesty."

"CCC?"

"Uh-uh."

"Not one of the foreigners!"

"I'm afraid so."

Betty took a big sip of her coffee. "That might not be good. No telling if he'd stay. He probably longs for concrete nightly."

"That's a point in his favor. He loves it here. Truly." Kate put down the towel and looked suddenly very focused. "He likes the things I like. More important, he doesn't find anything I say stupid or unusual because a woman said it."

"Maybe that's how he attracts women. It could be just a line."

Kate shook her head. "It's not. He wouldn't dare." She flashed her eyes at Betty. "That's how sure I am."

"My...you are in love. Of course, I'm terribly happy for you. I've never seen you so worked up about any man. Even with David."

"I was never in love with him, no matter what village tongues might say." She traced the rim of her coffee cup. "Am I that obvious?"

"Well, there is a certain glow. Tell me truthfully. Did you come to this revelation before or after you single-handedly rescued him in the mountains?"

"Does it matter?"

"To village tongues it might."

"Before. I mean, I noticed him. He even asked me out once, but I said no."

"Why?"

"Because I didn't want any commitments after David's possessiveness. It made me so uncomfortable. I can't stand being the little woman."

"Does he know you care about him?"

"No."

"Will you tell him?"

Kate nodded, then slowly brought up an adjacent problem. How she had saved his life. When she finished, there was a long silence.

“Well, it’s no one else's business. You did the right thing.”

Kate hugged her arms. "I’m sort of embarrassed. Not about what I did, but the feelings I have, having done it. He - he was in so much pain and so disoriented. It was the most pleasing thing to hold him and reassure him. Am I wrong to feel that?"

"No. But don't get it mixed up with other feelings. Not when you don't know how he feels."

"Would that really be wrong?"

"Don't lose your head until you really know."

"It's not my head that I'm worried about. It's my heart. I feel so silly and giddy. I positively melted when I saw him today."

"You saw him?"

"Yes. At the camp infirmary. He's quite banged up."

"Will he get medical leave?"

"Yes. And Betty... he's going to stay with Cory until he's better mended."

Betty rolled her eyes. "Young lady, you're in trouble now."

"I know. Isn't it wonderful?"

Betty beamed and they both laughed.

CHAPTER 13

Hardesty moved down to the Alford store the following evening. Spinelli and Staubach came over to help him back to the barracks to gather his things together. Moving stiffly, he made it across the parade grounds without assistance, but he was about as limber as an axe handle. His left leg was heavily bruised and scratched from his fall and pinning by the tree, but more alarming, while his shoulder began to hurt less, the leg seemed to worsen. Despite this, however, Doc was confident there would be improvement in the next few days.

The rest of the squad was back from the day's work at the campground and along with McGill's and Spenser's squads in various states of dress when Hardesty came in.

"Hey Park! Guys. Look who's here."

Joisey Squad crowded around, careful not to bump him.

"Where's the rescue party?" Werner asked.

Someone whistled. Another made an hourglass shape in the air. The ribbing continued until Hardesty warned them to be careful. "Watch it. That's a lady you're talking about. And she's Miss Alford to you."

"That's right," Spinelli said who had a vested interest in her sister.

“But is she Miss Alford to you?” Golden asked.

Hardesty gave him a weak grin.

Spinelli helped to pick up the duffel and put it on the bed, while Staubach gathered the things Hardesty wanted to take with him for his leave. Pointing with his head and body, he indicated what gear would be for storing in his trunk and what would go. Lorenzo rummaged around for him and in doing so, the notebook full of clippings fell out. Lorenzo reached over to help, but quietly, Hardesty got there first and put his foot on it.

"Please," he said to his young friend, "Could you put it back in?"

"Sure, Park." Lorenzo picked it up and carefully stuffed the edges of some articles back in, then laid it in the trunk. He put the items Staubach had found for Hardesty in the duffel. He gave Hardesty a puzzled look, but zipped up the bag for him.

“Thanks,” Hardesty murmured. He straightened up in time to see McGill over by the stove staring at him. The Tarheel looked at him intensely before averting his eyes as he went over to his side of the barracks, but Hardesty was sure McGill had seen the notebook. He decided he would be more careful. Some of the things in the notebook could be misunderstood and even damaging.

"You ready, Park?" Mario asked.

"Sure..." He looked around at his buddies. "You have an election yet? You should, you know. Someone has to be straw boss."

"That okay?" O'Connell asked.

"Sure. You’re not being disloyal to me or anything like. It's the rules. Besides, you fellows can take care of yourselves. It's time some of you take on more responsibilities. That's what you're here for. Golden can set up the election. You might as well do it tonight.”

"You gonna vote?" Werner asked.

"Sure. I'll get a slip of paper and do it now. Or leave it with Spenser until you're ready..."

The boys huddled around him. It was like he was leaving for good, but Hardesty wasn't going to have everyone get down about it. "I'm just going down the road. Like I'm going to see my Aunt Maude."

"Aunt Maude isn't a looker with auburn hair by any chance?"

Hardesty laughed.

"Wish I had an Aunt Maude," someone said.

"I do" Werner said, "and it ain't no picnic."

"Think I'll let a tree fall down on me," Lorenzo announced "and see what comes along."

"Aw, all you think about is dames," Staubach said. "Ever since the dance it's dames, but all you'll attract is raccoons."

"Maybe not. Maybe he has the technique right." Mario lifted up Lorenzo's encased arm as he stepped over to get the duffel. "I'll get it, Park."

"Thanks," Hardesty gave them a reassuring smile, but he felt weak. Staubach must have seen him sag. He took it as the cue to go.

"Gotta go, boys. Taylor's supposed to have a truck ready. Time to put him back to bed. Doctor's orders."

"Where exactly are you staying, Park?" Golden wondered.

"Over the general store. Cory Alford, the owner's son, has an apartment there. I won't be holed up too long. Maybe just a few days so I can get the kinks out, then I'll probably be out and about. Come down if you can. I'm sure you can ask to see me."

"Planning to go to the city?"

"I can't afford to go. I'll just stay around here."

"For three weeks?

"It's what the doctor ordered," he replied.

The squad followed him as he limped out the door. Larsen and some of the boys from Spenser's squad called encouragement.

"You take care, boys," Hardesty said after he was settled in the truck. "Don't let the natives get you down. That McGill and his crew gives you a hard time, you give it back." He leaned against the open window where Spinelli stood close to the side mirror on the truck.

"When's the test, Mario?"

"Friday."

Hardesty smiled at him. "You'll do fine. Have a bull session with the others."

"Maybe I can see you before?"

"Trust yourself. You'll do fine. Just..." Feeling suddenly nauseated, he stopped in mid-sentence and sagged back against the high seat of the truck. His eyes closed in pain.

"Park?"

Hardesty's eyes fluttered open. "It's all right. I'm just tired. Just tired." he muttered. He didn't really like all the fuss.

"That's it. Where's that Spense?" Spinelli hollered as he pushed away from the truck and into Joisey Squad hovering close by. "Park's sick. Get him out of here."

"Hold your horses. I'm coming," the straw boss said. "Clear the way, boys." He climbed into the cab and shot a glance at Hardesty.

"You still among the living?"

"You can count me in."

"Good. Might be rough driving down. The springs are going in this truck, so hold on."

Hardesty held on. Gritting his teeth, he closed his eyes to the jolt as the truck roared to life and started out towards the gate. He raised his hand to the boys, then swore as the front wheels plunged in and out of a rut. He was leaving, but he wasn't sure if he was leaving intact.

"Why, David," Caroline Alford said. "How nice to see you. Come in, come in."

"Sorry to come in the back door, but I guess you didn't hear me out in the front."

"I just came in from hanging wash. It's such as pretty day."

Callister commented that it was. He wiped his shoes on the doormat and came into the kitchen. Caroline washed her hands at the sink.

"Make yourself at home. Would you like a bowl of soup?"

Liking the way things were going, he said yes. It was important that he have an ally in the family.

"Did I hear that you've been in Seattle?" Caroline asked as

she dried her hands on a towel. "My, that was fast."

"Just one night, but I had some time to look around."

"How nice. I haven't been in some time. I only go when I take the train to see my family." She brought over a steaming bowl for him. When he was settled, she sat down opposite him and began to peel a pot of potatoes.

Caroline Alford was a pretty woman and despite her hard life, she had a certain beauty that transcended her outward appearance of housewife. Callister heard she had helped build up and run the business at their store, allowing her husband to tend to the fishing end of it. Alford had always done some guiding on the river and had one time been a ranger until he broke both legs. Caroline had saved the day. Yet she had come from upper class stock. He wondered where that put Kate. Callister talked while he ate, sharing some of his adventures down in Seattle with her. "Went to the university while I was there and took a boat over to one of the islands. There're still ugly signs the Depression's on. I saw that rambling shanty town of tumbled construction they call Hooverville."

"That's the original one," Caroline said. "Did you know that? Seattle also has the original Skid Row."

"Times are still tough."

"I know."

They talked about that for awhile. The lumber strike had continued and the economy was still unsettled and many families in their county were on relief. The WPA and CCC projects had done a good deal in relieving the situation by putting men and young men to work.

"Indeed, they have," Caroline said. "There are a number of our local boys at Kulshan and in some of the other CCC projects around the state. One of my best friend's sons is doing a WPA project building street curbs and sidewalks up in Lynden. It's a farming town north east of here. You can begin to guess at the misery when you know they come from so far. Like those East Coast boys. Imagine how displaced they must feel. One of my neighbors saw a boy the other day staring at the poor pasture around her house where her horse and cow graze. The dear thing thought he had gone to heaven. So green, he said to her. He hadn't seen the farms in the valley."

"I understand that Karin has taken a shine to one of them. That Mario Spinelli."

"Do you know him? Bob saw him at the store and said he was polite."

"He's one of the New Jersey boys. His whole squad is dubbed 'Joisey Squad.' They're a mix of Germans, Italians, Irish -- even a Jew."

"That's the squad Cory was talking about. So green they didn't know an axe from a mattock, except for that young man who's staying with him. Mr. Hardesty."

"Yes, that's the squad."

"What is this Spinelli boy like?"

Callister measured his words carefully. "He works hard and is all right in his classes, but if you want a candid opinion, the boy, like the rest of the squad, is a little on the rough side. You know, the tenement background."

"Oh," Caroline said. "He's been in trouble?"

Callister hedged his words. "I honestly don't know, but if I had a daughter, I would have restrictions."

"We do. They've always met at the store under Bob or Cory's eyes."

Caroline became quiet, concentrating on her bowl of potatoes.

Callister gave her a moment then said, "Mind if I ask about the arrangement with Park Hardesty?"

"As far as I know, he's doing all right. He's quite immobile, but fortunately has mostly slept. Cory had to feed him the other night, but I understand that in the next week the doctor will rebind the shoulder so he will have use of his uninjured arm. He really should be under the care of someone. I have a mind to ask Betty Olsen since she's married and could look after him until he's more on his feet."

"How did Cory get himself into this? Was he pressured?"

"Oh, my son is always taking in strays. This was his idea alone. He's known the young man for awhile and they get along famously. Mr. Hardesty is also not like the others. He is more mature and according to Bladstad, educated. Not some street smart boy from an east coast city. If Cory likes him, then I shall too."

Callister wanted to say something, but felt that it wasn't the time or place. If she had a favorable opinion, he would work quietly to undermine it if he had to. Caroline must have sensed something, because he found her looking at him curiously. "Do you know him well, David? You're rather quiet about it."

"Oh, I'd rather not say anything."

"But -"

"It's a rough crowd he's in with. He acts accordingly. I'm not one to gossip about the camp and its affairs, but there was a fight at one of the spike camps some time back. He gave a fellow quite a beating."

"Is the enrollee all right?"

"Yes ... but there have been altercations before."

"Isn't that all a part of the life there? After all, I knew men in the Forest Service after the war and the camps were hard then. I'm a woman. It's quite beyond my realm of things, but men will be men. It has always been so. Just as long as they don't fail in their responsibilities to society as a whole." She tossed the last peeled potato into the pan next to her bowl and standing up, took it to the stove. "Cory has invited him into his home. For now that is good enough for me. Times are so hard. We must have a little kindness towards each other."

Callister watched the slump of her shoulders and regretted saying anything. "I hope I haven't offended you."

"Oh, David. You've done nothing of the kind. I know that you were being considerate by being frank."

He got up from the table and took his empty bowl to the sink. "Thanks for the soup." He paused then asked, "What's Kate up to?"

"She's been up in the hills gathering samples for an artist. She should be down tomorrow."

"Don't you ever worry about her?"

"All the time. But you have to let go. I've decided that she will always be the lovely lady she is and the choices that she makes for herself will be all right."

"I didn't know you were that modern."

"Oh, I've been a New Woman for years. And I earned the vote. With Kate, it depends on the day. I just hold my breath and hope that something sunk in." She turned to him. "Do something for me, David. Be her friend. Sometimes I'm afraid that she'll never come down from the mountains."

CHAPTER 14

Hardesty lay back on the pile of hay and felt it bite into his skin under his shirt. It was cool and dim in the barn like it always was and he watched sleepily as dust motes floated down through the single shaft of sunlight piercing the gloom. He was wearing his college clothes but he had on caulks and his CCC cap. Somewhere off he thought he heard a robber jay squawk at some intruder. It was strange being home from school and back to the squabbling and competition again. Nothing had changed between his brothers, and though it was generally done good-naturedly, there was always an underlying tension, especially with his brother Paul. They were so close in age - too close - and he felt the jealousy. Being the youngest, he just wanted to get along, instead of always getting mad when he got pushed too far, but Paul seemed to jump the gun all the time and expect the worse. Even when Hardesty meant well by him.

I meant to do well by you. The thing with Marie....

Hardesty's shoulder felt heavy, so he shifted his weight. The barn door opened and closed behind him, but he couldn't move. He knew, though, who it was before he saw her. He smelled her perfume and the faint woman scent every man who came close to her tried to ignore.

I'm ignoring you, Marie, he thought, but she heard him and came around to face him.

"There you are, John."

Hardesty's heart sank. She was the most beautiful woman he'd ever seen and hoped to talk to. She had a full-figured body that strained at the simple cotton print dress she wore. He counted every button from her throat to her waist and followed the line they made between her full breasts. Her skin was smooth. Her complexion was rosy-cheeked, but her cheeks didn't compare to the dark eyes framed by the sun bleached blonde hair. She was a wild French-Canadian woman, as fresh and as earthy as a clear autumn day and she was Paul's.

"I hear you were home," she said.

"I've only been here a bit."

"You look very fine, I think. School agrees with you. So tanned, so muscular."

Hardesty looked at himself, surprised. All he had done was push a pencil.

I know what you are doing, he thought.

"Do you?" she said out loud.

"Paul should know."

"Will you tell?"

"Better from me, than someone else. He's my brother."

"I'm not with him anymore."

"He never said."

She came dangerously close. Hardesty felt weak.

"You're such a hypocrite, John. Because you know what you want."

In one motion she lifted her dress skirt, and straddled his lap. Hardesty groaned and sank back into the hay. She had nothing on underneath. Her bare flanks felt hot against his lap and he forgot to breathe for a moment as she undid her top and exposed her full, ripe breasts.

"See..." She took one of his hands, making a little sound in her throat. "Tu est fort..." She laughed when he took his hand away and proceeded to undo his shirt. "My," she said when she saw the hard muscles of his smooth chest. "You have been working outside."

"Arrete, Marie."

"Arrete, arrete. Tu est fol. You don't want me to stop. Look at you. Like a stray chien." She suddenly seized his face in both hands, clamping her mouth on his. "Mon cheri!"

He was aroused, but he was angry. She shouldn't have come here. He hated her. Hated himself. She tried to pull away, but he wouldn't let go, so she began to pound him on his shoulder. It felt like heavy lead and it itched.

"Bitch!" he spat and let go. Then he saw her face.

"Park!" she cried out and he blanched. It was Kate Alford dressed in a Forest Service uniform. She was holding the front of the torn shirt closed and she was frightened.

"Kate," he whispered. "Kate!" He reached out for her but bumped his head on some hard surface. The pain exploded, traveling down to his bound shoulder. When he looked at where she had been sitting, she was gone.

"Kate." he groaned. "I'd never hurt you." His forehead stung, but it didn't feel as bad as his shoulder. He grimaced in pain and rolled onto his side. The hay was gone. He was lying on something soft. A crow called somewhere and when he finally opened his eyes, he was lying on a sofa eyeball to eyeball with a hand-made coffee table.

Outside, the crow called again on the other side of the second floor window, then rustled away from the cedar it had been sitting in. Hardesty heard a door open and close as someone came into the apartment. He looked at his watch on the table. It was three in the afternoon. Another day slept away. Since coming to Cory's apartment three days ago, he had slept almost constantly, making up for sleep lost in the noisy camp infirmary. And rest he had. Almost twenty-four hours in the first day. The truck ride down had been torture even with Spenser taking care on the ruts that blemished the gravel road to Frazier. When he finally permitted assistance getting upstairs to the bed set up for him, he was exhausted and nauseated. He had barely lain down before he was sound asleep. Cory had checked in on him from time to time, but it was almost a day and half before he woke up and ate something. By then he was very hungry.

Hardesty rubbed his head against his pillow. He must have hit the coffee table in his sleep. Some sleep.

He hadn't had a dream like that since he was a teenager and it certainly was full of mixed metaphors. The thought of Kate Alford like that made him ashamed. He had recognized that he was growing even more attracted to her after she had visited him in the sick bay, but not in that way. He would never make her feel cheap. He cared for her.

Not like Marie Bertin.

The first time he saw Marie was up at Lacey's, a run-down speakeasy pretending to be a roadhouse. It hung slightly over the edge of Cooper's Creek like a cautious toe-dipper, its pilings green and smelling of creosote and slime. The interior wasn't much better with its flaking white-washed walls and fly paper scrolls hanging from the ceiling with last summer's catch. Cigarette smoke colored like dirty-water drifted up to the rafters above the card table and billiards. Under the haze, men long down on their luck leaned over their cards and drinks. Some were farmers still in their coveralls, others in jackets, caps, and pants as drab as the Depression.

The only bright spot was Marie draped against the walnut-stained bar, a strap on her red knit dress slipping off her slim shoulder. Molded by the cloth, her full breasts thrust out, taunting anyone bold enough to take his eyes off his cards.

"You lookin' for someone, cheri?"

"I was looking for my brother, Paul Hardesty. I was told he works here."

"Paul. *Ma foie moi*, that is very nice that he has such a brother. He never say."

Marie came away from the bar, her hands on her hips. She moved like an elegant cat and the cigarette smoke under the shaded ceiling lamp seemed to part, then close behind her as she came over and planted herself in front of him. She looked him up and down.

"What are you, a bank-ere? Such nice clothes."

"They're not much. I've been away at college."

"*L'université*? My, how nice. I never see such things here."

"Look, is my brother here nor not?"

"He is, how you say, indisposed."

"Then I'll wait."

Marie cocked her head at him. "Very nice. The brother waits. I wait too." She sat down in the nearest wooden chair and taking his hand pulled him towards her.

"Hey, Polaski. Get theez nice young man a drink."

Footsteps came into Cory's little living room, then stopped before moving quietly to the window to close it. Hardesty turned his head.

"Sorry, son," said Bob Alford. "Didn't mean to disturb you."

Hardesty struggled to sit up. "No, it's all right. I've been awake for awhile. About time I got up." He looked around for his slippers by the sofa and gingerly slipped into them. He had been sleeping in his robe, undershirt and pajamas for the last few days and he knew he looked disheveled.

"Cory been treating you right?"

Hardesty laughed, fully conscious of the new growth of beard on his face.

"Absolutely. I haven't been abandoned. He's the perfect host. He's let me have the run of all the sleeping accommodations."

"Well, you are looking much better. For a moment there, I wondered if you'd ever move again."

"I wondered too. I fell off a runaway horse when I was a kid, but I wasn't bruised or busted up like this."

Alford came over in front of him. "Want a soda? I brought one up from the store."

"Gee, thanks."

Alford opened it up with a bottle opener and then poured it into a tin cup.

"Say when. I don't mind pouring it in ya."

"Thanks." Hardesty leaned over and took a long sip from the cup, then sat back. Alford put the cup down on the coffee table and sat in a chair near the window. Outside the day was bright and sunny. A nice day to be out.

"This working out for you? My wife Caroline thinks you ought to be watched better."

"I'm fine. Doc's going to give me a new set up in a week. I think the break's coming along. Didn't tear anything around the collarbone and I've behaved. When he said to stay still, I stayed still. I want to get back to camp."

"But this could take another month."

"I know. I hope to at least do something in the camp. I probably won't be able to go out with my squad for that length of time, but once I have use of my good arm, I can at least work in the office."

"Must seem as tame as mashed potatoes being here."

"Oh, I appreciate all the neglect. I wasn't getting any sleep in the infirmary. Too much company."

"Speaking of company, you had visitors late yesterday, but you were asleep, so I let it go."

"Who?"

"Some boys from your squad. They came down after work. 'Course one of them has a vested interest in all my fishing tackle."

"That wouldn't be Spinelli?"

Alford nodded.

Hardesty turned away. His grin was so big it hurt his scratched face. "The kid's all right. He comes from a pretty tough neighborhood, gangsters and all – but he's making an effort here. He wants to go on in school and make something of himself. And he speaks fondly of his parents. He's not from a broken home."

"You know about him and my daughter?"

"Yes, sir."

"Do I have anything to be worried about?"

"No, sir. I've already talked to him about that."

"Oh?"

"It seems to be a family concern. Your other daughter asked me the same question a few weeks ago."

Alford laughed. "Kate," he said under his breath, but Hardesty heard him.

"Been fishing?" Hardesty asked.

"A little. There's a small summer run of steelhead going up. Cory went out this morning before breakfast."

"I fished when I was a kid, but I never was one for eating them. I like steelhead though. That's a fine eating fish. I got my first taste in Oregon. The Rouge River is one of the best fishing rivers around. My camp was right near there."

"Steelhead is good eating, but I like the fight in them too." They talked easily for awhile about fishing and the area in general, and once again, Hardesty got the impression that there was more to the shopkeeper than met the eye. He had an even nature, but he came across as someone who would do well in a pinch. Especially out here in this wilderness. As they talked, Hardesty found that he liked him very much.

"You want some more soda?"

"Sure." Hardesty let Alford hold the cup for him while he drank. When he finished, he asked Hardesty if he would like help getting cleaned up.

"I probably should at some point."

"Look," said Alford, "I'm going to take my wife's suggestion and have Mrs. Olsen come and help you. She can give you a shave and clean you up. She's not only one of our favorite teachers, she has done some nursing. It would be the proper thing to do."

Hardesty started to protest, but Alford wouldn't hear of it. He would give her a call and have her come over at four if that was all right with him. Hardesty decided that he had no choice.

Betty Olsen came over an hour later and with Cory's help, got Hardesty into the small bathroom for a shave. With some prodding she got him to sit still a little longer and wash his hair. When she was finished, Cory helped Hardesty change into a new pair of pajama bottoms, then guided him back to the sofa where he was propped up with pillows.

"Feeling better?" Cory asked.

"Like a new man, though I feel like I've had been scrubbed with pine soap."

"A necessity, old man. All that grit. Now you look half human." Cory looked at his watch. "Gosh, I've got to go down to the store and help Dad out. Betts here is going to stay and fix up some grub for you. While she's at it, you can talk about fifth grade science. I told her that you've been reading Kate's old books."

Forty minutes later, Betty served him a solid meal of liver and onions along with boiled potatoes. "It was on special downstairs in the meat locker," she said. "You need it." She cut up the meat into tiny pieces and fed him at the sofa. Between bites, they carried on a conversation.

"So you're Jack Turner's sister," he said. He acted like being fed by a married woman was the most normal thing in the world, but he was going to have to get used to his situation.

"That I am, his darling kid sister." She smiled at him impishly, the dimples in her rosy round cheeks working over time.

"You teach science?"

"It's fifth grade curriculum, but I love it. Actually, when I can, I have Kate Alford come with me. Last spring, I did a two-day overnight with my kids and she helped me out."

"You know her well?" Hardesty took the piece of meat she offered on the fork.

"Honey, everyone in this community knows each other well, but you could say that we're extra special friends."

"I'm glad," he said. "She's a nice person. Saved my bacon for sure."

"That annoy you?"

"Annoy me? Are you referring to the continual kidding because she rescued me? Why should I be? She was cool-headed and calm in a difficult situation. I was a pretty heavy load for her to pull and get up on the ridge to safety. After that, it got worse. It was her quick thinking..." He didn't finish the sentence. A wave of exhaustion swept over him.

"Want to finish this before it's cold?" Betty held out a forkful of liver and onions for him.

"Yes, ma'am." He grinned at her and a new friendship was sealed.

For the next few days Betty came to help him. While he waited, not wanting to be cooped up, he began to gingerly make the trip downstairs to walk around on the lawn behind the store. Going down to the river, he would often sit on the rocks and watch the birds and other wildlife flit around by the water's edge until it was time to return to the apartment. Betty Olsen had become a quick friend and unwittingly, he began to tell some things about himself. Not only of his life in the other camps, but the revelation that he had been to college "until the bottom fell out."

"Is that why you joined the three C's? The bottom fell out?"

"Yes," he said and left it at that because it was the truth.

"What did you study?"

"Biology, mostly, though I took some botany and chemistry courses as well."

"Well, you can't avoid botany around here."

One evening after coming back from a walk, Betty was late. Unable to do much, Hardesty lay down on the sofa and dozed. Sometime later, he woke to the sound of the apartment door opening and someone stepping in.

"That you, Mrs. Olsen?"

"No, it's me. Kate Alford." She came into the room and stopped at the end of the sofa.

"Well, hello. You're looking better. Pain gone? It looks it."

"I'm feeling better," he said as he sat up.

"Good." Kate cleared her throat. "Hope you don't mind, but Betty couldn't come, so I volunteered."

Hardesty didn't mind.

While she cooked some fresh trout and potatoes for him, they sat and talked at the apartment's tiny kitchen table. He hadn't heard anything from his squad in days and she informed him that they had gone back to the spike camp. "As for you, I think Doc said he was going to come down this evening."

"Oh? No one's said anything."

"The patient's always the last to know."

"I guess. What about you? Cory said you finally were gathering those plants for that artist."

"I've been collecting things for him. I take up one of those tree-planting bags and fill them with soil and moss. I put the plants I collect in it for transporting down to his studio."

"Why doesn't he go up there himself?"

"Probably the expense, but equally the hike. Sometimes the mountains and forests seem so daunting. I tried taking him there a year ago, but after a night of getting socked in and nearly freezing to death on a glacier, he is no longer an enthusiast."

"He should go with that hiking club from the city."

Kate laughed. "They're out of his league. Some of the members have a few years on them, but they can out-hike anyone."

She brought him his dinner, but he could tell she was a little nervous with the prospect of having to feed him.

"You don't have to do anything. I can wait for Cory..."

Kate laughed softly and looked down at her hands. Her auburn hair fell forward on the shoulders of her simple dress. Hardesty thought she didn't look like the woman who knew how to take care of herself in the woods and mountains. She looked vulnerable and a little lost. She picked up the fork and continued to look down away from him. It was such a plain gesture, but it tugged at him.

"I'll manage," he assured her.

"No, you won't. You'll starve to death." Her head shot up and she grinned at him. "I couldn't let that happen." She leaned over to the coffee table and speared a piece of fish.

"Open up."

Doc arrived around eight in the evening, asking to see Park. He found him sitting by the window looking out on the dirt street below.

"Stay where you are." Doc took things out of his medical bag and set them on the coffee table. "Please," the old man said when Kate began to back away. "I need a no-nonsense woman to help me out."

"What are you going to do?" she asked.

"Redo the straps and sling so the man can at least scratch his chin."

Hardesty remembered the last session with the doctor and inwardly groaned.

The double sling was carefully loosened, then removed.

"It's been two weeks," the doctor said. "Time enough for a good set to take hold."

Ordering Hardesty not to move his left arm out of its position on his chest, he freed his right arm for the first time since the collarbone was set.

"You may hold his hand if you like, Miss Alford, while I tackle his other side."

Kate took his hand. Hardesty remained quiet, but when the doctor began to manipulate the straps tight against his bare chest, he clenched hers in pain.

"Sorry." He stared at the cedar tree outside, but his hand clutched her fingers tighter as Doc secured the cinch so that his shoulders would stay back in position. One final pull and Doc announced that he was done.

"Now you're not to use that free arm in any way that will disturb the shoulder, but things should be easier now. Over the next few days, you can take your left arm out of the sling, especially at night and be completely free." The doctor helped put the arm back in the sling and pulled it tight.

"Are you all right?" Kate asked. It was another way of reminding him that he still held her hand too tight.

"Sorry," he murmured as he released her. He felt lightheaded and sweaty.

Doc checked the set up of the figure eight strap one more time, demonstrating once again his talent for kneading bread. When he was finished, he gave Hardesty a rambling account of how he would have to continue to be bound for at least one more week. If he was to return to camp within that time as planned, he would have to have light duty.

"Are you his nurse?" he asked Kate.

"Actually, Mrs. Olsen has been. She wasn't able to come this evening."

"Well, if he has an ounce of sense, I would see that he continues to spend some time in her care or with a family. Perhaps your mother. This leave idea is not the best one. You should have stayed at the camp."

Doc became all business as he put his materials away, taking a short time to listen to Hardesty's heart and feel his pulse. "You've been feverish?"

Hardesty shook his head no.

Doc asked Kate for a glass of water and gave Hardesty something to drink. He was relieved when the doctor finally left.

He felt like he'd been punched with one of Spinelli's boxing gloves. He was aware of Kate going down with Doc and aware of her coming back up, but he just couldn't move from his chair.

"Are you well?"

"No, I'm afraid I am not. Would you mind helping me to the bed? I'll sleep in my clothes."

Kate helped him up. He felt unsteady, as if he had a relapse. When he was seated on the high, old iron bed in the small bedroom, he just sat there.

"Park?"

"Hmmm?"

"I'll get your slippers." She took them off and put them away, then came back to help him. "You should lie down now."

She came close to his face as she tried to direct him. Suddenly an emotion as jarring as electricity passed between them. He felt it was like the dance all over again. The feeling of oneness. The joy of being together as they stepped out across the floor.

"Kate." Quietly, he leaned over and softly kissed her on her mouth. She closed her eyes and sucked her breath in.

"That's for helping. You've been a saint," he said.

"I haven't done anything..."

"Yes, you have."

"Park..." She brushed a hand against his cheek and did not pull away when he kissed her fingers.

He wondered if she thought it somewhat comical to have a man trussed up like a pig on the way to market make a pass at her, but she did not object when he pulled on her dress skirt with his newly freed hand and brought her closer to him.

"Miss Al-fee-ord."

"Mr. Hardesty. You look like you're going to fall asleep any moment. Did the doctor give you something?"

"Unfortunately, yes." His eyes felt dreamy. "Damn medicine man. He doesn't know the power of manipulation."

"Are you referring to the kiss?" Kate's eyes were sparkling now.

Hardesty laughed and shook his head. "Not particularly. It's not generally a thought a man candidly reveals to a lady." He pulled on the dress and she moved closer to him. "God, you're beautiful."

"Thank you," she said, "but I think you better lie down before you slide off the bed."

Hardesty swayed lightly towards her.

"You must lie down, Park. Before you fall down."

Agreeing with her, he scooted listlessly back on the bed, then laid down in an awkward clump. She found a wool blanket folded at the end of the bed and put it over him. He watched her drowsily with half-closed eyes.

"Are you O.K.?" she asked.

"Uh-huh. Just sleepy. Shoulder hurts."

"Shall I go?"

"Would you mind staying? Just for a little while."

Carefully, she sat down next to him on the bed, her hand not far from his side. As he drifted slowly off, she adjusted the blanket around his shoulders and turned off the lamp next to him. Her face floated before him, then faded only to come back as another when someone kissed him on the side of his mouth. Hardesty stirred.

"Kate," he murmured. "Have you seen Holly?"

He didn't know the words left her cold.

"You touch any of my stuff and I'll beat you to a pulp."

"Ah, lay off, Kolbrowski. Larsen ain't done nothin.'" Mario leaned over the edge of his upper bunk and glowered at the enrollee from New York. He was one of four from a squad housed over in a tent next door. Even in the main camp, they did not regularly mix with Joisey Squad. After four months, Mario and his crew had made a reasonably good adjustment to camp life in the woods, much better than the boys in the barracks next door. In their first week at Kulshan, one of them had quit, causing about three others to request a ticket home as well.

Mario had been a bit frightened and worse-- homesick-- when he first got here, but he had weathered his first few weeks and had entered a new stage where he was taking pride in the work he did and the way the work shaped him. He was not a tall boy, but the robust life in the CCC camp had hardened him and he liked the way he looked. He had joined the ranks to provide income for his family, but lately he had acquired a new reason: the search for knowledge and refinement. For that he could say thanks to Park Hardesty.

Mario rolled back on his stomach and continued the sentence he had been composing on the yellow tablet he had bought at the canteen. He had the only top bunk in the tent to make room for the whole squad. The damp, musty canvas roof barely cleared his head. Outside a large beetle banged blindly against the cloth.

He missed Hardesty. He'd known him over four months now, and during that time his opinion had widened and changed.

And I used to think you were some smart prissy from a middle class WASP family.

In fact, the Pennsylvanian could hold his own both in the workload and social matters such as camp disputes and group dynamics of a squad.

Mario grinned.

Man, Hardesty had put down McGill at the river with a skill of a street fighter and he should have won the boxing match. Who cared where he came from? Camp life had formed and toughened Hardesty just as it was painfully forming him and the boys of Joisey Squad. Now they could hold their own in work and in their position in the camp. Mario was proud of that, but now he wanted to try something for himself. He wanted to write.

Lying on the top bunk, night after night he composed his stories and articles with a pencil and notebook. He wrote of the streets, but he could also write about what it was like to be so far from home and undertaking this new life. Once he had the bug, he couldn't stop, but it wasn't for several weeks before he felt confident enough to put something into the camp paper. So he would take his little pieces and show them to Hardesty when they were alone. The sessions ended after Hardesty was hurt. Mario almost stopped writing altogether until he received a note from his friend two days after he had tried to see him at the store. It was one of encouragement and a warning to stick to business. It was important for both his objectives. And Karin Alford was definitely one of them, so he started writing again and put the first new piece into the paper, a poem.

Forest Lessons

In these deep dallying woods I walk
Far from the giant concrete forests I have known
To see the wonders of the land and streams
And wield the woodcraft I've been shown.

"Did you hear me. Larsen?"

Mario rolled over and glowered at Kolbrowski. "I said lay off. Beat it."

Kolbrowski gave him the finger and left the tent.

Mario sat up and dangled his legs off the bunk. His head fit under the tent ceiling without him having to bend over.

Larsen was OK. He was one local enrollee he really liked and he was looking forward to going home to his house during the next leave – if they were to ever get out of the spike camp. Fire season was in full force and they could be called away any time. For two months they had been organized into flying squads – units - that could leave for fire fighting duties in any part of the state. Traveling by bus, they could get out in a moment's notice.

"Anyone hear from Park today?" Staubach asked as he ducked to come into the tent. He was carrying a stack of papers and a book on car and truck maintenance.

"No one's come back from Kulshan. According to Bladstad, Doc let him out of his trap the other day. He can use his right arm now. He's got another few weeks to go, though."

"Wonder when he's coming back?"

Staubach shrugged. "Less than two weeks, I heard. Crawford over in mess says he might be able to do some cooking and eventually go out with us. No fancy stuff, though."

"Gee, what a lousy break. I can't see him hanging around camp doing nothing."

“He’ll find something,” Golden said.

The squad gathered around Mario's bunk, making plans for the evening. There was little to do in the way of classes up here, but after chores were done, they would have time to themselves. O'Connell had devised a fishing rod and had gotten some tackle when he was down in Frazier. He and Lorenzo were going to try it out.

"We're going to play ball," Costello. "The team's shaping up for a game against the high school down in the valley. They're going to play at the elementary school or something."

"That a fact?" said Mario.

"Yeah and you should be playing, instead of being so high and mighty and writing all the time. You've changed, Spinelli."

Mario stared. "Says who?"

"I do. You're soft."

With lightening speed, Mario was off the bunk and at Costello's throat. Grabbing onto his shirtfront, he slammed his squad mate against the side of the bed. "Don't you say nothin’. If you want me to play, say so. But don't call me names."

"Now who is hot," jeered Kolbrowski who poked his head back in.

"You stay out of this! This ain't your affair." Mario felt his face getting hot.

"No, I guess not. You guys are all weird."

The squad took offense en masse and stormed Kolbrowski spilling him onto the ground outside. A few of McGill's group saw the action and joined in. Mario grabbed Kolbrowski and rode on his back, his arms right around the enrollee’s neck. As boys grabbed onto them like iron filings to a magnet, they slammed back into the tent making the canvas look like an enraged amoeba from the inside.

Mario and three others thundered to the tent platform floor.

"Are you stupid? Williams is coming!" said Larsen. “The camp commander’s coming!”

Mario tried to disengage himself from the pile, but Kolbrowski pulled him back.

“I said stop,” Larsen shouted. “Staubach give me a hand.”

Mario felt himself being tugged and then lifted up.

"Time out, boys," Staubach said. "That's enough."

Williams and two other forestry officers appeared a short time later. The tent was in reasonable shape. Some of the beds were out of line but upright. A mattress spilling its contents of hay was covered with the legs of some boys occupied in reading and playing checkers. The only things that they couldn't hide were their bruised faces.

"Who started this?" Williams barked.

No one said anything. The place was deathly quiet.

Williams made a face. "Not talking, huh? Well, you boys settle your dispute, but do it properly. There's no busting up camp property. Staubach," he ordered, "get your boys cleaning up your area. You too, Spenser. Where's McGill?"

"He's in the warehouse," Costello said.

"Well, get him in here. I want this place back in order by dinner. Get that broken chair under that bunk over to the shop. You're to come to mess cleaned up and dressed properly. If you can't get going in two seconds, you're all grounded with a week's worth of KP. Now get moving!"

Mario and his friends moved along with the other squad members, the fear of peeling potatoes for fifty other guys extremely high. But once Williams was gone, the pace slowed and the mouths worked again.

"It's all your fault, Costello," Mario grumbled.

"Well, it's true. What's books gonna get you?"

Mario had trouble getting the right answer out to someone who wouldn't listen anyway. They crabbed at each other as they did their chores until Staubach told them to shut up. Eventually, McGill showed up. By then Joisey Squad was sullen and subdued.

"What's eating them? Mario heard him ask Johnson, a squad mate.

"Literacy."

Mario felt a sudden surge of dislike for McGill, then worry. What if he had found a weak point in the squad?

While Joisey Squad had its first falling out, Kate was experiencing problems of her own. Just when she was realizing that Park Hardesty had similar feelings for her as she for him, she had the rude shock of some other woman being thrown back at her. That he should say her name twice under stress or illness meant that person was deep in his mind. Some girlfriend from a past of which Kate had no knowledge. Some woman he cared about. Who was he anyway? Only an enrollee from a government camp thousands of miles from his home and background. Some of the boys were rough. Even if Hardesty were older, he could have as difficult a life as some of the enrollees from poor backgrounds. After all, that was why he was here: to help his family on relief or support himself in some way while aiding a parent. She knew nothing about him. Only that she loved him. There it was said. She loved him. Which made it all so crazy.

She always thought of herself as a sensible person. Clear-headed about what she wanted for herself. The time spent with David had been stifling. She had not been herself. Then Hardesty arrived. He had acted decisively at the river with the bear, but later showed interest in her as a person, not some helpless female. As their acquaintance grew, he seemed to enjoy their verbal sparring as much as she did but he also listened to her. He made her feel important and intellectually equal, not like an odd woman who shouldn't be speaking her mind or expressing her knowledge of things a woman shouldn't bother with. The dance had flustered her because she found it annoying that after stating that she wouldn't get involved with any man for awhile, she found that she wouldn't mind seeing him again. Even when she told him no. But the storm. She remembered his helplessness and how he had cried out the woman's name. How he had stared at her hair and then recoiled when he thought her this person. Who was Holly? And why was he afraid of her?

The day after she had put Hardesty to bed she went over to see Betty at her house. Her friend was getting ready to go to the lumber mill where her husband worked. Even though the strikes had been settled in most of the state, this mill was not back to capacity. Betty had been worried about how far their money would stretch, but they considered themselves lucky because they did have money to worry about. When she saw Kate, she led her into the dining room where she had been putting some bills together on the dining table.

"What are you doing here? I thought you'd be with Mr. Hardesty."

Kate shook her head no. "Cory's going to do that."

Betty gave her a funny look. "I thought everything was all right."

Kate looked away.

"Gosh, did he make a pass at you?"

Kate smiled, then sighed.

"You are in bad shape. He's got you that mixed up?"

Kate put her hands on a chair back and leaning into it, kicked at the rug. Betty picked up her bills and sorted through them.

"I wouldn't be so concerned, Kate. You're not in virgin territory when it comes to that--getting kissed. Are you worried about something else?"

Kate snorted. "He's not after my butterfly collection – yet. It's just. Oh, dammit. I just can't make him out. Just when I think that things are going swell, he ruins it." Kate twisted her hands.

"In what way?"

Kate told her about the storm and his strange ramblings, then the incident the other night. "It's not a very comfortable thought thinking that he's kissing you and dreaming of someone else." She bit her lip and walked over to the front door. Outside, it was overcast but warmish. "Isn't it strange. The first real man I like and he has to be so complicated."

"Maybe there's an answer," Betty said as she put some bills into a cardboard file box.

"How will I find that out?"

"Ask him."

Kate looked at Betty like she was hearing a message from a savant. It was a simple answer, but so obvious.

"Look," Betty said. "If he really is a decent man, and I think he is, he'll be honest. There is nothing to lose. If he doesn't tell you the truth, then don't waste your time with him."

Kate stayed quiet so her friend asked her to tell her what had happened that evening when Doc came over. When she finished, Betty looked thoughtful.

"Sounds like things are going very well, even if he made a pass all trussed up." Betty grinned. "From the way you talked earlier in the evening, I think you have the makings of a nice relationship. You can set the limits the way you want, but first you've got to talk to him." Betty looked for her hat. "If I were you, I'd go over before feeding time and go for a walk with him. Be honest. Tell him what is troubling you."

Kate leaned her forehead against the screen. "That simple?"

"Uh-huh. Honesty is always the best policy. It's kith and kin to love."

CHAPTER 15

When Kate didn't show up the next day, Hardesty was disappointed. Cory came to help him, but it wasn't the same. He began to wonder if he had offended her. After Doc had given him the sleeping pill, his head had become all muddled and he wasn't sure exactly what he said. He only remembered that he had kissed her.

She was sure skittish. A beautiful, no-nonsense woman who could take care of herself and others in rugged terrain that would make some men blanch. She seemed unsure about herself when it came to matters of the heart. He wondered what had happened between her and Callister. He remembered how she had acted after the education officer cut in at the dance. She had become subdued, not herself. He hated that because it was one of the things Hardesty admired about her. Her unconventionality. He smiled thinking of how she had cut him out from the tree and got him to the top of the ridge. That was unconventionality.

Hardesty spent the next two days on his own learning to adjust to his new set up. Occasionally, he would take the left arm out of the sling, but he found that his shoulder tired easily, so he continued to use it. The use of his right arm, however, gave him more freedom and he began to spend more time downstairs.

He was beginning to feel much better now. The bruises on his leg and torso were healing and the stitches were ready to come out. As the end of his second week of leave approached, he took to walking through the little hamlet and exploring trails along the river. Sometimes he encountered people from the community and they would visit. They were curious about him being an easterner and from the CCC camp, but generally accepting. Being a guest of Cory Alford didn't hurt. His presence in the store became routine and he was often seen with Bob Alford. But he still didn't see Kate.

One day, not long after Doc's visit, Hardesty took a canteen and a book and followed a trail out along the other side of the river. Crossing it at a low point, he made his way over and up to an area where he could look down on Frazier and the narrow valley around it. Largely forested, he could see the breaks in the trees where the homesteads were and the place that was called Frazier. Easing down on the edge of a sharp hill, he sat and read for an hour before dozing off, only to be awakened by the sound of metal clinking on the trail above him. Standing up, he saw to his surprise, Elsa, Kate's horse. The Appaloosa was standing still, its reins dangling down. When he clucked at it, it turned its head and pointed its ears down at him.

"Kate?"

There was no answer. Hardesty climbed up through the trees to the trail and came alongside the mare. Touching the mare on her neck, he moved to the front and took the reins.

"Good girl," he said then looked around for the woman. The trail appeared deserted, but down it a ways he heard movement in the brush. A few moments later, Kate appeared.

"Oh," she exclaimed. "You are here. I went looking for you on the overhang, but didn't see you."

"I was down there," he pointed. "I must have dozed off."

"Ah." She came up to Else and stroked the mare's nose. Hardesty gave her the reins.

"You were looking for me?" he asked.

"Cory said you were up here."

"Did I miss lunch?"

Kate laughed. "I don't know."

"Well, I missed you."

Kate looked at him sharply and blushed.

"You didn't come," he continued. "It wasn't something I did was it? My head. It got a little mushy."

"No, not exactly." She fiddled with the bridle. "It wasn't anything you did."

"But I offended you some way."

"No." Kate sighed. "Oh, gosh. There's a place further up here. Could we talk?"

"Sure. Got to get my canteen and book, though."

"I'll get them," she said. When she came back, she put them in one of the saddlebags on the mare, then walked the horse up the forested trail to where a bridge lay over a creek, rushing down to the edge of the hill. Above it, some large flat boulders lay in the creek bed. "Let's go there," she said and helped him make his way over to them. After he was settled he asked her what was wrong.

Kate sighed again and he wondered what was really troubling her.

"I kissed you. I apologize," he said.

"You needn't. I didn't mind."

She smiled softly at him. Hardesty smiled back, then picked up a cedar twig lying next to him on the boulder and played with it in his free hand. "Then what's wrong?"

"Remember when I told you that you had been out of your head up there during the storm?"

Hardesty looked her carefully. "Yes."

"You were talking about someone. You were so ill, I didn't mind. But you did it again when I was here a few days ago and it made me feel uncomfortable that you had kissed me, but were thinking about someone else."

"And who was this person? What name did I say?"

Kate hesitated for a moment like she was weighing something. "Holly."

"Holly?" Hardesty felt relief. "That's all?"

"Yes."

He grinned at her. "You needn't fear any competition. She was only fourteen years old."

"Fourteen?"

"Yeah, just a kid. The daughter of a friend of mine."

Kate stared at him in horror. "How awful!"

"Why do you say that?"

"Because you said she was dead. You were quite upset about it."

"Oh." It was Hardesty's turn to be stunned. For a moment he stared out into the alder and cedar lining the creek. He clamped his teeth, the old sensation of having no control over his life worming its way through his gut.

"I'm sorry, Kate. No wonder you've been troubled."

"What happened? How did she die?"

"She died from overexposure in the woods and - other complications." His voice became very quiet. "It was a difficult time for me. I had only been out here a couple of months. Not at all used to being in the wilderness. I was in the search party. She was just a kid. Sweet too. It was the first time that I was exposed to something like this." He waved his hand at the trees. Kate put a hand on his sling. "It still bothers you."

"It does. I'd almost forgotten though." He turned and smiled wanly at her. "I am sorry. I obviously said things not fit for a lady's ear."

"You were ill."

He nodded his head and was silent. Kate cocked her head at him.

"I'm glad you told me."

Hardesty sighed. "You know, you don't know anything about me. If you're uncomfortable, if you don't want to see me, it's all right with me. I'd understand."

"But why should I do that?"

"Maybe we don't come from the same place and it's not just because I'm from the other side of the States. My family's not like yours, Kate. My mother got ill when I was a little boy so we went to live on my grandparents' farm where she could be looked after. My father was gone a lot. He was a salesman for a petroleum company in western Pennsylvania. My parents might as well have been divorced because when he was home, there was a lot of tension. And when he was gone, there was little contact. There was a great deal of competition for his attention. I was the youngest and had to invent ways to earn it. I excelled in school, something my brothers were not interested in, but after a time my father stayed away longer and longer.

Hardesty broke some needles off the twig in his hands. “After the crash in '29, he didn't come back at all. During that time, there was a lot of trouble in the home. Except for my mother, I felt increasingly outside of the family circle. When I won a scholarship to college, I was relieved to go." He looked point blank at her. "I haven't been back." He waited for a response, but when she didn't reply, he went on. "I’ve had a rough background, Kate. Maybe I'm not suited for you."

“What is your mother like?”

A warm glow filled Hardesty’s chest. “A wonderful woman. Educated, reads a lot.”

“And you haven’t been back.”

“No.”

“And what are your brothers like?”

“Just like folks around here, married to the land. They’ve pretty much settled down in the area. Harry is a mechanic. Jim’s a farmer - works at my grandfather’s farm. My other brother - we had a falling out.”

“She’s using you, Paul. Every time you go out on those little drives with her, she’s taking contraband.”

“She’s only selling cosmetics door to door. She says I’m the most thoughtful man she’s ever known because I go along to protect her.”

“While you’re inside those houses with her, someone’s outside lifting the real goods.”

“She loves me.”

“She’s like our queen cat at the farm. She’s loves anything spelled M-A-L-E when in season.”

“You better watch your mouth, buster. Marie’s my girl.”

There was an uncomfortable silence. Every little trickle of the creek, the movement of the horse, little gnats whining by seemed too loud. Hardesty felt miserable. He was glad when Kate spoke first.

"What would you like to do if you weren't in the CCC's?"

"Go back to school. I had to eventually drop out to help the family." He cleared his throat. "At least, that is what I tell myself when I am alone on my bunk and looking up at the springs underneath the bed above. Funny thing. I didn't expect to fall in love with the country out here. It's changed how I see things. Which is good. I was an arrogant sod." Hardesty rubbed his hurt shoulder, then said softly, "I guess I've grown up. I care immensely about things that are not abstract and I have gained confidence in my place in the world."

"Like *Tamius striatus*."

Feeling hopeful, Hardesty laughed. Sitting upright, he threw away the stick. "You weren't listening."

"To your reasons for me not seeing you again? I was. It means nothing. You haven't scared me away. Everyone has stories to tell. These are hard times."

"Tenacious, aren't you?"

"Understanding, I hope." Kate crossed her legs and traced the seam on one of her riding pants leg. "I enjoy being with you, Park. I think you're a wonderful, considerate man. I want to know all about you. I want to talk to you and be with you. I appreciate your being honest about yourself. A lot of people don't bother. They're too conceited. It takes a lot of thought – and energy. By the way, are you hungry?

For a moment, Hardesty was puzzled. "Yeah."

"Then let's go home for lunch at my house. Cory can be our camouflage. You'll be his guest so my mother won't suspect us."

"Of what?"

"Caring for each other."

The remaining days of Hardesty's leave were spent with Kate. He continued to stay at the apartment, but there wasn't part of a day and sometimes an hour they weren't together. It was headstrong medicine for him, for he not only improved his health with his walks with her, but for the first time in his life he was falling in love with someone who was his equal and more. She did not disappoint him with her intelligence and wit, but her grace and charm sharpened by her woodcraft were equally captivating, They were constant companions and as the days passed, their caring for each other deepened into love. When out of sight of prying eyes, they held hands and leaned into each other when they walked.

Once they took horses and they rode out along the river to an ancient smokehouse erected one hundred years ago by Indians in the area. Inside the large structure made of hand-hewn cedar planks and massive cedar posts, salmon had been dried there up to a decade ago, the families meeting for the celebration. Standing in the cool, dim interior, Kate explained the history of the place to him and how it was important to the people who now lived down river in permanent clapboard homes. There were simple carvings of Coast Salish nature on the posts and in the rafters, a shovel-nosed canoe made out of a single cedar log. Outside, in the warm summer sun, she showed him the thimbleberries now past their prime and ripe huckleberries. They sampled them for a bit. Hardesty put a couple of them in her mouth and kissed her.

"Watch out for sow bears," she teased.

"Is that your totem?" He pulled her to him and lifted up her chin. "It would be fitting." Kate smiled at him. "That's for you to find out." She backed away from him and slipped through a break in the bushes. His left arm still in the sling, he ducked and followed her in. On the other side of the trees and brush there was a meadow.

"We should bring the horses here," he commented.

"They are here. This curves around from the smokehouse." She looked across the grass.

"I used to come here with Cory and we would play for hours. It's a sort of a prairie. The trees were so big in the old days that pioneers always looked for prairies to build their homesteads on. That way they didn't have to work so hard to cut the massive trees down. It's also dry here. Of course, the Indians claimed this place. They still do."

"You want to sit?"

"Sure. A lot of birds flit through here."

He took off his canvas jacket and put it on the ground. Kate sat down on it, Hardesty just taking a corner. They sat close, neither saying anything as they watched the wildlife that flourished here.

"Say, look at that. Was that a weasel?" Hardesty asked.

"No, I think it was a ferret."

Hardesty laughed and rubbed his forehead. "Same difference. I knew a guy who had never seen anything other than a rat. Thought the first squirrel he saw out here was a rat."

"No, really. Don't you have parks back east?"

"Sure we do, but not where he was from. He was from Hell's Kitchen. All he knew were rats."

"What about you?"

"Oh, I've seen them both. My grandfather's farm."

"I'm so-o-o glad. *Rattus pennsivannalus.*"

"That's the genus." He found a clover flower next to them in the grass and put it in behind her ear. Kate sat very still. "That should do," he said.

"You think so?"

"I know so." He smiled softly, then leaning over, kissed gently her on the lips.

"That was nice."

"You think so?"

"Um-huh."

"You know I'm crazy about you."

His put his free hand on her shoulder and made a gentle circle on the cloth of her cotton shirt with his thumb. He took his other arm out of the sling and turned her shoulders towards him with both hands. He kissed her on the mouth and opened it.

"Park."

He was glad she did not object when he gently pushed her back onto the jacket and lowered himself on her. As he enveloped her in his arms, the smile on her face lifted him up. It made him want to cry. He didn't deserve this happiness. He certainly didn't deserve her. The dream of Marie in the hay and the man with the half face hovered like a cold splash of water.

"I love you so much, Kate." He stroked her hair. "Darn it! I wish I didn't have to go back to camp. I want to stay right here with you-- forever."

"Forever is a long time, Mr. Hardesty. Are you proposing?" Kate's pony tail had come undone. She reminded him of some gal selling Coca Cola on one of his brother Harry's calendars.

He grinned. "Yeah. I guess I am." He brushed a bit of dry grass off her cheek. "I can't offer you much at first, but I'll find work and when I can, finish school. Bladstad's talked to me about doing something with the Forest Service." He moved his body off of hers and lay partially in the grass next to her. He took a strip of inner bark from a red cedar tree out of his pocket. He had found it on the dirt floor of the smokehouse. Lying on her back, Kate showed him how to separate it into finer strips. "The Coast Salish Indians made baskets from this. Rain cloaks and hats as well."

Hardesty played with his pieces of soft amber colored cedar and after braiding a couple together tied it around her wrist. "A promise," he said. "To marry you. Miss Al-fee-ord, will you be mine?"

She lay there so peacefully, her hair splayed out behind her like a fan.

"Yes," she said, then laughed when he caught his breath in relief. He took the hand with the bracelet and kissed the palm. Kate reached up to his head and pulled it down to her mouth.

"I love you, Park. You're the nicest thing that's ever happened to me."

Hardesty returned to Kulshan on the twenty-ninth of July. He had spent the remaining hours of his leave with Kate in the apartment talking and making plans. They had decided that they would keep their engagement quiet for awhile. He really needed to finish his tour and if necessary sign up for a final one. Their engagement would complicate things even though CCC boys got engaged with local girls all the time. They would meet instead on the weekends at her parents' cabin. If anyone was to know it would be Betty or Cory. Kate was to look into forestry school programs at the university in Seattle or the Normal School in town for him and herself as well. If Kate wanted to return to school, they would do it together.

On the day he left, Staubach came down to the store in a camp truck and greeted Hardesty and Kate on the front steps.

"Hey, Park, you're looking great."

"I'm doing pretty good. I'm free of the sling and will lose the straps soon enough."

Cory and Bob Alford came out to say goodbye. Hardesty knew that neither had any inkling of what was going on between him and Kate, except that he was "seeing her."

"Come again, Mr. Hardesty." The elder Alford shook his hand.

"Thank you. That's very kind."

Hardesty eased into the passenger side of the car. Kate closed the door. "Bye, Kate," he said through the open window. He touched his wrist and she answered by rubbing the cedar bracelet he knew was underneath her flannel shirt.

"Bye."

Callister was in the administration building when the truck came in. When enrollees began gathering around the passenger door, he wondered out loud who it was.

"Park Hardesty's back," an enrollee typing at the table said.

"Really? Looks like a movie star showed up."

The bell on the typewriter pinged and the enrolled threw the carriage back across the machine to start a new line on his government form. "Well, the guys like him, especially the foreign crowd, but I heard someone's sweet on him back in Frazier."

"Anyone I know?" Callister asked, a dull feeling stirring in his stomach.

"Uh, that redhead." The enrollee stopped typing.

"And how do you know?" Callister could feel his face flush and his voice sound harsh, but he didn't care.

"Someone in town told me. They've been going on walks around the place. Uh, I left something in the supply room. I'll be back." The enrollee jumped up and slipped out of the room as fast as he could.

"Coward." Callister waited until the boy was gone then marched down to his end of the building. Shutting the door to his office he swept every book in his sleeping quarters from their shelves.

Never, he vowed, would he let Hardesty get close to her. He didn't deserve her. To that end, Callister would do everything in his power to make life miserable for that enrollee from Pennsylvania.

He would never give up Kate.

CHAPTER 16

The day Hardesty came back to Kulshan, Joisey Squad returned to full complement for the first time in a month. At evening mess when he took his seat along with the others, the rest of the corps broke into applause. Grinning, he saluted them, then sat down at the head of the table. Golden immediately began passing the bowls of steaming food around.

"What have you been eating, Park? Hospital food?" Spinelli asked as he helped himself to mashed potatoes.

"Champagne and steak – liver, that is." Hardesty put his napkin in his lap and grinned.

"All the soda he wanted," Lorenzo said. "Pretty soft, living over a store."

"How's that redhead?" Golden asked.

The questions came fairly fast, so between bites, Hardesty set them straight. "What's the low down on the work assignments?" he asked. "Back to spike camp?"

"I don't think so," Staubach said between gulps of milk. "Bladstad has a project out in Cedar Canyon. Repairing some bridge and maybe some regrading. You going?"

"I don't know. I'm supposed to talk to Taylor after dinner. I'm not supposed to do anything heavy for awhile."

"Hope you can go, Park," Staubach said.

Hardesty grinned at him. "So do I. Maybe as bull cook. We'll see."

"Well, whatever happens," O'Connell said, "we're glad you're back." He lifted his glass of milk at him. "Here's to Park and Joisey Squad."

"To the squad," they all shouted. They clinked their glasses together and then downed the milk so fast they had white mustaches. From the other tables came hoots and hollers, followed by pounding at the tables.

"Nothing's changed," Hardesty said above the noise.

"Nope." Spinelli twirled spaghetti onto his fork then slurped it. "But we're at peace with Spenser's squad. Watch out for McGill, though. He hasn't given up yet. Last week, one of his boys tried to stuff Lorenzo down the latrine at Big Fir. Staubach flattened him. Better walk in two's."

Hardesty looked around the hall until he located McGill and his squad. The big Tarheel looked point blank at him and raised his half-empty glass of milk at him, then poured it slowly into his soup bowl. When he was finished, he turned the glass upside down. Hardesty wasn't sure what symbolism it was supposed to represent, but knew it was directed at him. He cheerily raised his glass back. The next few weeks were going to be fun.

After dinner, the squad dispersed for evening duties while Hardesty headed over to the camp office. Inside he found Taylor going over files in the cabinet behind his desk. Hardesty stood at attention until he was told to stand at ease.

"Welcome back, Mr. Hardesty."

"Thank you, sir."

"You're looking well. I saw Bob Alford the other day. He said that you were healing nicely. You made quite an impression on him."

"I hope a good one. The family was very kind to take me in."

"I'm glad you are aware of your social obligations. You've made an impression on other members of the family as well. A certain young woman. It is, of course, none of my business, but I trust you will keep the camp's reputation in mind when you deal with members of the opposite sex in our neighboring communities."

"I do, sir," he answered simply.

"Good. Now to business." Taylor put a file on his desk. "I talked to Doc and he suggests light duty for you for awhile. You can do it in the mess or here at the office."

"Any chance I can go out with my squad? Say bull cook?"

"It's a possibility. If there's heavy lifting, Doc will probably say no. But after a couple of more weeks, I'm sure it will be okay. How much longer are you to remain trussed up?"

"Doc is being cautious. The shoulder strap could come off now, but he wanted to be sure I don't stress the new bone growth around the break--something like that-- so I suspect another two weeks."

"Let's say two weeks then. In the meantime, I'm assigning you to Crawford and his mess crew. How are you at peeling spuds?"

"About as good as spudding trees. I'm experienced. Rather that than pearl diving for dishes."

Taylor chuckled. "That's what a tree soldier's for. Go to the wilderness and learn useful occupations. You can start tomorrow."

When Hardesty went back to the barracks, he found Spinelli up on his bunk writing. Except for an enrollee snoring on his bed across the room, the barracks was deserted.

"You done with evening chores already?" Hardesty asked.

"Night off. Thought I'd do this."

"You passed the test? Alford said you had come by the store, but by the time I got to feeling better, you'd all gone to Big Fir so I never heard."

"Yeah, I passed. Thanks to you." Spinelli sat up. "Thanks for your help." He extended his hand and Hardesty shook it before sitting down on the lower bunk.

"So what's next?" He punched his musty pillow and eased down on the bed.

"You mean with Miss Alford?"

"No, the test." Hardesty chuckled, knowing that he was

capable of making a similar mistake.

"I got one more to go," Spinelli said. He became quiet. Hardesty could hear his pencil scratching above him, then being tapped on the writing tablet. Spinelli cleared his throat. "You see Karin Alford at the store?"

"Once or twice." He didn't mention seeing her at their home because he didn't want to hurt the boy's feelings.

"Was she looking all right?"

"I'd say she was."

"Damn," Spinelli whispered.

"Trouble?"

"No, just haven't seen her in two weeks. I heard from a fellow who was madly in love with a girl he met at a dance, but when he was gone fighting fires for two weeks, he came back and found her engaged to someone else."

Hardesty grinned. "I think you're safe. She's not the flighty type."

"You talk to her? She talk about me?" Spinelli leaned over the side of the bunk.

"As a matter of fact she asked about you. I gave her a favorable opinion, especially about your studies."

"I showed her a poem I wrote. She liked it." Spinelli laid back down causing the springs to whine. "We don't get no – any – chance to be alone. We're always watched like I'm some sort of germ."

"It'll come in time. Folks are serious around here. They don't want their daughters running off with unknowns."

"I wouldn't do anything to hurt her. She's the nicest girl I've ever met."

"Keep that word "girl" in mind. She's sixteen."

"...maybe if I were to go with you. You like that redhead, don't you? Karin's sister? The one who can buck wood better than Sammy Kolbrowski."

"Anyone can buck better than he can." Hardesty grew serious. "Maybe I can see what I can do. Maybe this weekend, we can take a hike down to Frazier together. Miss Kate Alford wants to show me the waterfalls up above the river. Maybe we can pack a lunch and all four of us go."

"Jesus, you'd do that for me?"

"Sure."

"How can I thank you?"

"Pass that last test."

Spinelli leaned over the bunk again. "Thanks, Park." He lay back down again making the bed sing. He put his arms behind his head. "Do you know how long we've been here? Month-wise?"

“Nearly five months. Hard to believe.”

"Tour's almost up, but you know what? I'm going to sign up again."

"Taylor will be glad to hear that. I'm sure Miss Karin Alford will too."

"I want to finish school. That's you, Park. I never thought I could do it."

"I'm glad I can help." Hardesty lay quietly on the bed below, and closed his eyes. As he listened to his friend talk, he remembered how school had saved him for awhile, but in the end, not being able to escape his environment and background. Only being totally wrenched away from it, did he finally become free. At what cost!

Paul, I never got a chance to talk to you. To explain. No one would let me.

Hardesty pressed his fists into his closed eyes. For all his paltry reasons for sending his check home, it would never be enough.

Worse, some day he would have to tell Kate.

Callister waited until Taylor shut the office door completely and went out the front porch. A few moments later, he could hear the sound of boots crunching on the gravel path a squad had recently improved. When he no longer heard them, hc warily came down the dark hall, careful not to step on the sagging wood floorboards in the middle of the space. When he got to the commander's door, he cautiously opened it up and stepped in. It was never locked. There was no need for that.

Inside, he turned on his flashlight. It was past lights-off in the barracks and Taylor had just finished his rounds. Although he could give good reasons for being in the building, Callister decided not to chance curiosity about the late hour. Making sure the blinds were pulled down, he made his way over to the tall file cabinet. He pulled out a drawer and began thumbing through the files. In the middle of them, he found what he was looking for and took it out. Sitting down in Taylor's wooden swivel chair, he opened the file and began to read.

It consisted of several pages, including information transferred up from Oregon. It listed his height and weight. His birthday was written as August 31, 1910. It noted he had been a junior at the last camp he was at which was news to Callister. As he searched for personal information, he felt frustration.

Hardesty had been out in the northwest since the summer of 1933. He apparently had signed up in eastern Oregon in a camp there. His acquired skills and aptitudes were listed, but there was nothing about his family background. When Callister looked for details about his origins, the file said only Zelianople, Pennsylvania. Weird sounding name. No list of siblings or parents.

Nothing, thought Callister. The files told him nothing. Hardesty might as well not exist. He flipped through the other pages and came across an interesting contradiction. His checks went to someone in Pittsburgh. An address was given in East Liberty. Searching for a piece of paper, he hurriedly copied the address down. He also wrote down the name of Zelianople. He could write there too. He laid the papers back in and was preparing to close it when he noticed a small envelope at the back of the file. Taking it out carefully, he opened it up and finding a small note card, began to read:

20 April 1935.

> Enjoyed my dinner with you last evening. Looking forward to seeing you again in a few weeks in Seattle. Please give consideration to what I said about my young friend. P. Hardesty was an outstanding junior at Rouge

> River. Don't let him buffalo you into ignoring him. He was a winner of the Honor Award. He has had a troubled background and has generally wanted to stay shy of it, but I find him worthy of my trust. To my knowledge, he has no criminal record. If you have any further questions, don't hesitate to write.
>
> Sincerely, Floyd Garrison

Callister turned the card over carefully, his heart pounding. There was something strange going on here. Troubled past, but one of the top men in the Forest Service was a friend. Garrison was widely respected. Callister wondered how Hardesty and Garrison met. Slipping the card back in, he mulled over the information. It wasn't any better than the other stuff, but he kept thinking that there was something odd about Hardesty.

Too good to be true, and not good enough for Kate.

He wanted something that he could use against Hardesty. Something he could take to Caroline Alford and let the family intervene. Before it was too late.

He felt sick about the two of them being together. What if he had touched her? They went for walks, an acquaintance in Frazier said. Why didn't Kate see?

I should never have given up, should have gone to her father and asked him for her hand the old fashioned way. Bob Alford liked him. I have prospects, Callister thought.

Hardesty is just an enrollee, some unknown on the dole. He could never give her what Kate needed – the security of a home and a man to protect her.

"Dammit!" Suddenly he seized the file and jammed it back into the drawer before he destroyed it. That wouldn't do. He pulled it out again and repositioned it before closing the drawer. He stepped softly out into the hall and closed the door.

Now what? He would have to find some way to get to Hardesty. To have someone watch him. Unexpectedly he had an idea. There was someone who could help him, someone who probably hated Hardesty as much as he now did.

Jonas McGill.

CHAPTER 17

Joisey Squad went with Spenser's crew for Cedar Creek the next day, leaving Hardesty behind to work in the kitchen. It was not painful duty. The guys who worked there were a boisterous lot and easy to get along with. He enjoyed the chance to do any sort of work after being gone so long. He fit easily into the routine and worked as hard as he could. For now lifting heavy cooking pots and iron pans was out of the question, but he could do preparation work and help with the cooking. That meant rising early, sometimes around four-thirty and working long hours from breakfast until lunch when the food was driven out to the squads. Since he couldn't do that yet, he would go lie down for a couple of hours before reporting back to the kitchen and getting the evening's meal underway. By the end of the week, he was ready to sleep his entire weekend leave away. But not until he saw Kate. Through Cory, he made arrangements to hike up to Kulshan Falls on Saturday. He would be bringing Spinelli. Kate was bringing Karin.

The hike was an easy rise up through thick forest, lined with sword fern and salmonberry bushes. While Kate and Hardesty led the way up the trail, Spinelli and Karin dragged behind, talking, talking. Hardesty thought it amusing, remembering his own stabs at immortality at that age with a special girl. Spinelli had practically dressed up for the occasion until Hardesty told him that it was all right to prepare for a hike, not a hitching. The two of them could enjoy themselves all they wanted.

"You be grateful. You're the first enrollee her parents had allowed the girl to go out with."

Kate did most of the carrying for Hardesty. He took a light rucksack with foul weather clothes, but couldn't tote anything heavier. At the falls, Kate gave him a tablecloth that they spread on the ground in a sun-mottled, shady spot under big leaf maple trees. Not far away, they could hear the roar of the falls as it fell some fifty feet into the pool below.

"Stay away, Mario and Park," Kate warned. "I'll show you the safest spot. Every other year some silly comes up from the cities and gets into trouble. Most often it ends in death."

"No fooling?" Spinelli said.

"No fooling. We'd like to put up a chain fence, but some fool would probably go under it with the same fatal results. So far, no enrollee's been lost."

"So how do you look at them?" Hardesty asked.

"Carefully. There's a couple of viewing spots, but they're difficult to see because of the way the hill slopes. You've got to approach the falls correctly. Then it's perfectly safe."

The two couples stayed most of the day. Before lunch they explored the area together, but afterwards, Spinelli asked if he could go with Karin to see a lookout she had told him about.

"Yes, you may," Kate said without hesitation.

"Do you think they'll be all right?" she asked after they left.

"Sure. Mario's a great kid." Hardesty said. "A good kid."

"Don't laugh. Sometimes I can't understand him when he talks."

"Do you understand me?" Hardesty asked.

"Oh, Park." Kate's eyes were sparkling.

They sat at the edge of the tablecloth and put the food away together. Eventually, he asked about seeing the falls again, and she showed him how to approach the lookout from the hill. One couldn't tell right off that they were plunging down to a slippery and drastically narrow lip without the warning signs. To the right of the signs, the hill continued on into solid rock and soil that jutted wide above the falls. It was not slippery but someone had erected a wooden picket fence around the space for safety. When Hardesty looked back up, he could see the trees around the area where they had been picnicking.

"Funny," he said. "It's not obscured here."

"That's why it's dangerous," Kate said. To their left the falls thundered down, raising a cool mist. Its power was tremendous for its size.

"I saw Niagara Falls once when I was a boy," he said. "This is pretty impressive."

“What were they like?”

“Well, for one, you could hear it over a mile or so away. There was this tremendous roar. The spray started drifting at you a ways back too. Still, that didn’t prepare you for what you saw. Of course, that's before I came out here. The mountains, I have found, are just as extraordinary."

Kate shivered in the sunlight. Hardesty felt the mist from the falls too. It was heavy and cool even on a day like this. Hardesty put his arm around her and hugged her, then asked if she knew the daily volume of water going over the falls. They spent the rest of the afternoon calculating that and talking about anything that came into their heads.

He couldn’t believe how at ease they were with each other. It was as though they had known each other for a long time and the afternoon passed quickly. Assured the other two were gone for awhile, they lay down on the tablecloth and talked, their heads conspiratorially close. Occasionally, they kissed and nuzzled each other as they visited but Hardesty was careful not to repeat his performance at the smokehouse. When Spinelli and Karin came back an hour later, they were examining different types of leaves on the blanket.

“Time to pack up,” he said. As they prepared to go back, Hardesty noticed once again a small cabin made of long cedar shakes. It was set back in the trees. It wasn't much larger than a shack, but would be serviceable. "That belong to anyone in particular?"

"That's Micah Thompson's. An old-time miner. He's had a claim on it since the early 1890s. My family has used it from time to time. Helps him on his grocery bill. Besides it's getting harder for him to get up here."

Hardesty stared at it as they passed.

"I'd liked to come up here sometime," he said above the fall's noise. He turned to look back at Kate knowingly and she smiled wistfully at him. They went back hiking side by side.

Hardesty was in the bathhouse when McGill made his first search. The squads were gone for the second week to Cedar Canyon. McGill had been given permission to stay back by the education officer to take a makeup test since he would be out of the camp for a couple of days. He had spent most of the morning in the office under Taylor's and Callister's noses, but when the commander left, he joined Callister in his office behind closed doors. It had nothing to do with education.

The education officer had approached him several days earlier. McGill detested Callister and had come reluctantly to his office for the initial talk. To his surprise, he found that they had something in common: Hardesty.

"What do you know about Hardesty?" Callister asked. "You've worked on projects with him. Anything unusual about him?"

"What do you mean?"

"Oh, had a little tip that Hardesty had some secret vice that might be injurious to his squad."

"Injurious? That mean miring his image in skunk cabbage?"

"That's a way of putting it. Perhaps he's keeping a still somewhere or maintaining unhealthy relationships when he occasionally goes to town."

"Didn't know you cared."

"Care enough to look the other way when it comes to sexual escapades on leave in town, but still monitor your health through monthly examinations and keep people soliciting for prostitutes away from the camps. Community standards must be applied up to and in the camps. Hardesty, however, is an older enrollee and could unduly influence the younger boys in his group."

McGill made a face. He didn't have a thing to say. Besides, he was leery of talking to Callister – who knew what his motives were? Then he saw it might be a way to get back at Hardesty. But it had to be good and not trumped up. That's when he thought of the notebook.

"Really?" Callister said. "Is it some sort of journal?"

"Don't know, but Hardesty sure didn't like it when it fell out of his duffel."

"You seen it before that?"

"Never. He keeps it hidden. There were things in it, though. Papers or something."

"Or something. Could you get it?"

"Are you serious?" McGill frowned. "Stealing is about the worst thing you can do here. If I was in spike camp, they'd make me run a gauntlet."

"He'll never know. You get it and bring it here. Try to get it back later. You could always blame it on another enrollee."

McGill stared at Callister. "You must want him bad."

"There's a reason for all this. You can understand my position, though. I'm on the staff here."

"And probably want to stay..."

"Oh, I will. This will never get out. I'll see to that."

McGill looked at the dirt under his nails. "How do I know you won't turn me in?"

"I won't. Unless you try to pull something on me. No one will believe you against me. You've been fighting Hardesty for months. Everyone knows how you feel about him."

"Why should I help then?"

"So you can get promoted to a better position in the camp. Say a junior or better work assignment. What do you think the testing was all about?"

McGill dug some dirt out from under a fingernail with his thumbnail, but he was interested. "When should I bring it?"

"Whenever you can. As soon as possible. The investigation is just getting started."

"I don't like you, Callister. You're too good for your own self."

"And you're too full of it. If I were another officer, you'd be in big trouble for that remark."

"I'm not afraid of you."

"I know and that will be your downfall. Taylor can only tolerate one more outburst from you. It's because of your family's plight, he has been lenient."

McGill blanched. His family was one of the few things he did care about.

"Help me on this and I will help you. Hardesty is up to something. Your assistance will be rewarded."

McGill looked sullen, but he had no choice. He wiped his hands on his pants. "You on the level about a position or least a better work project?"

"Sure. We can talk about it this coming weekend. First, see what you can do about the notebook. Bring it here and leave it in my lunch box." Callister looked around."I'll put it under the desk."

"I'll see what I can do." McGill got up, making sure Callister realized that he was much taller and heftier. The education officer might look handsome, but he didn't even come close to the workload of even the newest enrollee. "See you soon."

McGill slipped into the barracks and watched the parade grounds for a moment. It was deserted. An office staffer got out of a truck and walked to the main office. There was no one else around. All the squads were out, including those who took the lunches out to the various projects. Hardesty was the only one on KP that didn't go. McGill craned his neck around, but didn't see him. Satisfied that he was alone, he began searching around Hardesty's bed, but after several minutes of going through the duffel and the mattress, he came up with nothing. The notebook wasn't around. He checked the bunk once again and any placc that Hardesty might put it, then approached the trunk. As he suspected, it was locked up tight. He tried working on the lock, but didn't have the materials for it. Going to the window, he saw to his dismay that Hardesty was on his way back to the barracks.

"Damn!"

He straightened up carefully around the bunk, then went to the stove and began fussing with the woodbin. Even though summer, it was still lit up at night to ward off the chill. Hardesty found him rearranging the low number of logs in the bin.

"Didn't know you were around," Hardesty commented as he came by the stove, wiping his ears with the towel slung around his neck. His hair was wet and his skin was flushed.

"Yeah, I'm going to stay in the next day or so. The education chief is helping me with some tests."

"Didn't know you were interested."

"I want to get ahead too," McGill said.

Hardesty continued to dry his hair. "You've got family in the Skagit Valley. I hear that's real pretty up near Rockport. Real good fishing there."

"Yeah. Who told you that?"

"Larsen."

"Well, pretty don't mean rich." McGill could barely contain his disdain. What would this foreign jerk know?

"I know what you mean," said Hardesty as he shook his towel out and hung it over his bed frame. "The area I come from in Pennsylvania is piss-poor too. It's known for its quaintness. All the folks with cars can drive through and look. Only a few can pocket what money is left behind."

"That a fact."

Hardesty's face softened. "I suspect that we're not unalike."

"Not likely. How's your shoulder?" Disdain for him or no, he still had to keep on Hardesty's good side.

"It's fine, thanks." After Hardesty finished dressing, he settled down on his bunk. "Soup's on at mess. You should go get it while it's hot. I'm going to take a nap." He closed his eyes, one arm behind his head. McGill watched for a few moments, but realizing that he couldn't do anything about the notebook until later, backed out and took off for lunch.

McGill's second attempt was more successful. After Hardesty left to prepare for the evening's meal and the barracks were deserted, McGill came back with the right tools and picked the lock on the trunk. Inside, he found what he wanted.

"Well, lookee here," he said under his breath as he picked up a small, worn notebook. Curious, he opened it up and found the first article about a car accident. There were other clippings. Spooked by a sound from outside, he hastily stuffed the notebook into his jacket and closed up the trunk. Pushing it back under Hardesty's bed, he walked calmly out the door and over to Callister's office.

Callister took the notebook home that night. After finding his bottle of scotch and a glass, he settled down in his two-room bungalow and laid out the contents of the notebook on his dining table. He had been hoping for some small thing that could be used against his rival, but what he found shocked him.

Hardesty wasn't exactly who he said he was.

Laying the articles out in chronological order, he pieced together a tragedy of the highest order.

A Mr. Paul Hardesty, age 24 and Miss Marie Bertin were involved in a fiery crash on January 18, 1933. Hitting ice, the car had skidded into a ditch where it burst into flames. Miss Bertin was killed instantly, but they had been unable to recover recognizable remains. Mr. Hardesty was trapped and severely burned before being pulled from the car. Rushed to a local hospital and eventually Pittsburgh, he was on the verge of death for several weeks before showing improvement. In a miraculous turnaround, the young man was beginning to respond to treatment despite hideous injuries.

Callister looked at the picture of the car in the ditch and a picture of the young man before the accident. He looked strikingly like Park Hardesty. There were several articles, each with a picture or two. The family was obviously well known in the area or it was just the most sensational event to happen in the area. The readers must have lapped the stories up.

There was a picture of the family taken a couple of years before. The grown-up offspring were all listed, including Hardesty from Kulshan.

Except his name wasn't Park. It was John. And the town

wasn't the odd Zelianople. It was Fair Chance, a rural place in southwest Pennsylvania. Since there were discrepancies in Hardesty's official accounting, Callister began to carefully pore over the articles.

As the weeks dragged by, the family's vigil for its badly injured son seemed to take on biblical dimensions. An absent father returned and while the parents grieved, a long smoldering scandal began to flare up involving Miss Bertin. Including several men, there were suggestions of immoral propriety, smuggled booze, and even murder. One of the last articles even suggested that her engagement to Paul Hardesty had been coolly calculated. Perhaps along with his own brother, John. The younger son was said to have disappeared after a confrontation with his father. His whereabouts were unknown. In all, it was a tragedy for everyone. At the time of the last article, Paul Hardesty was still in critical condition, unable to give his account of the disastrous accident and the preceding events.

Callister flipped it over back and forth. What did this have to do with anything? He spread the articles out on the table. He wasn't sure what had actually happened, but he felt a moral indignation that Hardesty was with Kate. The man was a lecher. Her parents should be told, but he wasn't sure how to go about it without earning Kate's ire. She could be so unpredictable, even when he was doing her a favor. He began to go over the second set of articles, his mind seeking a way to make this work to his advantage and perhaps use any information in the next group of articles. He was disappointed, however.

The second set was short, but to his surprise, he read the story of a fourteen-year-old girl who had been brutally abducted while returning from a walk in the Oregon wilderness. There had been a massive search that involved some squads from the CCC camp at Rouge River close by. She was eventually located, but died several days later from overexposure and some injuries she had sustained. The article mentioned the memorial service for her and noted that some of the enrollees at the camp had been questioned. In the end, however, all had been absolved and no charges filed against any of them. There was no mention of

Hardesty in the article, but it did say that the Holly Garrison girl was the loving daughter of Floyd and Lily Garrison. Again a connection to Hardesty. Recalling Garrison's note to Taylor, Callister wondered if he had been in one of the squads that searched for her. Whatever it was, he resolved to concentrate on the intriguing mystery of Hardesty's family background in Pennsylvania. The very fact he used a different name was suspicious. Callister would write to those addresses in that state and try to find some answers, and then somehow tell Kate.

He shifted through the pages of the journal. At first the entries just mentioned the weather and locations of places as Hardesty passed through to the west, occasionally describing them in detail.

Feb. 15

Hitched a truck to Pella, Iowa. Was as cold and snowy inside the cab as without heat. Window broken. Got job shoveling snow. Wyatt Earp said to be born here.

March 3

Month came in like a lamb. It's hot enough to cook eggs.

There was little feeling in them, except for a telling of a near mugging at some hobo camp in the Midwest. Hardesty seemed to travel everywhere and anywhere riding trains in ways that Callister had only read about.

He flipped through the notebook, scanning over each entry. By spring, Hardesty was in New Mexico and then Nevada contemplating going to California for work, but at the last moment opted for eastern Oregon. Penniless and friendless, the entries at last revealed his true feelings of tortured morose and loneliness. There was anger too. He found work at a relief camp and as soon as he was able, applied to the newly formed Civilian Conservation Corps. He was accepted and joined the corps at one of the first camps in the Northwest by summer.

He kept some entries for awhile in late 1933, then stopped.

Except for one lone entry in January of 1934, and a recent one announcing his arrival at Kulshan, the entries ended for good. Yet this entry written with a pencil was telling, perhaps intended as an essay for the New Year. It said simply:

> After a tragedy such as this, it is ironic that I now find myself with a friend and that for the first time in a long time, I have some purpose in life. I was taught that God will forgive me, but what I want more than anything else is for my brother to forgive me. It is my greatest fear that I drove him literally to do what he did and the burden of that will never go away until I am at peace with him.

Callister closed the notebook, making sure the clippings and medal were put carefully back in the way he found them. He felt no compassion for the writer, no degree of understanding.

He didn't care. He only thought of Kate.

CHAPTER 18

Hardesty returned to the field the following day, driving the lunch truck out to Joisey Squad for the noon break. There he found crews from three additional squads walking in from where they had been regrading the canyon road and clearing brush and trees along the river for a campsite. Hardesty pulled off to the side where the dirt road had been widened to a generous turnout and parked. By the time the boys were up to the trucks, he had already dropped the tailgate and was unloading the large metal containers of hot soup with the help of an enrollee from the kitchen.

"Hey, Park!" yelled Spinelli as he came up. "Whatcha got?"

"Split pea soup and corned beef sandwiches" He carefully set his container down, mindful of his shoulder.

"Need help?"

"Naw, I'm okay. You could ask Jimmy, though. He looks winded. Not used to the wild life."

The enrollee named Jimmy grinned. He was relatively new, from a small town in southwestern Washington. Spinelli went over to help him.

The food was set up on a folding table and as soon as it was ready, the squads lined up for serving. It was a hot, August day, the high mountains around them clear of clouds. In the sunlight, the glacier field that fed the river glistened like icing with rhinestone fragments. When the boys were served, they sat down with their plates along the road and riverbank. Joisey Squad stayed close to Hardesty at the truck.

"How're things going?" he asked Staubach.

“All right,” he said as he wiped his tanned hands on his work pants.

"Everyone getting on?"

"Sure.. 'cept Costello. Always complaining."

"That a fact?" Hardesty asked. He wasn't straw boss any more, but he felt a continuing nurturing role towards them all. “That doesn’t sound like Costello.”

"Not complaining," Costello grumbled. "Some people are just too good for us anymore."

Hardesty sensed some tension and concerned, decided to get at it right away, but the disagreement was getting ahead of him.

"I like my classes," Staubach protested.

"Ain't you." Costello looked pointedly at Spinelli who sat on the ground with his legs straight out. His plate was on his knees and he ate one-handed while the other held a book. He was so lost in reading that he didn't hear the argument about him, not even when Staubach called out his name.

"This bug you, Steve?" Hardesty asked.

"Makes me feel like a jerk."

"You're all right. Each to his own."

Costello made a face.

"Why don't you come here and get a second helping of soup?" Hardesty asked.

"I ain't ready."

"Sure you are." Hardesty said it in such a way that it left little room for him not to come.

The boy got up and self-consciously stepped over the legs of his mates stretched in every direction like pick-up sticks.

"Need some help," Hardesty said. He beckoned for Costello to put his plate down and they ambled to the front. While Hardesty opened the door, he continued talking.

"Not my business, but I was wondering how you were getting on. You passed your test?"

Costello looked stricken. “Heck no. Didn’t even try.”

"I thought you were going to." Hardesty motioned for him to pick up some flats on the truck floor and slowly got the whole story out of him. All the boys in the squad had gone ahead on their high school diploma except him. He had been having trouble.

"I could help," Hardesty volunteered.

The boy shook his head. "I dunno. What's the point? Can't use it when I go back."

Hardesty wanted to argue that he could but decided to let things lay. He was going to ask him about home, but McGill butted in by the tailgate.

“Hey, I’d like some seconds.”

"On the table." Hardesty instructed Costello to take the flat back to the rear end of the truck. When he came back with his own load, he saw Costello going off to sit with McGill and thought that an interesting development.

The squads finished up and brought their plates back to the truck where hot soapy water had been poured into a big metal tub for washing. The other enrollee began cleaning up and putting away food while Hardesty organized the dishes. Golden came up to him with his cup and plate and remarked that washing dishes wasn't much for the champion of Joisey Squad.

"It has its days," returned Hardesty. "I should be back soon – I hope."

From the front of the truck came an excited murmur from twenty-five lusty throats that worked its way down to the serving table. Hardesty looked out, and to his surprise saw Kate Alford sitting astride Elsa. She stopped the mare and - not seeing him - peered over the crowd of admirers. "Anyone see Mr. Bladstad?"

"He hasn't come up yet, Miss Alford," answered Spenser as he walked over. "Not until later. You want to leave him a message?"

“Yes, please. Thanks.”

About ten hands offered her paper and pencil. Taking what

she needed, she thanked them all. She freed her right leg from the stirrup and wrapped it around the pommel of the saddle while she wrote. She had her thick hair tied in a single braid under a green felt hat. With her flannel jacket, Hardesty thought she looked like something out of *Field and Stream.* The boys wore their own approval on their sunburned faces, bantering awkwardly with her like she was some movie star. Hardesty thought she had a lot of poise especially after Elsa got excited when an enrollee accidentally poked her nostril when he petted her nose. The mare danced a bit, but Kate kept her from planting a hoof on any toes. The mare eventually calmed down. Kate finished her note, asking Spenser to see that Bladstad got it.

"Will do," he said. The boys kept hanging around. Afraid that the mare might be startled again, one of Bladstad's forestry assistants ordered them to clean up and get ready to go back to their work sites. It was almost time anyway. Reluctantly, they said goodbye and began to move away, eventually leaving only Spenser and Kate. Hardesty pulled back and went back to his dishes, but he could hear everything.

"Damn. You'd think some of them never saw a horse," Spenser said.

"They probably haven't," Kate laughed.

"Want coffee?"

"That sounds nice."

Hardesty heard her get down, her boots scraping on the rocky road, and walk down towards the tailgate.

"Park!" she exclaimed when she saw him. "You're out."

"And about." He grinned impishly at her for he was up to his elbows in suds and hot water. He had rolled the arms of his regulation shirt up and he had his cap on backwards.

"Any coffee left?" Spenser asked. He seemed oblivious to any connection between them.

"Sure, Hank. Miller can get it for you." Hardesty yelled at the enrollee to get a thermos for them. "Our best china for the lady."

Kate laughed. She led the horse away and let the mare graze at the river's edge away from the truck. When she came back, Spenser had a speckled blue and white enamel cup for her.

"My, Wedgwood," she teased.

"Only the best, Miss Alford," Spenser grinned. Hardesty thought he seemed anxious to please her, wanting to talk to her and hold her attention. Kate happily complied but he felt her watching him as he put away containers and utensils on the back of the truck. Eventually, Spenser had to go. He gallantly whipped his CCC cap off his head and bowed.

"See ya."

"Bye," laughed Kate. When Spenser was out of earshot, she added, "He's nice."

"Yeah, he is." Hardesty removed his apron and told the other enrollee that he could have a break. He poured himself a cup of coffee and sat on the tailgate.

"How have you been?" he asked.

"I'm fine. I'm still getting those samples, but I'm almost done." She eyed him curiously. "Are you going back to the squad soon?"

"Hopefully, day after tomorrow. The strap's coming off tomorrow."

"Oh, Park. That's wonderful."

"I don't know how much a change it'll make. I won't be doing any hard labor for a couple of more weeks, but I could come out and at least be bull cook. Which means I can tramp out with the squad and make their lunch."

"Did you sign on again?"

"Yes, I did. Yesterday."

Kate looked thoughtful. "That okay? That's what we agreed on."

"Yes." She came over and leaned against the tailgate. Her shoulder brushed his. "You're looking well. Even tanned. Missed you," she murmured.

Hardesty looked around and finding them completely alone leaned over and brushed his lips on hers, sharing a tender kiss. "In time. Maybe this weekend." He wanted to say more but he didn't trust their privacy. Not wanting to do something that would cause comment and put her in a bad light, he stroked her cheek and resumed his place again next to her.

"It might be longer than this weekend," Kate said. "Bladstad wants to see me. Charlie Benson broke his leg yesterday – he mans the lookout over by Chapel Ridge. I think Bladstad wants me to take Benson's place until fire season is over. They can't spare anyone right now."

Hardesty took the news with mixed feelings. It would be the closest she could come to any job in the Forest Service and he was happy for her, but it could also be weeks before he saw her again. "That's great, Kate. How soon?"

"Tomorrow or the following day."

"That soon ..."

"A-huh. Betty Olsen is going up with me to check it out. I'll take Elsa and another horse. Take what I need."

"This place habitable?"

Kate laughed "It's like the Grand Hotel. You've seen them before..."

"I've built them before. Hauled the lumber up by packhorse down in Oregon. The CCC's there built four."

"This one has a grand view."

"Can I come? I'll bring my bedroll." Hardesty grinned mischievously at her. "And a tent."

Kate smiled weakly at him.

"I'm only teasing."

"It's all right. A tent is fine, although convention may allow for a bunk. I wouldn't want you to freeze." She didn't avoid his eyes. Hardesty once again admired that quality in her – her directness.

"I'll bring a tent and a roll." He got down from the tailgate. "I have to get back to work."

"I do too. I'll try to leave a message, Park. So you'll know."

"Thanks." He stayed close to her. He could smell the sweet scent of the horse on her and the dust. It reminded him of the horses at his grandparents' farm and the dust motes in the barn that danced over the haystack when the sun poked through the slats.

Marie.

"You come see me, John? I think I like that."

"You can think what you want."

"I think you want me."

"Just quit it, Marie. And stay away from my brother. You're using him."

"Ooh, you are so angry. I like theez."

An old pang of passion that was now as cold as the January snows she had died in stirred in his gut, but he knew that what he had felt had been nothing more than lust. The beauty next to him was a wonder. Far more real than any of the girls at Lacey's all gussied-up for show and a good time.

"I'm go-ing to close the door. Maybe you not so mad."

God, what made a man make the choices he did? And what was the relentless power that never would let him forget?

"Park? Let me know about your shoulder, will you?"

"Sure, Kate. You'll be the first." He looked around for any stray enrollee, then pulled her to him. "I love you, Kate."

"I know. While I'm up there, I'll stitch a pillow that says so."

"Don't leave out the forget-me-nots."

"Or the chipmunk coat of arms."

"I thought it was a bear."

Kate giggled as she leaned against him, then stood stock still when he quietly took off her hat and using it as a screen, gave her a full kiss on her mouth.

He put his arms around her and drawing her to him, whispered, "If I don't see you for awhile, I'll send something by carrier pigeon. Whatever time I've got off, I'll try to come." He released her from his arms, holding onto one of her hands.

"It won't seem too long, will it?" she wondered.

"Eternity, but I'm proud of you, Kate. One thing about you – you think and do what you believe in."

"I believe in you."

Hardesty flushed, moved by her comment. It had been a long time since someone had said that. Except for Garrison and his wife Lilly. And Bladstad. "I'll walk you to your horse."

After she was gone, Hardesty resumed cleaning up. The other enrollee had finished up his share and gone with his pole down to the river to fish. Somehow, he had managed to fall asleep against the rocky bank. Hardesty smiled. He was feeling lazy too, having been up since 4:30 a.m. preparing food. Stretching, he looked for a place to take a leak before he did a final loading into the truck. They were due back by 3:00 to get the final preparations for dinner started. He spied an area where at least there was some growth of alder and willow saplings along the road in the clear-cut. He decided to go there.

The day was hot and the dusty road was a reminder that it had not rained since mid-July. Coming back onto it, Hardesty buttoned up his pants and started back when he heard voices on the road around the bend.

Odd, he thought. None of the crews were supposed to be around, but then the air was clear and voices carried far. He turned away then stopped. The voices were arguing.

"You never said," one of the voices protested.

"You never asked. Look, you're in this now."

"Maybe I don't want to be."

"All right. No hard feelings then. Here, take another swig."

Hardesty was paying attention now. That was McGill's voice and with him was Costello. His first inclination was to stay where he was, just ignore them, but a rising irritation made him turn around and go up. He didn't like McGill hanging around his crewmate. It portended trouble for the squad. When he got up there, his instinct was right. Sitting on a boulder, the Tarheel and Costello were sharing a flask.

"You boys on holiday?" Hardesty kept walking up.

"None of your beeswax," McGill growled.

"I'm no saint myself," Hardesty said, "but drinking distilled liquor at two o'clock in the afternoon is not regulation."

"Go to hell, Hardesty. You've been out of it for a month."

"Do what you want, but Steve has work to do."

"You ain't my straw boss no more." Costello's voice trailed off.

"No, but I'm your friend. McGill's just asking for trouble."

McGill stood up. "You're too high and mighty, pal." He marched down to Hardesty and took another swig. "You want to talk about it?"

"We had our talk a couple of months ago. I believe it was a draw."

"Don't think so now. I'd have the advantage. I heard you're still trussed up."

Costello leaped up, his eyes darting between the two. "Hey, wait a minute, McGill."

"You pipe down." The Tarheel's arm shot out, slamming his hand palm out against Hardesty's shoulder. Grunting from the pain, Hardesty fell back, but anger propelled him forward. Regaining his balance, he charged and nearly knocked McGill flat. Roaring, McGill came back at him, but Hardesty met him punch for punch. Scuffling and throwing blows, they finally broke away.

"Don't lean on me, McGill. I mean it."

Wiping his mouth, McGill stared at him. Slowly he circled around him again. Hardesty held up his fists and watched him carefully. His shoulder throbbed, but he stood his ground. Eventually, McGill made a face and spitting on the ground, stepped back.

"Park?" Costello cautiously asked.

"I'm all right. Go back to the work site, Steve, before you catch it. McGill's not going to do anything."

"And you?"

"I've got to take the truck back. See you at mess tonight." The boy hesitated, but Hardesty was relieved that he appeared drawn back by loyalty to him. He waved him on. As soon as he was out of earshot, Hardesty turned on McGill.

"I don't know what you're up to, but you stay away from that kid."

"What are you, his mother?" McGill said.

"Costello hardly needs mothering. He's as street smart as you are in the woods. Don't misjudge him. I'd stay on his good side."

"What if he wants to be with me?"

Hardesty had no answer for that. "I can't make him stay away, but if you persist."

"You'll what?" McGill spat as he half-circled around. "I don't think you're in any position to say anything when you're a lying son of a bitch. I know a secret about you."

"Secret?"

McGill's eyes gloated. "Using a false name. What are you doing, Hardesty? Stealing someone's government check?"

"I don't know what you're talking about."

"Yeah, I'll bet. That's what I can't stand about you foreigners. You're sneaky, lying sons of bitches." McGill moved away from him. "Don't try anything funny. It'll only get you in deeper shit." He headed back down to the truck, his heavy boots kicking up dust on the road.

Hardesty watched him go in disbelief. Now what in the hell was that all about? What had McGill meant by false name?

As he followed him down, a heavy feeling began to sink into Hardesty as he pieced the puzzle together. When he got back to the barracks forty minutes later, his suspicions were confirmed. The little notebook was gone.

Stunned, he sat back on his haunches feeling totally dejected. Nothing in the articles was shameful. It was a private grief and guilt he felt. He had chosen to use his middle name when he signed up for a new start. Garrison had understood, but others might not. In the hands of someone like McGill, that and the articles could be misinterpreted. Staring at the empty space where he had placed it on the tray in his trunk, he felt sick. Suddenly his past was threatening to consume him again.

The medallion.

Did someone take that too? Panicking, he ransacked the remaining items of underwear, socks, and kit and found the medallion in the little tobacco sack in which he had hid it.

He looked around the barracks. It wasn't much, but this world, this organization where he had carved out a new life was important to him. He couldn't imagine what he'd do without it. What would he do if he was forced out somehow?

Joisey Squad returned to camp around 4:30 and after showering, made plans for their free time over at the canteen. At the counter, Staubach found a note from Hardesty waiting for him. "Come see me," was all it said. After grabbing a soda, he headed over to the mess hall.

Hardesty was in the kitchen putting some large pans into the oven. When he saw Staubach, he waved at him and joined him outside on the back step.

"Smells good, Park. Smells Eye-talian."

"Lasagna." Hardesty wiped his hands on his canvas apron. "About ready to eat. Thanks for coming, Jeff."

"Something on your mind?"

"Just feeling a bit out of it still. I'll be glad to go out with you, even if it's bull cook." He leaned his back against the screen door, setting his mouth tight. "Got a problem, though."

"Shoot."

"Someone got into my stuff while I was gone."

"You're kidding."

"Wish I wasn't. I'd like it back."

Staubach was nonplussed. "There's been no problem with stealing, at least not in our barracks while you were gone. Some of the other boys have reported an occasional theft of cigarettes or food from home, but that gets taken care of quickly."

"I know. Someone got into my stuff, though. I just found it missing."

"What do you want me to do?"

"Look around. Listen. It's personal stuff, not something you can hock. I don't think it's gone anywhere. McGill might know about its whereabouts."

"You think he stole it?"

"Might have."

"Jesus. Is it important to you?"

"It's personal -- a notebook that I kept during my first years out here. That's all."

"No shocking love notes?"

Hardesty grinned. "No, not even a French postcard."

Staubach beamed. "Then they can't get you on a morals charge."

Hardesty said no then wondered if that was the truth. The sheriff back east could have got him on a morals charge if he had wanted. Hardesty hadn't stayed around long enough to find out.

"I'll keep my eyes peeled."

"How do you like being straw boss?" Hardesty scratched his back against the screen.

"It's great, but you're a hard act to follow." Staubach brushed something imaginary on his shirt, then said, "Have any trouble today? One of McGill's boys was acting funny. Said there was some kind of fight after we left. You get hurt?"

Hardesty shook his head. The camp grapevine was busy again. "No," he replied. "Let's just say our Tarheel friend was testing the waters after a month's respite, but stubbed his toe going in."

Staubach chuckled, but he looked concerned. "McGill's been rough lately. Going after some new enrollees at the spike camp. He doesn't bother us as much, but I don't trust him. He's never forgotten how you tripped him at the river and nearly beating him in the fight. The newcomers hear about it right off and he can't stand it."

"What about Costello?"

Staubach made a face. "I can't figure that one out. Costello started hanging out with McGill a short while ago. Maybe I haven't been such a good straw boss. There's been some tension."

"Don't blame yourself. Costello sounds like he's been having trouble with his classes. It's making him sensitive and hard to get along with."

"Him and some others. That Callister. He'll seem like your friend, then really lights into you if he thinks you're stupid or something. He has no patience for eastern kids."

"Maybe we're too close to home. Callister isn't from around here."

"Really? How you know that?"

"His accent and what Cory Alford has said. How's the squad on the whole? You getting along?"

"Yeah, sure. We've missed you, though. You brought out the best in us."

"Thanks." Hardesty straightened up. "Say, you want a piece of cake to munch on with your soda?"

"Gee, that would be swell."

Hardesty went in to get a slice. When he came back, he was carrying a cloth napkin with chocolate cake in it. The icing was rich and dark. Staubach wowed over it a bit, then gobbled it down. Hardesty wished him good health and went inside.

Callister parked in front of the Alford home and got out just in time to see Kate go in. Bounding up the stairs, he called into the hallway, but got Karin instead.

"Hi, Mr. C.," she exclaimed as she came barreling out the door. "If you want to catch Kate, you better do it now. She's leaving."

"Leaving? She going somewhere?"

"She is. I've got to check on the cow." She half-bounced down the steps, leaving Callister to wonder exactly what had gotten into her lately. He did not decode the blaring signs of adolescent love. She was already at the gate, when she turned and said it was all right to go in. "Mom's there too."

To his dismay, he found both women in the kitchen along with Cory. There was no privacy at all, but he greeted them warmly anyway.

"Why David," Caroline exclaimed. "How nice."

"Didn't mean to barge in."

"Not at all. Kate's just putting some final things together."

He watched Caroline make what appeared to be an evening meal of sandwiches while she talked, passing them out to her brood of grown children like a dealer dealing cards. Kate was by the sink filling up a canteen. She was dressed for riding, a heavy all-weather jacket with a hood hung over her chair.

"You going somewhere?" Callister asked.

"Chapel Ridge," Kate answered. "I'm going to cover for Charlie Benson until they can get a replacement. Hopefully, it'll take the rest of the fire season."

David looked at Caroline, but she made no comment other than to remind her daughter brightly that she could take what reading materials with her from the bookshelf in the living room.

"Why doesn't she just ask for the daily newspaper? Cory

suggested. “A mountain goat could take it up.”

Caroline glared him down. Kate giggled.

“Why don’t you sit down, David? Thanks for the suggestion, Mom.” She put aside the canteen and opened the top flap on a canvas knapsack set on the drain board.

"What are you taking?" Callister hadn’t heard about this development at the camp office.

"It's pretty well stocked already, but I'll take a few extras. I might do some more collecting while I'm up there, so I'll take materials for that." She took a polite bite of her sandwich. “How *have* you been, David?”

“Busy. I’ve been down to Skagit at the Darrington camp.” Callister wanted to say that he had missed seeing her, but he wasn’t about to say that to her here. “When are you leaving?”

“Tomorrow morning. I should be up there by eleven.”

She went on to talk about the assignment, stopping once to ask Cory to pass the pitcher of milk. She seemed very excited and self-assured. Her face glowed with a beauty that disturbed him and made him fall in love with her even more deeply. He listened to everything she said, but without really listening. Rather, he watched the movements of her hands and the way she tossed her head to make some point. He forgot there were others in the room and saw only her. He didn’t see Cory’s eyes narrow to the points of a cat’s eye.

After lunch, Kate helped her mother clear away the dishes and wash up. Callister hung around to talk. When they finished – to her dismay – he followed her out to the small moss-covered shed where she kept tackle for her horses. Nestled under thick cedars on the other side of the house, the building was an old structure made of thick cedar planks. She went in and lit a lantern for better lighting while she organized the last of her gear. She didn't intend to be rude, but she had work to do and didn't talk much. Callister for his part seemed distant, like a dry storm brewing on the far of the mountains.

"You really going to do this?" he finally asked.

Kate stopped. "Of course. It's no different from what I've

always done. I can man the tower just fine."

"You'll be alone."

Kate said nothing at first, but she felt a rising irritation as she thrust some of her gear into a saddlebag. David was doing it again. Trying to control when he had no right. No man did. She was a person, not some trinket. "It's not like I haven't done this before."

"It's not safe."

"David! Just stop it. I know when it's dangerous and when it's not. It's been drummed into me since I could walk."

"I didn't mean that."

"Then what do you mean?"

His dark brow scowled. "It's not safe."

"Because …"

"The camp at Kulshan is rough. It's no telling with some of the boys from back east."

"There's rough and there's rough. Honestly, David, don't you remember the first year the boys were here? Remember that kid who thought himself so tough that he threatened to trash out the store?"

"Yeah, I heard about that."

Kate laughed. "Right. My mother, daughter of polite Portland society, without a word, put a .45 on the counter and when that kid taunted her, saying she didn't know how to use it, my mom went right outside and knocked off a couple of cans. No one said anything after. The incident's legend."

"But this new crowd is different," Callister said.

"Which one? The new group of boys just inducted last week?"

"No. The one called Joisey Squad. Those kids from New Jersey."

Kate stopped what she was packing and just stared.

"That Spinelli boy, for example." He launched into what Kate thought sounded like something taken from a file – something most wouldn't know about. "The boy's from a tough neighborhood in Newark. His parents are immigrants, for gosh sake. Some of the boy's relatives have been in trouble with the law. A cousin's been in jail."

Kate paused to think about what he said, then remembered Park's confidence in the boy. "Has Mario been in trouble?"

"Well, no. His father's a greengrocer, though. Not the same class."

Kate sighed. "You could call my dad a greengrocer – when in season. Mario has come to our house twice. He has been both courteous and respectful. My father has permitted him to take Karin out at least once. Only a week ago, he went with us to the falls. He's a very nice young man."

"Aren't you concerned for Karin? Some of these people are easy with girls. After a time."

"Of course, I'm concerned, but I've been reassured that the boy's all right by his old straw boss."

"Hardesty?" Callister tensed, his voice becoming guarded. "What does he know?"

"Quite a lot, David. He knows about each boy in his squad. He assured me that the Spinelli boy had never been in trouble with the law. Really, David, this is too much. It has nothing to do with me. No boy from the camp is going up there to molest me. The only danger at Chapel Ridge is dying of boredom."

Callister tried to make a joke out of her comment. "Are you prepared for that?"

"Yes," she answered. "I've got enough books to last two months."

He put his hands up. "Peace," he said. "It's only that I care about you, Kate. Truly."

"I'm flattered that you care and it's very nice, David," she said returning to her task, "but please don't see it as some way to insert yourself back into my life. I don't appreciate that. I have never appreciated it. I thought I made it clear months ago." She took her gear off the worktable and laid it over a low stall door, then looked at him. "It's over."

"I can offer you a good life. Times are very hard."

"I'm confused. We were talking about manning a fire tower, not a proposal of marriage." Something like a tightening cinch caught in Kate's chest. "Let us be friends, David, but only that. If you have difficulty with it then perhaps you shouldn't come here unless on camp business."

Callister's face reddened. "That's it? The past two years is left at that?"

"God, David! You make it sound so awful. I've liked our friendship. It's been nice – but from the very beginning I clearly stated that it could be never nothing more than that. You're so pigheaded sometimes. You think only of yourself." She made to move away from him, but Callister took her by the arm and swung her towards him. His fingers pinched.

"You're the one who is pigheaded. Look at you. You're throwing yourself away in a backwater community that will never go anywhere or be anything or care one hoot about some woman who thinks she has to fulfill herself by running around in the woods like a man. It'll never wash." He pulled her to him. "I'm willing to leave this place, even in these hard times and take you wherever you want to go. Please say yes, Kate."

"No." Kate pulled back only to be gripped tighter. "Stop it!" She tried twisting her hand away. "You don't understand, do you?"

"No, I guess I don't." He let her go when she pushed on him. "It's Hardesty, isn't it? I heard that he might be seeing you. That true?"

Kate held her chin up, glad at last the truth was out. "Yes."

"You serious about him?"

"I don't believe that is any of your business."

"Well, he's an enrollee and my business is the camp as you so amply put it. I guess it is."

Kate wanted to spit daggers at him, but he had a point. She reined in her anger, but something wasn't right. David wasn't right. He looked at her in strange way, his eyes smoldering with an odd light as though it would be a pleasure to crush her. She began to be conscious that he was looking at her neck where the collar on her shirt was open. Yet she would not back down.

"So?"

Callister started like he had come out of some reverie, but his words were full of venom.

"Hardesty is camp business and the camp has a code. When an enrollee comes down here, he has an obligation to the community he's serving in and an obligation to the camp. Hell, Kate, you don't even know who he is. Do you know who he is? What exactly do you know about his background?"

"I know enough and whatever else you have to say about it, it really is none of your business."

"He tell you everything? There's more to a man, you know. While you're so busy trying to emulate one, you haven't a clue as what his true nature is. Especially that bunch up at Kulshan. You think all those boys joined up for money and a place to eat and sleep? You think they're all here to get religion from the woods?" He stepped closer, his voice rising. "If I did something, what better place to come and hide."

"Are you hiding?" Kate mocked.

Callister laughed harshly, but did not rise to her bait. "No, but I think Hardesty is."

Kate stared at him in disbelief. She could see that he was jealous, but this was too much. "Enough! I've had enough! I want you to go."

"As you wish. I only want to show that I do have your interest at heart. You ask him, Kate. If you're so fired hot to see him, you ask him why he doesn't use his real name and while you're at it, ask him where his checks go home. Ask him what trouble he was in back home. Taylor's interested too, by the way. It's just come to his attention."

He came away from the stall and brushed against her as he passed her. Instinctively, she shrank away. His words had been as harsh as if he had hit her. Near the door he turned back and whisper, "Stay out of the woods."

"Damn you! You leave him alone."

"Leave who alone? God, you're starting to stampede the slugs." Cory braced his arms in the door frame, flicking his eyes at his sister to determine what the difficulty was. "You two having a discussion or an argument?"

"Neither. David was just leaving."

"Good, because you have company on the porch, Kate, and

Mom wants you there pronto." He gave her a nod and the excuse she needed to get out. She slipped past him as quickly as she could without looking like she was bolting. Out on the path she turned around to listen to her brother as he talked to Callister.

"Stay," he said quietly. "I want to get something straight or rather, I want you to get something straight." Kate thought she heard David swear.

"I don't know what you two were discussing," Cory went on, "but it was clear to me that you were upsetting her – which is something you seem to be doing on a regular basis the last few weeks. Now, in the interest of civility and civilization, I propose you cool down for a bit and just leave her alone. Then when you see things clear, I ask you not to come around here anymore. You're not welcome here."

"Ha. Your mother might have a say in that." The words came out only part-way out. Cory must have grabbed him.

"You know, Callister," Cory said in a voice as tight as clothesline wire. "I've decided you're as shallow as a puddle after a soft summer rain. Stay away from here and from her. You got it?"

At that moment, Kate dashed quietly under the tree boughs to the porch where Hardesty was waiting. She turned slightly when she heard a loud, "Aw, you're all nuts." Callister was yanking his tie back into shape as he worked his way out to the rhododendron hedge in front of the house. Their eyes met for a moment, then his strayed to Hardesty up on the porch. He scowled and left.

Kate watched him stomp off to his car and once it was started tear down the road leaving a billowing trail of dust. She didn't know whether to laugh or cry. What was wrong with him?

She never finished the thought. Hardesty called out to her. But she had been shaken.

CHAPTER 19

There was a dance that night at the Grange down the road. Having commandeered Bladstad's car for the evening, Hardesty had planned to take Kate out. All thoughts of a pleasant farewell evening before she went up to the tower were, however, in apparent jeopardy when he found her coming out from under the cedars next to the house. Her face had been livid. She wouldn't explain though, not even when he caught a glance of Callister taking off, so he let it lie and hoped that she would take him up on the dance.

"I'd love to," she said with clenched teeth, then gave him a peck on his cheek. "Sorry. I'll tell you what happened later."

While she went up to change, she invited him into the house, putting him ultimately under the scrutiny of her mother. Hardesty knew that Kate had never said a word about them. He wondered what her mother was thinking right now about them as he stood in the doorway. Had she heard the shouting match in the stable as he had from the porch? Seen Callister's angry departure? And here was Kate going off to a dance.

Hardesty decided Mrs. Alford was a sensible woman when she invited him into the kitchen for coffee.

While she found him a cup, Hardesty stood at the back

screen door and watched the heavily forested hills and mountains across the river. He was content to study them without being rude to her and when he turned to take the brew, he commented on the peaks. "Some view."

"Didn't you see it the day you came for lunch?"

"No, ma'am. Not in this light. They look sharp in this light."

Caroline drew up beside him. "They are beautiful and every time I see them, no matter what time of day, I feel renewed."

In the long summer evening light, the snowy peaks high at the top were bathed in apricot hues and were as distinct as the jagged edges of a broken bottle.

"They can be cruel, but I love them just the same."

She turned and looked at him, like she was trying to divine his innermost secrets. Perhaps she did. Perhaps she saw that he loved her daughter.

"Do you have mountains where you live, Mr. Hardesty?"

"Yes, ma'am, but compared to the ones around here, you'd probably just call them 'hills'. They have sand, though. You can get lost in them just as easy. We've got poison ivy, copperheads, and rattlesnakes that can blend into dry leaves on the ground. We've got lots of creeks that are like rivers and deep gorges that open up like a surprise at your feet. It's different under foot, though. The duff's different. We've got tons of leaves on the ground and pines, not the stuff from the cedar, fir and alder. You can rattle around more easily, make a lot of noise."

He sipped the coffee politely, hoping he was making a good impression. He was wearing his dress uniform and had taken a shower before coming over.

"I went back east once to see my great aunt one summer in New Hampshire," Caroline said. "I remember the White Mountains. I rode the cog train there. Do you know about that?"

Hardesty said that he did.

"I remember the humidity and the thunder storms after the heat built up," she went on, "and, oh, the fireflies. I loved their little lights. Such gentle little things. They were as light as a sunbeam."

Hardesty grinned.

“Why, what are you thinking, Mr. Hardesty?”

“That you are like Kate.”

Cory came into the kitchen, nodding his head at Hardesty. "You got her to go?"

"Yup."

"Great. Let me get Mary and we'll all go. You don't mind?"

“No.”

Cory brought over the coffeepot and poured some more in his cup. He winked at his mother. "It's like high school, isn't it? Only you don't have to wait up."

"I reckon I don't, but I probably will anyway." She looked up at the ceiling.

“What is keeping Kate? Is that the bath water running?” She looked at Hardesty. “What time will it be over?"

"At two," Hardesty said. "I promise to get her back right after it closes. There's no need to wait up."

Caroline patted his arm. “Would you like some cake?”

Hardesty started to answer when Cory let out a loud whistle. Everyone turned to look at Kate, but Hardesty did not see Caroline watch him on the sly. All he could see was Kate and how she had dressed up in an outfit that made her seem light and airy. When her eyes connected with his, he felt weak in the knees. This thing called love was incomprehensible. He felt a shivering thrill even though there was a hint of danger.

They stayed at the dance until nearly one, and then headed back in Bladstad's car. About a mile before the Alford home, Hardesty stopped the car and asked if Cory wouldn't mind driving it back to the house.

“I'd like to walk with Kate for a bit. I'll have her back on time.”

“Sure you and Kate don't need a chaperone? You could walk in front of the car. The headlights will keep you from tripping over raccoons in the dark.”

“Mind if I decline?” Hardesty got out and helped Kate slip around the steering wheel. Cory took over and after giving the horn a toot, drove slowly off, leaving behind a trail of red tail lights that disappeared in the deep dark of the forest.

When they were gone, Hardesty removed his uniform jacket and put it around Kate's shoulders. "You're not cold, are you? You think this is nuts?"

"I think it's lovely. Besides, I'm about as overheated as you can get from dancing. My, the place was jammed."

"It was, wasn't it?" He surveyed the gloom around them. Overhead, he could sense where the giant treetops of firs opened to the sky. There was a nearly full moon somewhere and it managed to put some light on the trees as well as the road. Kate put her hand through his arm and they started forward.

The dance had been fun. A band of musicians borrowed from a larger settlement had come and there was quite a mix of people, including some enrollees with time off. Hardesty had Kate's dance card appropriately filled for him, but she had been a favorite and was often on the floor when he was not. He didn't mind. Rather, he watched her with some amusement. He felt confident about his feelings for the woman he loved, but more importantly, confident about her feelings for him.

She looked so lovely to him, dressed in a peach-melon chiffon affair that complimented her hair and throat so wonderfully, but it made him grin to see her strong arms peeking out under the soft caps of her sleeves. He knew her legs were strong too from all her hiking and riding and it excited him. Everything about her excited him. When they were dancing together, they laughed and played to the faster tunes. When he held her close on the slow songs, they were quiet and he never felt happier. This, even while he was wrestling with some vexing problems stemming from the stolen notebook. Would McGill blab and spread things around before he had a chance to talk to her? That's why he wanted to be alone with her. It could be weeks before he saw her again.

"Park, you want to stop at the river?" They had been walking for ten minutes and were coming closer to one of the first houses near her home. Hardesty said he'd like that and let her lead him towards a trail she knew. When they came out laughing and spilling at the river's edge, they found a spot on a rocky bank where she wouldn't soil her dress. It was fairly light in the open space of the riverbed and they could see across into the bushes on the other side.

"Comfortable?" he asked.

"Uh-uh." Kate leaned against him and giggled when he put his arms around her.

"Say, isn't that the smokehouse over there?"

In the shadows the ancient cedar structure stood black against charcoal further down the river. The prairie along the river's edge was like a knife blade in the strong moonlight.

"Good eyes," she laughed. "You want to go there?"

"Do you?"

Kate hesitated for only a moment. "I'll go, but my shoes."

"I'll carry you."

"You think that's wise?"

"Naw."

They found a place to ford and made their way down. Picking her up in his arms, Kate put her arms around his neck and they joked and sloshed their way across. On the other side, he put her down, but Kate stayed close. She took his hand now and led him up into the damp grass.

Inside the ancient structure, they found a lantern and a camp blanket. He quickly put together a fire to ward off the chill. "Having fun?" he asked.

"Oh, yes. Such a date! Did you see that deer? It made me jump when it leaped out on the road."

"You jump? I don't believe it."

Kate laughed. "Oh, there are still things in the woods that scare me. Dad says if you weren't scared, you were foolish. The mountains and the forests are always trying to outdo you. We watch the city folks come up and try out skiing at the new mountain lodge and we wonder it they will ever make it through the first hour. Winter's the hardest, but the summer is deceiving too. The passes aren't free of snow and ice until around July and the good weather up there is so short. Down here, it's the cold and the damp. People just don't realize how quickly they can become deathly cold from getting wet. How quickly a sunlit morning can turn to rain."

Hardesty said he did. "A tree can be pretty mean too."

Kate squeezed his arm. "But you beat it."

They visited for a spell, but she became quiet as they sat feeding the fire. For awhile they didn't talk.

Hardesty pushed an ember in with a stick. "Penny for your thoughts?"

Kate pulled her knees up. Hugging her arms, she became quiet again. He let her be at first, but he began to sense that she was worried about something.

"Kate? Are you cold?"

"No, I'm fine."

"You're awfully quiet," he pressed. "Didn't you enjoy the dance?"

"Yes. It was wonderful. I don't know. It's David. Just something he said earlier today that's bothered me."

"I wondered about that. I could see you were upset. He say anything about the fire tower job?"

"Yes, and he was shockingly angry about me going up there, but that wasn't the only thing that upset me. He's also terribly jealous."

Hardesty tinkered with the fire, looking back at her over his shoulder as he waited. He had a sense odd of foreboding. "It's understandable. No man likes to be crowded out by another."

"Is this what this is? One man crowding out the other? Over me?"

Hardesty straightened up. "Oh, no, Kate. I never meant that. He just has to let go, on your say-so. After all, you are the one in charge of your feelings and ultimately, your life and body." He put a cedar branch on, causing the fire to snap and crackle. "So, he's been saying things about me?"

"He wanted to make an issue with your name. Something he had just learned. Said you might be hiding something. Honestly, I never realized how very narrow-minded he is. He actually sees people grouped together in classes, with some having more importance than others. For someone who is working with the three C's, I'm surprised. He thinks most of the out-of-state boys are degenerates, with police records, and poor upbringing."

So Callister had been looking around. Had McGill said something? "I've been in several camps now, and I know some of the boys have been in trouble no matter where they came from, but I've also seen boys turned around."

"But why he has made such a big deal about your name? He said to ask you about it. Are you using your real name?"

"I'm not sure what he means by 'real' name."

"Do you have a middle name?"

"Sure, I use it all the time."

Kate looked at him funny, waiting for the answer.

"It's Parker," he finally admitted, curious about her interest and more importantly, Callister's. "My first name is John."

Kate was at first taken aback. "You don't look like a John. You look like a Park."

"Complete with campgrounds." Laughing, he threw another stick on the fire.

"Have you always gone by Park?"

"No, not until a few years ago when I went to college. There were too many John's. Someone started calling me Park and it stuck. I didn't mind. It's close to my mother's maiden name Parker. When I was away from home, it helped me to establish who I was as a person on my own."

"So you're not hiding."

Hardesty's face was serious when he looked at her. "Everyone hides some time in their lives. Everyone wants a change or new beginning. Some actually try for it. Things were bad at home. I was glad to leave."

Kate became silent, pulling his jacket tighter around her shoulders.

"As far as I know," he said in a soft voice, "I'm not in trouble with the police. I used my second name because I wanted to start over." He cocked his head at her, looking for any sign of rejection.

"David implied that you were in trouble."

"Callister seems to be unduly interested in me all of the sudden. He give a reason?"

"No, but he did say that Taylor had been informed and was

interested, especially about your government check."

"What the hell for?"

"I don't know. Are you in trouble?"

"No, Kate. The only person I'm in trouble with is myself. It has no bearing on camp life." He shifted his weight from his cross-legged position on the ground

"But something bad did happen?"

Hardesty sighed and moved slightly away from her. He wasn't sure how this subject got started or if it had to do with McGill. He was surprised about Callister. He had never felt any animosity from him before. What he did know was that he had to answer her. To keep things straight between them.

"Park, who are Paul and Marie?"

"Where'd you hear that?"

"The night of the storm. Who are they? Is that the trouble?"

After a long silence, he said, "Yes."

Kate sucked her breath in, leaving Hardesty wondering where he should start and how much he should tell. He wasn't ready to tell her everything. Maybe never would because it was sordid and would surely offend her. He finally found his voice.

"You want to know?"

"Yes. I want to know."

Hardesty sighed. "All right, Kate, but it's not something I'm proud of." He dug the heel of a boot into the dirt floor, then began.

"Paul's my brother, barely a year older than I am and we were real close. Despite that, because I was the youngest, my life was generally arranged by my brothers. Sometimes Paul and I had some real good spats, but we always made up and always helped each other out." He paused. "I did particularly well in my schooling. Good enough to get a scholarship in science at the University of Pittsburgh. Paul was taking a stab at it too, trying to find work so he could go to business school, but with the Depression ..."

He picked up a stick and tapped the dirt floor with it. "Anyway, the only place he could get work was at a road house. He made sure no one knew, especially our mother, but I found out during Thanksgiving vacation. Paul had been working at Lacey's, a speakeasy during Prohibition and now a dance hall of pretty low repute. I kept that information to myself for a couple of weeks, but then I found out that some person was taking advantage of Paul. I thought I could remedy that, but my tactics backfired.

"I told you she was my girl."

"And I said she was using you."

"We had a terrible argument. The accusations just flew. Paul ended up beating me up."

"Are you satisfied? Got your jollies?"

"He became despondent. One night, someone showed up at the house to see Paul."

"I am leaving, Paul. I am very sorry for what has happened. I think I go home now."

"They spoke on the porch for some time, then he came inside. We argued again and he hit me good. Knocked me down. They got into his car and headed out in the snow to the train station. He had been acting wild earlier, drinking. A mile down the road, the car crashed and Paul - Paul was nearly burned alive. His passenger was killed, but he survived in the worst way for weeks, clinging to life in horrific pain."

"Park! How awful!" Kate put her hands over her mouth.

Hardesty cleared his throat. His voice had become thick.

Kate put a hand on his shoulder. "What happened? Did he die?"

"No, he didn't die. Just hung on. My father came back and accused me of meddling in Paul's affairs. I was called a liar and cheat and was asked not to see Paul again at the hospital."

"Don't you ever come back."

"In the end, I was held responsible for the crash. Funny, I didn't blame them. Secretly, I felt I was responsible too, but not in the way they thought. I'm afraid I acted rather badly on his part. It wouldn't surprise me if I learned he was trying to kill himself the night he went into the ditch."

Hardesty jostled the coals around. They looked hellishly red in the huge, dark space and they angrily shot up little sparks into the night.

"I was kicked out of the house by my father who in this instance had no business being there, but there was some stirring up going on at Lacey's and he insisted I should be long gone. There was too much grieving over Paul. It was not my finest hour."

"What happened to your brother?"

"He's alive, but his burns - he got pretty heavily burned on the right side of his face. His fingers and toes were burned on that side too. My aunt says his hand is bad."

"You haven't been back to see him?" Kate stared at him in disbelief.

"I haven't been back and I don't write. Only my check. It goes to my mother through my aunt near Pittsburgh. They haven't a clue where I am. When I left, I ran until I stopped out here."

They stayed quiet for what seemed to be long time. Finally, he shifted his position. "I warned you that my life was rough. Not like yours or your folks. It turned ugly when my father abandoned my mother when she became ill. After Paul's accident, it only became worse."

"You make it sound so awful."

"It was awful. It shouldn't happen to a family. My mother didn't deserve it. My grandparents didn't deserve it. No one deserved it." Hardesty looked away from her. "I betrayed my brother. While I can argue that my intentions were to help him, what I really did in the end was to hurt him. It was the same old tension between us."

Hardesty rubbed his forehead. He was getting a headache. Kate stood up and moved away from him, an action that hurt him almost physically.

"Kate," he whispered.

"I'm sorry," she said. "I can see that this is very hard, but I must ask. Who was in the car with your brother?"

"A woman. Her name doesn't matter."

"Was it Marie?"

He paused. "Yes."

"Who was she? What was she to you?"

Hardesty hung his head. "Nothing. Just some woman at a roadhouse. My brother was in love with her, but I discovered she was a fraud. She was using him to cover up some bootleg activities."

"What did you do?"

"Prove to him that she was trouble."

Kate's face at first was puzzled, but it filled with sadness.

She's guessing what it means, he thought. When she hugged her arms and moved towards the opening to the smokehouse, something close to grief engulfed him. At the dark edges of the fire, she threw off his jacket.

"Kate. Where are you going?"

"Home."

"For God's sake, let me take you back."

"I can manage."

"I know you can, but isn't this what Callister wanted? To break us apart? Because he's doing it. I'm sorry I offended you. There isn't a day I don't feel remorse for what happened to Paul, but it happened and I have to go on and live with it. It reflects nothing on you." He watched her take off her shoes and more by instinct than by sight make her way out. "You'll ruin your dress."

"I'll survive..."

"I can see that," he said wryly, "but what about the rest of the family? I'll get the entire Alford household in an uproar if I don't get you back on time and in one piece. One family in an uproar is enough."

"Is that what you are concerned about? Public reaction?"

"I'm concerned about you. Don't go, Kate. Village tongues may wag and you'd lose your chance to man the tower. You've taken a risk once before."

"Before?"

Hardesty smiled softly. "All that talk after rescuing me during the storm around Frazier. Behind that teasing some nosed around a little further at the edge of respectability. What folks don't know is how close they were and how you far you went in saving my life."

Kate stiffened as her cheeks reddened in the light of the dying fire.

He straightened up and came closer to her.

"I remember what you did for me, Kate," he said softly. "Just a few fragments, but enough to realize later that was what saved my life. You made me warm."

“Oh.” Kate straightened up, trying to act dignified.

"Kate. I'd never tell. It took moral courage over correct behavior to do what you did and for that I'm deeply moved and eternally grateful. No one has ever done anything like that for me, Kate. Ever." He choked off and kicked his boot into the dirt floor. "Look, you're upset and I understand. We can talk about it or we can say goodbye. Just let me get you back before there's more excitement than either one of us knows what to do with. I don't want you to lose that chance with Bladstad."

“Did you sleep with that woman?”

“Yes. I slept with her.”

Kate stood at the gaping maw of a door with one shoe in each hand and bit her lip. Her features seemed washed out by the dying firelight, so he could not tell where her tanned face and auburn hair separated, but he could see her eyes as they weighed his answer.

"Park, who is Holly again? How does she fit in all this?"

"Why do you ask?"

"Because you said her name and Marie's almost in the same breath."

"My friend's daughter."

"Holly...."

"Holly Garrison."

"Was she at your last camp?"

"Yes. Her father was - her father is Floyd Garrison."

"The Floyd Garrison?"

"Yes. Kate."

"Please, I have to think this through."

"I know, but listen. It's the only chance I'll have to explain to you. Garrison saved my life," Hardesty said under his breath. "He turned me around when I was running as far as I could go.

He saved my life, made me think I was worthy again, but until I met you, I have felt so damned. I need you, Kate. More than anything else on earth."

"Hmm." She hugged her arms. "Need is a strong thing. What do you want, Park?"

"I want my brother to forgive me and I want to have you. I want to have you for my friend, my wife, to be with me when I wake up in the morning, to walk in the woods with me -- looking for those bears."

She smiled faintly, the corners of her mouth lifting up.

"Want is a strong thing too," Kate said quietly, "but some things you will have to make happen. Some day you will have to face your brother."

"I know, but he may never want to speak to me again. And I wouldn't blame him."

"But you can try. You can write him a letter." She cleared her throat. "But first, you can walk me back," she said, "but I'm not promising you anything."

He had her back at the house just slightly after two. They had walked back on the road under the canopy of giant Douglas fir and cedar, but neither said anything. When they reached the house, Kate turned and said goodbye to him at the hedge of rhododendrons. On the second floor of the house, a lamp burned near the window, and then suddenly went out.

"Someone's light just went off." He pointed to a window on the left.

"Why that's Karin. I wonder if she's all right."

"I better scram. The whole Alford family's waking up. Good night, Kate. Despite everything, it was a fine night."

"Yes, yes it was," Kate said.

"If there is anything more I can say…"

"I think we'll leave it at this." Briskly, she handed his jacket back to him. "Goodnight, Park."

She made no mention of seeing each other soon or of her trip later that day. No invitation to come in. Hardesty felt heartsick. His shoulders drooping, he accepted her final words with the nodding of his head. Crestfallen, he backed off, the chilly night of the forest swallowing her up as he walked to the car. There was only the sound of his shoes crunching on the gravel near the hedge. He got into the car and tried to start it, but it failed. He tried again and this time it was successful. He looked through the windshield. He could barely make her out in the dark morning air when he started to pull away.

"Park!" he heard her cry. "Park!" She made it to the passenger's side just as he was moving out and banged on the window. He stopped the Model A abruptly. She tore open the door and climbed in. "Darn you, Park Hardesty! Don't you dare listen to me. Don't you dare go. I couldn't bear it."

Hardesty managed to get the car turned off and the brake on before they fell into each other's arms.

He crushed his lips on hers as she curled her pliant body against his on the seat and kissed him hard in return. It became a contest of wills, as their passion rose because she was a strong as he was. Against the flannel back of the seat, they necked and entwined in the tight space until at last they lay quiet in each other's arms.

“Forgiven?” Hardesty said as he stroked her hair.

“Forgiven.”

“Thank God.” He nuzzled her face. "I'm going to have to smuggle you inside," he eventually said as he sat up. "Wasn't that a light downstairs too?"

"I think so, but I'll manage, though. Don't you have to get back to camp?" She sat up next to him and smoothed her clothes back in order.

"I've got a special leave for tonight. Duty calls at four. I'll just stay up."

"Kitchen again?"

"One last time. Bull cook on Monday."

Kate smiled. “Oh my gosh. Lights.”

They hit the seat and froze until a truck passed, making its way down the road through the forest. It was the milk truck from Frazier on its way south for its morning run to a dairy. Its lights sliced the top of the interior of the car, then slid down off the hood before it disappeared into the dark. When they felt safe, they sat up hurriedly, laughing so hard that they nearly collapsed against the seat again.

"Why don't we elope?" he suggested as he twisted his body around the steering wheel.

"And get you drummed out? Just a little longer, Park. We need to plan and save."

"On five dollars a month, we should come out ahead in about thirty years. I'll have to give up sodas." He grinned at her. "All right, Beauty. I'm going to have to start a fire, just to get your attention up there."

"You could call."

"Sure and have the entire camp listen in. Damn. I nearly forgot." He reached up to his visor and pulled a little package of folded tissue from out of a pocket there. "This is for you while you're up at the tower. I wanted to engrave a fire bucket, but they don't do that kind of work in Frazier, so I guess you'll have to settle for this." He placed it in her hands. Inside, when she opened it, was a little pewter bear, small enough to wear on a bracelet or around the neck.

"Thought you might need your totem. Bladstad says it can get lonely, but when you're not on the phone to headquarters, you can commune with the bears." He groped for a flashlight on the dashboard and shined it on her hands.

"Oh, Park, it's lovely. Truly."

"It's a poor excuse for an engagement ring. I didn't win the prize in the candy box, but hopefully this will do."

"It does." She put a finger on his lips and traced an edge of his mouth. "I'm crazy about bears. Ever since that first day. My hero."

Hardesty snorted. "Realistically, you probably would have come out fine, although Elsa would have been hard pressed to come down out of her tree. I didn't know whom I was dealing with at the time. There's no one quite like you, Kate Hardesty." He had slipped when he said her name, but she must have liked it because she smiled. She turned his wrist and tried to read the numbers on his watch's dial.

"Oh, my gosh. I think it says nearly three. I better go. I'll be all right." She straightened her hair and took the jacket he offered to make her look more presentable. Hardesty got out and came around to open her door. They embraced again at the gate before he walked her to the porch. Inside, a light burned in the kitchen like a beacon in a black hole.

"Think it's your mom? I'll speak to her if you like."

"I can manage." She took his hand and for a moment wove her fingers through his as her mind stayed distant on some thought.

"Park. I'm sorry for that awful scene at the river."

“I'm the one who's sorry for subjecting you to my uneven past.”

Kate silenced him with a hand on his lips. "Then we're both sorry. I can't say I fully understand, but I know you have been making amends all along. It must have been very hard to come here, not really knowing exactly where you stood back home, but it must have suited you. You have won many friends here: Taylor, Bladstad, Spenser, even sour Williams up at the spike camp. Your name counts for something."

“My name…”

Kate smiled. She rubbed his thumb with a finger. "I was thinking though. If you ever need to talk to someone, talk to my father. He's a wonderful man. Before he met my mother, he was a bindle stiff, a logger, and backwoodsman. I'm not supposed to know, but he's seen the rough side of life too and is not immune to listening to others talk. If you feel you need an ally, he'd be a good one to talk to. Especially if David makes trouble for you. My father has known Taylor personally for years."

“Thanks. I've been planning to anyway. I think it's about time he got to know my intentions."

“And Paul?”

“I promise I'll write to him.”

Hardesty made it back to camp by three-thirty and for appearance's sake, laid down on his bunk with his uniform on. He had less than thirty minutes before he would have to go to the kitchen and begin putting the Saturday breakfast together.

Coming into the cool barracks, all inhabitants appeared to be sleeping heavily. From a far dark corner, a lone sleeper broke wind and turning, went back to snoring. Taking off his shoes, Hardesty started to lay down when he noticed that Mario appeared to have rolled over to the edge of the bunk. Further scrutiny in the dark revealed, however, that the covers had been arranged to look like someone was sleeping in it. Mario was not there. Damn. On his bed, Hardesty's tired brain mulled this over.

Normally, he would have left it as a prank, but when he remembered that Karin's light had gone off only a short time before, he wondered if he should be worried about Mario's absence. As if to confirm his suspicions, the door to the barracks opened stealthily as someone attempted to enter quietly into the room without detection. However, just when things were going well, the third board in from the door creaked.

"That you, Spinelli sneaking in?" Hardesty whispered sharply into the dark. "If it is, you have some explaining to do."

For a pregnant moment, there was silence as someone searched frantically for a good answer then finally came forward and said, "Oh, hell." It was Mario all right.

"What are you doing back so late?"

"Maybe it's the other way around. I'm early and you're late."

"I had leave. You're AWOL. Wouldn't have anything to do with a certain Miss Karin Alford, would it? She was up late I noticed at her house."

Mario coughed quietly and crept over to the bunk. He didn't answer until he had climbed up to the top of the bunk and the bedsprings stopped shaking like metallic jello. "It wasn't nothing."

"Nothing at three in the morning in the middle of a national forest is not the same as Newark, New Jersey. Different community standards."

"You ain't - aren't - hurting." Mario was always working on his speech.

"I'm a big boy. You're a kid." Hardesty shook his head.

"We didn't do nothing," Mario whispered loudly. "Karin, she's a nice girl. We just talked, sort of. I wouldn't do nothi -

anything--to hurt her."

"I know you wouldn't, but you'll both get in all sorts of trouble you didn't know existed."

"You telling, Park?"

"No, but I hope you're more discreet and careful. Like meet her at her dad's place in the afternoon. You're too reckless. So far, the camp's maintained a pretty good record. Sneaking out of the camp doesn't enhance its image. If Taylor got wind of it, it'd be the cat-o'-nine-tails for sure and an assignment from hell – like moving all the outhouses twelve feet in every camp from here to Big Fir and back. That'll take about six months with time off for good behavior. You'll stink so much, all the lavender soap and rose water in the world couldn't bring Miss Alford back to you."

Mario laughed softly. "Thanks, Park. You're the best friend I ever had." He punched his pillow and the bed whined as he settled into his camp blankets.

"Sure. Just don't let me catch you slipping up again. You'll wish Taylor caught you first."

"I promise." There was additional wheezing from the springs as he settled down, then a final twang from an errant wire. Hardesty listened drowsily for more, then fought the sandman off for the next twenty minutes before he left for kitchen duties. For the first time in weeks, there were no ghosts stirring over by the stovepipe. Spinelli was sleeping like a baby when he left, no doubt dreaming of babes in the woods.

CHAPTER 20

Kate made the long trek up to Chapel Ridge, arriving at the fire tower around one in the afternoon with Betty Olsen and Cory in tow. The two young women had planned this from the beginning, but Cory had come along at the last minute in order to report back for posterity how things were going. News had leaked out about Kate's assignment, so that by the time of departure from Alford's, a number of friends had gathered to see her off. The idea was more than novel and somewhat amusing, but the fire season had been underway for some weeks and flying squads from Kulshan had done their share of spelling the fire lines in districts east of the Cascades. With Charlie Benson gone, word was that Bladstad had debated if he should send some CC's up to the tower until a replacement could be found, then decided that Kate would do. She knew the backcountry intimately. Bladstad might get hell from headquarters, but for now, his mind was made up. She would man the tower.

"My, how times have changed," one of the gentleman well wishers said as they gathered near Alford's. "To think it was only two few short summers ago they put that fire tower up there. I remember when all we had up at Chapel Ridge was a stump with the dial on it and a tent in the woods down below to run to when it rained. Now Kate's going up."

"That's the CC's for sure," another answered. "Like the way they put in fire roads and three permanent fire towers. Fires are way down."

"She'll do a good job. That little gal knows what she's doing."

Bob Alford listened to the talk from the top stair of his store while he waited to see Kate off. He was very proud of her. To take part in fire watching. Many parts of the state were over-logged, with snags and debris just waiting for lightning to strike. In 1910, a fire nearly burned out the whole Northwest clear to Montana. His daughter was going to do her part, her one dream.

But what I have created?

Here she was a beauty to match her mother and Portland society, off on a horse for several weeks to stay in a 10 foot by 10 foot building miles back from the edge of civilization. Working his way down through the light crowd around her, he came up to give her some final words and was struck by her poise and confidence as she sat atop Elsa. She had always been unconventional, tagging along beside him as a little girl with all sorts of stories in her head, yet as focused on a task as any boy and better than most.

She had always wanted to be in the Forest Service, hanging on to the anecdotes the men would tell around the stove in the general store and begging to go on days he packed horses for them. Alford had taken her along and taught her what to do. But no Forest Service for her. He wondered if that would change. There was disturbing news in the papers about matters on the continent and Hitler's Germany. Time would only tell if there was unfinished business from the Great War. Women had worked in factories then. Why not in the forest now?

Alford looked at his daughter and felt pride in her. She was dressed in her usual riding togs with a felt crusher hat. She smiled when she saw him and he saw something different. She looked content.

"Are you all set, *lille gjente*?"

"*Ja*, Papa," she teased back. "You haven't called me that in years." She leaned over and a little necklace slipped out from her throat. It had a little silver bear on it. He looked at it curiously while she visited with him, then watched her tuck it back in when Cory finally arrived on his horse with Betty. Alford nodded to his son, then turned back to Kate.

"Give us a jingle when you get up. At least let Bladstad know."

"I will. Cory can fill in all the details."

"Kiss?" Alford asked and was rewarded with a hug. The little bear swung out.

"What's this?" he asked.

"It's from Parker Hardesty." She sat back up, her eyes teasing him as she stuffed it in again and took Elsa's reins. "He might be coming by to see you."

Before Alford had any chance to even say, "Oh?" she was gently urging the mare and the packhorse she was leading forward.

The fire tower at Chapel Ridge was typical for its size. Though built close to the ground, it had a commanding view of the country in all directions. The area around it was wide-open with meadows for the horses to graze on. Now that it was August, the flowers were in full force, creating a kaleidoscope of dizzying colors as the land plunged away from the fire tower to the woods. Below it, the forests stretched out broken from time to time by exposed canyons and ridges as they rose towards the higher mountains. Here and there creeks worked their way through, their stony sides ash-white in the midday sun.

Cory got off and surveyed the tower itself. Built of fir, its corners were anchored down with ground wires from the shake roof into the earth itself. A telephone line made of insulation wire came away from a wall like a long clothesline, following the curve of the hill down into the trees. Near them were a wood shed and an outhouse.

Betty and Kate got down and began to unload the horses while Cory unlocked the fire tower door and went inside to make a quick inspection. When he came out, he went around to the windows and raised up the wooden shutters that served as window awnings. Each side of the building had paned windows that stood at waist high, but only one had allowed enough space for a door to be put in and a place for a bunk. It was quite austere, but the view was breathtaking.

"Charlie probably left some wood for the stove, but you'll have to hustle more for yourself. Kerosene lamps looked low too. Should check the storage room in the wood shed. I recall Charlie stored his flammables there." He finished opening the last shutter then helped them organize the pack bags.

"What's for dinner?"

"Mom sent up fried chicken and other goodies. There's even lemonade," Kate said. "I want to check the instruments, call down to the camp, then lunch." She walked to the stairs and let her eyes sweep over her new domain before they settled on Cory. "What?" she asked.

"Nothing," Cory said quickly. "Nothing I can't wait to tell half of Frazier. You look like you swallowed a bird and enjoyed the whole gulp going down." He beamed at her. "You did it, kiddo and I'm proud as punch. Now if Bladstad can get away with it."

"If you're not too proud, why don't you help me with this pack?" Betty grunted as she pulled a saddlebag off the extra horse. "What did you put in this Kate, an anvil?"

"Canned goods. Charlie didn't get it all up the first time because of the snow."

To an outsider, it would have been hard to believe that there had been snow just a few weeks ago, even with the lack of rain, but it was true. In early July, an ice pick would still have been required to get past some of the trail. Kate helped Betty with the gear and together they went into the lookout tower. Cory followed them in.

It smelt musty inside with an ancient waft of cigarette smoke imbedded in the camp blanket draped over the iron bedstead. Kate went to a window and slid it open, letting in the cool, mountain-sweet air of the afternoon. She inspected the little cook stove with an oven big enough to put in some biscuits. On the side of the stove, someone had laid a fire in the fire pit. Mountain courtesy. She closed it up and began to unpack the lunch their mother had put up for them.

The afternoon sun had worked itself up to a good burn and even up here it felt hot. There were little white clouds encamped around one of the peaks nearest them, but the rest of the mountains were clear. As they sat lunching at a tiny table looking east, Cory remarked that for local color, it was sure hard to beat.

"Too bad that movie company awhile back was a pack of whiners. They had to choose some other locale lower down because the star couldn't stand being away from his trailer more than five minutes. Might have mussed his hair. Maybe his knee-high boots would've gotten scraped too. Next time I see a newsreel about the making of adventure movies," Cory said, "I'm going to ask who did the adventuring for them." He chomped his chicken hungrily before going on. "Dad ever say how much he got from all that? Three dollars. Three dollars a day. And him taking all the chances."

They spent the rest of the afternoon checking out the premises. After Kate got on the radio and called headquarters they went en masse down into the trees where the horses were grazing in the shade. About a quarter mile down a trail, there was one of the peculiarities of nature: a hot spring set up in the mountains. Nestled near a little creek that wended its way through an open glade, it had been encased by the Forest Service long ago with sides and a platform made of fir planks so bathers could sit on the side and swing their legs if they wanted. On the count of three, the three of them stripped out of their shirts and pants to swimming attire underneath, throwing off their boots in advance. Cory was the first one in, followed by Betty, then Kate. It was hot and smelled suspicious, but the thick water felt wonderful on their dusty, stiff bodies. It had been some ride coming up.

Kate sat at the edge and put her hair up. She opened up a bar of soap and tossed it to her brother, then slid in next to Betty. The two women laughed as Cory began vigorously rubbing his head with the soap. "Fleas," he reported and splashed at them to get the imaginary buggers off.

"Go on," Betty said and trudged to the other side of the walled-in spring. The three friends carried on for more than twenty minutes, then finally settled down to a lively discussion about the approach of summer's end and the start up of school in Frazier.

"I'm going back, of course," Betty said, "and I'm looking forward to it, but lately - oh, dash it all, I'd like a family."

"I thought Carl was baby enough," Cory said.

"He's been weaned. I've trained him to pick up his dirty clothes too. He puts them in the basket now."

Cory laughed. "That's what you get for playing high school basketball." Carl had been on the nine-man basketball team in high school. The Olsen and Turner families were the original homesteaders still on the land. The Alfords were relative newcomers, homesteading since 1907. The Olsen, Alford and Turner kids were fast friends.

"Of course, Carl's folks came direct from Norway," Betty said. "I don't think his grandfather ever spoke any more English than was required to wrangle over prices at the general store down in the valley. In those days, that was all they had." She smiled, her dimples working overtime again and making Cory wish he had been the one to ask her out to that high school dance first long ago.

"Carl still working?"

"He has that job at the mill, but they're talking like they'll have to shut it down again. We'll just get by while we wait, but Carl says it'll take a war to get it to reopen again."

They climbed out and sat on the edge of the spring to dry off. A couple of old stumps were close by with huckleberries growing out of the crew cut-like tops. In the old days, the trees were cut high on springboards and even after all the years they still bore the rounded tops made by crosscut saws and springboard notches in the side. The first harvest had been made about 1905-6. The fires had come not too far after, so the trees around the spring were all new growth.

The friends spent a quiet evening watching the sun fall into the west and go down. The long twilight that followed was beautiful. Soon Kate was setting the fire and getting the lanterns ready.

At nine thirty, Cory went outside to return to the tent he had pitched down near the horses. Kate came with him.

"You never said anything about Callister," Cory said as they marched down the grassy slope.

"I didn't want to."

Cory stopped. "Well, I did. I told him to lay off."

"Cory!"

"Well, you're my sister and he treats you like horsesh-manure.

Kate snorted, but didn't say anything more. What could she say? In reality, she was glad Cory had said something. David had been acting so odd. Yet that was a feeling, not a fact other than the way he had grabbed her by her arm.

They started walking again. A slight breeze had come up with the balmy, cool freshness of night. It was still light enough to see things clearly down to the woods and the high peaks all around that were receding into purple, jagged teeth. "How's Park?"

"He's fine."

"Enjoy your walk?"

"It was fine. Why don't you desist?" She grinned and looked away, trying to suppress a laugh.

"Oh, I'm just warming up as brother protector. I think he's sweet on you. In fact, I know he is. Point is, what about you?"

"Is this a quiz?"

"This is a query. The test comes later. Couldn't help but notice how he looked at you last night. A sure goner."

"I never thought of him that way. Am I that dangerous?"

"Most of Camp Kulshan would say so. 'Course on a given day the air out there is so rarefied anything female with legs." Kate pounded his arm at that. "What I'm aiming at, is that I hope he's treating you right and that you're doing the same. I like him. Always have."

Kate's mouth curled into a smile. "I'm glad. That means a lot to me because I like him a lot too." She turned to her brother in the dying twilight. "I love him, Cory. He's asked me to marry him."

Cory stopped. "No kidding. I'm happy for you, Kate. Hardesty's a good guy. When would you do this?"

"Not until after next year. His tour will be up then. He wants to keep sending money to his mother as long as he can. Feels the family needs it."

"That okay with you?"

"Yes. We've been making plans about what we'll do when he gets out."

Cory stopped at the halfway point to the horses. "You say anything to Mom or Dad yet?" "No. Everything had happened so fast with coming up here, but Park's planning on seeing Dad." She hesitated for a little bit. "Do you think Mom and Dad will accept him?"

"I don't see why not. He's not like the usual outside men in the CCC's. He fits in here. Dad likes him already. Told me so when Hardesty was mending at my place."

Kate hugged her arms. "I know Mom likes David. I think she has always had hopes for him. I think she will be disappointed." She started to say something about David's behavior in the stable, then let it go.

"I think she will be happy for you." Cory squeezed her around the waist. "Heck, she may be so elated that you're finally going to get married that she'll give away door prizes to celebrate."

"Some help you are," Kate snorted.

"Never mind me, Katie. Hardesty's smart and has some college education. That will sit well with her."

Kate shook her head in exasperation, but she was happy. Park had an ally with her brother. She wondered if he needed more than that. What would her parents think if they knew the nature of his family trouble?

Cory kissed his sister on her forehead. "Look, I better go. I'm going to make an early start in the morning. Got to help Dad with some Seattle types on Monday." He gave her a hug and waving, took off down to his tent.

The two young women went to bed not long after, Betty

putting her sleeping bag on an extra mattress on the floor. They didn't sleep, though. It had been several weeks since they had really visited. Being married, Betty wasted no time getting down to the main point of the discussion: Park Hardesty.

Kate told her about the dance and what had happened before with Callister. "He said awful, spiteful things about Park. Unfortunately, some of it's true, but not in the way he put it."

"What was it?" Betty asked. Kate told her about Park's brother and the accident. "He was seriously hurt."

"But not Park."

"Oh, he's hurt. But in here." Kate laid a fist on her heart. "David implied that he was in trouble, but Park says it's more the matter of being in trouble with himself. He really regrets what happened."

"I'm surprised that David is so vindictive. There must be more to it than that."

"Park says there isn't, but it wasn't his finest hour."

"What do you think will happen?"

Kate shrugged. "I don't know. I don't think there's anything to worry about. Park can take care of any problem."

Betty wasn't convinced. "It wasn't over some woman, was it? Not one of his ladies in his delirium the night of the storm?"

Kate shrugged. She didn't want to talk about it anymore, but Betty was the more practical of the two. "So it was. Maybe it is serious if someone got hurt. David might know some rule about enrollee conduct."

"Oh, I wish you'd stop. I wish everyone would stop speculating." Kate sat up in her bedroll. "All that I care about is that Park loves me and respects me and I love him."

"Maybe he's in trouble back east over this. The police."

"He says he's not, but -" Kate sighed. "He's been using his middle name since he first signed up in Oregon."

Betty sat up like a mousetrap going off. "You're kidding."

"Do you think that's odd?"

"I should think so. But then again, who knows about these outside men, these foreigners. Maybe they do that all the time when they signed up for relief work. No one would really check.

Maybe that's what David is worried about."

"Only thing David Callister is worried about is his standing with me, which is over, over, OVER! Do you know that he had the gall to tell me that I shouldn't come up here? That I was some woman running around in the woods acting like a man? God! If I were a man, I would have floored him." Kate was so livid she trembled on her bed. Betty burst out laughing.

"What's so funny?"

"You've finally come to your senses and told off David."

"Well, it's more than tell off. He tried to stop me. Physically grabbed me."

"No."

"He did. I'm glad he's gone."

"It still doesn't change the mystery with Park, though. Lord, Katie. What have you gotten yourself into?"

"A lifetime of happiness, I hope. I love him, Betts. He's asked me to marry him."

"Kate. Really?"

"Yes."

Betty chewed her lip in the dark and rustled around in her sleeping bag. Kate could barely see the gray outline of her pajamas in the gloom as she drew her knees up to her chest, but couldn't wait for her friend to speak. "Well?"

"I think it's fine. I'm really happy for you. Just from talking to him, I think he's a decent, honest man. Not given to airs like someone else we know. All this other stuff - just go slow."

"Why?"

"Because you just don't know."

"Did you and Carl know?"

"Honey, we've known each other since we could lick ice cream cones together."

But when did your friendship turn to love? You had nine guys in your graduating class. Weren't there only eighteen of you altogether? The field was definitely limited. You must have been more like siblings than anything else. How did you know?

"Like you, probably," Betty confessed. "The goose bumps got noticeably pricklier when he walked by. Before I even knew."

"Can I ask you something real personal?" Kate asked.

"It depends." Betty's voice sounded bemused.

"Did you ever go all the way before you got married?"

Betty sighed lightly. "Kate, it's just like you to come out and be all direct. You dear girl. You're the most beautiful, strongest person I've ever known, yet you're such an innocent." She laughed. "We just sort of grew into each other. One day we were teasing on the porch of your dad's store, the next we didn't know what had hit us. I had always liked him, but suddenly there it was. I noticed everything about him for the first time. It was like lichen growing on my mind. The thought of him accumulated everywhere. The next thing we knew, we were talking about getting married." Betty's dimples must have deepened with the idea. Her smile was so wide that Kate could sense it in the dark. "It happened natural-like. A loving expression of how we'd be together married. Of course, being a biology teacher puts you in a certain frame of mind, but there are ways to protect yourself. Which you know. And Carl provided. The rest we didn't need any road map for. We made it up along the way." Betty giggled under her breath. "We still do."

Kate shifted on the bed. Betty finished her thoughts for her. "Park's a handsome man. He looks nice from the back."

Kate laughed. They had had conversations like this before, only this time this was someone she really cared about.

"Did he ever ask about your butterfly collection?" Betty asked.

"Betts. Okay. We came close once, but he drew away. Like he was afraid of something."

"Sensible man. He oughta be. If he does anything to hurt you, I'll kill him myself and pickle him along with my other specimens of slug life. So it's up to you. What are you going to do?"

"I'm going to marry Park Hardesty. As soon as he can talk to Dad, we'll set a date."

Betty felt it was the sensible thing to do, but as it turned out, Hardesty wasn't able to get around to the subject for a while.

CHAPTER 21

Joisey Squad left for the wilds again on Monday, taking along Hardesty as bull cook. Being bull cook had its place in a squad. When the boys were out and away from an area where the lunch truck couldn't get out, the bull cook's job was to furnish the fixings and put up meals for lunch. Then, more often than not, for the remainder of the afternoon, the bull cook could rejoin the squad and finish the rest of the day's work with them. Doc thought that Hardesty was up to that point where he could participate again in moderate work, so gave his approval to go out. Hardesty was elated. He had been chafing at the strap for so long that he was beginning to forget what it looked like out in the trees. For weeks, they had looked like some tall skirting around the main camp, blocking his way back to the mountains. He wanted to get in them again. When he left with the camp truck to take them out to their job site, he took along a fishing pole. Lunch, he was told, was in those streams.

The new assignment was repairing some trail damage from the storm weeks ago. In addition to downed trees and limbs, there was also a small slide across the trail. It had been closed for the length of time that Hardesty had been recuperating and was the last to be fixed. They took the truck out to a trailhead then hiked in two miles to the job site. While the boys organized the tools to do the job with the forester assistant, Hardesty looked around for a place to set up a cook hole. When he had that determined, he bid them farewell and went off to inspect the creek. He had about two and half hours to make a dent in the fish population or else.

He set up his gear on the low bank and prepared for battle. As luck would have it, though, he got his first strike within minutes of setting up. Just as Bladstad had foretold, this creek was inhabited with fish so sociable that they were just lining up to jump into the pan. About an hour and a half later, he returned with enough fish to satisfy a crew of twenty.

The forest around the kitchen area was fairly open, allowing a glade of sword and lady fern to grow around some of the large hemlock and red cedar that stood on guard there. Hardesty cleared a spot to build a fire pit and set about gathering the wood to fuel his cook fire. Some cedar kindling, some shavings of pitch wood smelling of turpentine were the ingredients for starting it and in a few moments the flames were crackling. He rustled through his equipment in his pack, found the coffee pot and filled it with water from the stream.

Logger's coffee: Fill a coffee pot with and add a freshly cut chip of alder to it. Bring to boil. Add coffee and return to fire. Let boil for one minute. Add cold water to settle the grounds and serve.

When the water boiled for its final time, Hardesty poured himself a cup and sat back to catch his breath. This was not the rough work of a swamp crew, but it had its moments of hardness. He rubbed his shoulder. The bone was supposed to be mended, but there were days when he ached, as though the ghost of the tree top that felled him was still around to remind him of the occasion. Above him, the heads of the old giant firs and cedars were obscured, but he felt the presence of the thin alders that grew like ash-mottled weeds between them. Just as he did of another.

Kate was thoroughly entrenched in his mind these days. Her headstrong nature. Her quickness of mind. Her loveliness. He couldn't look at anything without seeing her there. Anticipating her – there. The long spindly trunks of the alders reminded him of her slim bare legs walking through the grass near the smokehouse.

He nursed his coffee for a bit, his head thoroughly disengaged from the task ahead of him, then began to methodically peel the potatoes he had brought in with him.

The forest is hot, he thought.

It had been dry for some time with no relief. He imagined Kate up there in the clouds, looking over her domain with binoculars, checking for any sign. Back home in Fair Chance, the humidity and heat would build up for a period of time, like a pressure cooker, then implode on itself with the arrival of thunderstorms that swept out the system with the soothing, cool smell of rain-filled air. Here it was just dry. The trails were dry, the big trees next to the clear cuts drooped, and somewhere up there, the sky was bare of clouds as the sun beat down. It made him wonder if he had become a northwesterner. After three days of sunshine, he almost prayed for clouds and rain. He got hot and irritable and wished it would all go away.

"Park?"

Golden suddenly appeared, helping a limping Costello down to the fire.

"What happened?"

"Pee-vee hit his toe," replied Golden. "I think he was trying to stab at a log and it stabbed back."

"Ouch." The tool had a nasty point at its metal tip. "Why don't you sit?" Hardesty said. He gingerly removed the caulk boot.

"Ouch," Costello said, then swore.

"Hey, you're going to live."

There was a big hole in the shoe leather near the top. Inside, the sock was bloody, but when he took it off and turned the foot, it didn't look too bad. Miraculously, the heavy iron instrument had gone between his big toe and the rest of his toes, scraping both sides. The toes now bled freely. Hardesty rustled around in his rucksack for his first aid kit. He gave Costello all the attention he needed, listening patiently to his version of the story, while Golden picked up the slack in the kitchen department and peeled some potatoes. Eventually, the toes were bandaged and the sock put back on.

"That should do it," commented Hardesty. "You can stay back if you want.."

"Naw, I'll go back. It's nothin'."

"Probably feels like it too. Do what you like. Check in with Doc when you get back." Hardesty was done with negotiating with him. Costello would do as he pleased. He stood up and put away the kit. The boy got up, made a wry face and mumbled thanks. "See ya."

Hardesty shoved his hands in his pants pockets and acknowledged him with a nod. The boy nodded back off and limped out into the forest.

"Hard head," Golden muttered.

"What's going on?"

"I don't know. Something's eating him. He's been sour for two weeks now. Glad you're back, Park. It hasn't been the same."

"You boys can take care of yourselves. You've already proved it."

"I dunno. Maybe everyone has a high lonesome. Homesick now that summer's nearly over."

"You all signed on again."

"Yeah, but it doesn't cure the low feelings. Some of the boys are talking about investigating a boarding house in the city some of the regular Forest Service guys were talking about."

"That low - "

"Aren't you?"

Hardesty laughed. "Not lately. Actually not for some time." He offered no more information, taking the peeler back. "Why don't you head on back too? Lunch is still a ways off."

"All right, but when I come back, you'll have to tell me your secret."

Hardesty returned to his work, but the camp seemed to be on a visiting tour because a few minutes later Bladstad showed up. He greeted him with a wave of his peeler, then went back to work.

"What's for lunch?"

Hardesty opened his creel and showed the sizable catch. Bladstad whistled. They had been already gutted and were ready for frying. Hardesty indicated that he should sit, then checked on a pan melting butter on the fire. Bladstad sat down on a log and they chatted for a bit as he worked, eventually arriving at the subject of Kate.

"Has she called?"

"She has." Bladstad chuckled. "I sense that this is not just an ordinary interest in fire towers," he continued in an amused voice. "In fact, there is rumor that the two of you might be an item."

"It hasn't been announced in *The Mountain Call* yet."

"But I take that as a `yes'."

"Yes," Hardesty answered with a steady voice, giving the forester an equally steady look.

"Between you and me, we're going to get married when my next tour is over."

Bladstad seemed surprised, then beamed. "Honestly? I'll - be. That's terrific, Park. I'm happy for both of you," he said. "What news." And then he frowned.

"This hurt my tour?"

"No, nothing like that. I did come up here on business, though – concerning you."

Hardesty's heart skipped a beat. Before Bladstad even opened his mouth to go on, he knew. "Anything particular?" He tapped the sizzling butter with his spatula, then finished slicing a second bowl of potatoes.

"Well, I'm not sure. There's been a flurry of phone calls between here and Seattle and one back east. Seems that there was an inquiry into your original induction."

"Find anything?"

Bladstad eyed him carefully. "I didn't find it so irregular, but Callister is sure acting funny. You have an opinion on all this?"

"Only that it's got nothing to do with the CCC's. He's a poor loser and he doesn't take no for an answer."

"Kate."

"Yeah." Hardesty began flouring up some of the fish. He laid about eight in the big pan, then put it back on the fire. The butter splattered. In a large second pan, he got the potatoes going.

"Still," Bladstad went on. "You weren't in some sort of trouble back east that would cause you to falsify your name?"

Hardesty swore. This whole deal was getting out of hand and he had McGill to blame. "Never. I never did such a thing. I'm legal all the way. Who the hell besides Callister is asking all these questions?"

"No one yet, but he's got a couple of people interested."

"On what grounds? What's his evidence?"

"I guess something showed up in the mail."

Hardesty snorted. McGill again. He wondered how Callister found out. Would the Tarheel have gone to him? Suddenly he remembered the day he had found McGill in camp. He said he was in for some testing. With the education chief. Were they in this together?

"So, am I crucified without any recourse?"

"I was thinking of hijacking you up to Big Fir. 'Til things cool down. I was also hoping that you might enlighten me. Your name, for example."

Hardesty's temper was becoming short. "It's John Parker Hardesty. I dropped my first name years ago."

"I guess that settles that bit."

"Is it a crime?"

"No. No, it's not a crime," Bladstad assured him. "Not anything worse than signing your name with an 'x' because you can't write and read. You've got a right to sign it the way you want – Charlie, Charles, Chuck."

"What are the other charges against me?"

"They are looking into who's getting the check. The addressee's not the same as on the check."

"Maggie Learner. My mother's sister in Pittsburgh. The check's in my aunt's name. Aunt Maggie passes the money on to my mom."

"Why?"

Hardesty was getting tired of explaining himself again. He wished they would leave him alone. He dug under the fish in the pan and turned them, then gave the potatoes a stir.

"Because, right now, I don't have a home," he snapped. "All I've got duffel, three changes of underwear, corks, and a uniform."

"Whoa. I'm on your side."

"Are you? The rooting section's getting a little rough." He banged the metal spatula on the side of the pan. "It's no one's business. No one's!"

Bladstad tried to soothe him. "Hey, I just was trying to figure out the spat of telephone messages that came in from headquarters at Camp Lewis."

"Doesn't make me feel any better. I feel like some criminal."

"Well, I'd like to hear your point of view." Bladstad shifted on his log. "Why don't you tell me? Now you know that it's regulations to get fingerprinted when you come in. They'll use your fingerprints. Any police trouble will come up."

"I'm not in trouble." Well, maybe, he thought. Marie Bertin.

"Hmm." Bladstad cleared his throat. "You said once that I didn't know you. That's true. I don't know much about you other than your papers and what Garrison said. So I think that you should be straight with me. So I ask again, are you in trouble?"

"No. It's just a family matter. I got into a fight with one of my brothers. He ended up getting hurt real bad in car accident. I left after that."

"How do you manage the check? Obviously, your family knows where you are."

Hardesty sighed, putting the spatula down on a flat rock next to the fire.

"They don't really know. I've asked my aunt not to reveal that. Just wanted to make sure my mom got her money. When I first went in the CCC's, I had to state where the money was to go. I wrote my aunt a letter, explaining what I was doing, that I was pretty confused and just needed some time. I told her not to tell what part of the country I was in. I also told her that I wanted my mom to get the money, not my philandering dad."

"That sounds a little irregular."

"It's not. I can state what family member I'm supporting. My Aunt Maggie helped raise me. My grandfather just passed away a year ago."

"Does she write?"

"She's written several times over the years. Keeps me up with things. Last heard from her four weeks ago."

Bladstad chewed his lip. "Callister is making some inquiries into your background, so I still think it might do some good just to head on up to Big Fir for a bit. I've got another assignment for the whole squad more pressing than this. In the meantime, I'll pass along what you've told me in case someone asks. I don't want someone messing around with my prize recruit for the Forest Service. Will you go?"

"Sure, I'll go. Can't be bull cook without my squad."

"Good. We'll get things smoothed out soon enough." He stood up, brushing off his work pants. He spun his cap between his hands. "I'm glad about you and Kate. She's needed someone who was accepting of her for herself for a long time. She's an original. I've never met a lovelier person. Will you stay here?"

"I'll go for that job in the woods you keep yakking about and get more schooling if I can."

"So you have been to school."

Hardesty went back to stirring the potatoes. "Yeah. I was working on a degree in biology as a matter of fact."

"Great. That fits into future plans for you."

Hardesty guffawed. He stood up and shook his hand. "Thanks for telling me."

Bladstad looked askance of him. "You told me everything?"

Hardesty thought for a minute. "Well, when I left home I did pinch a couple of bucks out of my dad's suitcase. If I had the time, I'd have asked my mother for a loan for bus fare, but he was ruling the roost by then. If he thought that was a federal offense, I wouldn't be surprised."

"Anything else?"

"No, except some of my personal stuff at camp was stolen while I was gone. It might have some bearing on the inquiries. It's no one's damn business, but my own."

"How personal was it?"

"I'll beat the living daylights out of the man who took it."

Bladstad snorted. "Don't think you're the type." He frowned. "I'll get a truck to take you up to Big Fir. The squad can collect their gear and head up tomorrow." He stood up. "Well, see you around." He started back to the trail when Hardesty said,

"Wait." Hardesty felt his shoulders sag. "Wait. I didn't tell you everything."

"Oh?"

He cleared his throat. "I'm sorry, this is hard for me. After all the things you've done for me I just don't want to disappoint you."

"You don't disappoint me."

"Callister would like it." Hardesty stood up with the spatula in his hand. "There was a woman. She was killed in the crash."

"Sorry to hear that."

"She was at the establishment. Lacey's." With his heart thumping, Hardesty looked at Bladstad. The only person who knew everything was Garrison. "My brother was seeing her a lot. I started on her too because I saw that she was using him. Wanted to prove it. Caused a rift between us."

"Heard this before. Happens all the time."

Hardesty gave him a hard, but bemused look. "Lacey's wasn't a church picnic. There was, in fact, bootlegging going on. My brother got caught up in it innocently because he was nuts about her. Then things changed. She cut him off, then all of the sudden came back asking for him to help her. I don't know what all happened. I know he was drunk. They got into that car during a snowstorm and then they crashed."

"I'm very sorry." Bladstad walked back to him. "You're worried about what Callister might dig up. Does Kate know all this?"

"I've told her everything except this." Bladstad was reminding him more and more of Garrison the reformer, although Floyd really knew the whole story.

Joisey Squad got up to Big Fir the following day as planned, but Hardesty didn't see the boys until he met up with them with lunch. Having proven himself the day before, they marched down to his field kitchen en masse and sat around the fire while he doled out the sandwiches and soup he had made up.

"You joining us later, Park?" Spinelli asked from his perch near the edge of a clear-cut.

"I plan to. I'll see what I can do with a shovel and mattock these days." He was in a subdued mood this morning and the boys noticed, especially Costello.

He worked with them on a project for a couple of hours, showing his stamina of old, but quit before they did to put the rest of his kitchen gear back into the truck. The crows had been busy. A hole had been nearly drilled through the back of one of the pie pan covers brought from camp. They had managed to get under the tarp to steal what was left over. At four-thirty, the squad left for camp.

It was good to be back at Big Fir. Hardesty liked the isolation and primitive nature of the camp, though its politics could be irritating if McGill and his crew should be around.

He was.

Hardesty was tempted to go and have it out with him. He wasn't sure if the notebook was still with McGill, if it was with him. Who knew? Maybe Callister had it. It didn't matter. There appeared to be a real effort to cause trouble for him. No one had ever questioned him before, except for -. Now there was a hurt as big as a log in his eye. God, was it going to be repeated all over again?

After they unloaded the truck, they hit the showers, crowding around the streams to get the last bit of dust off of them.

"Man, I can't remember it being so hot and dusty," one local enrollee said as he came into the showers. "It feels like the woods are dry kindling waiting for a match."

Hardesty looked at the wide welts of sunburn across the already tanned necks and bare backs as the enrollees turned their red, brown and white painted bodies under the water. He hadn't seen it this bad either.

He dried off then stayed back and shaved, taking time to converse with Golden who really did want to know his secret of life and good mental health.

"It true you're sweet on someone?" Golden asked. "Is it the redhead? You spent a lot of time at the store."

Hint. Hint. Hardesty offered no clue, just an amused grin.

"What do you think about the girls in Frazier?"

The only answer Golden got was the sound of the razor on his ex-straw's boss's face.

When Hardesty was finished, he wiped his face and finished dressing. The bathhouse was nearly deserted, the only sound a stray shower dripping onto the concrete floor. The other Joisey Squad mates had left.

"Life treating you okay, Golden?" Hardesty asked as he put on his regulation undershirt. He would forget about the shirt. It was too hot.

"Got a letter from my folks. Things are going OK, I guess. My brother Simon's going to have his Bar Mitzvah." He explained what that was.

Hardesty was interested, but his only knowledge of religious rites of passage was that of a friend who'd been baptized at a Baptist church. To a Presbyterian like he was, jumping into a swimming pool in the flush of adolescence would have been the last thing he would have wanted to do. A Bar Mitzvah sounded more civilized. No swimming pool.

Golden started to ask him something when there was a commotion out on the small parade grounds by the canteen. Through the multi-paned window Hardesty could see a large bunch of boys come tumbling out of the building, pushing and hollering. A glance showed that half of them were from their squad. Costello was in the middle. Staubach was on the outside trying to maintain order.

"Park," Golden said. "What's going on?"

"Disagreement over job assignments looks like."

"Looks like a brawl to me. Hey, that's Kolbrowski and Larsen in there."

“So it is and some others from McGill's and Spenser's squads.”

The yelling and shoving was attracting other enrollees. When Hardesty saw someone start to take his belt off, he knew the offense. Stealing.

"Time to go," he said slipping out the bathhouse door. “The kangaroo court’s in session.”

He strode over quickly, circling the group. Staubach had separated some of the crew, forcing his way into the center where an indignant Spinelli looked as though he was going to throttle Costello. When he saw Hardesty, he yelled out something that Hardesty couldn't make out until he got closer. "Your notebook. Costello had the notebook."

Some of the boys from McGill's squad began chanting, trying to make a double line. Is it the heat? Or are we all nuts? Hardesty thought.

"Hold on," he shouted and plowed his way through to accused and accuser. "Run this by me again," he said when he had pushed some of the others away. "Someone found my notebook?" he asked Staubach.

"Yeah,” Staubach said pointing to Costello. “There it was as bold as daylight. Some nerve. We unload our gear the truck brought up and there he is standing in the room holding it in front of him like he owned it."

"I didn't take it," Costello shouted as hands shoved him around. "Honest to God, Park. I just found it in my duffel."

"How come you got it?" Spinelli spat back. "You bastard. You oughtn't have taken it."

"I didn't," Costello appealed to Hardesty. "Honest."

"Aw. He just wants to get off light," said Kolbrowski as he plowed his way in. "You know what the punishment is for stealing. The gauntlet."

"Park," Costello shouted. "I didn't take it." A couple of enrollees started to pull him out of the crowd and to the side. Costello fought back.

Hardesty felt a yank on his shoulder as Kolbrowski started to pull him out. Some of McGill's group looked like they would get their fun regardless.

Stealing was the worst offense at a spike camp. Running a gauntlet and getting hit below the waist by belts was the prescribed punishment. Hardesty had seen the sentence carried out in several different places, and generally, there wasn't a stealing problem ever again from that person.

Hardesty wondered, though, if he had been robbed or exposed. He stared at the boy, not quite believing his guilt, even as Staubach continued to light into him for stealing from their former straw boss.

"I seen Costello. You and McGill."

"What about McGill?" one of the Tarheel's mates countered.

"Why don't you go and mind your own business?" Hardesty advised the enrollee as he pushed against the crowd. Hardesty reached out to Costello and pulled him back to his side.

"This is a family affair." He nodded to Staubach to clear the way.

"Not without justice," shouted Kolbrowski.

"Justice? Go milk another crowd. The lynching is adjourned." He managed to get Costello to the edge of the crowd with the aid of some of his confused squad, but Kolbrowski wasn't finished.

“Hey, stupid,” he yelled as he flung himself across a couple of boys and hit Hardesty on the back with a fist.

Its force hurt Hardesty’s shoulder as he was thrown against Costello in front of him. Together, they nearly fell to the ground, but were pulled back when Joisey Squad exploded with indignation to his stab-in-the-back assault. They were able to break loose. Getting away from the developing melee, Hardesty herded Costello into their tent and spun him around against a bunk.

"Where is it?"

"Jeff has it."

"And?"

"I found it in my duffel when I opened it up. I didn't even know what it was until I opened it up and found some newspaper clippings inside. Your name was underneath on the first page."

Well, thought Hardesty, it was definitely the notebook.

"I'm sorry, Park" Costello said, looking point blank at Hardesty. "About everything."

"You've been keeping some strong company."

"I know. I found that out. Those guys are sharks."

Hardesty let out a loud breath. "So what am I to do?"

"Just believe me. I didn't take it."

Hardesty looked out the tent flap to the fight outside. It had stopped before it had really started. He rubbed his shoulder, smoothing away the ache that had developed there. The squads were separating, maybe because Williams was on the office porch looking mildly concerned. One of the enrollees turned and looked back at Hardesty. It was McGill and he was smiling. No one said anything, but Hardesty knew right then that McGill had done it.

"I believe you," Hardesty said.

Costello looked relieved. "Thanks."

Hardesty shrugged. "No hard feelings. Let's let it drop. You want a soda? I've got an extra five cents," Hardesty asked.

"S-sure, Park. That would be swell."

By the time the rest of the squad was back, they were coming out from the tent.

"Hold onto the notebook," Hardesty told Staubach. "Steve and I are going for a beer. Birch, that is. After that, who knows? Maybe a jump in the river after mess to cool off."

The two went past them and without saying a word, Joisey Squad turned as a unit and followed them out. The crisis was passed. They would be a team again and nothing would touch them again. Which was a good thing. In the next few weeks, they would need all the cohesiveness they could get as the forest heated up.

Bladstad kept Hardesty out as long as he could, but by week's end, Taylor was asking for him, so Joisey Squad returned to Kulshan. When Park was done showering and his hair combed, he went over to see the commander. The ex-policeman was looking more and more like Pershing these days, his white moustache and military bearing a study in discipline. He indicated for Hardesty to stand at ease.

"How're you doing? Collarbone back to normal?"

“Yes, sir.”

“Good. It’s a pleasure to have you back out in the field, Mr. Hardesty. Damn lucky, you know. Down in Skagit and in some of the other camps, they lost a couple of boys this summer through accidents. One was a snag falling on an enrollee during a fire mop-up. Sure glad you came out of this all right. I was frankly worried."

“I feel fine, sir. It’s okay being bull cook, but I’m enjoying doing some work too alongside the cooking.”

Taylor made some remark about the coming weekend, then changed the subject abruptly. "I had a phone call the other day. There was some inquiry about your original induction papers. Seems there might have been some problem with your check going home. Have any words on this? Such as your name. There’s been an inquiry into that."

Hardesty gave him the information he needed, answering the questions a little more patiently than he had with Bladstad. He gave his name, the party the check was sent to, and answered other questions.

"Headquarters is terribly slow." Taylor continued, “In investigating your original papers, the name discrepancy came up, but I see that it's a misunderstanding. They did, however, discover that there had been a request at police headquarters in Pittsburgh to locate you about two days ago. Were you aware of that?"

Hardesty tensed. “No,” he answered carefully.

"Then you don't know," Taylor said. "I'm terribly sorry, but your father has passed away."

Pow. Funny how words could hit hard. He had been expecting the names Paul and Marie Bertin and here it was news of his father.

Hardesty had to almost analyze his feelings. What did he feel?

Did he care? He was surprised that he did care. With further exploration, he realized that it was for the lost time and the time he didn't have with his father over the years. He remembered the last time they had been together at the hospital where Paul was so close to death

"Get out of here. You don't belong here."

Taylor watched his face, but Hardesty gave nothing away.

"Well, I am sorry. Life's sometimes all bad luck, isn't it?" Taylor pushed back against his desk. Hardesty stayed still.

"You know Floyd Garrison."

A statement. Hardesty looked up sharply.

"Yes, sir."

"That's extraordinary. He's a remarkable man. He seems to know you well. Even wrote me about you a time back."

Hardesty made a wry face, betraying his annoyance at his friend's good intentions.

"Floyd said you had had a hard time before you came, but had made a good go of things."

Hardesty sighed. "The man's a pest."

Taylor laughed. He found his pipe and began stuffing it. "Well, he sent in quite a recommendation to headquarters. When the inquiry came in about your induction papers, it took awhile for the head to catch up with the tail. I think that things will all work out."

"Then everything is all right? I won't get limbed or whatever you do in this tree army?"

"Yeah," Taylor answered. His eyes were as close to twinkling as his military demeanor would allow. "I am curious, though. How did you get on David Callister's laundry list?"

"He thinks I stole something of his."

"Did you?"

"It was never for the taking. Ask her and she'll say so." Hardesty straightened up. "May I be excused, sir?"

Taylor stood up. "Yes, you may. What are your plans for the evening?"

"There's no instruction and I'm not doing any job. I thought I'd walk into Frazier."

"Shall I notify certain parties in Pennsylvania about your whereabouts?"

Hardesty looked straight at the commander. "No. No, thank you. I'll write them myself." There were some final words and then he departed.

Bob Alford was in the storeroom when he heard movement at the back counter. Half-expecting Cory there, he sailed out some remark about how low the river was and the necessity to navigate only in a certain section when the drift boats were hired out. When he didn't get a response, he poked his head out and saw Park Hardesty reading an advertisement for some fishing tackle on a post.

He might be coming by to see you.

So here's the young man Kate had hinted some affection for. Alford had noted the surface staying qualities when Hardesty was recuperating upstairs in the apartment, but there had to be something deeper to strike his daughter's heart.

"Sorry," he said lightly. "Thought Cory was about."

"He was. I just saw him off with John Turner and another fellow."

"Carl Olsen, most likely. The mill's been shut down again. It's too dry to cut trees."

He took off his apron and closed the stock room door behind him. "I'm done," he announced. "You want a beer?"

"Gee, thanks. That'd be nice. I'm of age."

"Look, why don't you come out to the back porch? Got a couple of chairs there and it's cool."

Hardesty hesitated just a bit. Probably wondering if Kate said something, Alford thought.

"I don't bite," he said. "Besides, we need to talk. There's a certain young lady."

He located a couple of bottles in the ice cooler and offering one to Hardesty, took him on the grand tour of the back of the store to a screened door that led out onto a wooden porch. Two bent willow chairs and crate served as a sitting area. "Make yourself at home."

“Some home.” Hardesty stood at the railing and peered through the large cedars that dotted the lawn going down to the river.

“That it is,” Alford replied. In the early evening light, it was cool and smelled of dry earth straining to hold what moisture it had to the ground. A raven flew up to a higher branch to observe them, disturbing the quiet babble of the river with its annoyed call. Alford watched Hardesty’s face soften when he looked up at the window of the room he had stayed in for nearly three weeks.

"Let me give you a hand." Alford opened the bottle with one lift of the opener and proceeded to get beer foam all over Hardesty's hand. "Aw, must be really cold in the cooler."

Grinning, Hardesty shook the beer off and took a long drink. “I don’t mind. Tastes great. The first sip’s always the best on a hot day.”

"It surely is. So, you're back in the woods. Dick says you haven't missed a beat. Bull cook, straw boss. You seem to do it all."

"I make a stab at it. At least it isn't anything new." He leaned against the rail. He was wearing his uniform shirt, which Alford took as an attempt to look presentable for him -- the first important man in Kate's life.

"You going to stay on? Study for the Forest Service? Dick says you are."

Hardesty took a sip of the beer and nodded his head. “What else has he told you?”

“That you’re his prized recruit.”

Hardesty laughed.

Alford moved over to the rail. A mosquito buzzed over his head. He brushed it away and took a swig of his beer. "Kate said you might come around. I understand that you two are serious about things. I assume that there is some progression in this.

"Yes, sir. I want to marry her. I love your daughter every much."

"And so do we. You'll understand if I act a little testy. Modern women. They're something, aren't they? First inkling I get of all this, is pewter bears. This is something I should know about?"

Hardesty suddenly beamed. "The bear? No, no great leap into the dark, just a focal point, maybe a starting point between us. That's how we got introduced." He cleared his throat. "I'll give her the best life I can, but I want you to know that I don't see her as the traditional wife behind the stove. Kate's more than that. She's a partner - and not in the traditional sense. There's a lot of things we've talked about. We've got similar interests in natural science and the outdoors. I'm going to finish school and she'll work on it too, then we'd both like to come back here to settle. We know that it will be hard to get work, but I am going to try with the Forest Service."

"Tell me about your family."

Hardesty hesitated, taking another swig of his beer. He started in cautiously. Alford wondered why.

"My mother's great. She was in college before the war. Even taught a year before marrying. She's pretty much raised my three older brothers and me, giving us the things we need. For me, it was science and books."

"What about your father?"

Hardesty looked pained. He faced away against the railing and seemed to stare at the line of holes running up and down the trunk of a hemlock like machine-gun bullets. Alford wondered if he knew a yellow-bellied sapsucker made them.

"Well, he's not like you." Hardesty turned around. "I admire you, sir. The way you and Cory talk to each other."

"I take it you and your dad don't get along?"

"No, sir. I don't think he ever cared about us."

He went on to tell about the disintegration of his family.

"When I was about two years old, my mother got ill. Her health never was good after I was born and it worsened. She became increasingly weaker until she couldn't look after us. My father began to stay away, saying work was hard to get, but the plain fact is, I think he took up with someone else. It was my mother's decision to move us to my grandparents' farm. She continued to fail, finally being confined to a wheelchair. But she always found meaning in life. Even after my father left for a final time. She's been my source of encouragement, especially about school where I've been the happiest."

"This what you left to come out here?"

"And never hope to have repeated. I'd never treat a woman that way." He clenched the brown bottle tightly around its narrow neck.

"You told Kate this?"

"Yes, sir. It's painful, but it's the truth. And while it has nothing to do with us, the past has ways of coming up when you least expect it. I'm not sure if I want to take her back there. There are too many unhappy memories."

Alford was thoughtful for a minute. "I can understand how families can collide. Mrs. Alford and I were from totally different backgrounds, but we fell madly in love after meeting at a dance in a small town outside of Seattle. She was visiting her uncle's family for the summer. Her rich uncle. We spent the summer getting to know each other so to speak and by the end we were convinced that there could be no other.

"What we didn't reckon on was her folks. Mine were from the old country in Scandinavia and they were thoroughly enchanted with her. But hers. It was a battle. We finally eloped. The century was new and so were we. We lived with my folks for awhile then I brought her up here after I got a job in the newly formed Forest Service. A rough life for a wife, but she adjusted. She's Portland's best, but she has some of her New England ancestors in her. Real pioneering grit. I bought the store just after the war. We've been making things work ever since."

"You ever see her folks again?"

"Not for a long while, but after her younger brother got killed in the war and a sister turned out a marrying fool, they got kind of wistful about their only grandchildren and the fences were mended. Caroline goes down once a year or two."

Hardesty was silent.

"Thing is I was straight-as-an-arrow with Mrs. Alford. Character counts, not the bucks. Want another beer?"

"Sure. Thanks."

"Anything else I should know?" Alford asked after taking a

swig of his beer.

Hardesty hesitated for a moment. "Kate thought I ought to talk to you. Said you've seen the rough side of life too."

"She did, did she?"

"Did you ever do something you've regretted deeply, something that would affect you the rest of your life?"

"There are a couple of things, but nothing that would destroy a life. I did some rough stuff before I met Caroline. It just went with the kind of work that I did when I was a youngster – working with logging crews. But that was life and it goes on."

Hardesty swallowed, then went on to tell him about his brother Paul and the blow-up over Marie Bertin. He left nothing out. He shared his feelings and his worst fears, then he talked about his coming out west, riding the rails and generally hiding from life and everything else that got in his way. He talked about meeting Garrison and his family, then he stopped.

"The rest you know. I came up here."

Alford had been quiet all the time, listening intently, sometimes asking a question, but nothing more. Finally, he said, "You tell Kate?"

"Almost everything. I didn't enlighten her with any minute details behind the blow-up."

"I've seen a cathouse or two. Even might thought I fancied one lady. It isn't new news."

"But Marie Bertin wasn't quite like that. She was loose, but she was particular about who she slept with. Now looking back, I think she did love my brother in her own way. Then again she could twist a man around."

"That gall you? Or just that you wanted it?"

Hardesty looked stunned for a moment, like he didn't expect such a crude remark or just the frankness.

"It's life, son. Some lessons are hard and you don't learn them all in college."

"My brother -"

"Now that's a hard lesson. One as old as the Bible. I'd say it's up to you to find out what's what. Where is your father these days?"

"According to Taylor, dead. A couple of days ago."

"Gee, I am sorry." Alford finished off his beer. "Maybe it's time to write to your brother."

Hardesty started to say something, but stopped. He looked sad.

"You take good care of my Kate. She's as strong and spirited as I was at her age. She has the same love of the outdoors and mountains as I do. It doesn't matter she's a woman. If the Forest Service opened its doors today, she'd be there. Caroline wants her to get out of here and have a life that's not so hard, but Kate's fit for here and if you stay - well, we wouldn't mind seeing her and the young ones from time to time." Alford was all grin and Hardesty had to smile too. "Course you'll name one after me."

Hardesty laughed. "Guess I better."

Alford clapped him hard on his shoulder. "Welcome to the family. Want to call Mrs. Alford on this?"

"Why don't we wait until Kate can call down. I was planning on calling her this weekend. Bladstad said it was okay."

Alford smoothed his hair down. "I'm going to get some more beer. You coming?"

"Yes, sir."

CHAPTER 22

Kate's first call was not to say hello, but to report smoke to the north of Chapel Ridge. The Osborne Fire Finder in the tower had been lined up on some of the features around the area. The blue smoke was coming off a mountain close enough to walk in. As soon as she reported to the dispatcher, she waited for them to call over to the other fire lookout. Once an intersection was made, the crews could go out and have a look-see.

"Smokechasers coming," she was informed after answering a call.

“Great,” she said and turned back to looking for other hot spots.

A fire, she knew, had a way of sleeping, getting underneath the duff where it wasn't seen, then coming out some other area unexpected. Lightning could strike a tree deep inside, then come out days later and really go to town. She spotted nothing else, however, and towards evening, she was informed that the fire was out and the area judged clean.

Kate's first week was a busy one. The forest was very dry now with no sign of rain. The air felt like dry skin stretched over bone and it was hard to believe that a region so well known for rain couldn't even come up with a sprinkle. She occupied her time reading, watching and feeding a chipmunk that scavenged under the tower legs. Sometimes, a series of rings brought the voice of a man at the fire tower to the east of the range near her. He was an older fellow--Kate thought he might be a veteran--who seemed to enjoy the novelty of talking to her. When he asked her to describe herself, she gave him the description of an old maid with bobbed hair and horn-rimmed glasses. It sunk his ship of aspirations, but he was lonely, so he kept calling once a day.

There were a few tense hours when smoke sign appeared to the northwest of her where there was a small mining outfit, but it was quickly put out by smokechasers. Then were other hot spots, but these were stopped before they did any damage or developed into fires. Then during the second week, she got a call from Bladstad.

"Hi, kiddo. A fire's broken out to the south of Frazier. I've got Forest Service crews on it."

"That bad?"

"'Fraid so. Got too much for smoke chasers after a day of trying. It stalled briefly two nights ago then raged in the mountains across the river from your folks' place by early morning. Frazier's full of smoke. Camp Kulshan's even worse. I finally had to send some of the more experienced squads out."

"You'll let me know?" she asked, wondering of Park would have been sent out with one of those CC crews.

"You betcha."

The fire went on for two days, then at six the third morning, Bladstad rang her up to say that the fire was under control. Countermeasures had worked and the final mop-up was underway. "Crews will watch it for a while, but looks like the danger is over. How's life up there? Is it hot yet?" he teased.

Kate said "Hrumpt."

At noon her phone buddy was back to chat a bit. "Some careless camper started it. Was out for a ride on a logging road."

"Maybe it wasn't a camper," Kate wondered. "The mill's laid off again. I saw lots of strange faces in Frazier the last time I was there."

"Our own Skid Row in Frazier," her phone buddy remarked

except it wasn't funny. Some of the men were friends.

The evening promised to be a nice one. It had become a bit overcast, but there was no hint of rain of any kind. It looked like September had arrived and stayed as some of the trees lower down had lost their green a few weeks early. She stared at the mountain range across from her, going on and on like hazy blue-gray humps of a sea serpent.

To the north in Canada, the clouds did seem to be building up, but the weather was supposed to stay dry. She turned away then back. Lightning was in one of them. She watched the dry heat of the storm work its way across the razorback edge of the nearest range. Most of it stayed above the border, but the wind started to pick up and part of the storm began to drift over like dry ice fog pouring over steps. She watched with fascination, even as she saw the occasional lick of fire jab out from the dark flat interior of the clouds. The storm continued on for nearly forty minutes, but didn't seem to drop any rain. She became distracted, watching out on the other hills. The lightning decreased. She was about to go and do something else, when she realized that there was smoke rising from a crevasse due north of her. It just about straddled the border, but was close enough to be on the American side. She brought out her glasses and studied it. The blue smoke was growing bigger.

She set up the fire finder and wrote down her findings. The storm had nearly spent itself as it brushed by on the mountains, leaving nothing but flicks of fire. She watched the smoke a bit longer, then made the call to headquarters. It was too late to send someone out. Still, there was a group of smokechasers camped out to the west of her. They would be contacted and if possible moved in the remaining light as close as they could.

"I'll be back first thing in the morning," Bladstad promised.

It was barely light, when he called again asking for her sighting. Going to the window, she stared with binoculars at the crevasse several miles away and reported that the smoke was still there.

"Stay in touch," Bladstad said. "The smokechasers are going out now and will report on the fire's progress. Hopefully, it won't be too bad. The fire above Frazier's pretty stubborn. Pretty taxing on the crews. Some are still tending the mop-up."

"How are my folks?" Kate asked.

"There was a run on ice and bandannas."

Kate lit a fire and made mush and coffee for herself. The smoke continued to widen and around eight, the phone rang out a series of shorts and longs for her.

"Kate? Dick here. It's going to be a hot day. It's a good one."

"They couldn't put it out?"

"Nope. We're going to have to call in more troops."

"Is Park going out?"

"He was cooking the last I heard, but yes, he's out. He left with his squad ten minutes ago. If this keeps spreading like I'm afraid it might, we'll have to dip south to get help. How're you doing, sweetheart? Is Murray over at Goat Heaven giving you a hard time on the phone? He's been beside himself since you arrived. A girl! What's she doing out here? Is she married?" Bladstad laughed, then said he had to sign off. "Take care."

Noon came and with it a stiff wind. Kate's eyes felt the strain of looking through the glasses all morning. Putting them down, she went outside and down to the area where Elsa was picketed. Even from here, she could pick up the waft of smoke. She went down into the trees and checked the horse's water, something that was piped over from a spring further over. It felt cool in the trees and she suddenly felt like lying down, but knew she couldn't. She cupped some water in her hands and splashed her face, letting the water run down inside her shirt. Sighing, she started to go back up the trail when she heard the phone ringing off.

She moved as quickly as she could, but was too late. The phone had stopped ringing. She was sure it was for her, so she waited a minute, then rang down to headquarters.

"Bladstad's not here," Bladstad's assistant said. "The fire can't be contained. He's gone out personally out to the site."

"How bad is it?"

"It was moving like a fire in a chimney and the crews had to be pulled back for safety. They're looking for ways to stop it, but probably can't until tomorrow. Bladstad's calling it a project fire now."

"How many fire fighters?" Kate asked.

"Not enough." Bladstad's assistant signed off wearily.

The fire consumed all the wood in the crevasse and when the wind turned downward, it moved that direction as well. Kate watched for hours and at some point could see the movement of fire fighters into the area. It burned all night like a grand torch parade, filling the dark with acrid smoke she could barely stave off behind her windows. At dawn, there was a call, this time Bladstad from a portable field phone.

"It still not contained completely," he reported.

From the window she could see that it was moving down near good fuel, most it of Douglas and hemlock. It was several miles away, but it looked impressive.

The battle went on most of the day and by evening, they had managed to contain it somewhat, but it menaced the stand like an angry lion. Kate hoped that somehow they could get it out before it reached the section. Once it got fuel, fires could break out and engulf the trees clear to their crowns and after that, it would be too dangerous to tackle in its present direction. She stayed wearily near the phone watching and waiting, occasionally breaking away to feed the chipmunk and herself or Elsa.

The third day seemed no better. There was, by now, the customary wake-up call from Bladstad along with a report.

"We're going to try to get their backfires up and running again and hopefully, this effort will put it out. The crews are exhausted, so we're bussing up new ones from the Columbia and eastern Washington. You're doing a great job, Kate," he said. "Keep us posted."

From the shelter of the fire tower, Kate watched and worried. There had fortunately been only one other fire started since the dry storm that had started this giant one and it had been smothered before it could take off, but she kept to her duties and watched for other possible problems. To the north again, there was a buildup of clouds, but they appeared flat and dry. At noon, there seemed to be some movement near the stand of fir and hemlock wall. Through her glasses she could make out ant-like figures of men working fire against the bigger fire. Suddenly, there was a rush of activity and smoke then, pouf, the fire went out.

For a long time, she watched, her breath caught. The steep hill leading up to the wall appeared silent with not a single movement when she spied some men running. The roaring fire of just moments ago seemed dead, although steam rose from some hot spots still to be smothered. The figures on the hill seemed to regroup again and move in two directions. Someone was pointing, maybe shouting. For more than a half-hour she watched. The figures eventually moved down and closer into her range and she saw for the first time that they were carrying something. Her heart stopped, making her stomach churn. Something was terribly wrong. She picked up the phone and rang up a signal, but there was no response at Bladstad's end. She tried again, but again no response. After waiting impatiently for another twenty minutes, she called again. This time she got through. It wasn't Dick Bladstad.

"Who's this?" an unfamiliar voice asked, surprised to get a woman on the line.

"Kate Alford. I'm manning the fire tower at Chapel Ridge. Who's this?"

"Neal Jeffries. Forest ranger from Rainier."

This could go for awhile, so Kate just cut through the preliminaries.

"Where's Dick Bladstad?"

"Who?"

"The Forest Service head for Camp Kulshan."

There was a pause as a hand was put over the receiver, then Jeffries was back on line.

"There was an accident -- ma'am. Bladstad got hurt."

Kate gasped. "How badly?"

"Don't know, but not as bad as some others."

"What's bad?" she asked.

"A couple of enrollees were killed."

For a moment she was stunned, fearing the worst, but she

recovered quickly and was soon asking him questions. "Who was killed?"

"A couple of guys from Kulshan. Some of the guys from back east."

"Oh, God," Kate said. Her mouth was dry, her heart skipped a beat.

Park, dear God please don't make it Park, she prayed. "You don't know who?"

"Sorry, I don't. Right now they were trying to get the hurt and dead out while mopping up the rest of the damage. It's pretty chaotic."

Kate put the receiver up to her cheek. Tears came to her eyes. She sighed and got back on.

"Can I call for you, give you any kind of support? Look, Bladstad set me up here and I've lived in Frazier all my life. I know those mountains, I know how to get people out, and I know who to call."

Since no one else on that end seemed to know what was going on, he consented and she signed off.

Kate spent the next couple of hours on line with headquarters at Kulshan and the fire crew coordinating efforts to get the injured and dead out and fresh crews in, all the while continuing her duty as smoke spotter. From her vantage point at the tower, she watched for telltale signs of the fire restarting somewhere else or any other problem. The day dragged on and on, but the miles of ridges and forests held and there were no more blue smoke tails into the sky. There was no more word on Bladstad or the dead CCC enrollees. Kate bit back the urge to ask the whereabouts of Park, hoping that he was still in the role of a cook. It worried her though.

Some of the boys from back east.

The words haunted her.

At three, she put her binoculars down and slumped back exhausted in her chair. The view across the way looked quiet now. The old crews would be on their way out with the dead and injured and in a little while she could call down and ask for some progress on Dick Bladstad. Maybe they would know. She stood up and put some tinder into her firebox and readied a fire for dinner. Outside, the chipmunk called a sharp warning, disappearing with a jerk of its tail. Kate listened for the robber jay that usually annoyed it, but heard, to her surprise, boot steps. Coming to the door she looked down and saw the figure of a man in dirty clothes and a blackened face. At first wary that it might one of the homeless men who sometimes camped in the woods, she looked again and realized that she knew him.

"Park!" she cried and flew down the steep ladder into his arms. "Oh, God, Park."

As his mouth seared her lips, he fell into her. She could feel the damp sweat of his body from his climb and the anticipation of seeing her, but there was also a singular weariness that seemed to bear down on his hard body. After a time, he stopped kissing her and just held her tight. Kate closed her eyes and just stayed silent against him in his encircling arms. There was an airy calm around them on the high open hill, broken only by the call of birds down in the trees and undergrowth. Drowsily, Kate rested her head on his shoulder and waited until he brushed her hair away from her face. She opened her eyes and put a finger on his lip.

"I was so afraid. They said some CC boys were killed."

Hardesty nodded his head as his hold on her stiffened. He seemed to collect his thoughts, then spoke in a low, hoarse voice.

"My squad's okay, although Golden got burned on his arm. Not so good for some others. One of the outside men -- Kolbrowski from McGill's squad -- got leveled by a widow maker. The CC crews were going in to mop up when the snag just came down like Niagara Falls and took out four of the guys. Couple of them came out with broken bones and burns. Kolbrowski was killed instantly, but another -- Hardesty's face contorted in grief -- "Jesus Christ, that damn snag took Hank Spenser."

Kate gasped. Her hands cupped her mouth. "Oh, Park, how awful. He was so sweet. I really liked him."

"So did I." He moved away, close to tears. He walked to the end of the tower and looked back towards the mountains where the fire had been eating up the forest only hours ago.

"Damnest thing," he murmured.

"How is Dick Bladstad?

"Broken leg. He was lucky. Like Golden, he was just brushed by the falling debris. He's in a lot of pain, though."

Kate came up beside him and slipped her arm through his.

"You look tired."

"Beat's more like it. In the end, I was fighting the fire too. It nearly went over our heads." He patted her arm with his free hand.

"Why don't you come on up, Park? I can make you coffee and something to eat."

"I'd like that," he said.

"Will you join the others?"

"Tomorrow. Everyone was given leave. I just sort of peeled off from the supply pack crew on the pretext of checking on some downed telephone line."

"And will you?"

"Yes," he answered. "First thing in the morning."

He trudged back to the ladder and picked up his rucksack that he had left there. Inside, he took off his boots and sat on the bed. Kate busied herself at the stove and talked to him, but eventually he grew silent. When she looked back a little later, she discovered him sound asleep. She looked fondly at the dirty face, then came over and put a blanket over him.

Hardesty woke about five hours later, well into the evening. Kate was at the stove preparing some concoction. He watched her for a while in a half-dreamy state, then remembered where he was. She retrieved a pan and put it on the top of the range with a clatter.

"Ouch," she cried out, jabbing her finger into her mouth. She shut the oven door and sat down on a chair next to her little kitchen table to nurse her finger.

"Burn your finger?"

"Oh, Park. You're up." She sucked her sore finger. "The person who invented crocheted pot holders ought to be hung.

They're useless. What are you doing awake? I thought you'd be out all night."

"Must have been the promise of food."

Kate laughed. "Well, the biscuits aren't burned. Only me."

"Let me see it. My first aid training might come in handy."

"Baloney." Kate sat down on the edge of the bed next to him. He turned her hand over and examined the index finger. There was a white line pumping up on the tip. He kissed it and pronounced it cured.

"Thanks. I think it's better already. Are you sure you don't want to sleep more?" She pushed his matted hair back from the soot on his forehead.

"No. I would like to clean up though. My clothes are stiff with dirt and sweat. I must smell like a mud pond at Yellowstone."

"Uh-uh." She kissed him on his lips. He put a hand around her neck and pulled her down, opening her mouth with his tongue. His hands moved again and began to explore her shoulders and back, forcing her down on him. She gave in and lay on top of him, but soon they were laughing.

"Boy, you're ripe. How about a swim? There's a hot spring down below. You could bathe there, then we'll have dinner."

"Sounds great. I haven't bathed in three days. Maybe it will take the ache out of my collarbone. You coming?" he asked.

"Of course. As soon as I change into my suit."

Elsa watched them come down with their towels and sleeping bag. The evening was still airy and light enough to see well and she swished her tail as they came by. There was a rub on her nose from Hardesty, but she didn't like the smell of fire on him and she pulled back.

"I must be bad," Hardesty commented as they went onto the trail in the mixed forest of fir and maple. "Even horses object."

"Nothing a bar of soap can't fix," answered Kate.

The water felt comfortably hot as they slipped in. Hardesty had stripped to his boxer shorts first, then watched Kate enter. She was wearing a simple black knit swimsuit that hugged her hips and had a tank top neck that slipped low. In the late evening light, he could see her nipples under the cloth. He smiled at her softly, then asked for the soap.

While he scrubbed, they talked about the fires.

"How was Frazier during the fire?" she asked.

"Smoky. I really wasn't able to get into town. It was pretty smoky where we were for a couple of days and Frazier was probably worse. The buildings are all right."

"What is really terrible up there at the wall?"

"I've seen a worse fire down in Oregon, but we didn't lose anyone." He became quieter as he talked, focusing his attention on his shoulders and chest while he bathed. He had become darker over the summer and more muscular since their first encounter with the bear at the river. He didn't mind that at all, but he was acutely aware of each strained muscle. And he was aware of Kate.

Leaning against the log wall of the hot spring, she fingered the little pewter bear on her neck and tried to keep the talk light. He began to wash his hair, slipping under the water to rinse off. Eventually, he considered himself clean. He put the piece of toweling she had given him for a cloth up on the wood platform that enclosed the top of the spring.

"How do I look now?" he asked.

"Scots-Irish. There are at least two freckles on your nose despite your tan. All that dirt. I forgot."

Hardesty laughed and slipped down to his shoulders in the water. Some water got in his mouth and he spit it out.

"God, that's awful stuff. No one's going to bottle it, I hope."

"No," Kate answered, suddenly shy. She fingered the bear again, but when she looked at him with the most wide and fearful eyes, Hardesty called to her softly. "Kate. Why are you over there?"

Slowly, she plowed her way over through the thick water and stood in front of him. His eyes lit up when he saw the bear and he smiled at her, but there was a prolonged silence between them, as an immense tension grew.

"I talked to your dad before all hell broke lose," he finally said. "It appears that I have passed the son-in-law test. He's given his consent for us to marry."

Kate brought her hands to her mouth and smiled. It was a little girl reaction that was not characteristic of her and it amused him. His throat tightened with the tender feelings he felt for her and what she meant to him. He fingered the bear on her breastbone.

"We can get married any time. Whenever you want. I'll quit."

Kate put her hand out. "No. I don't want you to. Besides, I want to be here as long as possible. I just love it."

"All right. I can handle the bachelor life a bit longer. There's that savings account we've got to work on."

He grinned at her, but they both knew they were circling around the subject that was really on their minds. Finally, he made the first move and tested the water so to speak, by touching her on a breast and squeezing it in his hands. It felt full and firm through the knit cloth. She drew her breath in sharply, closing her eyes when he reached for her and began to kiss her on her mouth and throat while he squeezed her breast. He moved his hands and mouth everywhere, then stopped and asked her permission to lower her straps.

"Yes," she said weakly.

With both hands, he pulled the suit off her shoulders and down to her slim waist, exposing her full, high breasts and flat belly, the hollow of her navel. God she was lovely. He was conscious of her immobility and reassured her with a kiss before he touched her again. He pulled her into his arms and he wondered if she could feel the tenseness in his groin as her breasts touched his wet, bare chest. They were not standing in water, but were somewhere else it seemed. The heat was their own, not the water's.

"If you think this is wrong, I'll stop," he said drawing back from her. Kate said nothing, he said, "I want to be the first and only. The only."

She brushed his wet hair away. "I love you, Park."

The heat was rising from the water into the cool evening air when he laid her down on the sleeping bag next to the spring. She cried out his name at the pain, but it was over shortly and she rose to meet his passion with some of her own. In the end, they lay together side by side, their naked bodies cooling in the fading evening sun.

"Are you okay?"

"I'm fine," she answered. She put a hand over her forehead.

He squeezed her shoulder and bringing her into his arms, rolled his leg over hers and they dozed a little. Later, they went back into the pool to clean off. He had been considerate of her and brought "French letters" for protection, but their passion for each other now as something primeval. They had stepped beyond all thought and reason. There were only the senses.

They dressed, Hardesty slipping into clothes belonging to Cory. Kate liked to wear her brother's undershirts and coveralls. They fit Hardesty somewhat, but at least they were clean. His went into the water for washing in hopes of being dried up at the fire tower.

Back in the tower they ate a hot meal and watched the last of the sun disappear in the west. In the east, in front of the windows, a moon came up and spread a pale light over the domes of the mountains. It was like magic, just as the evening at the spring had been. They touched each other often and made light jokes of things, even as his wrung-out wash went up over the stove.

Once, she took his hands and looked at the scars on his palms.

"I've never noticed them before." He told her the truth about them and how he tried to get his brother out. Marie Bertin too. She kissed each one, making him want to cry.

Later, he brought up a final load of wood in the dark and played with the fire while she lit a lantern and set it on the table.

"This is like being in Rapunzel's tower with no escape," she murmured as she leaned against him.

"The world's definitely at our feet and we're free." They stood at the windows a long time watching the shadows of the moon slip across the landscape below. Then, finally, they could not ignore each other anymore and blowing the lantern out, went to explore the thing called making love again on her bed.

CHAPTER 23

Callister watched the trucks bring the tired crews back one by one. The injured had been back for only a short time ahead of them and the infirmary was full. In the woodshop, a temporary morgue had been set up while Taylor waited for an ambulance to come up from the city and take the bodies in. In the meantime, the next of kin were being notified and paperwork signed. It had been a hell of a week. He asked his assistant for news of the outside squads and was told all were back except for that Joisey group. They had stayed back to help on some telephone line trouble and would be in at noon. "Where's Hardesty?"

"Don't know. He split off, I heard." The assistant gave Callister a funny look when he wasn't looking. "Should be down shortly."

"From where?"

"How the hell should I know?" the assistant snapped. "I'm not his booking agent."

Callister shot him a testy look. “How’s Bladstad doing?”

"Bad night, I heard, but he's awake. Didn't you see him?"

No, thought Callister, I didn't want to. He and Hardesty were too tight. And Bladstad was a personal friend of Kate and... His pencil broke in two. He tossed the pieces on his desk and said he was going out to check on the crews. "If you see Taylor, tell him I'd like to talk to him again."

He checked in at the infirmary, thankful to find Bladstad sleeping. The others were awake, reading or visiting in their beds. Golden was propped up, trying to read without his glasses. One of his lenses had been broken and they were trying to get it fixed. His face was scraped, but outwardly he didn't look like a six hundred pound snag had tapped him on the way down. He was too near-sighted to see the education officer watching him. He was having enough trouble looking at his magazine. Callister made a clean sweep of the room then backed out. At least McGill wasn't here.

He went outside and walked along the recently graveled path to the barracks. He stopped at number one and went inside. There he found a number of the local boys lying on their bunks. Some of them were asleep, an unusual sight at the camp during the day, but he knew that they were exhausted. Over in the corner, he spied McGill's red head. He was smoking a cigarette. When his eyes connected with Callister, he stood up casually and walked over. At the doorway, he brushed Callister's shoulder and went out. A few moments later, Callister followed him. They went off in different directions towards a path in the woods behind the baseball backstop. McGill went down about hundred feet and stopped to tie his boot on a large downed hemlock. His cigarette dangled out of his mouth as he laced up hand over hand until he was done. He completely ignored Callister, something that made Callister mad.

"You see Hardesty?" he barked.

“Yeah, he was there the whole time. Cooking mostly, but had to get on the line to help when things got rough. That was a surprise. Hardesty knows what he’s doing and he sure didn’t lose his head. Saved a few of those foreigners, for sure. And a couple of my buddies to boot.”

“I’m not interested in Hardesty’s communal contributions. What about Big Fir? What happened when the notebook was put back?”

"Nothing," McGill said. “Nothing happened. No one blew

up. Still, Hardesty isn't going to forget, though. He knows I'm behind it."

"Question is, stupid, does he know it's me?"

McGill stood up like a shot. "Don't call me stupid."

"And don't underestimate me. You'll be out. Where's Hardesty now?" You little prick, he thought. I'd love to slap you down. But McGill was a big young man, so he knew it would be better to get him on camp regulations.

"That gall you? He's not with his squad. He left before they did." McGill smiled slyly at him. "No telling where a man might go in these woods. Maybe he took a look-see up at Chapel Ridge. I would if I had half a mind. Then again he might be bringing the supply pack back. He left with that crew."

"Don't play games with me, McGill."

"And don't underestimate me - David." The Tarheel's eyes were steady, but his jaw was tense. "If you want me to do anything else about Hardesty, why don't you just let me settle my own score with him without advice from you." He came around Callister and brushed him on purpose.

That did it. The weeks of frustration since Kate went up to the tower boiled up in Callister and he exploded in anger. He grabbed the enrollee and swinging him around, landed a solid punch on his jaw.

"You insolent bastard, I didn't come up from the streets of Chicago to get fucked by you, McGill. You stay in line. If I can't get you thrown out, then I'll do you myself. Understood?"

"Yeah, I get it."

Callister watched McGill stomp off down the wooded trail to the main grounds. For now, things were under control. Still, he wondered if it wasn't time to bring out the pistol he kept hidden in a locked drawer in the office and start carrying it. He wouldn't underestimate McGill's hatred for him, like the bite of an ugly knife wound.

Hardesty got back around noon, coming in with the supply train. Once the horses were turned out, he came back to the barracks before heading off to the showers.

"Hey, Park. Is Spinelli back?" Larsen from McGill's squad asked as Hardesty came in.

"He'll be down," he said. "You two taking off again for Mount Vernon soon?"

"Yeah, my folks like him. He's kind of funny, though. He thinks we live like kings with our little house and fields. He stares at the grass and always says how green it is."

"You have to see the tenements back east, to understand," Hardesty replied. "It can break your heart."

"You come from there?"

"Naw, I'm from farm country like you are. Only our villages are a lot older and you're more flung out." He picked up his towel and kit. "Let me know when they're back. We'll go see Golden together." He smiled at Larsen and went off whistling.

The bathhouse was deserted. Hardesty took the opportunity to shower alone and get the most recent trail grime off him. He had left early in the morning from the tower after having been up more than half the night with Kate. It had been a wildly passionate time that had left them aching and breathless, but sometimes there was no sex.

Everything seemed passionate to them. They had talked in bed and finally got up and lit the stove and lantern and ate toast at the table completely naked. They were up before the crack of dawn to watch the sun come over the mountains and thought that passionate too. It was passionate making pancakes. Passionate feeding each other in the doorway while *Spermophilus lateralis* waited for his double helping of syrupy crumbs. Passionate walking hand in hand down to greet Elsa with a bag of grain.

Hardesty decided that he had never known passion because it increased ten-fold when it had to do with being in love with a woman with whom he wanted to spend the rest of his life. He loved making love to her, showing her things and finding how easily she responded to pleasure. He wanted to go hiking with her back in the mountains and stay away for days. He wanted to show her Boston and New York City and their rich cultures. He wanted her to meet his mother.

A shadow appeared in the door, then quickly stepped in. Hardesty didn't see it until he turned around in the water to get the soap off his back. The shadow came forward, but Hardesty knew who it was before it turned into flesh.

"Do you mind, sir? Privacy is poor enough around here without having people gawking at you."

Callister came over to the wall and just stood there while Hardesty turned off the shower and groped around for his towel. He attacked his ears and upper body first, slipping the towel around his waist after he was done. He walked to a sink to work on his whiskers, giving Callister a quizzical look. "You have a problem?"

"I just wanted to look at you and see if you took your pecker out recently."

The razor clattered into the sink. "Beg pardon?"

"You heard me, you bastard. You couldn't stay away from her, could you? You went up there."

Hardesty looked at him in disbelief, then in sorrow and shame for him. Up until the scene with Kate at her house, Callister at least had had his respect all these months. He wasn't a bad education officer, even if he was a bit narrow-minded. But this.

"Look, if you want to give me a spelling test, I'll come over. But anything outside of your department is off limits. That includes Kate Alford."

"Is she suddenly your department?"

"No, there is nothing sudden about this. It just got around to your attention a bit late."

"You fucked her."

"Listen, I don't care if you're staff and I'm a lowly enrollee. You'll speak respectfully of her or I'll slam you so hard you won't see the ground coming."

"Why should I care?"

Hardesty picked up his razor and pointed it at Callister. "It's not that you should care. It's that I care. Kate and I are engaged. One more comment like that and you'll be singing falsetto for impugning her reputation."

Callister's face froze into a mask from an exotic travel reel. "Engaged? Since when? You just ask?"

"No, I didn't just ask. It's been over a month now. You're just a little slow in picking up the signals." He scraped at his light beard of four days and rinsed off. "By the way, her father approves."

"You hadn't the right. Not to come in. You hadn't the right."

"You don't get it, do you? Kate's not some item you pick up to show off. It's not a matter of a right. It's the matter of the privilege of getting to know a hell of a person who is named Kate Alford."

"You fucked that Marie Bertin, I bet. You fuck that kid down in Oregon? That Holly Garrison?"

Hardesty flew from the sink to Callister and slammed him against the wall, but Callister was surprisingly strong and he pushed back on Hardesty by grabbing his ears and pulling on them. It was a street-wise move that threw Hardesty off guard for a moment, but if they were going to play dirty, they might as well get on with it. He slammed Callister in the groin and the hold was released. Callister staggered back gasping, but straightened up enough to put up his fists. He made an attempt to circle and close in.

Where did he learn that? Maybe the smooth veneer he presented to the world wasn't so deep. Hardesty suddenly felt tired. Four days of driving fatigue he had gathered out along the fire line seized him. Callister was in no shape to pummel him, but a feather could knock him down at this point.

"I don't want to fight you, but I will if you press me," Hardesty growled at him. He was a bit vulnerable in just a towel and he tightened it just in case.

"You can't afford to. I have Taylor's ear."

"I've already talked to Taylor. You're out of luck."

"Not when he learns that you were investigated for rape two and a half years ago in Rouge River."

Hardesty lowered his fists slightly. "Where did you hear that?"

"I just know."

"Knowing isn't exactly the truth."

"It might be to someone. Taylor might not be the only one interested. Maybe Kate ought to know."

Hardesty sighed. He felt defeated without having to duke out the last round. He stepped back from Callister and looked for his gear. At least Hardesty's weary brain knew one thing. Callister had been the receiver of stolen goods. Maybe McGill wasn't far behind.

"You leaving?" Callister asked.

"Yeah."

"Pity. We were having such a good chat."

"Maybe. Too bad we aren't up at Big Fir. You'd been run through the gauntlet so fast for stealing that you'd see religion in about two seconds."

"Stealing? This is only the privilege of knowing someone like you, John Parker Hardesty. When it comes down to it, you'll never get what you want."

The fire season got a reprieve that night with the first real rain in weeks. It pounded down on the roof at the rec hall, making it hard to hear over the telephone. Hardesty let it ring away and hoped he'd get the one he needed. He didn't. On the other end was a woman's voice and for a moment he didn't answer.

"Hello? Is anyone there?" The rain must have sounded like a snare drum over the line. He almost let it go but in the end didn't have the heart.

"Hello, is Floyd around?" he asked in a loud voice.

"No, I'm sorry. He's at a meeting right now in Oregon. He won't be back for days. May I ask who's calling?"

Hardesty panicked, wanting to hang up, but he could hear Floyd admonishing him and knew this was a part of his test for jumping back into the human race.

"It's Park Hardesty, Lily."

"Who? I can't hear very well."

"John, Lily, John Parker Hardesty."

"My land. Oh, you dear boy. How kind to call."

Hardesty leaned his forehead against the window frame. Was this kind? This sweet woman who had pulled him back from the edge so long ago? To come back into her life and stir things up again? They had lost their daughter and ended up with him. Not that he was to blame. Only that it was the turning point on his scale of worthiness. They called him a hero and all he felt was helplessness that he couldn't have done anything more for them.

Sweet Holly. Hair the color of Kate's.

There had been an investigation all right, but she had lived long enough to set it straight. He found her and kept her alive until the main rescue party arrived. After the funeral, Floyd had taken an interest in him and over several months had been able to get him to open up. From a quiet yet deeply angry young man to someone who could be trusted to be straw boss and higher positions of authority, he became a tree soldier and a leader of men.

"It's so good to hear your voice, but honestly you'd think you were calling from a tin can."

Hardesty laughed. It was so like her. She was a lot like Betty Olsen in outlook on life. A take-care woman with a lot of kindness and mirth even in the midst of tragedy.

"They call it rain, Lily. It finally broke out here."

"Oh, my. The fires up there. You didn't get scorched, did ya?"

Hardesty laughed again. "Just about."

"Well, it's good to hear you. When are you coming down?"

Hardesty thought about it. "Soon. I'd like to bring a friend too if you don't mind."

"One of your squad buddies?"

"No, this one is more presentable. She's of the marrying variety."

"Oh, Park, how nice."

"Look, could you do a favor for me?"

"Of course," Lily said.

"I need to talk to Floyd as soon as feasible."

"Anything wrong?"

"No, everything's all right. I just need to talk to him."

"Will you come down then?"

"No, I need to speak to him first."

"Then it is important."

"All right. It's important."

"Now, that's better. I hope to speak to him soon. Perhaps tonight. I'll have him get in touch with you at the camp."

"Thanks --again," he said.

"What? I couldn't hear that."

"Oh, yes you did. I said I love you!" He signed off with a big grin and put the receiver back only to see McGill staring at him as he came in.

"You cow sick or something?" McGill sing-songed.

"Depends on interpretation." Hardesty went over to the canteen and flipped a nickel on the counter. "Coke," he ordered, taking the bottle opener with him. He spied *The Mountain Call* with Spinelli's latest article on the front and picked it up too.

McGill bought a soda and came around to the other side of the pool table. Hardesty ignored him and went over by the window to stare out at the parade ground where some of the enrollees were maneuvering across the rivulets in the road. McGill stood behind him and took a big swig of his soda. The sound irritated Hardesty. He wanted to flatten the big jerk for all the trouble he caused, then thought that maybe it wasn't McGill. Maybe it had been Callister all the time. McGill could be just a pawn.

Hardesty stared at his soda bottle. He wanted to drink it, but he kept thinking about Callister. Something about him wasn't right. Not just some jealous problem, but a real irrational disturbance. Kate had told him how he had acted toward her in the horse shed. Almost violent enough to unsettle her. She felt partly to blame for his mood swing, but Hardesty said he was a big boy. Callister just couldn't go around manipulating her any more.

"Can I ask you something?" McGill burst into his thoughts like a bulldozer.

"Depends."

"No, I'm serious."

Hardesty turned around to look at what a serious McGill would be like.

"Got to thinking out there yesterday. How you handled yourself on the fire line. I decided that it was safer down on your end."

Hardesty was wondering if this was supposed to be some sort of compliment or was he being greased for some future onslaught. He decided to take the compliment with a grunt and let it go at that.

"No, I mean it. That Kolbrowski had no sense. Thought he knew everything, but there he went right into the line of fire. Look what happened. Bladstad had to go in and he got hurt. You were cautious. You have good fire sense. Where did you learn that?"

Hardesty realized that McGill was serious. He shrugged. What the hell. It was turning out to be a strange evening since he got back. He'd not only been accosted by Callister in the shower and phoned Floyd, he had actually written a letter to his mother asking after Paul. Now that was a first. Now here was Old Tarheel himself asking about fire credentials. Hardesty finally decided to let him have both barrels.

"I was taught by Floyd Garrison down in Oregon. At my first camp."

Hardesty knew Garrison's folks were from McGill's neck of the woods and Garrison was highly thought of there. His war record notwithstanding, he had made a name for himself in the Forest Service. He had a solid reputation and was a favorite son.

"That a fact?"

"Yes. I had Sunday dinner with him all the time."

McGill made a face.

"No, it's true," Hardesty countered. "He's a friend as well as mentor."

"How come you didn't talk to him when he was up here before?"

"We did. Only it was kind of quiet like. He knows I'm gun-shy around high-muckety-muck folks."

McGill gave him a funny look. He didn't quite believe, so Hardesty gave him an example of Garrison's philosophy about fires and forestry. McGill listened. They were actually talking to each other, a condition that ended when another enrollee came in from outside.

"Gotta go," McGill said.

"What? Have to man the still?"

McGill gave him a "you're dead" look, but somehow Hardesty thought the old spark was gone.

The memorial service for the CCC boys was the following day. All that could, attended. Afterwards, Joisey Squad went over to help Bladstad get settled in his own place. His wife, Amy, was there with their little son Andy who was now a crawling expert. He took an immediate shine to his father's cast. Bladstad grimaced when the little boy tried to pull himself up to stand by holding onto the cast.

"Maybe you should lay low at the infirmary," Hardesty said.

"And miss the Andy Olympics?"

The boys were invited in for lemonade and cookies. The little bit of home was very much appreciated and they stayed for an hour. When they were done, they went back to the barracks to wait for dinner.

"You see Karin yet?" Hardesty asked Spinelli as they sat on the front step.

"I hope to. We're still figuring it out. How about you?"

"I talked to Kate by phone this morning. She's doing all right after her heavy involvement over the last four days."

"Don't you miss her?"

"Sure, but she's there and I'm here. We can handle it." He took a swig of the Nehi soda he had picked up at the canteen.

Mario looked thoughtful. "When I get paid, me and Karin are going to a picture show. We'll take the stage into town."

Hardesty said distantly that that would be nice, but he wasn't really thinking about them. He was thinking of Kate.

CHAPTER 24

"Get up now, Spinelli," a voice said above Hardesty's head. When Mario didn't quite move fast enough, the voice said, "NOW!" Opening one eye to the commotion, Hardesty was blinded by the yellow orbs of flashlights going by him at his bunk level. Someone shook Mario and a few seconds later the befuddled enrollee dropped down to the floor in his undershorts and undershirt.

"Get dressed," the voice ordered. Hardesty was awake enough now to recognize it as the assistant camp officer, Henderson. He watched as Mario hurriedly dressed and put on his jacket. There were two other staff officers next to him and when he saw them, Hardesty became wide awake. There was real trouble here for these men were not called unless there was a security problem.

"Where are we going? My folks aren't sick or hurt are they?" Mario asked sleepily.

"Taylor wants you."

"Now? At what, three in the morning?"

"Now." Henderson made sure Spinelli's bootlaces were tolerable, then pushed on him to move.

"What's up?" Hardesty asked.

"Go back to sleep. You'll know in the morning." Henderson was in no mood to discuss anything. He left Hardesty speechless.

"Park?"

"Jeff?" Staubach had been awakened by the exchange of voices.

"What's going on?"

"I don't know." It worried Hardesty enough to get out of bed and go over to the window.

It was pitch black out, but over by Taylor's office the porch light was on and a car was parked next to it.

"Isn't that the police chief's from the county?" he asked Staubach when he came over.

"Christ, it is."

They were completely puzzled as they watched as Mario was led up the stairs and marched into Taylor's lit office. Behind them, Costello whispered from his bed, wondering what was happening. Both enrollees just shrugged, but Hardesty had an uneasy feeling. Even though Mario had been in bed at lights out, Hardesty suspected that he had attempted one of his harebrained meetings with Karin in the woods later on.

"We're still figuring it out."

Something must have happened. Maybe someone saw them and was now reporting it. He went over to Spinelli's bed and felt around.

"What you are doing Park?"

"Just checking the lay of the land."

"Anyone wake up earlier and see Mario gone?"

Costello, who was now joined by Lorenzo, said no. "Maybe he took a leak."

"And got caught." Staubach shook his head.

"He was sound asleep."

"But maybe not for long," Hardesty said out loud. He went back to the window. There was activity over by the stairs. Doc was coming out and getting into the truck. He drove off with whoever was in the car.

"Jesus," Staubach swore. "The whole camp administration's awake. What the hell is going on?"

A clue appeared a bit later when a truck came into compound and pulled up in the front of the camp office. Hardesty didn't see it initially, but his stomach dropped about ten feet when he finally recognized it. It belonged to Cory Alford. Heartsick, Hardesty realized that there could only be one conclusion. Mario was in trouble because of Karin. Cory wouldn't be there if it wasn't the case. And if the sheriff was involved...

A half hour later, Henderson came over to their barracks. He looked straight at Hardesty when he came in. "Taylor wants to see you."

"You gonna say why?

"Don't give me grief, Park. Just go." His face was very serious and upset. Hardesty got dressed and followed him into the cold early morning air.

At the office building, a light was on in the hall, sending out cheesy yellow glow through the screen door. The screen door whined when he came through in front of Henderson. He was directed into Taylor's office. The camp officer was standing going over some papers. Sitting near his desk were Cory and one of the camp police officers. When Cory looked at him, Hardesty was astonished to see that he had been crying.

"Cory," he cried out. "What's going on?"

Cory stood up and cleared his throat. "Was wondering if you could help out here."

"Sure, anything." Hardesty looked from Taylor to Cory and back.

"How well do you know this Spinelli kid?"

"Well enough. He's a good kid. One of the best in the squad."

"You know he's been seeing my little sister."

"Of course. He's even gone with me and Kate."

"Did you know that he has met her out in the woods outside of the camp? At night?"

Hardesty chewed his lip, but he told the truth straight out. "Yes."

"Jesus Christ!" Cory slapped his hat against his thigh as he looked heavenward. "There it is. It's gotta be him."

"Cory, what's going on?"

Cory's face contorted in grief. "Didn't he say, the little bastard?" he spat out. "It's Karin. She was raped. Just awhile ago."

"Good God." Hardesty swallowed hard. He stared in disbelief while at the same time his mind raced ahead. He knew he had to act fast before things got worse. "Cory. I'm so sorry. I don't know what to say. Where is she?"

"At my folks. She came crawling back, her clothes all ripped and bloody. My kid sister!" he raged. His hunched his shoulders and drew his fists in.

"That why Doc went down?"

"Yes. We're waiting for Dr. Erlholm to drive up from the valley."

"Did she name him?"

"No, she can't talk right now. Too hysterical. But Spinelli was seen coming back into the camp from the road about 1:30. They put two and two together when the call came up at the camp." Cory ran his fingers through his hair and Hardesty saw that they were shaking. He patted his friend on his shoulder.

"Cory, I don't know what say, except I can't believe it's Spinelli. Is there anything I can do? Who's with her now?"

"My mom. Betty Olsen's on her way over too. When they can, they'll call Kate."

Hardesty's stomach tightened further. Poor Kate. She would be devastated. It could also put an end to her assignment up there. He turned to Taylor. "What's the camp's response?"

"Spinelli is being held here in my office until the sheriff can make a determination. If there is just cause as there seems to be, he will be turned over to the local authorities. It is out of the camp's hands. This is too serious a charge."

"It can't be Spinelli," Hardesty said. "He cares too much about her."

"He's not a local boy, Hardesty," Taylor interjected. "His values. - "

"- are as good as yours." Hardesty finished the statement. "Look, have you talked with him? Have you let him tell his side of the story? He told me this afternoon he and Karin were trying to get together. They're young kids, both of them. I don't believe it was anything serious. I lit into him some time back the first time I caught him sneaking in. He talked about responsibility and I believe that he had stopped. But these fires."

"You're sticking your neck out pretty fancy," Henderson commented.

"He's a squad mate and worth it. This could ruin him as much as the girl. At least wait until your mother can talk to her." He appealed to Cory and for the first time, an element of caution was entered on Spinelli's behalf. Hardesty turned to the commander. "Look, hold Spinelli. Keep him under lock and key, but you should be looking for clues and possibly another party."

Taylor looked at Hardesty with approval. "Well, at least someone has his head on straight. Where do you suggest, Cory?"

Cory couldn't answer. He was too upset. Hardesty spoke for him.

"Try the path between here and the Alford home. Ask Mario, for God's sake. Get him involved. Have him show you where they liked to meet and determine the way she went back. Maybe he's walked her home. I wouldn't put it past him. Sir, I'd like to talk with him."

Hardesty found a shaken Spinelli sitting on a chair in a narrow supply room. His face was ashen and his mouth tight and turned down. He looked miserable.

"That true about Karin?"

Hardesty nodded yes. "Looks like you're a prime suspect."

Spinelli shook his head and swallowed hard. He couldn't speak for awhile, his dark eyes retreating back into a face that had lost its dark tan, but eventually he found his voice. "Honest to God, I left her on the trail just a short ways to the house." He turned his mournful eyes up to his friend. There were tears in them. "We didn't do nothing. And I didn't do anything to her."

"You've never slept with her?"

"No! Never. She's a nice girl."

"Sorry, hard question." Hardesty reassured him with a light smile. There wasn't much to say, but he believed the boy.

"They probably think because I'm Eye-talian and a foreigner

and I come from back east I'm oversexed or something."

"Not since you started your literary career." I'm a foreigner too, he thought. All of us East Coast guys are.

"That's just it. Karin and I would talk for hours. She likes books and likes to write too." He was thoughtful for a minute then added as if it would help, "All we did was smooch a bit."

"It's not illegal to smooch."

Hardesty asked him a few more questions and listened to his responses. "Can you tell which direction Karin went on the trail? They'll look for clues to her attacker there."

"She was heading back towards the big cedar tree next to the house. Trail starts back about two hundred feet from the curve in the road."

"I'll tell 'em. You thirsty? I'll get something for you to drink."

Mario kept his head down and nodded. "Uh-uh. How long will I be here?"

"Until the sheriff makes a determination."

Hardesty located Cory in Taylor's office and related his conversation with Mario. "He didn't do it, Cory. I was sure before and I'm sure now. You've got to look for clues on the trail. Do you have any idea what direction Karin came in from?"

Cory thought the south side of the house.

"Maybe she was abducted." The whole affair was pretty disgusting. Hardesty turned when the main door to the building creaked open and Taylor came back in with some other men. One of them was David Callister. He shot a glance at him.

"One of your boys is in trouble, I hear."

"It'll clear up, just like rain," Hardesty said back. He ignored him and asked Cory if he was going back to his house. "Could I come? With the camp's approval, of course."

"Friend of the family now?" Callister asked. "Maybe your boy's been taking lessons from you."

The little group froze at Callister's tone of voice.

"Really, David," Taylor said. "That's quite enough. We're all under stress here."

"He doesn't belong here in this conversation, though, sir," Callister retorted. "He's not staff."

"Well, as family friend, you may go with Mr. Alford, Mr. Hardesty."

"Thank you, sir," Hardesty said. Callister was steamed, but Taylor gave him something else to do as they left. Hardesty hoped the matter was settled.

Hardesty returned to his barracks for breakfast. The camp was awake now and the awful story was going around. Some of the boys stood on the parade ground talking in little groups. Others stood on the porches of the camp buildings. The whole company was in a state of shock and felt personally assaulted themselves. Boys would be boys, but there was a line between fun on the weekend and this. Everyone knew the Alford family, so it was personal.

Hardesty didn't feel any better either. In the kitchen of the Alford home, Bob Alford had grilled him over the affair. Was the boy the one? How long had he and Karin been meeting like this? Hardesty felt the heat as much as his young squad mate and when Sheriff Bonner arrived in his official car, it brought back ugly memories from Rouge River.

Caroline was visibly absent for a long time, but finally came down around five. Her face looked ashen from crying and circles were under her eyes, but she held herself well. "Karin has a statement to make, Mr. Bonner," she said to the sheriff. "She is quite distressed that Mr. Spinelli has been detained. He is not the one. She said that he would have defended her in every way."

Hardesty felt an immense sigh of relief. Now only the rest of the camp was to blame unless some other clue came forward. Bob and Caroline went back up, leaving the younger men.

"Want some coffee?" Cory asked. He didn't wait for an answer and poured two, then opened a flask from his pocket and put in something. "For strength." Hardesty took a taste, then had a thought.

"Where did you get this stuff?"

"It's around. I think Jack Turner picked it up."

"Are there any new faces in the area? I heard the mill let off a bunch of people."

“There were a few,” Cory said.

"How about the fire? Did that bring in some new folks? Especially someone who might be camping out in the woods. What about the campsite they discovered? Wasn't it a point of origin?" Hardesty kept thinking about the still he was sure existed and decided he'd talk to Costello. He owed him something.

Noon brought only the sheriff back to the camp. Hardesty was working in the kitchen when he saw him go into Taylor's office. A few minutes later, Spinelli came out, carrying his jacket over his arm. The camp assistant followed him and they went back to the barracks. There was no activity for a bit, then Callister came out with Taylor and the sheriff. Hardesty disgustedly unloaded some garbage outside in the can and went back in. Moments later they drove off.

Lunch came and went, but he didn't see Spinelli. It was an overcast day, the woods enjoying its reprieve from the sun. Hardesty took a break and sat on the back step. There was some work in progress on the grounds, but no details went out. The camp was temporarily closed. At four, he was back inside getting ready for dinner when one of the kitchen crew came in and said Taylor wanted to see him. "Pronto." He took off his apron and walked over, brushing his hair with his hands.

A small army of men was inside Taylor's office, including the sheriff.

“Where's Spinelli, sir?” Hardesty asked.

“He's been released. I sent him to the city with the supply clerk for a breather while the investigation continues. Family's request. They didn't think he should come around just yet.”

"How's Karin?" Hardesty asked.

"Physically, she's improving. It's been a hard day for the family, though, despite the support."

Hardesty stood at attention waiting to be told to stand at ease. There was a tight tension in the room. The door opened and shut behind him and Callister came around into his view and gave Taylor a file. The officer opened it up.

“You been through this before, Mr. Hardesty?”

"I don't know what you mean, sir."

"This - tragedy." Taylor arched an eyebrow as he took out a sheet of paper.

Hardesty glanced at Callister. So, Callister's behind this, he thought.

"You'll have to elaborate, sir. I'm lost."

"Rouge River, 1933. The summer of the first CCC camps. There was an incident in which a young girl was abducted. She managed to escape and hide, but sustained injuries. I believe you know the family well. Floyd Garrison. Hmm?" He looked at Hardesty.

"Yes, sir. I told you I knew him," he answered carefully.

"It's come to my attention about your part in the rescue. Very commendable, but it's news to me that you were also investigated for the crime. This true?"

"Yes, sir."

"Under those circumstances, you never would have been admitted here to this camp, but for some reason your paperwork was removed. Your record was unblemished."

Garrison, he thought. Did he know that this incident would dog him like this?

For the next half hour, Hardesty was stripped of all dignity as he was ordered to sit and be grilled by a hostile panel of camp officers and policemen. Since they had no clue about the recent attack, they wanted to know all the details of the first. Sheriff Bonner was especially hot to get some answers and Callister made sure all the sparks dropped on Hardesty.

"What was the nature of the interrogation, Mr. Hardesty?" the sheriff asked. "Mainly the sequence of events."

"Sure it didn't have something to do with the abduction itself?" Callister sneered.

"No. We were already out. She was several miles from where she had been last seen. So were we."

"So you were out on assignment," Sheriff Bonner said. "When were you and your comrades asked to partake in the search?"

"On the second day after she had gone missing."

"So she would have been suffering from exposure."

"Yes, sir."

"Were you alone when you found her?" Callister asked.

"What does that have to do with anything?" Hardesty answered.

"Because you could have played funny with her," he snapped back. "While she was lying helpless, you could have taken advantage of her. Or you could have done it."

Hardesty jumped out of his seat towards Callister. "That's a damn insult, Callister, and a damn lie." Some of the staff grabbed him by the arms and held him back.

"That's enough, Mr. Hardesty," said Taylor. "You too, David."

"The story's always been wrong." Hardesty was near shouting. "The girl wasn't raped, just roughed up. She was smart and got away before anything worse happened and hid, but she had a terrible head wound."

"And how would you know that?" Callister sneered.

"Because - her father told me about the medical report." Hardesty let out a sob. "Ask Garrison that question if you like, but every time you ask, you just hurt him more." Hardesty calmed down. "May I make a call, sir?" Hardesty shrugged off his handlers.

"Not now. Later." the commander answered. He looked uncomfortable. "I want to know more about the investigation."

"I've explained what happened at Rouge River before. I found the girl first. I had been out west only a short while. I kept her protected as much as I could until the rescue party found us, but her physical condition continued to deteriorate. The investigation was only a formality. The girl exonerated me personally. Honest to God, I'd never to do anything to hurt any girl."

"I've had to review material from Pennsylvania." Taylor pulled out another sheet. "Do you have anything to say about any aspect of this? Did Garrison know about that?"

"He knew everything."

"What was your relationship to this Marie Bertin? It appears that a bootlegging operation was exposed after her death."

"What does it have to do with this?"

"Answer the question."

"My brother worked at her establishment, but he was - unaware of its illegal operations."

"The police said that there was a romantic attachment. Did that apply to you as well?"

"My brother loved her. Was blind to her. I - I made a mistake.

"You seem to have difficulty with women all the time," Callister said. "A record of abuse and excess. They never did find the abductor in Rouge River. No woman is safe." He turned to Taylor. "I hope Bladstad has come to his senses. Kate Alford should not be up there."

"She's on her way down." Taylor watched Hardesty as he stiffened with anger. "How much do you weigh?"

"About a hundred and sixty-five."

"The girl said the man was tall and heavy. Not a description of our Spinelli, but you could do." Taylor swallowed. "However, it is my opinion that there is not probable cause in this matter. The sheriff would like, however, to keep things open on the Rouge River affair. He will not have a final opinion on this case until more investigating is done. I would like to see or hear something on Rouge River by tomorrow. You are, therefore, confined to the infirmary, until further notice."

"Why?" Hardesty exploded. "On what grounds?"

"Mr. Callister has presented a reasonable scenario," interrupted the sheriff. "It will be looked into. In the meantime, you will wait here in this building. It is preferable to jail, I'm sure."

"I'm afraid that it is more than that, Harold," Taylor said to the sheriff. He looked at Hardesty, his eyes sad. "There was something else on this wire." He tapped the sheet. "Did you know a Jacques Polaski?"

"Heard of him. Saw him once or twice. He was part owner of Lacey's, but I think he did more than bartend. He was running bootleg."

"You know this for a fact?"

"I saw him take cases out of a truck my brother was hauling around."

"A crook, then. Was he someone seeing Miss Bertin on a personal basis?"

"That's why I was upset. She was using my brother to hide the deliveries."

"Upset enough to kill Polaski? Would you feel bad to know that he's dead?"

"Dead?"

"His remains showed up a month ago. Found at the base of some sort of Lover's Leap in a state park. They just made identification. He'd been shot." Taylor cleared his throat. "Coroner figures it was around two years ago. About the time of your brother's car accident. Tell me, when was the last time you saw Miss Bretin?"

"Minutes before. She came to the house with my brother. Her car had broken down. He picked up something then left with her for the train station. That's all I know. What has it got to do with me?"

The sheriff got up. "That's what we're going to find out."

Hardesty almost expected handcuffs, but none appeared for now. "You will see him set up in a secure area?" the sheriff asked Taylor.

"There's always the supply closet," Callister replied. He was smirking.

Someone brought Hardesty dinner at seven in his cramped quarters. It was cold and greasy so he had no stomach for it. A phone call to the Garrisons earlier brought no answer and he wondered if Lily was away for the evening. Whatever, he was in big trouble. All of it fabricated. Even after it was worked out as he felt it would, he wondered if the damage would be permanent. How would this look to Kate and her family? He felt wretched, forever damned.

Sometime later, he heard thumping outside of the door, then a knock. "It's open," called out Hardesty. "I think the barbed wire is down."

"This how they treat my recruit?" Bladstad said as he limped into the space. "Jesus, I'll speak to Taylor right away."

"Why don't you save some words for Callister? He's been studying Fascist philosophy."

Bladstad looked for a box to sit on and eased down, rearranging his leg and crutches as he did so.

"You should be in bed, Dick," Hardesty said. "You look ill."

"I am. Couldn't sleep worth a damn last night. Not since this morning. Hell. That's what it is. I can't believe they've done this. What's this about Pennsylvania?"

"I don't know. Some guy my brother knew was just found dead. Two years after the fact."

Hardesty shrugged and leaned against shelves of office supplies and cleaners. Bladstad noticed his tray.

"Want some real food? Amy can make some up."

"Thanks. I'm all right. Can't eat anyway." He rubbed his shoulder and sighed.

"You're not going to take this laying down?"

"It appears I'll take it sitting down." He reached for a box of typing paper and taking out a sheet, began to assemble a paper airplane. "It true that Kate's coming down?"

"Yes. She should be down by now."

"She won't be able to go up again, will she?"

"Probably not. Headquarters was just getting wind of the assignment. Highly irregular, despite the excellent job she did."

Hardesty sighed. He toyed with the plane then shot it out the door into the hall.

"Let me get you some coffee."

"All right, if you're going to make a fuss about it. I'd like to know when Kate is down. I'd like to see her."

Bladstad hobbled out and a few moments later an enrollee brought in a cup of coffee. "Hi, Park. How's the weather in here?"

"Fine. There's no chance of rain."

Bladstad came back. "I just called the Alford home. Kate's back."

"Can she come?"

"Might not tonight." Bladstad tried to explain it away, but Hardesty wasn't fooled. Bladstad apologized, but he looked guilty. "Don't mean to depress you any further, but I think Callister was down there giving advice."

"The bastard. This is what it's all about, you know. Kate. Him and Kate. Me and Kate. That's all. Poor Kate. She really liked it up there." He sipped the cup gratefully. "One favor, Bladstad. Find out where I'm sleeping. Doc's examining table is better than this."

They talked for a bit. Bladstad carefully brought the subject around to Rouge River. Hardesty talked willingly about it and for the first time, he let the old loneliness and despair flow out of him. Bladstad listened sympathetically.

"You see Garrison when he was up here?"

Hardesty nodded that he had.

"Look, I can't stand this. They've no right to do this to you."

"Oh, let it be. I'll get Garrison in the morning and he'll straighten things out. Just make sure they're still searching and get me a pillow."

Hardesty was led into Doc's office at nine. By then he was pretty stiff. He was allowed to go out and relieve himself and then was marshaled back by Henderson who was taking his duty seriously. "Wake me in the morning," Hardesty said as he lay down on the examining table. "I like my coffee strong."

"Keep that up and you'll only get water."

"'Night."

He waited until the door closed then sat up. The dark room was sterile and smelled of antiseptics. It started a rich headache in his temples, a worthy counterpoint to his collarbone, which ached out of proportion to the rest of his stiff body. What a day. He hoped that he could reach Garrison first thing in the morning and get it over with. Callister was having a field day, which Hardesty hoped was soon to blow up in his face. He wondered though, how he managed to get back into the Alfords' good graces. Cory must have had a change of heart. Had Kate? There were voices in the hall next to the infirmary and then someone was unlocking the door. "You decent?" Henderson asked.

When he got an answer, the door opened. Standing next to the camp assistant was Kate.

"Kate!" Hardesty slid off the table and came over to her. She was dressed in her riding clothes and looked tired and disheveled. "I don't know about this..." Henderson stated, "but Bladstad said..."

"Thank Bladstad." Hardesty gave her a ghost of a smile.

"We won't be long, Mr. Henderson," she announced. "We'll be quite all right." Meaning, close the door. Henderson closed the door.

"Kate. I'm so glad you've come..."

Without warning, she came up to him and slapped him on the face. He stepped back rubbing his cheek.

"That's for not telling me the truth." She came close and pounded his chest with the flat of her hand, her eyes close to tears. "And that's for - Oh, God, Karin." She finally broke down, putting her hands over her face. "Why? Why my sister?"

"Kate." Hardesty gently took her by the wrists and pulled her hands away from her face. "Kate." He brought her into his arms and holding her close, he rocked her. Eventually, she stopped crying and laid her head on his chest. He continued to rock her and finally, she was quiet.

"Why don't you sit down? I'll locate the light."

"Don't. I'd rather not be seen. I'm so ashamed. I let her go out with him."

"It's not Spinelli - "

"It's the freedom it allowed."

"I think we both had our own bout with freedom -"

"We're not kids, though."

"No, we're not."

Kate wiggled free and blew her nose. "Why are you in trouble in over what happened in Rouge River?"

"I'm not in trouble. They just imagine it. Callister imagines it."

"But those charges."

"I told you enough, Kate. You didn't need to know the details."

"I want to know. Tell me again about Holly," she sniffed, wiping her nose on a bandanna from her pocket.

"I told you that I found her."

"You didn't tell me that she had been abducted and that a whole community was in an uproar over finding her. You didn't tell me that after the second day, squads of boys were called up to help in the search. You didn't say that you had already had been out in the field with five boys and you just turned around."

Hardesty stared at her. "God, Kate, you don't think I'd do that?" He felt suddenly ill and tears sprang into his eyes.

Kate bit her lips. "No. No, I don't - think that. I'm sorry. I didn't mean - I just expected to hear the truth."

"It's very sordid. I didn't want to offend."

"- any female sensibilities. Oh, blast, I hate that. And you know better. I hate being treated that way." She folded her arms and leaned against the examining table. "What happened?"

He told her how they had split off and how he got lost right away because he was new to the camp. "I guess that was good, because I don't think she would ever have been found."

Hardesty's voice grew quiet as he described how he found her. "Christ, she was only fourteen. I had seen her around the camp. She was a sweet kid. A lot of the boys who were homesick thought of her as their kid sister."

He cleared his throat to go on. "I built a shelter for her and got a fire going and kept her awake until help came." Tears rolled down Kate's face.

"I got questioned because I was in a party that had been out when she had been abducted. And because-." He paused. "Because there was blood on my hands." He held them palms up. The scars from where he had been burned in Paul's accident looked pink and wrinkled. He sighed. "She kept bleeding from her head. There was nothing I could do other than keep pressure on it with my shirt. Back at camp, we were grilled during several sessions, but just before the girl went into a coma and died, she woke and was able to tell her father about me finding her and caring for her. She also had sort of a description of the man who hurt her. He was never found, but may have been one of the countless out-of-work men in that area."

"That's why Garrison became your friend? That you helped his daughter?"

Hardesty's eyes welled up. "Poor Holly. Poor Floyd and Lily. It just wasn't fair. It's not fair for Karin either."

Kate whimpered in her throat. Putting a fist to her mouth, tears rolled down on her hand.

"How's Karin?"

"Oh, on one hand, she's very strong and I think will pull through this, but on another... She keeps asking for Mario."

"Your parents should let him see her. It would do them both good."

"Nothing will ever come of it. It was just a summer thing."

"I think it was a friendship thing. Two nice young people. Just a harebrained thing to go sneaking out."

"Karin has never done anything like that before."

"Karin hasn't been sixteen before."

Kate smiled behind her fist, then sniffed loudly. "How are you?"

"Fine since they let me out of the closet."

"You don't seem upset being here." A light from a post outside lit her face.

"Oh, I'm upset, but it's going to be all right. Seeing you made it all right."

Kate bit her lip to hold back tears and then came into his arms. He kissed her slowly on her mouth and bunched her thick hair in his hand. She kissed him back and for a moment, passion flowed between them. Finally, he leaned back against the table and just held her.

"I love you, Kate Alfjord."

"I love you, John Parker Hardesty."

Her words made him whole.

CHAPTER 25

Hardesty was up before Henderson came in to get him. Though he slept reasonably well on the examining table, he awoke early out of habit from working in the kitchen.

"Can I make my call again?" he asked as he stuffed his shirt into his pants.

"Sure, Park," Henderson said, but when Hardesty called Garrison again, there was still no answer. Subdued, Hardesty came back into Doc's office. Outside, he saw Callister talking to a staff officer on the steps.

"What's he up to?"

Henderson shrugged. "Beats me. He's sure gotten mean lately. I thought he was going to organize a lynching party last night."

"For who?"

"Spinelli first, then you. He was particularly aiming at you."

"Any more word on the Alfords?"

"We had some searchers out yesterday. Picked up some boot prints down around the trail near their home. Didn't match Spinelli's. His went as far south as the house. These boots prints were found just a few feet from where his stop and to the south of the house on the other side. Also found a bottle of booze.

Homemade variety."

"What happens to me?"

"I think Taylor is planning to take you to the big city."

"To jail?"

"I honestly don't know, Park," Henderson said softening his voice. "I think he just wants to satisfy the sheriff and maybe Callister. Seems the education head has been busy probing headquarters down at Camp Lewis."

"Figures." Hardesty sat on a chair and redid a bootstrap. "When's breakfast?"

"It's on the way over."

Hardesty ate by himself, but he was hopeful that he would connect with Lily or Floyd. He was feeling much better since seeing Kate and oddly enough, what Garrison had predicted was coming true. Things had a way of working themselves out. Even if they came with different results, you could get through life as long as you owned up to it.

There was a discussion out in the hall next to him and Hardesty recognized Taylor talking to Callister. Someone went out the front door, but a set of boots came back to see him.

"How are you doing?" Taylor inquired as he closed the door.

"I'm not starving. Is it true I'm going to be hauled out of here?"

"We're leaning that way, but I wouldn't worry. Sheriff Bonner thinks it a worthwhile endeavor. I'm not so inclined, but after this awful business, headquarters is asking questions so I must go along just to keep the camp's good name intact. Were you able to reach Garrison? One word from him and this would be cleared up, I know."

Taylor walked over to the window and cleared his throat.

"You have to understand. I just can't ignore those police reports from Pennsylvania."

"I wasn't in trouble. I just got up and left."

"Let me finish. There were inquiries about bootlegging and a dead woman's involvement. A woman you apparently knew. And now Rouge River and this new development about this dead Polaski fellow."

"That's news to me, sir. Honest."

"I believe you, these are serious charges against the man who did this to the Alford girl. Rouge River just has to be cleared up before I can say that things are all right with you here. Garrison has absolute faith in you. That's enough for me, but the others…"

"Will I be gone long?"

"Say about two days. You'll go to Camp Lewis and talk to people there. If the sheriff's deputy insists on taking you, I'll send Henderson so you're well represented."

"Am I to be jailed?"

"No. Detained." Taylor looked uncomfortable, but tried to be positive. "I've called on one of my friends there at Camp Lewis. You'll be staying with him at night."

Hardesty pushed his tray away at the little table he was sitting at and got up with his cup of coffee. "Any progress on the search?"

"Well, there were boot prints. Some bottles of distilled liquor. Bad stuff."

Hardesty was thoughtful about it. The still again. He was tempted to say something about it, but thought he'd try to speak to Costello instead. He owed him a turn.

Hardesty tried the Garrison home again, but no answer. He walked to the office again and was about to self-imprison himself when Bladstad came banging up the porch steps and into the hall.

"Any news? Hardesty asked.

"Unfortunately, yes. Bad news from the radio. Garrison's apparently been involved in a car crash, which is why he couldn't be reached. Coming home from the train, he was hit by another car. He's now enroute to a hospital in Seattle where he's to undergo surgery."

"Damn." He thought of Lily and what she would be going through.

"I'm sorry, Park. I'll try to reach Mrs. Garrison for you, if it will help."

"Would you?" Hardesty tried not to show his disappointment

and concern. He didn't relish going to Camp Lewis and having to get grilled again. He'd rather help in the search here.

As it would turn out, he went anyway that evening in the deputy sheriff's car. Leaving from the camp office building with his head somewhat high, he was seen off by a few of his friends in Joisey Squad.

Kate heard word of his leaving from Bladstad. When the car passed by their place, she watched from Karin's window on the second floor.

Caroline was in the kitchen when Kate came down with Karin's dinner tray. Kate put it on the table, then put the dirty dishes in the sink.

"I'll do them, dear," her mother said, but Kate insisted.

"They took Park into the city," she said.

Caroline cocked her head at Kate as if she was trying read her mind. "I'm so sorry. What do you think will happen?"

"Park thinks they'll realize that it's a mistake and will come back with egg over all their faces. David's in particular."

"Do you want that? Poor David."

"Don't. Don't feel sorry for David Callister. He's been very - difficult lately. He insists on having his way with me."

"Insisting?"

"He won't let go. He can't accept the fact that I love someone else. Lately, I think since he can't have me, no one can. He's behind all this trouble with Park. I know he is."

"That is a very strong thing to say, Kate."

"But it's true. I - I don't trust him anymore."

"He didn't approve of you being up there, did he?"

"No."

"I wasn't sure myself, but I was very proud of you in the end. I suppose that's the difference. Your young man could see through it all and know what was best for you." She came over and put a hand on her daughter's shoulder. "Do you know when you will go back?"

"I won't. It has been made clear to me that I can't. David has seen to that."

Caroline gasped. "But how when it means so much to you?"

"Well, it's not Forest Service policy, as he has probably so aptly reminded them. God, I could strangle him." She threw the washing sponge down into the soapy water in disgust.

Caroline gave her a kiss on her cheek. "Maybe another time."

"We'll have to declare war on somebody before that happens. People like David don't think women belong up there." Kate untied her apron. "I need to put some things away in the shed. Are you going back up to Karin?"

"For a bit. When she wakes, maybe you could sit a spell."

Kate took some scraps outside for the chickens then went out to the shed. Across the river, the sun was slipping down the face of the mountains streaking their tops from peach to misty blue. Under the cedar trees, it was dim and cool. She hesitated for a moment, listening for the sounds of the evening forest. She heard no intruder, no footsteps and after a time, went inside. She lit the lantern and finished putting away the rest of her gear.

It was not a happy task for her. In the last thirty-six hours, her life seemed to have crumbled around her. While she grieved for her sister, she also grieved for herself. The first love of her life had been tested, her confidence in it shaken to her core beliefs before she felt vindicated in that love. Hardesty had been tested. It hurt to see him suffer before his renewed self worth finally won over the insinuations of others.

And she had been tested. She had been so happy at the tower, knowing that she had done her job as well as any man. She had handled herself very well under difficult conditions and she had made a difference. Now that was over. She wouldn't be going back. Someone in the Forest Service would be going up instead. She folded away her poncho and stacked some gear in a pile for storage in the small tack area, then prepared to leave. She would spell her mother for a time with Karin. She picked up the lantern and started to go, then froze.

Had she heard something?

For a long moment she stayed still, keenly aware that it had been only yesterday that Karin had been attacked. When she thought she heard movement again, she carefully moved to her gear and pulled a knife out of its scabbard and placed it behind her. There was heavy, dense silence again then the crackling of a twig. Kate held her breath and waited for the approach of a shadow to the low door.

"Cory Alford! You scared me half to death."

"Sorry. Didn't think you should be alone out here."

"What were you doing? Sneaking around like Daniel Boone?"

Cory laughed. "I wasn't sure if you were here or in the pasture. Need some help?"

"Not really, but you could put that stuff over there into the tack box."

Cory complied. "Have you seen Dad?"

"No, I haven't."

"He should be down. He's been talking to Taylor. Maybe we'll get some news on this business."

"I hope so. I want it to be over." She brought out the knife and put it away. Cory's eyes widened.

"Are you all right?"

"Yes."

"Kate, I'm sorry about Park, and I'm sorry about the tower." He looked at the stored gear.

"You gave them the best, kiddo. I've heard nothing but good things."

She ran her hand over Elsa's saddle. "Well, it's not the worst of my worries."

"But they are a singular part. I talked to Bladstad and he was unhappy about the way things turned out for you. Said they didn't give you a chance. The stir over Karin was just an excuse. Women at the towers are just as qualified as men. You've proved that. You could have gotten a rating just like any other."

"Did Dad say anything about Park?"

"He was interested in this latest development as he put it, but said he was leaving it up to your judgment about it all. `You knew your young man best', I think was the quote. Here's hoping Park's back soon. The way Callister has been pushing this makes me sick."

Cory picked up the lantern. "How about coffee? I'll play you cribbage."

They stepped out into the space under the trees and for an odd moment felt a strange lack of sound, then suddenly a crash as something heavy moved back through the path going north of the house.

"Who's there?" Cory shouted.

He ran towards the path and stopped. Kate came rushing up to him and he held her lightly around the waist. The salmonberry bushes were still shaking at the edge. Lowering the light, he checked on the still muddy ground from yesterday's rain and found a newly made boot print. It was easily recognizable. About everyone up at Kulshan had one.

CHAPTER 26

The assembled squad looked about as forlorn as you could get as they sat on log benches next to the camp parking lot. With Hardesty and Spinelli gone and Golden and Werner injured, Staubach had called a meeting to discuss ways to improve morale, but found himself in a discussion on how to help in the search for Karin Alford's abductor. While the camp and the sheriff were going about it their way, the enrollees had their own ideas.

"I don't care what those clowns think," O'Connell said - meaning the police. "No one here woulda done such a thing. We got too much going on around here. Folks have been real nice, putting on baseball games at the high school, inviting us to picture shows or church picnics. Even dances. We're here almost every weekend cuz it's too far to the city, so we got to behave. I wouldn't want to get on the town's bad side."

"So, what are we going to do?" Staubach asked.

"Well, we ain't going to sit around here," Lorenzo said. "What about all those new guys in Frazier? The fire sure brought some ticks out of the woods."

"You mean the hobos? Bladstad said that's because the mill closed."

"I seen them," Lorenzo said. "Tripped over two last week while we were out doing trail. Makes you wonder if they started the fire down here."

"I wonder if they came around to the still," Costello said. "It's not very big. McGill's been stashing it for weeks in a shed just outside the camp. I don't think anyone knew about until Kolbrowski sold some juice to some outsiders. There could be somethin' going on between the still and the bottle found down near the Alford home."

"Why don't we take a look?" Staubach said. "Maybe someone was using it when neither McGill or Kolbrowski was around."

They put on their rain gear and headed out for the still. The way up was steep, initially through stinging nettles and devil's club, but the trail, though in poor condition, showed some signs of regular use. When they were in the trees of big leaf and vine maple, it began to drizzle lightly.

They found the outbuilding about ten minutes later. It was an old cedar plank cabin, its corners carefully notched for good fitting. It had been abandoned long ago for better quarters. The windows were boarded up and the roof was covered with moss and dead leaves. Inside, they found a lantern, but Costello had brought a flashlight just in case. It revealed a single room with an old cook stove and bench. It was littered with trash, but there was no sign of the still.

"Damn!" Costello said. "It's gone. It was right there."

They searched around anyway and came up with a tobacco tin and a ticket for motion picture house in the city, but nothing else. Discouraged, Joisey Squad bunched outside wondering what to do next.

"It's all your fault, Costello," Lorenzo said.

"Yeah," O'Connell said. "You should never have sided up with McGill."

"Aw, leave him alone," Staubach said. "You've given me an idea. I think I should see McGill. Instead of fighting with him, we'll ask for his help."

"What the hell for?"

"Because maybe he has ideas about who was out here."

There was a lot of yelling about this, but the boys began to see his way and agreed to start back. While Staubach talked with McGill, they would try to find out more about Mario and Park's situation. Suddenly, they didn't look so lost now without their squad mates.

McGill, it turned out, had been on a similar mission. It had taken a lot of soul-searching --if one could call it that on his part -- but he finally decided to go see Bladstad at his home. Since yesterday afternoon, his conscience had been bothering him. The attack on the Alford girl had unnerved him, hit a chord. He came from a community even smaller than Frazier and he had in his own way certain propriety about what was right and wrong. He wasn't sure exactly how he was going to approach the problem without getting singed himself, but he had to say something.

He thought he knew who raped Karin Alford.

He had done some snooping of his own, especially after learning a bottle of homemade brew had been found down around the Alford home. He had gone down the other night to look around himself and nearly got caught by the younger Alford. But he was sure he was right. After Kolbrowski got himself killed, some of his local friends may have come back to take advantage of the situation.

Bladstad was in his living room with his foot propped up on an ottoman when McGill knocked. He was more than surprised when Amy let him in. McGill had a reputation for being a tough man on a fire line and he was a good worker, but his other reputation for brawling and bullying less aggressive enrollees gave Bladstad a headache. In another outfit where the commander was stiff Army regulation all the way, McGill probably would have been kicked out. Still, Taylor believed that the CCC had something else to offer than a job in the woods. Bladstad understood him too. Understood the kind of down-under-the-belly-existence McGill had lived growing up in his area of the Skagit before and during the Depression and what being at the camp meant to him.

He sat up and invited the Tarheel to sit while Amy went to get something hot to drink. The day had started out damp and cool and had progressed to rain. McGill was already dressed for it. Bladstad showed him where to hang his gear.

"Nice of you to drop by," Bladstad said. As if this was a social call. There had to be something on his mind.

"How's the leg?" McGill mumbled.

"Coming along." Bladstad said, then smiled. "Have a seat."

"Oh, I wasn't staying long. Just had something on my mind I thought I ought to pass along." He cleared his throat. "Too bad about Kolbrowski. Spenser too."

"Yes. I'll especially miss Hank. He was hoping to go into the Forest Service. Good candidate too."

"Kolbrowski was a bit rougher, I know. I didn't like him at first, but he fit in well as an outside man could."

"Something on your mind about the accident?"

"No, it ain't that. Getting hit by a snag is all part of the life. I had a great uncle taken that way. He was an early pioneer down a ways." He decided to sit down after all. He looked embarrassed. "I was thinking about the Alford girl. How it's going to affect the place here."

"It is a terrible thing in itself, but yes, it's put a cloud over the camp."

"I don't think it was one of the boys. In fact, I'm sure."

Bladstad looked sharply at him. "You know something?"

"Hmmm." Carefully, he began to talk about the still. "Rumor is that some of the boys set it up and made hooch from it. Tried some myself. Trouble is, some of the boys were into sharing it with locals."

"You referring to Kolbrowski?"

McGill said nothing, but he knew Bladstad took it as yes.

"What does this have to do with the Alford girl?" Bladstad asked.

"Night after the accident, someone got into the still. Could have gotten drunked up pretty good with what was there --so I've heard."

Bladstad nodded his head. Of course. "What makes you think

this person hurt Karin Alford?"

"'Cuz of that bottle found around the Alford place. I found a second one last night."

Bladstad was sitting up now. "Where?"

"Just north of the house. Up the river trail a ways."

"You're sure?"

"Got it right here."

McGill took out a small cloth wrapped package. Inside was a squared bottle. "Didn't think I should touch it."

"Good man," replied Bladstad more than a little excited. "You think you know who used it?"

"Pretty sure. Brings his own every time. I couldn't find the cork but I can see the writing on it. "Squamish."

"You know what he looks like?"

"Big man. Grizzled hair and moustache. He got laid off at the mill about five days ago. Name's Baldwin."

"You see him around?"

"Last time was before the fire. He come for his stuff. Complained about the prices." McGill knew he was incriminating himself now, but suddenly didn't care.

"Do you know where he lives?"

"He was living with some fellows out across the river. About where the fire started above Frazier."

Bladstad started to drag himself forward and out of the chair. "I can't go, but could you show someone the still?"

McGill blanched.

"Look. You did a good thing coming forward, Jonas. I'll try to keep you out of it. Why don't you draw me a map and I'll talk to someone about going up there. In the meantime, I'll talk to Taylor and notify the sheriff." He gave the enrollee an encouraging smile. "Jonas McGill. You know, I've always known you're capable of doing good things like this. You could do us all a favor if you behaved like the real human being I know you are, at least once in a while. You've got potential."

McGill rubbed his hands together like he was washing them off, then got up to go. "You hear anything else about Hardesty?"

"Didn't know you cared."

McGill shrugged. "Just curious." He went over to the screen door. "If things don't work out for him, ask Callister about it."

Things moved quickly after that and it was why the still was gone when Joisey Squad showed up. By then, the sheriff's office and a volunteer group of Forest Service employees had taken off in trucks and were fanning out into known places where some of the idle men were known to meet. Bob and Cory Alford were notified and joined in. At Kulshan, the camp tried to return to some sort of normalcy. Around three, a baseball game was announced between the defending champions of a series two weeks before and two squads from Spenser's barracks. Most of the camp turned out, filling the baseball field with cheers of hope.

CHAPTER 27

Callister listened to the noise from the office porch, then went back into his office. On his desk were papers he had been throwing out or sending down to Camp Lewis. Some of the boys from spring were gone while others were ending their tours soon. Except Joisey Squad. Since their arrival in March, they had remained not only intact, but were becoming a first class group much to his annoyance. Recent events hadn't changed them much and from the look of things, Spinelli would at least return. What would happen to Hardesty, he didn't really know or care about, but the tension in his stomach that had plagued him in the last few hours warned him that maybe the outcome that he wanted - getting him as far away from Kate as possible - might not come to fruition. Hardesty kept coming back like a bad headache. That realization made him nervous.

He stuffed some paper into an envelope marked Camp Lewis and sealed it up. Others he threw into a waste paper basket. He stopped at the sound of cheering coming through a window. Looking across the parade ground, he thought of his life here. He had come out of desperation when things fell apart in Chicago in '33 and took on this assignment. He had done a good job here, he knew, but he had always planned to move on because Frazier was too small, too stifling. Then he met Kate Alford.

What a mistake that had been. He should have been more careful.

When she said she didn't want him, he should have let it drop. Only he couldn't let it drop. She had inflamed him in the worst way from the first time he saw her. Her beauty, her intelligence. She shone like a new copper penny on a stone slate and he wanted to have it. Put it in his pocket and bring it out to show. A wife like that. He hadn't counted on her turning him down or continuing to turn him down as he attempted to change her mind. He should have let go. That was his first mistake because getting angry over being rejected by her may have jeopardized his position here. His second mistake was getting that moron McGill involved in stealing Hardesty's stuff. He should have done it himself. If Taylor should find out …

Callister crushed the piece of paper he was holding in his hand and tossed it into the pile growing at a forty-five degree angle in the metal basket.

That damned Hardesty.

At the back of the building someone came in and scuffed his way to the main office. A few moments later, Callister's assistant poked his head in. "There you are. Just got some word on the telephone. The search has been expanded to south of here. The sheriff's picked up some good clues."

"Taylor still out?"

"Looks like he'll be gone all evening. You going to mess?"

"Naw," Callister said. "Think I'll get a tray and eat at my desk.

They talked for a few more minutes, then his assistant left. Callister returned to his work, ignoring the sound of the front door screeching followed by its accompanying bang. When it repeated itself again not long after, he was still lost in his paperwork. He wasn't aware of the thumping noise nor that he was being watched until the door framed Bladstad's lean body.

"Dick. I'm surprised to see you about. Aren't you supposed to be tied down or something?"

Bladstad swung into the room and hopped to the nearest

chair that could accommodate him. His face looked tired and pale, but his eyes were very bright as they burned with a mixture of displeasure and exasperation. Clearly not liking the disadvantage sitting down gave him, he drew himself up as best he could and without the usual pleasantries, asked Callister where he had obtained records for Hardesty's file.

"Headquarters, of course," Callister replied but the forester wasn't convinced.

"I never saw such records and I know every one of the enrollees. How did you find out about the difference in Hardesty's signed and given name? The deposition of the check? Why did you think it was necessary to ask?"

"Why not? There was a deception here. As education officer."

"There was never any deception. His papers are legal and correct. I suspect a personal interest here. Why else dig so deep? The records from Rouge River were outstanding."

"You're blinded by friendship, Dick. You have placed a lot of faith in him and now you are tested."

"You're the one who is blinded, David. You've been a good education officer, but you have failed to be honest about your reasons for failure in personal matters. If you can't bend something towards your way of thinking, you generally don't invest any more time in it. But when you can't see that bending won't work and you continue to go at it, you blame some other for your failure. This time you've gone too far. I've reason to believe that you have used coercion and theft to get what you want. Correct me if I'm wrong."

"You are wrong and I resent any suggestion that I've done something inappropriate." Callister got up in a huff.

"You forget my position here at the camp," Bladstad barked. "And to whom you are speaking. This has been all over Kate Alford and that's the sorrow of it. You just couldn't look up long enough around you to see that she was not for you. For you it was a game, a question of wills, not wants. She didn't want what you had to offer."

"How dare you," Callister said. He felt his face reddening, the burning sensation going beyond his cheeks.

Bladstad cut him off. "What's done is done. Hardesty's going to be down at Camp Lewis for a couple of days. When he comes back - which I'm sure he will - I want you to write up a report detailing his work under you. I'm sure you will say something good."

"And if I refuse?"

"You'll be transferred. I'm not callous enough to get you canned, but there's your choice. You're going to have to do something to clear up the mess with Hardesty."

Callister stared at him, but he knew that Bladstad as head Forest Service officer had as much authority in the camp as Taylor. He could appeal to the commander, but that could backfire if Bladstad made good on his threat. Briefly his temper flared and he started to say something but then had stopped. He was defeated.

Bladstad watched him coldly. "Agreed?"

"All right."

"Good. If we're going to continue to work together then we must have an understanding. Stick to your teaching. You're lousy at politics." Bladstad struggled up into some sort of standing position and stuck his crutches under his arms.

"Maybe you ought to take some time off, David. It might do you some good. I'll put in a request to Taylor."

"I suppose I must."

"It's a good suggestion. Take a couple of days to write your report, and then take a week off."

So I'll miss Hardesty's triumphant return to camp, Callister thought bitterly. Quietly, he told Bladstad he would take the leave, and politely followed him out into the hallway. As soon as the forester was out the door, however, he gave him the finger.

Hardesty came back three days later. During that time there had been an arrest by the sheriff's office. In a makeshift forest camp ten miles south of Frazier, one J.T. Baldwin was arrested and taken into custody. After a day of grilling, he finally broke down and confessed to the assault on Karin Alford. A fingerprint check revealed a match on those found on the bottle

McGill had collected and though the girl could not identify Baldwin's face because of the dark, she had remembered his sour breath and that he had a mustache. Around his face and cheeks there were attempts to cover up scratches, but he could not hide the spots where hairs had been torn from his upper lip. They matched those found on the girl's chest. In addition, J.T. Baldwin smelled like a sewer.

There was bittersweet rejoicing at the Alford home. Karin was making great progress and in a turn around, Mario was allowed to see her upon his return to camp. His visit was emotional for Karin, but his acceptance and friendship boosted the girl's sense of self worth and it was decided he could come again. Caroline even had him stay for dinner before he returned to Kulshan, though he received some stern lecturing from Bob.

There were questions, of course, about Hardesty. No one had heard a word about him since he went down to Camp Lewis. Bob Alford could see the hurt in his daughter Kate's eyes, but he could offer no comfort other than saying that things would work out. Garrison's accident had made news in the paper and it was reported that he was out of surgery and making good progress. Perhaps he was able to make a statement about Park. Bob watched Kate mope around and realized that she was also hurting from having been wrenched away from a job she had enjoyed doing. His normally strong daughter had been having a series of setbacks that were taxing even her. For the first time that he could remember, her confidence was riding low. She would stay away from the house, sitting out on the bank of the river or go out to the pasture and curry her mare. She seemed listless and without direction and wouldn't speak. Towards evening, though, there was relief when a phone call came for her. It was Park.

"Park!" she cried into the phone, then looked everywhere in the hall for some privacy. With her parents, brother and some cousins that had come to help craning their necks to see her reaction, it was not in view. She said, "Oh, bother," and waved them away.

"What?" Hardesty asked on the other end.

"Oh, gosh. Nothing. How are you?"

"I'm fine. How's Karin?"

She could feel him relax at the news that an arrest had been made and that her sister was doing better. When she told him about Spinelli, he said, "Good."

"And you?" Kate sat down on a wooden chair next to the phone table.

"I'm coming home. I was able to go and see Garrison at the hospital. His wife Lily was there. She was able to arrange for me to go with some Army type and get things cleared up."

"Are they?"

"Well, the Oregon part is. Someone's going to be very embarrassed. Garrison was very upset and so was Lily. They said it all was old news and unnecessary."

Kate laughed uneasily. "The whole week has been unnecessary. But what about the charges in Pennsylvania?"

Hardesty sighed. "I may have to make a statement, but I'm holding out that any connection to the whole deal will exonerate me. Just hope that my brother is cleared as well."

"Are you coming soon?"

"Yeah, I am. I'm looking forward to another hot bath."

Kate went instantly silent.

"Kate?" His voice sounded like he was talking through a tin can.

"Uh-huh?" She tried to keep her voice serious, but it began to break down into light and music. She was having trouble keeping from laughing.

"I love you. I've missed you in the deepest sense," Hardesty said.

"I know. I've missed you too. Will you leave today?"

"I'm getting on a train at noon, but probably can't get to the camp until early tomorrow." He was silent for a minute. "I'd like to see you right away. After all this I'm thinking of quitting again. I won't change my plans, but I just might see if I can get into school this winter."

"Shhh. Don't talk." She looked around for any eavesdropping relatives and then whispered into the phone, "Meet me at the falls. Do you remember how to get there? I'll go up ahead of you to the old cabin there. It's time it was swept out again."

Hardesty said something suggestive for his answer, which made her giggle and feel wildly happy that he would want to possess her that way. Fall cleaning would never be the same.

They cooed into the phone a bit more, ending with good-byes to Mr. and Mrs. Hardesty. When she put the phone down, Kate was all smiles. For a moment, she gently brushed the telephone with her fingers, but her solace was only temporary. "Everything all right?" her mother asked from the kitchen.

"Yes! Park's coming home."

McGill seemed to take the news like a shock of cold water in the face.

"There's no appeal?"

"None. Enough has been tolerated. You're dismissed." Taylor kept his face hard, but he had mixed feelings about the whole affair. It was Callister again, but the education officer was right. Enough was enough. Running a still could have meant discipline entailing loss of weekend leave and some extra work, but McGill had gone too far in his insubordination. The only recourse was to dismiss him.

He watched with some pity the big young man square his shoulders, and like a shudder, stiffen all the way down his back. "It ain't my work?"

"No, you're an excellent woodsman. You were absolutely indispensable on the fire lines."

Taylor looked down at his file for focus. "Your family has one more check coming to them. You can sort out your gear, but the boots and clothes are yours. You may stay through Sunday if you wish. We'll arrange transportation home for you."

McGill chewed his lips. "I know I was kinda rough, but I liked it here. Nothing I can do?"

"No, not this time."

McGill shuffled his feet. "It ain't my grades is it? I didn't meet the grade?"

"I don't know what you mean, but -"

"Callister. It ain't Callister is it? Seeing he has a thing against me."

Taylor looked at him curiously. "I don't know about that, but I'm afraid that there is no recourse." He moved the papers around his desk, then stacked a batch real hard. "It's over. This interview is over." Taylor gave him his best soldier dismissal, then went back to his work. McGill worked his mouth for a bit, then standing at attention, turned and left the office.

Out in the hall, McGill stopped to blow his nose on his bandanna, afraid to show his face outside. He felt like he had taken a mortal blow. Canned! He was miserable and ashamed of being disgraced. Most of all, he began to feel a rising hatred.

Was it Bladstad? The forester had promised that he would keep the information to himself, but maybe he didn't. Thinking it over, though, McGill knew that he could trust Bladstad. He was an honest, evenhanded man who had gotten on him before, but usually tried to make things constructive. He had given his word and the Tarheel felt it was good.

Maybe someone blabbed, McGill thought next. Someone from the group. A possibility when questions were asked. Question was, why was there no recourse? Why didn't he get a chance to ask for a more lenient punishment? Who had pressed for dismissal? As he stepped outside and composed himself, he thought of Callister's threat. It had to be him. The little shit had to have his way in order to cover his own tracks. Hardesty, he was sure, would be back.

Thinking about his betrayal, McGill's teeth began to grind. He looked around the parade grounds. The camp was into the evening hours, the late August night turning cool as the sun slipped behind the trees. Some of his boys, he knew, were over in the canteen while others he could see out near a maintenance shed looking at some truck engine. Suddenly, he felt lost and lonely. It oughtn't have happened being kicked out.

Callister.

His anger stirring deep inside, his first thought was to look for the bastard, then cooling a little bit, he decided to go talk to

Bladstad and see if he could help. Avoiding his mates, he slipped behind the office and headed in the direction of the forester's home down the road from the camp. When he found the back trail that paralleled the road, he disappeared into the trees. It was to no avail. Bladstad had gone into the city for a doctor's appointment. By the time he returned to the camp, he discovered that Callister was gone as well, leaving the Tarheel to stew in his anger for the rest of the night.

CHAPTER 28

Kate left for the cabin at six-thirty on Saturday morning, leaving a message with Cory at the store that she would be gone for a day or two and not to worry the folks about it. She just needed to get away. Having not told anyone when Park would be arriving, she left open the possibility of him slipping away unnoticed - she hoped. She saddled Elsa and headed over to the river crossing where she encountered Henderson, the camp assistant, on the bridge. He was about to leave in his truck for the fishery down the road.

"When's Dick getting back?" Kate asked.

"Dick's getting home this noon, I think. City doctor was going to look over the leg."

"No problem, I hope."

Henderson said no, then wished her a good day. Although overcast, it was supposed to hold and not rain. Kate said goodbye, then pointed her mare towards the trail that veered away from the riverbed and up to the falls.

Callister arrived at the store only a few minutes later. The previous day he had gone to talk to a school official down in the valley about books, and had stayed overnight with an acquaintance. He had stayed away on purpose, hoping that McGill would be gone by the time he got back to camp. In that way he would be avoiding any nasty confrontation. Callister had planned, on his return, to keep a low profile and get the report that Bladstad wanted on Hardesty done. He didn't know that Taylor was allowing the Tarheel to stay an extra day if needed.

The store door was slightly opened when he came up the wooden steps. Inside the big room was empty. The lights in the back over the fishing tackle counter were on, but everything else was unlit. He went over to the cooler, opened the lid and helped himself to a soda. Taking out some change, he placed it on the counter where the cash register was. Next to the post where an ad was tacked on, he found a folded piece of paper. Its tack had fallen off. He turned it over and saw the name "Cory" in Kate's handwriting. Obediently, he picked up the tack and began to pin it back on the post when curiosity got to him. He hadn't seen her in days and he was still burning from Bladstad's remarks about failing with her. In one swift movement, he opened the note and read it, then pinned it back. He knew where she had gone. The Alfords had use of an old cabin there.

For a moment he stood there, not thinking about anything in particular, then on an impulse, decided that he would go up there. He had no idea what he would do when he arrived, but he made the decision to go. Overhead he heard the floor creaked as someone walked across the apartment above. Backing away, he quietly took his bottle and retreated out the front door.

Callister got back to his office and checked in with his assistant, then changed into his work clothes for hiking. By eight-thirty, being Saturday, the camp was in various stages of unrest. Now that restrictions were over since the arrest of Baldwin, enrollees were lining up for the camp bus into the city for weekend leave. More were going than usual since the break in the hot, dry weather. He saw some of McGill's old squad get on. Then he froze at the front door. McGill was still here. Standing on the front porch of his barracks, McGill had stopped to light a cigarette. One of his squad mates, Larsen, came over and shook his hand. Some words were said, then the boy walked over to the bus. McGill watched them for a moment, inhaling rather than smoking the cigarette with long drags. Finally, he flicked it to the ground and rubbed it out. Callister waited until he went back inside, then quickly grabbing his jacket and small knapsack, slunk outside around the back of the camp office. When he felt he was safely out of view, he continued around until the last building near the gate and slipped out the same time the bus came down. Callister had to step aside. The bus driver honked at him playfully and some of the boys waved, leaving him exposed to the notice of everyone else left on the parade ground. He did his best to ignore them, hoping that he wasn't seen, but he was. McGill caught him just as he turned the corner at the gate.

The bus met Hardesty's car as it passed through Twin Forks. Only one vehicle could cross the bridge, so the bus stopped and waited. Some of the boys from Joisey Squad recognized the passenger in the car and ordered the bus to wait further while they greeted him. The windows were pushed down while the boys hollered hello to their ex-straw boss.

"Seen Mario?" Hardesty asked as he leaned out the car. Ten voices told him he was up at the camp doing extra duty for being AWOL at night.

"What's for dinner?" Golden asked.

"Beat's me," answered Hardesty. "My apron's been taken away. It's back to bucking and falling again."

Some of the boys drummed the outside of the bus with their hands in approval until the bus driver told them to desist or walk back to camp. The drumming stopped and the bus moved on. Lorenzo was still leaning out the bus waving when someone yanked him. "See ya," he yelled and was gone.

Hardesty was dropped off at the camp office and went in to check with Taylor as he was instructed to do. He was anxious to leave as soon as he could. His trip in Seattle hadn't been a complete bust. Lily had arranged for him to go home with her after everything was officially straightened out and they had spent most of the night before he had called Kate talking about his future. Lily was quite determined about it. They would help in any way they could, even with school. When he told her about Kate, he had been given something to give her: a lovely pearl ring that had been Lily's when she was younger. The Garrisons had married late. Their daughter Holly had been their only child.

"You're like a son, John," Lily said and he had been moved to tears.

Taylor was on the phone when he came in. He was talking about a new bunch of enrollees about to descend on the camp in a matter of days. He smiled up at Hardesty and signaled for him to stand at ease. When he was through, he took the file of papers Hardesty handed him.

"Welcome back," he said as he flipped through them quickly.

"Thank you, sir."

Nothing else was said, but the older man indicated that he wanted him to get settled back in as soon as he could.

"Part of your squad's on leave. Staubach and Spinelli are staying back. You can have the weekend off as well, but here, if you don't mind. I think Bladstad wants to see you when he gets back."

Taylor stood up and shook his hand.

"You've been through a lot in the last week, but you took it like the gentleman I knew you were, Mr. Hardesty. It's a pleasure to have you back."

Hardesty nodded his thanks. "Anything I should know about?"

"The case is closed. I guess the only casualty is McGill. He's been dismissed." Hardesty raised an eyebrow, but he was more curious about Callister.

"Is Callister around?" he asked.

"He's been down in Twin Forks. Just got back a few hours ago. Just saw him a little while ago. You going? I'll walk you out."

At the front door, Taylor asked what his plans were.

"I'm going to just laze around, I think, until dinner. Simmons said you had a movie in the canteen tonight, so I might take it in."

The trail to Kulshan Falls was beautiful in the cool morning air. The trees seemed greener since the rain returned and the ground was ripe with little black slugs. On top of some of the old cedar stumps, huckleberries went through their last gasp. Callister stopped to eat a few and catch his breath. The earth smelt deep and musty. The freshest smell, he thought. To him, it was what the Midwest wasn't. No bittersweet smell of hog or stockyard cow, no humidity that turned you into a damp rag two seconds after walking out the door. Here it was rain fresh and there was nothing like it. He wondered why he thought about it. Maybe because he had taken so much for granted. Just like the camp and his position there. He shouldn't have taken it for granted.

He suddenly thought of Kate. It never occurred to him that he might have taken her for granted too. Instead, he thought of all the trouble she had brought him. What had possessed him to get involved with a woman who dressed like a man and clamored around the mountains like a billy goat? What amount of gall did it take to think that she could just dismiss the experience of Forest Service veterans and ask to man a tower? He couldn't see it. As he tromped along the trail any original intentions to make amends to her - in order to preserve his neck - began to dissolve into bitterness.

The bitch.

She had distracted him and just about ruined his career. He felt the strange gnawing in his groin like when he argued with her in the shed. It disturbed him. The image of her disturbed him because he had never met a woman as beautiful as Kate Alford. She seemed to float in front of him, her auburn hair lying on her shoulders, her breasts swelling under a flannel shirt and the slim, neat waist flowing to rounded hips. She had rejected him and taken Hardesty instead. Slept with him, he was sure. It made him sick.

The cabin was deserted when he arrived. He stopped to catch his breath. Unlike most of the camp, he did not always get out and work hard. He went out into the woods only when he had to and although he had been up some of the trails to see the projects, he went more like a tourist. He put his rucksack down next to the little porch and went up to the door. It was slightly ajar, but no one was inside. She had been there, though. Her gear was on the bed. Back outside, he looked down towards the falls that poured over the rocks to the river below. Its roar was constant, a muted background to the other sounds of the deep woods. He heard a Steller's Jay and in reply, a crow in the Douglas fir and hemlock that crowded out the vine maple and other smaller trees around the cabin. But it was remarkably still. There was no wind. He stood for a moment with his hands in his pockets and listened for any sign of the woman or her horse, but there was nothing.

Where was she?

He stepped down to the path that went past the cabin and above the treacherous head of the falls, and looked for any sign of her passing. Under the duff, he could see where hooves had cut into the mineral part of the soil. They appeared to have been made a little while ago because the marks were not wet from a rain last night. Standing on the hill that sloped down to the ridge's edge, he saw the signs warning about the drop to the base of the falls. From where he stood, he could not see the ledge that jutted out over the water's deadly rocks down below. He looked for her across the ravine and realized that no one could probably go over there. She would have to be on this side and was, though higher.

Restless, he made his way back to the cabin and attempted to sit down on the porch, but anxious, he got up and went inside. On the little cook stove just big enough to make biscuits, he found a warm coffeepot and helped himself to a cup. The cabin was sparse, but clean. It boasted a single bed and a bunk bed built into the wall and a small kitchen table crudely made of young alder and some planks. A couple of shelves and jelly cupboard had been slap dashed together as well, but it gave the cabin a certain charm. In a coal bucket, he found some old issues of *Saturday Evening Post* and a *Seattle Times* and he sat back and read. He became absorbed in an article and would have stayed that way had a flock of crows not begun to make a racket outside. Cornered something, he thought. Maybe an owl. They tended to harass something they didn't like or feared. When they kept it up, he got up and went outside to look. It wasn't anything spectacular.

Only McGill on the porch.

Callister pulled back in shock.

"Expecting someone else?" the Tarheel spat. "Like maybe a lady? She ain't around, you know. Looks like she went up the trail a ways."

"How long have you been here?" Callister growled

"Long enough."

"You have no business being here."

"No, you're the one with no business. This ain't your place and that Alford girl sure ain't your business. Me, I'm looking at mine right now. You!"

"I don't know what you mean. School's out, McGill. It's the weekend."

"Oh, I'm not bound by camp rules any more. Remember? You got me canned, you bastard." McGill advanced a little further. Callister wondered if he could shut the door on him.

"You did it to yourself, stupid. Taylor couldn't find an excuse for you anymore. Not with all the troubles surrounding the camp. Operating a still connected to a heinous crime. Made the camp look bad."

"That a fact? Or is it an officer trying to back-pedal as far as he can go without crashing on the rocks? You're not so clean yourself. Stealing an enrollee's private belongings and trying to manipulate records for your own end. That's conduct unbecoming an officer."

"You're out of it McGill. You've been dismissed. You've no recourse."

"Recourse. Now that's a big word I like to hear. I asked Taylor about that and he said I had no recourse. But you know, I do. I'm going to beat the shit out of you Callister. And if anyone asks me about it, I'll just refer them to a little notebook I happen to know about. There's a wealth of information in there, I'm told. Might figure in on Hardesty's latest troubles. Oh, I've got recourse. Right here."

With unbelievable speed, McGill charged. Callister tried to slam the heavy fir door, but it gave way easily under McGill's onslaught throwing Callister clear across the room against the kitchen table. McGill was not far behind and when he landed on Callister, the table collapsed on its front legs, sending them to the floor. For a moment, both men were stunned but Callister disentangled himself from the wreckage and slugging McGill on his face, rolled away to his feet. His back throbbed with pain.

"You fucker," McGill screamed as he got onto his feet.

Callister jumped back to avoid his rush then grabbed at McGill as he came by causing them to twirl and slam like drunken dancers into the jelly cupboard. A tin lard can full of fire makings and a salt box rained down on them, but they held their grip and twirled over to the bunk beds. Grunting, McGill broke loose first, showering Callister with verbal as well as physical abuse. Callister held his own, but he was tiring quickly. He found an opening and hit the Tarheel in the belly and face, but that made McGill even more mad. When they crashed to the wall by the small bed and nearly collapsed on it he knew he had to stop McGill or he would be beaten to a pulp.

"You getting satisfaction from this?" he yelled at McGill.

"Why not? You're a mess, Callister," McGill taunted. They both were back on their feet circling the tight space with battered knuckles. One of McGill's eyes was puffy, but Callister knew he had cuts bleeding freely now.

"It won't matter too much in the end. You're still out."

"Don't count your lucky stars yet. This is only the beginning. I've changed my mind. I'm going to see Taylor when I get back. Let's see, I'll deposit you somewhere and get a head start."

Callister's eyes widened. McGill took it as fear, but he was wrong. In the corner near the door, Callister saw tools stored for outside. He drew McGill as close as he could without making him suspicious, then grabbed a shovel.

"You'll get no start," Callister yelled and raised the shovel.

McGill saw it coming at him and put his hands up to protect himself, but Callister fooled him and instead of hitting his head, struck him with the flat of the shovel in his middle. Crying out,

McGill grabbed his stomach and with a grunt, Callister hit him again on the side of his face, felling him to the ground like a tree.

There was an immense silence. McGill was on the floor face down in a lump. When he didn't move, Callister pushed him with his foot, but there was no response. The Tarheel was out cold. For a long moment, Callister stood there, his breath coming in short gasps as the enormity of what he done. Sweat poured down into his eyes. He wiped it back with his shirt sleeve, then shaking, he knelt down and felt McGill's throat. There was little or no pulse. His eyes were shut tight and his mouth was slack. When his wrist was lifted up, the hand dropped back like a rock. Callister began to panic.

Looking around the cabin, he realized the extent of the damage their fighting had done. The table was busted along with a chair and the stovepipe on the stove was knocked out of whack. It looked like a herd of elk had come through. Or a bear. A bear could wreck a place like they had. He looked down at McGill and tried to think of something plausible to explain it all away, but couldn't. What if he was dead?

A few minutes passed, but he was running out of time and finally grabbing the unconscious McGill by the heels turned him around and started dragging him out the door. He had no idea what he would do with him or where to put him. He got him out on the porch, then stepped down to look for any sign of Kate. When he saw none, he went back and lifted McGill off the porch by the shoulders and pulled him off. He was very heavy, dead weight that strained Callister's tender back, but he lugged him down onto the path and stopped. Where was he going? He should be put into the trees and covered, but - He looked down towards the signs warning <DANGER> and knew his answer was there. The roar of the falls seemed louder in his ears as he dragged the Tarheel down toward the hidden ledge.

"David! What has happened?"

Above him on the trail, Kate sat on her horse. She had watched in horror as Callister moved the body down the path. Carefully, she dismounted, dangling the reins in her hands. He dropped his burden on the slope and calmly walked up to her, like this was an occurrence that he dealt with on a daily basis. Disposing of evidence.

"What have you done?"

"Hello, Kate. I came looking for you."

"What happened? That's McGill. The enrollee from Skagit."

Callister looked back, and nodded. "He followed me up here and attacked me. The cabin's all busted up, but I managed to get away."

Kate watched him warily. Maybe it was his voice. It didn't sound right. Under the calm, there was a flat pool of deadness.

"Is he badly hurt?" She noticed the marks and cuts on Callister's face. McGill looked worse. It was strange seeing him lay head down on his back. It didn't look natural.

"I don't know. Honestly, Kate. You came at a bad time."

"I did? How did you know I was here?"

"A note. You left it at the store." He came closer to her. "I wanted to talk to you, to apologize -"

Kate looked around him. "David. This is so unlike you. What has happened? Can I help you?"

"Too late. You're too late."

She swallowed quickly, then composed herself. She never should have gotten off Elsa. He advanced up to the mare's head and took hold of the bridle.

"God," he said as if he was noticing her for the first time. "You're so beautiful." He pulled on the reins, making her move closer to him.

Kate became very still, vaguely wondering if Karin had ever been aware that she was in danger like she knew she was now. She became icy calm, as if she were watching the progress of a coiled snake about to strike. She must not do anything to disturb him further and cause him to go for her. She didn't draw back when he reached out and touched her cheek with his fingers. He stroked it a couple of times, then began to draw them down her throat and shoulder. He slid his hand down until his palm rested on the top of her breast.

"Oh, Kate. We were such friends."

"I know. I enjoyed our times together. Look, it can happen again."

"Really?" She let him touch her breast while she moved her right hand back along the pommel of the saddle where she kept a small knife. He leaned into her and kissed her softly on the lips.

"I wanted to do that."

Kate did nothing. She was frozen now as her hand secretly worked the strap of the knife.

"I wanted to do more, but then you wouldn't let me. I wanted to do good for you, but instead all you've done is get me into trouble." His hand stole behind her neck, then suddenly he grasped her hair viciously. "I'm not sure if you're worth it anymore." He jammed his mouth on her lips and tore her shirt open, but Kate was ready. The knife came out and bit into the top of his shoulder. He cried out and instantly released her. Kate shouted at the mare and the mare moved into him while she backed away from Elsa with lightning speed.

"Bitch!" Callister roared when he got his footing. The mare was between them, turning her body like a shield. Kate held her knife in front and tried to predict which way to go.

Down the trail she saw two things: McGill who was beginning to stir on the slope and Hardesty. He had just hiked into view, dressed in his CCC uniform and cap. He carried a knapsack and a walking stick. He did not see McGill at first, but he was aware that something was wrong. She was relieved when he caught her eyes and then the direction of her head pointing down the slope where McGill lay. Then McGill groaned. Hardesty stopped dead still in his tracks, careful not to draw Callister's attention, but the education officer must have seen something in Kate's posture and he turned.

"Ah, the hero arrives."

"What's going on?" Hardesty asked as he walked up. "Looks like you and McGill had a go-at-it." He nodded at Callister's bleeding shoulder. "Who won?"

"Does it matter?"

"It might to McGill. Why don't you let Kate take a look at him. See if he's all right."

"Why doesn't she stay?" Callister spat.

Kate moved into view from behind the mare and Hardesty saw the tattered shirt and her knife for the first time.

"Kate." Hardesty's voice was sharp.

"I'm all right." She advanced warily down, saying, "Come, Elsa."

The mare moved like a big dog going down around Callister, keeping Kate from him.

Hardesty came up towards them, dropping the knapsack as he walked. He kept the thick cedar stick close to him. When she and the mare were safely past him, he came opposite McGill and looked down. Kate followed his gaze. One side of McGill's face was red, quickly turning to a heavy, wide bruise. It already was swollen.

"He attacked me," Callister said. He watched Hardesty with narrowed eyes. He couldn't stay still. He worked his mouth and hands constantly.

Kate's heart began to pound hard in her chest. This wasn't real. This was a nightmare.

"I guess so," Hardesty replied. "I heard he got canned."

He turned his body slightly and gave her a smile. She gave him a tentative smile back so grateful that he had come in time.

"Look, don't make things worse," Hardesty said, "Let's help him up to the cabin. You can explain things up there, Callister. Kate, why don't you look for my first aid kit in the knapsack. We can fix him proper."

Callister hesitated.

Kate wondered what was going on in his head. Everything certainly was unraveling for him. He would be ruined. Even without his touching her, there was McGill. Kate looked at Callister, but she wasn't afraid any more. There was only pity.

McGill groaned. He was rolling his head around now, trying to move. While Hardesty watched Callister, she made her way down the slope and knelt beside the Tarheel. She heard Hardesty talk to Callister behind her in a soothing voice. McGill moaned loudly as Kate tried to turn him over.

"Shhh," she said.

Suddenly, she heard scuffling behind her.

"Don't be crazy!" Hardesty yelled.

She turned to see Callister running full force at her, a look of pure hatred on his face. The whites of his eyes were like those of Elsa's when she was afraid, bright white circles encircling dark pupils. His mouth was opened like dark questioning "O", but no sound came out. In his hands was a thick stick raised up high.

In five awful strides he was nearly upon her when Hardesty grabbed him by the arm. Callister tried to shrug him away and then fought to gain his footing when he hit the slope wrong. He went down on his rump hard, dragging Hardesty down on his side with him. Both men tumbled and began to slide forward on the duff and rock as they went under the warning signs and jackknifed towards the ledge. Hardesty tried to hold back against the downward plunge, pulling Callister back with him, but his boots failed him as they hit rock slippery from mist around the falls.

"Park," Kate shouted. Then she began to scream over and over again as soon as she realized she could do nothing to keep him from going to go over the ledge, but she tried anyway.

Scooting down on her rear, she was able to control her own movement down, but Hardesty was ahead of her –flailing out his arms to grab onto anything. For a brief moment he seemed able to hold back his dreadful plunge, even as Callister came sliding to the edge of the ledge and grabbed onto him. Callister continued to slip, then was over the edge.

Kate could not see Hardesty's face as he fell, but she saw Callister's. It was one of horror and of accusation. He seemed to look especially at her, memorizing her face, then shot off the ledge. He took Hardesty with him.

"Park! Park!" she sobbed. She came to a stop and half crawling, found a low huckleberry bush to grab. She stopped screaming his name, her throat raw and torn. She shook all over. For a moment, she heard no sound, just the roar of the falls to her left and boiling water underneath. There were no others. Cautiously, she scooted down as safely as she could and tried to look down, but all she could see was the water and rocks on the other side. She could not see below her.

"Park!" she cried out helplessly, then pulled back when she heard a moan above the falls. Scooting carefully away, she backed up the slope until she was up by McGill. The Tarheel was awake now.

"Miss Alford," he said in surprise. "Were you calling me?"

She patted his shoulder, then sniffed. "No. Can you move back?" She helped him into a sitting position and gave him support as he moved to safety. As soon as he was settled she got up.

"Where are you going?" he asked when she started to go down the trail.

"It's Park Hardesty," she cried. "He's gone over the ledge with David Callister." She was near to tears again, but she told him to stay. "I'll be back."

She took Elsa and led her down to where the ridge dropped. There was a trail there, she knew, that would lead down to the water. She tied the horse off, and slipped off some rope. She made sure she had her knife, then ducked under the trees to the overgrown path down to the rocks.

The rain of the past few days had swollen the river and she was glad for it. It would make the pools under the falls deeper, though the water's rush would be more powerful. She didn't really know what to expect, except the inevitable. Unless they fell clear, they both were probably dead. She climbed carefully down a trail half rock and half soil. When she reached the water, she began to trek up over the large boulders that lined the river. The banks on either side of the water were steep and were either sandy or rock-faced. At the top, the roots of hemlock or maple sometimes drilled through the soil, sometimes sticking out into space. It was like a cross section of a porcupine. All the spines were on top, and the tips were evergreens.

She made a turn in the river's course and could hear the roar of the falls coming closer. The first pool was right before her and she held her breath as she approached. Face down, floating in the water on the far side, was a man. Only his hair was showing. His shoulders were below the water, but she could see the uniform of the CCC's billowing out around the body. Involuntarily, she sobbed, slapping a hand over her mouth in grief. She slogged through the water knee-high, being careful to keep her footing against the current. She came up around the body, biting back the urge to throw up. It had been badly hammered by the rocks and was bloody around the shoulders as well as skull. The water around him was turning red. Taking a deep breath, she grabbed onto an arm and turned the body over.

The blue eyes were open, staring up at the overcast sky. It wasn't Park. It was Callister. The forehead was caved in and his right cheek was torn, exposing meat and bone. She wondered if he had died instantly. She reached down and closed the eyes, then stood up and looked further upstream. She was weeping now, the hot tears running down her cheeks, but they did not weaken her resolve to see it through. She stepped back into the current and plowed her way around the rocks to the next pool. There were large boulders here, some of them obstructing her vision. She looked for signs of Hardesty, but saw none and so continued up. She went as far as she could safely go and saw further ahead the edge where they had fallen. The water was deep in the center of the pool, but there were boulders submerged at its edges and up the sides of the cliff. David must have hit rocks before he went into the water. The bank between the water and the ridge was very narrow. If Park had fallen further out or landed on David … She could not see him. She visually searched the pool the best she could, but there was no telling if a body was submerged there. Saddened, she began to make her way back to where David's body was. The water was cold and she was becoming chilled. A raven called above her and she thought of the stories about it. She would give anything to fly on its back and look for Park.

"Park..." she cried. She almost tripped over the outstretched hand. He was lying on his back behind a boulder, the current pushing him partway up on the gravel edge. His eyes were half-opened and his nose and mouth bloody. The water's rush had nearly torn his shirt off and she could see the cuts and scrapes on his solid chest. His skin was a curious pale color. She wondered how she had missed him, but the boulders were almost the color of his uniform. She was afraid to touch him, to confirm the news she already believed, but as she bent down to examine him, she leaned on his side and he groaned. The mouth went slack and a little trickle of blood rolled down out of his mouth and into the gravel. He was alive.

"Park" She made an effort to move him out of the water, but when she tried to lift his shoulders, he cried out in agonizing pain, grabbing onto her blindly. He opened his eyes wider and looked at her distantly.

"Kate?"

"Oh, sweetheart, I'm right here. I'll get help."

He tracked her with his eyes, but he couldn't speak. He swallowed hard. Finally, he gasped out. "My side. I can't breathe. Damn collarbone's gone again too." He gulped air as he talked.

She did everything to stay calm. I've done this before, she thought. I can do it again. She pulled his shirt apart and felt around his shoulders and side. The collarbone was broken, perhaps in the same spot and some ribs appeared broken. There could be internal injuries as well. He was extremely uncomfortable as she probed, pulling in under her touch.

"Where's Cal-llister?" he asked.

"Further down. He's dead."

He nodded his head gingerly. He didn't appear to have any head injuries. His bloody mouth may have come from biting his tongue on impact. His bloody nose from striking the water hard. Whatever had happened, he had come out of the initial trauma. But how would she get him up to safety? He was in danger from being cold and wet as much as his injuries, but she was afraid to move him. Besides, he was too heavy.

"Kate," he said hoarsely. "How's McGill?"

"Sitting up. He came to a little while ago. His face is a mess, but I think he'll live. I'm surprise his jaw's not broken or his skull. He still may not be all right."

"I've-- got to get up on -- top."

"I know. Can you stand it?"

Hardesty gave her a faint smile. He tried to scoot up further on his own, but the pain was too much. His face turned white. She thought he was going to black out.

"I've been beached," he said, trying to make light of his predicament, but his eyes betrayed his pain and fear. "Try - again." He asked for her support in lifting his legs out of the water. She got behind him and started pulling him back.

"Auhh," he screamed. His cry unnerved her and when he lost consciousness, she hunkered down beside him in despair.

"So here's the other one."

Kate couldn't believe it. McGill was up and walking. His face was swollen like one big bee sting, but other than that, he was mobile. He came over and knelt beside them. He examined Hardesty thoughtfully.

"Are you sure you should be up?" Kate asked.

He nodded yes. "My head aches and my face is on fire, but I can walk." He felt Hardesty's throat for a pulse. "He's all broken up, isn't he?"

"Yes."

"I'll take him up for you, then go get help."

"You'll carry him?"

"We'll figure it out. It's the only way out."

"Park. Park." Something warm touched his lips and he swallowed it. A chair creaked next to him and then he felt the warmth of a fire popping in a stove. He opened his eyes and saw Kate sitting next to him, then began to drift. It didn't last long. The driving pain hit as he caught his breath and he moaned. Kate leaned over him and stroked his brow. "I'm here, Park."

"Hurts," he whispered. "Hurts to breathe."

"I know. I'm getting help. Just hold on Park." She squeezed his hand to reassure him.

"How - did I get up?" he asked, his breath a raspy rattle.

"We put you on a stretcher we made out of some poles and blankets. Elsa helped too. It was hard getting you up on top."

An image of falling through the air then rocks and foaming water jumping up to meet him flashed before him. It made him shiver. Gingerly, he moved his legs under the blankets. He had no clothes on. He listlessly turned his head. His wet clothes were hanging next to the cranked up stove.

"Where's McGill?"

"He took Elsa to get help. It's going to take about an hour round trip at the minimum. He said he would get them to hurry."

Hardesty started to drift and lose consciousness again, but a stabbing sensation in his side brought him back as he tried to breathe around the pain.

"Paul," he groaned. "Paul."

He was aware that Kate was soothing him, but behind her the man with the half face was taking form again, looming in the corner of the cabin. Hardesty stared at him transfixed. His labored breathing became more difficult to endure.

"Paul. I'm sorry." His eyes welled up and a tear fell away. "Sorry..." He sighed and closed his eyes, hoping to avoid the pain, but a little while later, he opened them again. Kate was holding his hand, stroking it. She smiled faintly.

"I love you," he said between quick breaths. He put what strength he had left in his hand and squeezed hers. Kate smiled back, but fear was washed all over her face before it faded away. He wanted to say something more, but he felt himself slipping away, getting weaker. Finally, he just drifted off and went limp.

CHAPTER 29

The man with the half face was waiting on the other side of the tunnel for him. The flames that licked around Hardesty were hot and seared his lungs. It was difficult to concentrate and maintain breath, but the crooked hand beckoned him to come on over.

"Through the fire and you will be free of it."

Through the fire. The tunnel shrunk and it was a burning car lying on its side in a snowy ditch and Hardesty was inside pounding to get out.

"Get out," the voice said on the outside."Get out to freedom."

He pushed on the door handle and it burned his hands. His hair was on fire. On the other side came another voice.

"Get out, Park. You can do it." He stared through the melting window and saw a woman with auburn hair. She had a wreath of lady ferns on her head and she was beckoning for him to come out. The fire bore a hole in the window glass and the sweet smell of the forest blew over to him. It beckoned him and pushing on the door he fell onto the snow and safety.

He lay a while on a cool whiteness. Slowly, he took a breath, terrified of the pain that had plagued him for so long. He was rewarded with a pain-free sensation that encouraged him to breathe deeper and take in -

Hospital smell. About as appetizing as a shot in the butt.

His eyes shot open and he looked up at a ceiling with a large twisted crack in it. It reminded him of a bear. Something rustled next to him and he was greeted grumpily by an efficient nurse who took his pulse and jammed a thermometer down his throat. When she was through, she spoke over her shoulder into the room and said lunch was coming. She left with a little silver tray. It was only when she was gone that he realized that he wasn't alone. Turning his head, he looked into the lovely, smiling face of Kate Alford.

"Miss Al-fee-ord," he said drowsily.

"Mr. Hardesty. You gave us quite a scare."

Had he? He didn't remember. He looked for his hand but it was hidden. The dream had been so real. He took another strong breath and Kate laughed weakly.

"Does it hurt, Park?"

"Strangely, it doesn't."

"Thank God," she said. "It was torture listening to you breathe. Day in and day out."

"Where am I?"

"In Seattle. They decided to bring you down here for treatment after you stabilized. Lily Garrison insisted." She sat down on a chair next to him, but he asked her over. She came hugging her arms over her short-sleeved plaid dress.

"How did I get out?" His arms were immobile again, the figure-eight strap trussing him up.

"McGill went and got help. Some fellas from the Forest Service and my dad came and got you out on a stretcher, then to the hospital in the city by a train that came especially for you. It was pretty touch and go. You almost - well, we'll talk about that later."

"How bad am I hurt?"

"You have a couple of broken ribs and collarbone. A lung collapsed and your insides were bruised, but you've gone through the worst of it and real recovery is on the way."

"Have I been here long?"

"Over two weeks."

Hardesty whistled softly. "I don't remember a thing. Well, maybe." There was a vague memory. "Was my squad here? Taylor maybe?"

"Yes. All of them came just yesterday. Some before. They're still around hoping to see you awake. You've been doped up a lot. Too much for company, but they still keep coming."

Hardesty shifted his head on his pillow and grinned at her. "You're the only company I want. Is that battle-axe gone?"

"Miss Stewart is very nice and has taken good care of you."

"Hmm." He pointed his shoulder to his mouth. "She can't cure me here." He smiled mischievously at her. "Or here. I'm completely helpless, you know." Kate leaned over and kissed him.

"I can see that. My father, by the way, says you can have your old room back at Cory's. When you leave here."

"Does he realize that it might be a permanent occupation?"

"Yes. Oh, I found this in your pants pocket. Floyd says you should keep it."

"It's Floyd now?"

"I only know the best people." She pulled out a chain. Dangling on the end was the bronze CCC honor award.

LOYALTY*CHARACTER*SERVICE

She hung it around his neck, then kissed him.

"What happened to McGill?"

"Better than I thought. Took some stitches, but that thick head of his - By the way, Taylor's going to give him another chance. He's being sent to a camp down near Darrington for his help in the investigation and for alerting the rescue party that came to get you."

He sighed. "Well, he's been through enough, the knucklehead. I guess he deserves it. Who came down?"

"All the boys...Let's see...Spinelli, Staubach, Costello, Golden, Lorenzo? The whole Joisey Squad." She brushed his shoulder with a finger. "Dick Bladstad said to say hello and there are lots of notes and cards. And there are others, too, Park. Others who have come a long way."

Hardesty looked at her curiously. He couldn't imagine, but his heart knew. His lips parted.

Through the fire.

He swallowed. What he had wanted, he now had and he was afraid. His eyes connected with hers and he knew for sure.

"It's Paul, isn't it?"

"Yes."

"God ... Have you… seen...him?"

"Yes. I've talked to him several times."

"He was here?"

"He came about six days ago. Floyd Garrison arranged it."

Hardesty looked away, concentrating on a chestnut tree outside his window. "How...did he look?"

"I thought quite well. Not so frightening. He has compensation and has been going to business school since January. He says he has a girl. Best of all, he was cleared of any involvement with that murder. Marie Bertin apparently did it. Why don't you see him for yourself?" Without a word she got up and opened the door, ignoring his stricken face. He would forgive her in time.

The man with the half face.

The figure outside the door rose awkwardly, but he did not shuffle as in the dreams. He looked more like Hardesty than Hardesty did. No two brothers could look so close and not be twins. He was tall and sandy-haired with dark green eyes. It was a handsome face blemished only when he turned his head to reveal the melted pink and white skin from ear to cheek and down his throat. If a hand were stiff, it was hard to tell. He came to the door and smiling at Kate, looked in.

"Hello, John. Where've you been?"

Forgiven.

Kate closed the door and left them alone.

EPILOGUE

Mario Spinelli stepped out to the landing of the old barracks and shut the door. The air was crisp outside, the hint of early autumn seeping into his aging bones. Somewhere off came the scent of wood smoke. He went back to his car and got out his camera, then walked around the grounds for a bit. The sun was still above the towering slate-gray mountains and it hit the tops of the big leaf maples near the camp entrance with a diffused light. A gentle wind stirred the leaves. It was time to go.

He started the car up and drove it back onto the two-lane road and headed down to the little settlement. Once across the log bridge, he entered into a picturesque village winding down from a summer of backpackers and campers in the national park. Some of the buildings were old, but several were new, geared to the yuppie crowd that favored it now. They wouldn't know it, but he had a hand in their coming. He passed a gas station and Alford's General Store & Deli and was back into the forest again.

When he got a mile beyond the town's edge, he slowed as he passed some of the old homes set back in riverside meadows and the cedars. There were more houses and cabins along the way than he remembered, but generally, it all seemed the same. At a particular house, he slowed down altogether, then stopped alongside a deep meadow lined by tall hemlock and fir trees. For a moment, he hesitated. He had planned this meeting over two years ago. Dreamed about it forever in his mind.

I shouldn't keep them waiting, he thought, but as he gazed across the road at the old house sheltered by a massive, ancient cedar, a powerful memory seized him. My tour at Camp Kulshan really began right here, he thought. Right at this house. We all started here, our hopes and fears, just newly held together by a thread of impending, strange adventure and budding comradeship.

Hardesty. Joisey Squad. He felt as though his chest would burst.

"Hey, mister. You all right?"

The old enrollee's gray head snapped up and he found himself looking a handsome youth of about seventeen. He was leaning on the car door, his face full of concern. Even with the auburn hair, the face was Hardesty's.

It brought bittersweet joy to Spinelli. The line went on.

"I'm fine," he answered as he rolled down the car window. "Just checking the address. I just drove up from Seattle this morning."

The youth looked around the interior of the car and saw the airline tags on the bags that said "Newark." He burst into a grin. "Are you Professor Spinelli?"

"That's not a name students use when grades go out, but generally speaking, I am. You must be Bob's boy."

Again a rush of emotion. He'd have to get a grip on things before he went in. He looked across the road to the house and thought he saw the screen door open.

"We've been expecting you. Grandma's pretty excited."

"So am I."

"Can I take anything over for you?

"Sure. That would be nice. Would you mind if I collect my thoughts, though, before I come over for you?"

"Sure." The small number of bags were collected and taken across the rural two-lane road now crowded with folks returning to the city. On the porch two women appeared, one with her hand over her brow.

Where had the time gone? It had been only yesterday that he had been the age of that kid and in remembering his stay here he knew the story of that summer had ended better than anything he could have written. Mario Spinelli smiled softly at the memory.

Hardesty was out of the hospital a month later. He and Kate were married around Thanksgiving with a large contingent from the camp attending. Reconciliation with his family followed. Then he'd done exactly what he said he would do. He went to school at the University of Washington, working for the Forest Service in the summer. He came on as professional in '37. He was reassigned, but remained with the Forest Service through the war years. Eventually, he became head ranger up around Kulshan.

It had been a very good, solid marriage with the normal highs and lows. A love affair that never dimmed, Kate and Park manned a fire station together a couple of seasons, even going twice with their three kids. She had finished up her degree sometime after the war and taught. Even worked for the Forest Service on her own some summers after they let women in.

A car whizzed past him, covering up the dusty smell of autumn as it goldened into the evening. Cars didn't whiz like that when he was young. Not on the original gravel road to Frazier. His eyes took in the stand of cedar and hemlock trees along the river's edge. Some of them had been planted when he was here. Now they soared against the backdrop of jagged mountains. The maples around the pasture were huge and turning color.

Time heals. Karin had gone away for awhile, but later she married and had a family. "It was summer thing," he said out loud, "But we were always first friends." There were the occasional Christmas cards, but he had started writing to her in earnest a couple of years ago after both their spouses died. He'd kept in touch with Park too, sharing his own academic advancements including associate professor of creative writing at NYU. For that, Park had sent him a cedar shake with a diploma scratched on it. It still hung in his den at his house back home.

They had corresponded regularly and over time, he'd came to know much of Hardesty's life before and since then with Kate, including what went on at the fire tower. The rest was writer's eye.

Spinelli reached into his coat pocket and took out an old brass medallion -- old, but cared for after all the years. Hardesty had given it to him before the squad left to go back East.

LOYALTY*CHARACTER*SERVICE

Honor Award C.C.C. The barracks, the trees, the smoke rising up. The images were all there.

"Best friend, you were special," he said out loud. Past and present were colliding together like the roiling clouds of that fire season.

That's why it hurt so much that Park wouldn't be here for this reunion. Just a couple years before he was to retire, he was killed in a plane crash during a forest fire. There was poignancy in that for he'd been doing what he loved best.

Spinelli gathered courage to look across at the sidewalk lined by large rhododendrons. The two women were walking down towards him and even in their elder years, Kate Hardesty and Karin Blaine were still beauties. It jarred his memories of that summer even more, though the camp had been closed since the early forties. The CCC ceased to exist after 1942.

Once he had written Karin about his friendship with Park and his time here:

> " I never knew a man could feel so damned yet
> turn his life around. Never really believed
> in redemption or had true friendship until I met
> Park Hardesty. All because of this place that
> I was privileged to be in with him. All because
> of the trees. That's what gets me sometimes.
> Our lives were changed forever - all because we
> were tree soldiers: soldiers for the trees."

ABOUT THE AUTHOR

J.L. Oakley grew up in Pittsburgh, Pennsylvania. After obtaining her BA degree in history from Kalamazoo College, she made her way west and eventually settled in Hawaii. In Honolulu, she studied weaving and did museum work. After meeting and marrying her future husband, they moved to Northwest Washington where they raised three sons.

Her writings appear in various magazines, anthologies, and other media including the *Cup of Comfort* series and Historylink.org, a "cyberpedia of Washington State history." Her historical novels- *Tree Soldier* set in 1930s Pacific NW and *The Jossing Affair* set in WW II Norway- were Pacific Northwest Writers Association Literary Contest finalists. She won the top prize in non-fiction with her essay "Drywall in the Time of Grief" at the 2006 Surrey International Writers Conference in Canada.

Oakley writes social studies curricula for schools and historical organizations, demonstrates 19th century folkways such as butter making and handspinning, and was the curator of education at a small county museum for many years. In 2006 she was project coordinator for a History Channel grant.

Currently, Oakley is working on her next historical novel, *Mistshimus: A Novel of Captivity* set in 1860s Pacific Northwest and continues researching the *Ann Parry*, a 19th century bark which brought the bricks for the construction of the Whatcom County Territorial Courthouse, the oldest brick building in the state of Washington.

Made in the USA
Charleston, SC
30 April 2011